Mark Roussel Mysteries
The Accused

Tricia Voute

To my parents who never stopped believing

First published by Blue Ormer Publishing 2024

Copyright © 2024 by Tricia Voute
All rights reserved.

No part of this book may be reproduced in any form or by any electronic or mechanical means, including information storage and retrieval systems, without written permission from the author, except for the use of brief quotations in a book review. It is illegal to copy this book, post it to a website, or distribute it by any other means without permission.

This novel is entirely a work of fiction. The names, characters and incidents portrayed in it are the work of the author's imagination. Any resemblance to actual persons, living or dead, events or localities is entirely coincidental. Tricia Voute asserts the moral right to be identified as the author of this work.

Paperback ISBN: 978-1-915786-23-4

Typeset in Vellum
Printed and Bound in Great Britain by Short Run Press Ltd, Exeter

Cover art by Gallowaycreate

"Mes amis, retenez ceci, il n'y a ni mauvaises herbes ni mauvais hommes. Il n'y a que de mauvais cultivateurs."

"My friends, remember this, there are no bad weeds and no bad people. There are only bad cultivators."

Victor Hugo, Les Misérables, 1862

Prologue

HE STEPPED BACK AS SHE FELL, HER HAND TAKING IT with her.

Efficient; that was his first thought. Not so hard, was his second.

Crouching with his hands on his knees, he leant forward and held his hand over her nose. Her breath had gone. The air was still.

That was that.

He glanced over his shoulder, just to check. You never knew. Perhaps he'd catch a glimpse of her spirit watching him, over there by the kitchen sink, startled by what had happened, angry too. It took them time to find their power, his grandmother had told him once.

But no one was about. All he could hear was a blackbird singing in the garden, trilling through its repertoire, improvising as it went.

He stood up. There was work to be done. First the washing-up gloves, then a quick wipe down of the surfaces. Toss everything into the bag and scarper.

Chapter One

His life has this peculiar feel to it, like flotsam caught in the surf that keeps rolling over itself, pointlessly. He misses the click of fingers and the beating of time, the sense that if it isn't going to happen now, then it never will. As for his edginess? Well, that's fading fast and if he isn't careful, he'll end up with a fishing rod, waiting for the pollock to bite.

Earlier, he was sitting on the rocks down by the gully, watching the swell rise and fall. A pair of strapping old ladies swam past him, their caps bobbing up and down. They stopped to tread water, and looked at him with scrunched up eyes. One of them waved a flabby arm over her head.

"Are you Lilly's son, Mark?"

He nodded.

"How is she?"

He gave the thumbs up.

"Send her our love."

"Will do," he shouted back.

They breast-stroked around in a circle and made their

way back to Cobo. As soon as they were out of sight, he jumped into the sea and swam in the opposite direction.

He hasn't been 'Lilly's son' for over thirty years. In London, he was called 'fucking bastard' or 'Bobby cunt' as well as 'wanker' now and then, but what really got to him was when his boss said: "Roussel or Rousseau? No bloody difference when it comes to you, mate." He never worked it out (French names? 'Noble savage'? The man needed to get down to a London sink-estate, 'mate'). He called him a *poseur* and that was that, in a nutshell.

Now he's taking the steps up to Burton Battery, walking over the gun-placement, along the path and down onto the road. Flowering weeds grow from the high granite walls. A crow squawks overhead. On reaching the top of the hill, he puts his back to the pine trees and looks out to the West Coast, at Vazon bay that curves round like a sliver of moon.

Up here, the silence isn't really silence – the sparrows are chattering in the hedge for one thing – but it's peaceful. He doesn't miss the noisy, concrete world of the city but he could do with a bit more of the mad dash energy of work, the information thrown at him, his mind racing through the options, up at night, trying to find the answer. He misses that.

And he's never much enjoyed fishing.

"Mark? Mark Roussel? Well, I never."

He stops outside the church yard. A woman in shorts and a t-shirt is walking along the lane towards him. She's familiar in a vague sort of way, but he's lost for a name.

"Viv," she says, coming up to him and holding out her hand.

He shakes it. A memory flickers.

"Viv Le Prevost. I've gone back to my maiden name. Câtel Primary School. Don't tell me you've forgotten?"

"Jesus!" The embarrassment. She was the first girl he ever kissed. His cheeks burn and he looks around to see whether he can escape.

"You've forgotten, haven't you?" Her smile's genuine, but she keeps her distance.

"Can I blame the sun in my eyes?"

"Not really. It's behind you."

"How about age?"

"Mine or yours?"

"Mine." Then he adds quickly (to be polite), "You're looking great." And she is, to be fair, trim and tanned from a summer by the beach. There's a sudden memory of taking her into a cupboard to see what she had under her knickers. He clears his throat.

"I'm a sucker for a compliment." Her eyes twinkle. "That means I forgive you, by the way."

"Right." A quick glance at his watch and then an apologetic smile.

"I'd heard you were back from the Met. Retired, is it? I'd have thought you were a bit young for that – and that's meant as a compliment in case you're wondering."

"My mother's ill."

"Yes, sorry. I heard. So, what's your plan?"

He taps his watch. "I best be going."

"You're not setting up Roussel's Detective Agency then? It's got a ring to it, you know. RDA for short, offices in the Bordage. I'd hire you."

"Whatever for?"

"My ex and all the money he's pinged across to the Cayman Islands."

There isn't much he can say to that, and he taps his watch again.

"And, yup, in case you're too polite to ask, I'm divorced.

Like 68% of the island." Her laugh is gruff. "It's a local hobby. He lives down the road with an ex-girlfriend of mine."

There isn't much he can say to that either.

"What about you?"

"Me. Married to my job, I'm afraid. Or was."

"Aha, another divorcee. Who was the guilty party: you or them?"

"It's complicated." This is far too much friendliness for a morning chat.

"Always is. From my experience though, it's better out than in – as the bishop said to the actress."

He laughs despite himself. "The last bishop I spoke to had his hand in the till."

"That's boring of him." She takes out her phone. "Give me your number. 07781 – what's the rest?"

He doesn't want to share it, but he can't think of a reason to refuse, so he tells her and a few moments later his phone rings in his pockets. He takes it out and puts it to his ear.

"Keep in touch," she says. "Better get to my yoga class." She points at the church hall. "I'm late." She steps away and walks along the lane.

THE HOUSE IS three hundred years old, built in the days when the family still farmed. Only four *vergées* remain which is enough land to worry about, as far as he is concerned. He likes cows, but only to look at, and few properties on Guernsey have two-acre gardens.

Weeds colour the drive, and stinging nettles are growing along the bottom of the granite wall. He walks past the hydrangeas towards the old Dutch barn that's attached to the side of the house and glows like burning coal in the morning sun. One section of the roof has collapsed revealing the rafters. The brickwork too is crumbling.

In its entirety, the property is six times as long as it's wide, and with imagination (and a hefty sum of money), he plans to turn the outbuildings into holiday lets. But he's keeping his ambitions modest for now. There's the old skiff to work on first.

He heads through the arch to the front garden and the old house whose windows are framed in granite. Inside, the smell of damp is overlain with baking. He hurries across the tiled floor to the inner hallway and the kitchen beyond where he finds Janice, holding a tray of brownies.

"God, I'm starved." He steals one and bites into it.

"I've put a polenta cake in the deep freeze," she says. "There's some shortbread as well. I thought your mother might like making the dough, but I got that one wrong." She smiles. "Don't worry, I like baking."

"That's something." He looks about the kitchen. "Where's Mum?"

She points to the larder.

He follows the trail of chocolate powder across the flagstones to the door at the end. Inside, the shelves are filled with tins of tomatoes and beans, outsized jars of flour and rice, boxes of pasta and a large tin of Cream Crackers – and his mother stuck in a corner, holding onto the walls for balance.

"What are you doing here?" He tries to pull her away but she throws him off. "Mum, you're staring at a wall."

"I like it," she mumbles.

"It's a wall, Mum."

"I like it!"

Janice is standing in the doorway. "Leave her. She'll come away when she's ready. I'm keeping an eye on her."

"But this..." He waves a hand in the air. "This isn't my mother." There's a crack in his voice.

"She'll be okay."

Really? A crumbling brain and a slow death? There's nothing 'okay' about it. Life isn't fair, he knows that. You can't expect a nuclear universe to care about suffering, and he's seen too much to believe in fanciful hopes like gods and crystals. Yet still ....

He kisses her his mother's head and leaves.

At the back of the house is another barn. He pushes through the door and fumbles against the wall to switch on the light. A bulb gutters in the darkness to reveal the old skiff, resting on two wooden saw horses with burnt paint on the floor. The issue is skill: the last time he hammered a nail into anything, it came out the other side and punctured his thigh. He ended up in A&E.

Still, he's inordinately proud of its striped sides, sandpapered to a smooth finish. True, paint is stuck to the seams and there's a rotten plank to deal with. It's broken away and today's job is to replace it with a piece of larch he bought at Norman Piette on the Bridge.

He rubs his hands together. He can do it. Belief's everything. Visualise the process, imagine the result. If he can cut a murderer down to size in an interview, he can saw a piece of wood in half; he's just needs to get on with it. That said, he also needs a shower. He's still covered in salt.

BBC RADIO GUERNSEY IS PLAYING, and he's only half listening as he measures the width and length of a piece of wood. He's working outside, his back to the stable door, the sun warming his shoulders.

"That was Neil Diamond singing 'America' from his album, *The Jazz Singer*. I hope you enjoyed it, Lindsay from Perelle. It's one of the most successful film soundtrack albums in history. Now onto the news that's got everyone talking: Pierre Bourgaize's returned to the island."

On hearing the name, he stops.

"He's here to finish his life sentence. According to the Chief Minister, that's common practice but many of you've been phoning in with your concerns. Mr. Tupper from St Saviour's wanted the islanders to have a say, while Mrs. Robin said the fear of the *sorcière* hasn't gone away and no one wants them back. So, what should we be doing about it? Phone in your thoughts while I play another track from *The Jazz Singer*. This is Ted De Vic on 'Catch up Guernsey'."

He remembers the case. It made national news with its lurid facts of ritual abuse and Satanism. At the time, his life was busy, investigating multiple crimes from his desk in New Scotland Yard. It didn't interest him then, and it doesn't much interest him now.

He switches the radio off and goes back to drawing a pencil-line down the piece of larch. Clearly marked, he pushes the jig saw along the grain, sawdust falling about his feet, until the piece of wood falls to the floor. Relieved to have cut it straight – yup, this is going well – he picks up the plane and uses muscle-force to shave off the uneven edges. Next comes the bevelling and once that's done, he carries his piece of artistry into the barn, pickled with pride. Who says Mark Roussel has two left hands? He mayn't be as practical as Odysseus (who made a bed *and* built a house around it), but everyone's got to start somewhere, and he's just fashioned a piece of wood for an old boat.

With a copper nail in his mouth, he carefully slips the plank in at one end and bows it around the ribs of the hull to meet the other.

That's when he sees it: the gap. An inch wide. He stares at it. He pushes the plank forward and then back. He measured the bloody thing; he cut along the line; he can't fathom the problem – but there's no stretching that piece of wood.

Chapter Two

DEAR VIV,
My mate has got together with this girl I work with, but I really fancy her and I don't know what to do. They've been going out for about nine months but things aren't good anymore and they're always at each other's throat. At work, she gets a bit flirty with me but I'm too embarrassed to look at her. I've got her photo by my bed and I can't stop masturbating to it. I'm twenty-five and she's twenty.
Yours, a frustrated labourer.

Viv: While she is with your friend, you need to stand back and wait. When the relationship finds its natural end, then you can decide whether you want to be with her or not. You need to be sure that you are attracted to <u>her</u> and not to the fact that she's unavailable; you might fancy her <u>because</u> she is with your mate and not otherwise. A question to ask yourself is why you never made a move when she was free. If she was in the office with you every day, you had lots of opportunities. For the time being, look elsewhere. Your friend is your *friend after all. As for the masturbation – tear up that photo and throw it away. To make it easier, imagine how she would react if she walked in and found you at it. Stop indulging and find someone else.*

BEING the island's Agony Aunt with a page in the *Guernsey Press* has its predicaments. Take this letter: she's a good idea who 'the frustrated labourer' is, and the thought of him masturbating is frankly disgusting. Then there was the man who complained about his wife's cooking; she was sure she'd been to their house for dinner and sympathised. She told him to kick her out of the kitchen and take over. The wife hasn't spoken to her since.

Now, she needs some advice herself because, let's be honest, bumping into Mark Roussel was no coincidence. She spied him walking up the hill the week before and the week before that. Orchestrating a casual 'oh, hi there' meant hanging around and studying her phone, saying to her classmates 'just coming – got a call to make.' Which is what she did, and when she later hurries into the room and gives her teacher an 'oops-sorry' smile, everyone is lying prostrate on the floor with their legs in the air. For the rest of the session, she tries to focus on her breath and fails spectacularly. Mark. She never wrote to him because life took over. First, she was getting married and then she was trying to save her marriage. After the divorce, she needed time away from men.

"Now ladies, I want you to stand with your legs hip-width apart and shift the weight onto your left foot."

She scrambles to her feet.

"Take hold of your right knee with your right hand."

She obeys, wobbling on her left leg.

The Accused

There were always rumours about him. His days in Indonesia and what happened to him over there. Now people are buzzing about the Met. He pissed off some bigwig and they've booted him out.

"Now take hold of your big toe with your right hand – left hand on the hip – and push that right heel forward and straighten the leg."

She shoves it out and topples over, falling coccyx-hard on the floor. "Fuck!"

The class turn to her.

"Sorry."

Up on her feet once more, she takes hold of her heel and holds onto it, knee bent and left arm out to stop herself swaying. Stuff the instructions; it's a miracle she's still standing.

After the lesson, the yoga teacher catches her by the door. "Anything the matter, Viv?"

"Lord, no. Just got an infection in my ear. Can't keep my balance. See you next week. Cheerie!"

Chapter Three

In the kitchen, Mark boils the kettle to make himself a coffee. It's his one indulgence, this refusal to drink anything but an Ethiopian bean from Yirgacheffe, the birth place of coffee. He orders it online and grinds it himself. It's a ritual of sorts, and today he's needing it because his spirits are down there on the barn floor with the plank of wood. A Boy Scout could measure better than he did. It's humiliating.

Retirement is absolutely and totally charmless. For years he said, 'when I retire' never really expecting to do so, always assuming he'd carry on until his heart gave out. Now, he's forty-nine and feels as redundant as an eighty-year old. It isn't a life – and it isn't a plan either. He doesn't have a plan, and forget retiring as a master boat-builder; he's about as practical as a one-armed monkey.

Mug in hand, he follows the sound of singing and spies his mother in the sitting room huddled in her chair head-to-head with Janice, pretending to follow the lyrics on Janice's phone, warbling 'Morning has Broken' in her broken voice.

He goes inside.

The Accused

"Come on, Mum. We're off for a drive."
He hates 'Morning has Broken'.

PORT SOIF'S flag flutters over the grassed dunes. He turns left and drives up the side-road past the half-moon bay towards the car-park, rattling over the stones to find a place between the Land Rovers and Mercedes. His bubble car might be duck-egg blue and inches above the ground but it has character and his mother loves it. True, it has shaken her into a bag of disjointed bones but she sits in the back like Queen-mug.

High above, a mackerel sky stretches out across the island. The sun is bright, and he takes his mother's arm to pull her out. With a hat pushed down over her head, he leads her down the steps to the kiosk garden and sits her at one of the picnic tables. He kisses her through the hat, telling her to stay where she is and not to get out.

"Are you alright?"

"I'm fine, Mum. You stay where you are, okay?"

"You alright?"

"I'm going to get us some food, so stay quiet and don't move."

At the kiosk, he keeps looking over to check on her, to ensure she hasn't fallen backwards off the bench or is preparing to bark like a dog for the sheer thrill of it. He gets the point that everyone needs to express themselves somehow, and if the body's slow and language limited, then why not bark instead? It makes sense. Babies do it. It's just not his mother. Or his mother as he remembered her. And it's embarrassing.

"What can I get you?"

"Two crab sandwiches, please."

"Brown or white?"

"One brown, one white."

The teenager calls out to the back, "Two crab sandwiches, one brown meat, one white."

"No, wait," he interrupts. "I meant bread."

"That's bread, not meat," the lad shouts over his shoulder, and taps out the amount in the till. "Twelve quid, please."

He pays in cash and takes a wooden spoon with a number painted on it. A woman is talking to his mother and he hurries past the picnic tables to rescue her.

"Hello," he says.

She's in her late sixties, possibly younger; it's hard to tell. Her slacks and silk shirt speak 'resident-rich', and the logo on her handbag is familiar. Moschino? Versace? A girlfriend splashed her redundancy money on something similar a long time ago and he's never forgotten it.

"You must be Mark."

He's taken by her teeth. Hollywood white and way too brilliant in the midday sun.

"You probably don't remember me. Cynthia, Cynthia Marshall." She holds out a hand and for a moment, he isn't sure whether he's expected to kiss it or not. An enormous gem-weighted bracelet jangles as he shakes it. "We met at Christmas drinks a few years ago. Government House."

"Yes, of course." The memory's non-existent.

"Your dear mother" – here she throws a glance in her direction – "she must be so happy to have you home." She leans forward a little and whispers, "I thought I'd have a chat but I don't think she can hear me very well."

"She can hear well enough, she just isn't interested."

"Oh." Cynthia's smile doesn't reach her eyes.

He gestures to the table. "Would you like to join us?"

"I'm sort of..." She points towards the car-park.

Mark nods, and this time her smile is pure relief. He's about to say, 'Don't worry' when the crab sandwiches arrive with napkin-wrapped cutlery and two glasses of water. His mother grabs her plate and draws it over, picking up a sandwich and biting into it, mayonnaise oozing out of the corners of her mouth.

Cynthia glances at him and then has the thought to unwrap the napkin and pass it to her, saying, "Here you are, Lilly." Then, glancing at her watch, she gives a theatrical gasp. "Hubby will be beeping the horn soon if I don't hurry along. He's waiting for me in the car. Lovely to catch up with you both. Ta-ra!" And she gives a gold-jangled wave of her hand as she hurries off.

Alone, he tucks the napkin into his mother's shirt and straightens her plate. He sits beside her and taps his sandwich against her own as he would a glass of wine.

"Bottoms up!"

She laughs, and crumbs spatter out of her mouth.

On the next-door table is a copy of the *Guernsey Press* with the Pierre Bourgaize story all over the front page. He leans across to take it and skims over the text. The case comes back to him now: the woman's body found hanging in the Pine Forest, the pentacle cut into her chest and, of course, the severed hand. The lad was nineteen years old when he committed the crimes and a College boy to boot (albeit a scholarship lad). This seems to enrage the article writer more than anything else, except the Chief Minister's agreement to have him back on-island of course. How is it possible that such a venerable institution could educate a reprobate? Quite easily, he thinks, having been taught at the same turreted establishment himself. Elizabeth The First might have founded it on good Protestant principles, but he remembers the bullies down by the sheds.

Guernsey has its fair share of villains – most of the elegant houses of St Peter Port were built by privateers – it just doesn't have many murderers. His mother always said, 'Beware of the Three Ms: Men, Masons and Methodists' but his mother isn't local and the great families of Carey, de Beauvoir and De Havilland left their Methodist roots long ago. Still, she has a point. His father used to counter it with the three Ws: Women, Witches and Winkles. He meant it as a joke, but it never quite worked because winkles are whelks, and witches don't exist.

And the family has never quite rid itself of superstition anyway, like most of the island to be frank. It comes in with the tide, usually ignored until a south-westerly gale throws the waves over the seawall and floods the roads.

He folds the *Press* and drops it on the ground, stretching back and putting his feet on the bench beside his mother. He has no time for those old tales told around the fire.

BACK IN THE HOUSE, he takes his laptop and types 'Pierre Bourgaize' into Google. Up comes a list of sites and he opens the ones that are contemporary to the murder. The first is a six-hundred-word article from the BBC, under the title 'Pine Forest Murder'. It includes a photograph of Pierre Bourgaize as he was eleven years ago (looking suitably malicious with greasy black hair) and one of Jasmine Gardiner. She was thirty-seven at the time, divorced with two children, both of whom were boarding on the mainland.

The Accused

Blonde, with a taste for fine clothes (though she is wearing a simple t-shirt in the photograph), she was found on the morning of Tuesday 15th by an old man walking his dog.

Next is an article from the *Guernsey Press*. It's short on detail but long on gossip. The island was scandalised; people were scared; there had even been a demonstration outside the Royal Court demanding the criminalisation of witchcraft. Some were talking about the murder of Fanny Le Page a hundred years before and a few mentioned the covens that existed on the island, but there was precious little about Jasmine herself. Her cleaner was in tears and her husband in shock. Their scant comments said it all: pretty lady, often seen in town, liked writing, had a red umbrella.

As for Pierre, he never had much of a chance. The evidence against him was strong: not only was he seen pedalling away from the scene of the crime with a black bag, but Jasmine Gardiner's hand was found in his garden shed. In fact, it was Pierre's father who handed him into the police.

A clear enough case. Charged and found guilty.

Back to the skiff it is then, except, no, that isn't going to happen. He has fastened a padlock on the stable door and has no intention of opening it until he has an architect by his side, advising him on how to turn the property into a holiday let. A man mightn't be a boat-builder, but he can be an entrepreneur. The problem is money; full-time care is expensive, and he'll have to sell his flat in London to afford the renovations. His mother won't suffer the upheaval of workmen in the house, and he isn't convinced that wanting to live by the sea justifies him living on a small island.

The water's the problem. It obsesses him. It always has done. In London, he used to head to the Highgate Ponds every weekend, in every weather, and down to the coast too, whenever he could. He holidayed by the water. He dreamt of water. A diver told him once that the dolphin was the man that had remained in the sea; we were the ones that turned to the land and always regretted it.

"Hello? Anyone at home."

He gets up from his chair and makes his way to the hall where he finds Viv standing in the porch, a plastic bag in her hands.

"Hi," she says.

Freckles have erupted all over her face and her hair is pinned back with a pair of sunglasses. An old fleece is tied about her waist and she wears a faded t-shirt and a pair of shorts. A quick glance down, and he notes the sailing shoes and well-shaped legs. Give it to her, this is no attempt at seduction but it's how he always remembered her – fearless and blithe.

"I thought you'd like a lobster. We've just got them off the Humps."

"Thanks," he said, taking the bag. Then he adds, pointing into the house, "Do you want a coffee?"

A smile cuts across her face. "I've got the old man in the car. Vernon Le Prevost, remember him? You dug up his cabbages."

"God, so I did."

"He's my great-uncle. He says to pop round one of these days. He wants to talk to you."

"About the cabbages?"

She laughs. "No. Pierre Bourgaize. He's got a theory. I said you've retired but he says you owe him one."

"Can't I take him a bottle instead?"

"There's no arguing with a fisherman, and he's got himself hooked on this one. Says he isn't guilty."

The Accused

"He looks pretty guilty to me."

"That's where you're wrong." With a wave, she hurries out of the porch.

He peeks into the bag at the unhappy lobster. "Janice!" he calls. "Can you come a moment? The thing's still alive."

Chapter Four

Yeah, he knows what people think of him. He can list the adjectives: perverse, nasty, evil, abomination, vile. Do one for every letter of the alphabet, except Z. He's a bit stuck on Z. He should write to the journalist at the *Press*; she got to 'w' with 'waspish', which is more creative than 'wicked' but not quite as good as 'serpentine'. Let's be honest, Lucifer wasn't buzzing around Eve's ear, annoying her, was he? She wasn't flicking her hand about her face trying to get rid of him. Hell, no. He wrapped himself about her body and did – well, it didn't take a genius to work that bit out.

Not that he'd know. Personally, that is. They bloody locked him up before he had a chance. Thank you, Guernsey.

Everyone said, 'Aren't you lucky going back home'. And he said, 'Fuck off. You call prison, home?' As if.

He's done some research on the word's roots, though. Just to be sure. He likes etymology, he likes words. It comes from the Proto-Germanic *khaim* which isn't the same as *hus* (that comes from the verb 'to hide'). *Hus* is a shelter. *Khaim* is a residence, somewhere you lay down or settled.

So, yeah, he was going to Guernsey, 'to *khaim*'. Didn't have a choice, did he? They put him on a bloody plane and told him to get off it. That was a shock, seeing the place again. It smelt of the sea, even up there at the airport. And he stood a moment with his eyes shut, breathing it in, like those wine buffs on TV, their noses stuck in a glass – 'I say, old man, I think I have stone and nettles.'

He caught a hint of seaweed, he did. But they pushed him on, his hands cuffed in front of him before he had a chance to catch anything else. That's when he glanced up at the observation window, just in case. There was a café up there. It gave his mum an excuse – 'Just popping off for a coffee, Dad.' Thought he might catch her face at the window, waving down at him, like other mothers.

The fuck she was.

That's why he's written to her. 'It's okay here, Mum. I've got a room to myself and I can see the gardens at the back.' He would have said more, but she wasn't one for that sort of thing. Give her the *Reader's Digest* any day, Dickens reduced to a few words: *Pip said, 'Hi Miss Haversham. I'm in love with Estella.' Miss Haversham got angry; Pip deserted his friends and then ended up saying he was sorry.*

That's about the extent of his mum's literary interests. Still, she'd get a moral from it, she always did. 'Say sorry, Pierre. Pip did.'

Yeah, as if.

Chapter Five

"Is that your gardener over there?"

"I don't have a gardener."

"The sexy guy that cuts your trees. I bet that's him."

She forces her eyes up from the chocolate tart on her plate. The portion's small, with fancy fondant swirls and toasted hazelnuts, and she's eaten most of it in one mouthful. She follows Libby's finger to a figure on the other side of the window, by the quay. He's framed in the dying light and beyond the parked cars, the yacht masts rise and fall. The sea is black and the lighthouse shines on the breakwater.

"I don't know. He's got his back to me."

Libby leans over the table and taps on the window. The man doesn't react and she taps again, this time harder.

"Sssh," Viv says, glancing at the other diners. Libby's been wine-tasting since seven, and is nicely pickled.

"Darling, faint lady never won fair man." This time she rams on the glass.

The man turns around. It's the gardener alright. Viv waves feebly, and stuffs a spoonful of chocolate pudding in her mouth.

"See!" Libby says. "He's coming in. What's his name again?"

"Tom," she splutters. "Tom de Carteret."

"Local, oh well. Can't be helped. Hello, Tom!" Libby turns sideward in her chair as he pushes through the door. "Why don't you join us."

"Ladies!"

He beams a flirtatious smile and she wishes to God he hadn't come in. Not because she dislikes him. On the contrary, there isn't a middle-aged woman on Guernsey who doesn't fancy a night alone with him, but she's old enough to be his mother (just).

"Another bottle of Chablis," Libby calls out to the waiter, "and a glass too."

Viv slings her bag over her shoulder and makes to get up. "I ought to be going."

"Nonsense!" Libby takes the bag off her. "It's very rude of you to disappear now that Tom's arrived. It is Tom, isn't it? You see, Tom agrees."

Tom smiles. "It's the weekend tomorrow."

THAT's the problem with getting old, everything takes so much longer to do. More cleansing, more face creams, longer with the dental floss, longer at the hairdressers. She doesn't walk so fast, she doesn't think so fast. And now the hangover – it just won't lift. Paracetamol, jugs of water.

Brandy is yapping at her ankles and she opens the door to let her out, leaning against the frame and noticing the line of washing she's forgotten to bring in. The morning sun stings her eyes.

Never again. Libby is off her contacts list. There's only

so much shame she can tolerate, and she's met her limit. Thank God for Tom. The memory's vague but at some point, he rolled her up and tossed her into his van.

She was singing Abba in the High Street.

Mamma mia: her to-do list is a mile long, and her head feels like it's on the rack. It's her great uncle's birthday and she's forgotten to send him a card. He won't mind if she turns up with a bottle of Scotch. It's the 'turning up' that's the issue.

She needs a shower and the strongest coffee possible, both of which she has before picking up the phone and calling him. He doesn't answer, so she goes back to bed.

THE AFTERNOON SUN is as hot as an oven and she steps back into the shade of the Forest Stores. Mark is walking down the covered walkway and when he spies her, he stops next to the crates of fresh vegetables. He draws his finger down over his nose and she can't decide if it's a gesture of awkwardness or just weird.

"I didn't think you shopped here," she says.

He shrugs. "I thought you were a Marks and Spencer type of woman."

"Touché. I'm meant to be buying my great uncle a bottle for his birthday. You?"

He points to the cabbages piled on top of each other. "You said he wanted to see me."

"Yes, but not about the cabbages."

He picks up a basket. "Pierre Bourgaize?"

"He has a theory. You look sceptical."

He searches for his words. "The man murdered the woman, he didn't put a spell on her."

"I agree, but old Vernon thinks it's a cover up."

"The Masons, was it?"

"Ouch." His sarcasm burns.

"Sorry. That came out wrong."

"Yes, it did," she says. "Look, for what it's worth I agree with him. I was Pierre's advocate's secretary, so I know what I'm talking about, more than old Vernon if I'm honest. The verdict was unsafe."

"He got a fair trial."

"Depends what you mean by fair. They did a sloppy job of it, and the island was going crazy about him being a witch. The Bailiff's guidance was pretty biased too."

"That's a serious accusation." She watches him inspect the tomatoes.

"It should have gone to the Court of Appeal."

"Why didn't it?"

"I don't know."

"It's a legal matter then."

"The police should have investigated further. They missed out a lot of stuff."

He drops six tomatoes into his basket and turns to the lettuces. "Have you evidence for that?"

"It's something you could look into."

He shakes his head. "Sorry. Roussel's Detective Agency's been turned down by the Inland Revenue."

"We don't have them over here."

"Okay, I'm retired."

"I get it, but what if he's innocent?"

"He got a fair trial, Viv."

"It depends what you mean by fair. Look, let's put it this way: go to the Pine Forest and check it out. He was a weedy kid. You'll see what I mean."

"I don't want to get involved."

She bites her lip. "Seriously, someone got away with murder, and the weird kid got lynched. It's about justice, isn't it, in the end anyway?" The word 'justice' catches him. She sees it in the narrowing of his eyes, and the slight tilt to the head. But he doesn't say anything. Awkward silence. He walks towards the entrance.

Quick, get in there, Viv, before he heads for the pasta shelves and you've lost him.

"How about meeting for coffee in town? For a catch-up. You know the Boat House? On the veranda. How about Friday, at eleven?"

He stops. "Is that a date?"

"It's an invitation – with one condition. You go to the Pine Forest."

"I've told you, I don't want to get involved."

"Just go. That's all I'm asking. You'll see the problem and," she adds for effect, "justice must win in the end or we're all fucked. Cheerie."

She walks back up the incline to her car. Brandy is wagging her tail in the back seat, and she gives her a vigorous rub on the head before sitting down and switching on the engine. Not until she reaches the traffic lights does she remember Vernon's birthday bottle; she went to the Forest Stores to buy it for him.

Chapter Six

THE OTHER SIDE OF THE ISLAND IS ONLY A FEW MILES away, but by the time he drives into the car-park, the weather has changed. A mist has come in, and the sea is hidden from view. It is probably localised (it can be raining at Pleinmont and scorching at L'Ancresse) but St Martin's Point is a faint grey line adrift in the fog. He parks his car beside an over-sized Range Rover, just to make a point, and lifts the canopy to step out. The air is cold and damp. No one's about, not even a seagull. There's only the deep rumble of the fog horn and a light coming from the kiosk. He strides over to it and greets the girl who leans out of the hatch.

"What is it?" she says, pointing to his car which is only just visible.

"Messerschmitt KR200."

"It's cute. I like the colour, what's it called?"

"Duck-egg blue."

"I meant the car."

"It doesn't have a name."

"Does it have pedals?"

"Yes."

"And an engine?"

"Of course."

"How about 'Tiddles, eh?"

"Tiddles?" He's aghast.

"You're a bit big for it, that's all," and then she adds quickly, "can I get you a coffee?"

He's struggling to smile at her. "How about a piece of gâche."

"You don't want coffee?"

"No."

"It's not instant, eh."

"Unless it's Ethiopian from Yirgacheffe, I don't want it."

"Suit yourself."

She turns away and steps to the back of the room where the fridge stands industrial-size with a door that is too heavy to open. After some tugging, she pulls it back and takes out a plate of buttered gâche covered in Clingfilm.

"It's nice to have someone to talk to, being up here when the weather's like this." She brings it over and puts it down on the ledge. "It's a bit creepy, is it."

He's looking at the Clingfilm. "You really should stop using that stuff."

"What stuff?" she says as she peels it back.

"That," he says, pointing to the Clingfilm.

"What's wrong with it?"

"Everything."

"Yeah? Well, can't do without it."

"Use a plate."

A dog barks somewhere close and he thinks he hears voices walking down the lane but he can't be sure; the fog dampens the sound and then scatters it.

"At least you're not up here alone with that Pierre guy

back on the island. Scary stuff, all that about the witches and everything. My gran spoke the patois, eh, and she knew all about that stuff. And the black dogs, she was always going on about the black dogs."

Mark is hungry and he points to the plate of gâche. "Any chance of having a piece?"

"Trying to keep the waistline down, is it?"

She holds the plate out for him. He takes a slice and they stand a few moments in silence as he eats.

"I put my money on him having some sick idea of trying to conjure the devil. That's what they used to do, the witches, is it. Maybe there's this group, like the Illuminati and they do all these weird things."

Mark laughs.

She isn't impressed. "My gran says he comes from the Queripels – through his mum – and she said they were all witches. My gran used to have a copy of the *Petit Albert* but I don't know what happened to it. You can't destroy them, is it – that's what my gran says – but hers disappeared alright."

"There you have it then."

"You don't know though, do you, eh? There's this ghost in my gran's house. He keeps turning the taps on at night."

He tries not to laugh this time. The girl is young, local. It's easy to believe in ghosts when the world's shrouded in mist. In the olden days – the days of Calvin – when most of the island was windswept and empty, the parishes were awash with fear. Witches flew above the clouds, making their way to the Catioroc to dance with the devil; they threw their spells this way and that, causing cows to dry up, children to itch with lice, and crops to fail. His grandmother told tales of shape-shifters and potion-makers, of the little people and malice, but she had said nothing of murder. Not even the infamous Marie Pipet had trodden that path. They were charlatans the lot of them, making money from ignorance and fear.

"What do I owe you?" he asks.

"It's on the house. You've kept the ghosts away."

This time he smiles, and pulls a napkin from the metal container to wipe his fingers. "Ghosts don't exist, you know. Neither do witches. You'll be okay."

WALKING through fog is rather like walking through a dreamscape; ill-defined objects drift in and out of sight, and sounds are muffled. If he looks down at his feet, he sees the steps of the path and the twisted gorse bushes either side. If he looks up, he finds himself in a cloud. Booming through the wetness, flattened and distorted, is the fog-horn. Now and then the mist thins a little and he makes out the path bending to the left and winding its way up the cliff edge. But as soon as it falls again, he's lost in eeriness. Stepping over broken twigs and old pine cones, he makes his way into the Pine Forest, looking this way and that for the tree, the gallows.

Then suddenly the mist lifts and the summer sun shines with all its strength. He sees the pine trees either side, their umbrella-tops thick and their lower branches ragged. Gorse bushes cover the hillside like knitted pile, and logs are heaped in stacks. He takes the path to his left and continues to tread over pine needles until he sees several bunches of flowers left at the base of a tree, not a pine but another species, bent against the wind. The freesias and chrysanthemums have wilted and are damp from the mist, and he kneels to look at them. Only one carries a card attached to the stems by a curled blue ribbon. It reads 'I'll never forget

The Accused

you, TX'. He peers up at the branch overhead. This is where they found her, hanging by a noose. Jasmine Gardiner.

The branch is high, and the tree is far into the wood. He's seen Pierre's photograph in the *Press*. Short and dark, like most locals, and thin, very thin. Unless he knows a spell to swing a corpse, he'd struggle to string her up.

He carries on along the path through the forest, following its steep curve upwards towards the old steps that lead up to the washing pond and the lane beyond. He walks through the opening onto tarmac and finds himself outside a house called Pine Forest Lodge. This was Jasmine Gardiner's home. It abuts the wood, its roof peeking over a high wall. Everything about it says, 'keep out', even the wooden gates, which are tall and iron-fringed. It's modern but stylish; open market, no doubt. Probably worth a few million. There are only two types of people who can afford a place like this: bankers and lawyers. Usually English.

A boy is sitting on a bicycle, one hand on the handle-bars, the other gripping an ice-lolly. It's dripping down his wrist, and he sucks the bottom of it.

"Does anyone live here?" he asks.

"My mum says it's haunted. My dad says it's too bloody expensive."

"So, the answer's 'no'."

The boy shrugs his shoulders and pedals away.

He looks back at the house. The perfect place for a murder: once through the gates, no one will see or hear anything. And close to the wood too – it's easy to steal a body down into them.

It just doesn't seem the kind of place that would open its doors to a witch.

Chapter Seven

THE ISLAND IS SMALL; TWENTY-FIVE SQUARE MILES AT high tide with an average speed limit of the same. He's going to bump into people. He's going to step on their toes. It's the reason he left in the first place. Are you a Roussel from Torteval or from the ones down at Bordeaux? That's the question. Your mother isn't local, is she? That's the other question. Thirty years off island and he's more English than Guern, and they'll remind him of it the moment he starts stuffing his nose into things.

Superstition – he loathes it about much as he loathes the hysteria that goes with it. It has power, and that's the problem. Once you fill the darkness with shadows, there's no shooing them away. He knows that from childhood. The invisible lurks everywhere, a blink away from being real.

And Viv's right, someone is stirring it up.

Whoever Pierre is – and whatever he's done – he's damned if witchcraft has anything to do with it. He agrees, it smacks of a cover up.

There's a case he remembered from childhood, when a woman committed suicide after her name appeared in the

Press. The details are lost on him now, but he remembers walking with his mother to her house, a ginger cake in his hands. She was associated with a series of thefts from a vinery. "There's a difference between a just person and a judgemental one," his mother said as they knocked on the door, the net curtains of the bungalow opposite twitching, "don't ever forget that."

But if he's going to separate judgement from justice, he needs facts. He needs to review the forensics and read the court transcripts. Without those, he can't do anything.

And there's the issue of Viv. He remembers what she was like at school, daring him to put cow dung in Sally Mauger's dancing shoes and making him dig up cabbages. She got him into trouble then; she might get him into trouble now.

Home is dark and the floor is cold under his feet. He takes the *Yellow Pages* from the table and angles it to the light, flipping through it in search of the Greffe, the registry office of the Royal Court.

"The Greffe, good morning."

"Good morning. I was wondering if I could talk to someone about seeing the papers on Pierre Bourgaize's trial."

"Are you from the *Press*?"

"No."

"May I ask why you want to see them?"

"I'm an ex-detective. From London. I'm looking into the case."

"Who's speaking, please."

"Mark Roussel."

"Hold the line. I'll put you through to the Strongroom."

'Moonlight Sonata' shrills through the airways. He

holds the phone away from his ear and waits until he hears a click and the music stops.

"Mr. Roussel. This is Timothy Sarre. I'm the Assistant Clerk of the Strongroom at the Royal Court. I believe we've met, at Jurat Martel's house, a few years ago. Christmas drinks. You probably don't remember."

He doesn't.

"I'm not sure I can help you. Has Pierre Bourgaize nominated you as his investigator? I haven't heard anything about the case being reopened."

"Not yet. I'm doing some soundings first, to see if there is a case. For that, I need access to the case files."

"Ah, well that's where we have an issue. Without his formal nomination, the Greffier won't agree."

"There's no point opening a new investigation unless there are grounds to do so. For that, I need the papers."

"I understand, but the rules are the rules. It's a bit of a Catch-22, I'm afraid." There's a pause. "To be honest – and of course, it isn't my place to say – but it's probably saving you a lot of wasted time. Pierre is guilty. No one doubts it."

"Have you read the material?"

"No."

"On what basis are you not doubting it then?"

There's a moment's silence. And a change in tone. "Is there anything else I can help you with?"

His 'no' is short, and he hangs up.

The question is what to do next. He's never been refused access to information before; but then he's never been outside the system before. Without access to the files, it's a non-starter. He takes out his phone.

"Hi Viv, it's Mark." Music is playing in the background, and the chatter of voices is loud. "Can you talk?"

"Bit awkward. I'm on a date."

"It's lunch-time."

"Lunch-time date, then. He's gone to the loo. I've time for a quickie."

Her chuckle disarms him. He forgets what to say.

"Do you remember when we hid in the cupboard? It was so cute."

No, it wasn't. It's embarrassing. "Look, it's about the case. I can't get to see the forensics or the transcript of the trial proceedings."

"Blimey. You went to Jerbourg?"

"You sound surprised."

"I am. I mean, I'm pleased but I'm surprised."

"Do you have any copies?"

"Of the trial proceedings?"

"Yes."

"Why would I have copies, Mark?"

"You could have made them."

"I'm not sure that would have been legal."

"Without them, I'm going nowhere with this."

"Why don't you use your old-boy connections? You're a College lad, you can pull strings."

"Not if it's against the rules. Look, what's the name of the SIO at the time?"

"The Senior Investigating Officer? He left the island ages ago."

"How about Pierre's advocate?"

"Vaudin, my old boss?"

"Yes."

"He's behind St Julian's Avenue. I can call him if you want and but be prepared for disappointment."

"How do you mean?"

There's a pause. "Sorry, got to go." She's whispering now. "My date's coming back from the loo."

"And?"

"I'm putting on a seductive smile. Shall I send you a photo?"

"Of what?"

"The smile."

Yes, no. He doesn't know what to say. "I'll call you tomorrow." He hangs up.

"Mark! Mark!"

It's his mother. She sounds distressed. He bolts up the stairs and into her room where he finds her sitting on the edge of the bed, her hands held out as Janice gives her a pill.

"What's the problem?" He's puffing.

"Nothing," Janice says. "She just likes the sound of your name."

"Right."

He watches his mother pop the pills into her mouth and start to chew them.

"No, Mum. Swallow." He flops down beside her and takes the glass of water from the bedside table. He holds it to her lips. "You must swallow the pills."

She continues to chew.

"Swallow," he orders.

Her brain is stuck, like an old record. He can't stop her even when she opens her mouth in distress and shows him the white powder coating her teeth.

"Have some water."

Three sips later, he watches as Janice lifts her legs and helps her lay down, covering her with the duvet and tucking it under her chin. He kisses her cheek and like a child after

The Accused

a happy day at the beach, his mother cuddles down, a grin on her face and sparkles in her eyes.

"Are you alright?"

"I'm alright," he says.

"Are you alright?"

"I'm fine."

"Are you alright?"

"Just rest, Mum."

"Good night."

"You're having a siesta, Mum."

"Good night."

"Mum..."

She rolls over and gives him her back. The sun is shining bright and the window is open, but as far as she's concerned, it's night and she's going to sleep.

Downstairs, he pours himself a glass of wine and takes it into the vine-house, sitting down on the old wicker chair and looking out at the garden. He thinks of his mother as he remembers her, boisterous, laughing, always singing songs and ready for a dash over the sand into the sea, splashing through the waves. Tears prick his eyes. He takes a gulp of wine.

The *Guernsey Press* is on the floor and he opens it to the puzzle pages. Here is something to distract him. He's good at puzzles. Always has been. Good at holding up a hand to Time and saying: Slow down, I've got a problem to think through.

Right now, the problem is Pierre Bourgaize. Whether he rattles the cages of the island's judiciary or not. People know people who know people. Pointing the finger is hazardous in a small community, and he's only just returned.

Not everyone gets what they deserve in life, he knows

that and, yes, he knows it's about justice too but he's never been able to define the word. It has something to do with fairness and equity, with levelling up and levelling out, but after that, he's adrift. It sounds like a noun but feels like a verb, something you do rather than something you seek. And he really can't bear the lazy conceit and unholy clamour going on in the *Press*.

Chapter Eight

The Priaulx Library is housed in a Georgian mansion set high above the town. He's never been here before, and he pushes open the front door to find himself in a dark space of panelled walls. It smells of dust and decaying books. The front parlours have been turned into one long room with the crests of the parishes hanging above a connecting door. Leather studded chairs sit either side of an old fireplace, and bookcases run from ceiling to floor, filling the place with a strange brooding as if the books themselves were alive with eyes to watch.

To his right is a large partners' desk and another sits perpendicular to it. Two women are beavering away, head down and bespectacled, filling in old-fashioned borrowing cards. Another is tapping away at a computer in the corner. He clears this throat. The lady behind the main desk is the first to lift her glasses onto her head and acknowledge him.

"Yes?"

"I was wondering if I could look at some past copies of the *Press*."

"If you give me the dates, we should be able to find them."

"1907 or 1908 to begin with. Anything on the death of Fanny Le Page. And then anything on Jasmine Gardiner's murder."

There is silence. The woman at the computer stops tapping and looks over at him, then glances at her colleague.

"Can I ask why?"

Not really. "Is there a problem?"

"We try not to encourage rogue inquiries."

"Do I look like a rogue?"

The woman forces a smile. She scuffles between the desks and the bookcases and holds out her hand.

"Mrs. Boxall. Head librarian. If you tell me why you're looking, I can point you in the right direction."

"I'm interested in the commonality between the two murders. Psychological profiling," he adds as an afterthought.

"Good enough," she says with pinched reluctance. "The cutting files is the best place to start. If you need more, you can search through the reels of microfilm upstairs. But it's best to give us a day's notice so we can set up the machine."

He watches her totter off through a heavy door into a back room and waits. The woman at the computer taps away, glancing down at some papers while the other takes a book from a pile, opens it, stamps it, moves it to another pile and begins again.

"Here they are." It's Mrs. Boxall. She's doddering down the corridor with three heavy ledgers in her arms. She drops them into his own and he reels. They weigh like granite slabs. "You'll find the Gardiner case in the top two. Fanny Le Page's death is in the bottom one. It was 1908, not 1907."

The Accused

He chooses a booth in the back parlour that's tucked between bookcases and lit by a window. From there he can look out onto a strip of grass and the lane beyond. With a notebook beside him and his phone on the desk, he begins with Fanny Le Page, opening the thick pages of the ledger and smelling the dust of Victorian England.

LEDGER NOT OPENED *in a <u>very</u> long time. Whoever knew the story, didn't come here to research it.*

That is his first note. The second is this:

Mr. Le Maitre found her hanging from a <u>pine tree</u> (<u>different to JG</u>) in the early morning, on his way to Bec du Nez to fish. Quote (in patois) "she was just a little thing, but I got the fright of my life."

DESPITE MR. LE MAITRE claiming not to be a superstitious man (he knew on good account that all the witches were at L'Eree), he did see a shadowy figure point a finger at him and mutter something strange. That was all it took. The next thing he knew, he was walking all the way to Jerbourg, on to Icart, up and down the cliff paths until he reached the Corbière. Only then did he remember that a man could march himself to death with the walking-curse. He wriggled out of his guernsey, and turned his vest inside-out to counteract the spell. Whence he stopped. Exhausted, he sat down on the rocks to catch his breath.

His tale is followed by another that spoke of an old woman who lived in a cottage near Jerbourg. She made no secret that she had the gift, frightening everyone with her threats and bad-tempered cackle. All the people thereabouts kept nutmeg in their pockets and sewed phials of quicksilver in their petticoats. Yet when the constables inspected her home, they found nothing. No black books, no potions, and it was agreed she had neither the wit nor the strength to hang Fanny Le Page from a pine tree.

With the tales of witchcraft exhausted, people's attention turned to foreigners. First the French, then the English. Later the army. One account stands out. A few *maisons de debauche* had grown up about the garrison at Fort George. It was rumoured that Fanny Le Page offered her services there. When the women were asked, no one seemed to know her but an anonymous note was handed to a constable by a young lad running errands. It mentioned a soldier. It gave no name or rank but said he killed her because she was a bitch. After this, the leads peter out. The soldier was never identified and the murder of Fanny Le Page remained a mystery.

He closes the volume and stretches, his arms over his head. Whoever killed Jasmine Gardiner knew the story, and whoever knew the story understood the island and its folklore. Resurrect the witches; remember the covens. Conjure shadows and bring back the fear. Islanders can hold reason in one hand and superstition in the other and see no contradiction. 'Witches died out with electric light', his father used to say as he tucked him up in bed, but even he – a realist and a doctor – had fallen quiet when his grandmother told her dark tales of a night.

Enter Pierre Bourgaize, weirdo-exceptional, the perfect scapegoat. He fits the story and the mythology. He sets tongues wagging. It's easy to see why they arrested him; it's not so easy to see why he was convicted.

And that's the issue. The evidence must have been convincing. He needs to get his hands on it.

He takes up the volumes dealing with Jasmine

The Accused

Gardiner's case, and turns the pages to find the relevant articles. Hanging, location, time of being discovered, how she was discovered, mutilations...he's right, the similarities to Fanny's death are too contrived for coincidence.

But that's where it ends. Pierre's DNA was found on her arm, the arm whose hand was severed. Nowhere else. Yet surely – as Pierre's Advocate pointed out – if he murdered her and carried her into the Pine Forest, we would expect more DNA contamination. We would also expect the fibres found on her clothes to match his jumper, but they didn't. They matched her husband's, except her husband had an alibi. He was off island at the time, with his mistress in London.

One article discussed the sail cloth that her body was wrapped in, indicating it was hidden somewhere between death and hanging. The question was where. In the garage, the Prosecution argued, without providing the evidence. It was speculation, yet the Defence never challenged it.

Reading on, death was caused by ingesting yew seeds. It was assumed she had taken them in a drink because there was a smattering of ground seeds found on the dishcloth, but there were no mugs or glasses left at the scene so, again, this was speculation.

What surprises him is the precise time of death: eleven forty-three in the morning.

As for the discovery of the body hanging in the Pine Forest: Mr. Duquemin went for a morning walk, as was his habit and found it blocking his path. He called his wife and then the police, and hurried back the way he came.

The case against Pierre rested on three crucial facts. One: everyone else had an alibi. Two: r de Carteret, a gardener, saw him pedalling fast out of the road leading to the house half an hour after the murder took place. Three:

Jasmine Gardiner's hand was found wrapped in a piece of cloth in the garden shed. Pierre's father discovered it and handed it over to the police along with his son. In the Royal Court, when confronted with this fact, Pierre declared himself a witch and shouted: *"la main de gloire!"*, which rather did it for him.

In his summing-up, the Prosecutor described Pierre as one of life's miscreants. His path was freely chosen, freely pursued. Emanating from a hardworking family and being of good intellect – a College boy, no less – he preferred the dark power of fear over common decency. He chose a life of malevolence, brewing his lies into noxious dreams and dreadful acts. He desired influence, he sought control. He practiced magic and chose a defenceless woman as his victim. He was an evil man and should be locked away for life.

The Advocate for the defence requested tests to assess Pierre's mental state but the Bailiff and the Chairman of the Jurats declined. There was sufficient evidence to convict him and reason enough to believe him sane. That we might not like how he thinks, they argued, does not mean he cannot think. Merely that we disagree with him, and deem him dangerous.

Mark rubs his hands down his face and holds them there. It's neat, superficially obvious. Except for a few troubling points such as how Pierre strung the body up on his own and the fact that a hand is not a body, and belief doesn't always translate into action.

He gets to his feet. Another thing is bothering him. Witchcraft isn't a method and it certainly isn't much of a motive either. Patently, many still think it is, but since it assumes the universe is ordered by supernatural powers and not a closed system of cause-and-effect, it shouldn't be

The Accused

considered in a court of law. That leaves another question unanswered: If Pierre killed Jasmine Gardiner, *why* did he kill her? No one has offered a reason.

It's true, of course, that Pierre proclaimed himself a witch. He dressed as a goth, and was seen prowling about the Foulon Cemetery at Halloween. But that didn't establish much beyond inclination. No Jurat with a grey cell in their head would make that mistake. They are eminent members of society, voted in by leaders of the community; they aren't meant to be swayed by fallacious argument, unlike twelve random people picked off the street. and told to decide on murder. It's the age-old argument for Norman law over English, but he can see some serious problems with it.

The grandfather clock in the hall strikes eleven.

He jumps up; he's late. He leaves the ledgers with the librarians and rushes out of the library, down the hill, across St Julian's Avenue and down again towards the harbour.

Chapter Nine

"Sorry I'm late." He kisses Viv on the cheek and sits down in the chair opposite.

"Ten minutes," she says, looking at her watch. A half-finished cup of coffee is on the table before her.

"Better ten minutes late in this world than ten years earlier in the next."

"Yes, well, it garners minus marks on my tally sheet."

He brings his sunglasses down over his eyes. The veranda gives onto Careening Hard, the last remnant of the Old Harbour. White-tipped waves lick the beach beneath them, leaving lines of brown seaweed and two fishing boats listing on their sides. At the far end, the Herm boat is backing out, its upper deck filled with people. He hears their laughter as the engines turn.

"Do you want to go to Herm one of these days? A friend's band is playing at the Mermaid next weekend."

He opens his mouth, then shuts it again.

"We can get the late boat back."

He looks down at the table. "I've heard there's a new

The Accused

chef at the White House. They're offering two for the price of one. Three course meal. Wine not included."

Viv raises an eyebrow. "My friend's playing at the Mermaid, not the White House."

He glances out at the Weighbridge Steps which are painted white and visible now the Herm boat has sailed. "I don't like the Mermaid."

"That settles it then."

"I was at the Priaulx," he says. "In case you wondered. That's why I'm late."

"Okay."

"I thought you'd be pleased."

"Not really."

He ignores her mood. It's always the best option. He learnt it from his mother and it's been his go-to with women ever since.

She calls the waiter over. "Do you want anything?"

"English breakfast."

"That," she tells the waiter, "and another double-shot cappuccino, please."

A French family are settling themselves at a table behind Viv. They must be sailors in their chic boating-gear and tanned faces. The children wear sunglasses and the father is struggling to raise the umbrella.

"It's a shame the island's lost so much of its heritage," he says aimlessly.

Viv looks over her shoulder to follow his gaze. "Blame the Nazis. Usually a safe bet."

He nods. "My father was evacuated. When he came back, he'd forgotten the patois."

"It's like all the old characters. You don't find them anymore. Everyone's horribly normal these days."

He arches his eyebrows.

"Remember old Can-Can? Dad said he was a liability. He used to take his wife in a box-cart at the back of his bike."

"God, yes! It was made of half a barrel, and broke loose and rolled her down St Julian's Avenue. That was before the roundabout."

"And Old Maggie? I never saw her, but she used to stand outside the town church in her glad-rags, waiting for Mr. Right to come along and marry her. Every week at the same time, poor love."

He smiles at the table, remembering characters like Stiffy Lawrence and Ring-a-ding Georgie; Mumblin' Lizzie and Mackerel Annie. There was also famous Steve Picquet, the hermit with his goats down at Pleinmont.

The waiter arrives with their order and Viv pops the biscuit that accompanies her coffee into her mouth. She sips the cappuccino and flicks the foam off her top lip.

"Did you ever hear the story about Taffy and the faeries?"

He shakes his head.

"It's a good one. Noel Trotter was a friend of my dad's. They used to name those motorbike mirrors after him: Trotter-spotters. Anyway, this old guy called Taffy used to phone the station at seven pm every evening, complaining about the faeries partying in his attic. No one took any notice of him. He hated the police but that didn't stop him calling. In the end, Trotter turned up at his cottage with a paper bag saying he was the Channel Islander Faery Catcher. He took a ladder and got into the attic and made a hell of a noise pretending to catch them. 'Got you, you bastards, you're under arrest!' When he came down, he told Taffy to tie a piece of string around the top of the bag, and took them back to the station."

He laughs. "I didn't know that."

"I tell you, we've sanitised everyone. If we don't like what they say, we put them on drugs and send them home."

"Doesn't look like it worked with Pierre."

"Probably because we never got hold of him."

"We?"

"It's what I do. Didn't you know? Counsellor, therapist. Call it what you will."

A herring gull lands on the railings a short distance away. It turns its yellow eye on them and hops closer, and then closer again. Juvenile feathers speckle its neck, but it's already cunning, looking away when he stares at it, and glancing back when he's distracted. He claps his hands and it hops indignantly onto the ground and waddles off.

"What do you think about Pierre's case then?" Viv says.

He sips his tea. "I can't go much further with it unless I get the court papers and the forensics."

"I called Vaudin's office, but he's away on holiday. They said he'll call you when he's back."

"Thanks. There's time. Can you remember what you read?"

"Bits of it."

"There wasn't any blood in the house, was there?"

Viv shakes her head.

"What about the Pine Forest?"

"Not that I recall. There was vomit, on the path a little way from the tree. I remember that."

"Whose vomit?"

"Couldn't say."

"Was it tested?"

"Not that I'm aware of."

He raises his eyebrows. "Right." What he means is 'negligent'. The vomit defines the scene; tells them about the state of the person who was there. "If there isn't any blood, we have two options. Either the mutilation happened elsewhere or, if it's done on-site, it happened at least eight hours after death. Was forensic evidence from the sail bag found in the wounds?"

"No idea."

"What about lividity?"

"You're asking me now."

"Had the blood settled about her feet? Or was it on her back?"

"I never saw the body."

"But the reports."

"I remember something about her being on her front first and then on her back. She was hung up a long time after death."

"Okay." He rests his chin on interlocked fingers and stares at the table top. "Lividity begins about two hours after death and discolouration becomes permanent between eight and twelve hours afterwards. A lot depends on the ambient temperature of course..."

"It was March."

"Yes, cold. That will slow it down. Rigor mortis would have set in already but not totally, so the body wouldn't have been rigid but stiff enough to make moving it difficult." He pauses. He's thinking about the vomit. "I'd say the mutilation was done in the Pine Forest. It would have been dark by then, so no one was about to watch..." He sits back and crosses his arms. "Pierre could have done the mutilation, he could have done the murder, but I doubt he could have moved the body on his own and strung it up."

"He had an accomplice?"

"That's one theory."

The Accused

"Blimey," she says. "You should open that agency, you know."

HE STANDS ASIDE to let an elderly couple pass, and then motions for Viv to follow him out onto the Crown Pier. Cars are everywhere. The whole island's come to town. The marina is a forest of masts and the air is filled with the smell of seaweed and diesel.

"What are you going to do now?" Viv asks him.

"Bits and bobs. And you?"

"Creaseys. I need to get a birthday present."

Over her shoulder, he spies a man cross the road and stride towards them. Late seventies with slick grey hair, expensive blazer, smart shirt... he's the last person Mark wants to meet. He bends to tie his shoelaces.

"Mark!" The man takes out his keys and aims them at a Mercedes. 'Ping' goes the machine and the lights flash yellow. "Perfect timing. We need to have a word."

"I'm in a bit of a hurry," Mark lies. "Let me introduce you to Viv Le Prevost."

The man keeps his hands to himself. "Guernsey's very own Agony Aunt."

"Always one to help the locals," Viv says without a smile.

Mark looks at her – what's this? Agony Aunt – Christ! What will she get caught up in next? He never reads beyond the first two pages of the *Press*, except to jump to the middle to do the puzzles.

"Your advice last Saturday," the man says, "was rather – how shall I put it? –provocative. 'No one's obliged to tell the truth.'"

"I thought you'd approve."

"A popular mantra in prison, just not helpful in the local newspaper."

"I encourage people to think for themselves."

"I've found that to be a dangerous habit, a man in my position and all that."

Viv is about to speak and he breaks in with a question.

"I hear you've been off-island?"

"A meeting in Jersey, Mark. That's what I wanted to talk to you about. There's a group of people I'd like you to meet."

"Can we discuss this later? I'm actually in a bit of a hurry."

The man smiles. "Of course. You must be very busy, having just retired."

"Rushed off my feet," Mark quips, and taking Viv by the hand, he hurries her along the pier, past the cars, to the far end of the quay.

Viv stops and retrieves her hand. "You know Jurat Martel?" Her tone is accusatory.

"Yup."

"You know he sat on the trial? He used to be the Principal of Elizabeth College, and was Head when Pierre was there."

"I know that too."

"He isn't the Mr. Perfect everyone thinks, you know. And he can't stand me."

"I got that impression. Agony Aunt and all that."

"It pays the bills. Just confess: how do you know him?"

"He's my father's second cousin."

"Blimey," she whistles. "That's not good."

"Not when I was a child, no. His mother was a superstitious old witch."

"Metaphorically speaking."

"She held séances. My gran used to take me along. The usual: 'can you get in touch with Fred for me?'"

"Fred being?"

"My grandfather."

"And?"

"And what?"

"What happened?"

"The door slammed shut and the candles blew out."

"No! Don't tell me!"

Mark stares at her. "The cat came in. There was a gale outside."

She shakes her head, laughing. "That's our Mark. Always the realist."

Chapter Ten

Mark is annoyingly predictable. Not one query about her lunch-time date. She thought of mentioning it when he turned up late – 'At least Phil got to the Octopus on time' – but that had a petty ring to it and he'd have probably ask, 'Phil, who's Phil?'

'A sad chap with a mole on his nose.'

'Right.'

'I didn't get off with him, you know.'

'Right.'

Not much of a conversation, that one. She could have carried on: 'that sad man happens to be a retired accountant with a beautiful house in Saint Saviours,' but there was no guarantee of a reaction. 'If I'd met him a month ago, I'd have accepted his invitation for dinner at the Nautique.' Except she hasn't accepted it, and to admit as much is a confession of sorts.

'Dear Self, forgive me for I have lied. It is two weeks since I was last honest with you. I fancy Mark Roussel and it is mucking up my life.'

She often encourages her clients to switch their internal

dialogue to the third person. It opens a gap between the self and their consciousness; it helps them hear what they're saying to themselves in a new way. Don't censure, don't edit. Talk, listen; you'll be surprised what you discover.

No one understands the dynamics of attraction. It's subjectivity at its most incomprehensible (and chemical too, all those pheromones). If push comes to shove, she'd say it was Mark's eyes that she fancied most. And his face which is just long enough not to be round. His hair, of course, beginning to thin at the top and not too grey, and that lopsided smile. But in the end, it's the eyes.

What's disappointing, though, is Jurat Martel. Family strings and all that. Not helpful when it comes to Jasmine Gardiner's case. Or herself, for that matter. There's history.

And there's all the Royal Court stuff too. It wasn't her favourite hang-out, and certainly not during a murder trial with the Bailiff perched in his golden chair beneath the Royal Crest. It was trial by superior men in purple robes. Not that she objects to the system; she understands its benefits. Still, it was intimidation by a sheer fact of numbers. Ten Jurats in funny black hats, five either side in a semi-circle with the council for the Crown and the defendant in the docks below. The Jurats not only judged the evidence but they fixed the sentence and delivered it too.

And who was the chairman of the Jurats? Martel.

And what did he do? He sat through the trial with a paternalistic 'I told you so' look on his face.

As she says, it isn't good news having Martel in his family.

AFTER VIV LEAVES, he buys a sandwich at Marks and Spencer's and sits on a bench. St Peter Port is a maze of quays and harbours, piers and pontoons. The yachts are bobbing below him now the tide is going out, and there's something mindless in watching the to-ing and fro-ing of people on deck. Over there, a woman's cutting a baguette and filling it with cheese, and over there a man's pulling the cork out of a wine bottle. It's colourful and quaint: the boats with their flags hanging off the stern, the pink granite wall of the harbour, the green hill in the distance, the painted shops, and the sea as it ebbs.

Suddenly, there's a whoosh of large wings and a black-backed gull swoops down and tears the sandwich out of his hands.

"Hey!" he shouts, jumping up.

The gull knocks its head against a bollard and topples down towards the water. He peers over the railings. A dazed bird sits on a deck below, the sandwich still in its beak.

"Bastard," he mutters.

The seagull looks up at him. It gobbles down the cheese and pickle and patters along the deck.

"That was *so* cool!" A boy looks over the railings next to him.

"They're greedy bastards," he admits.

"My dad says they eat the ducklings."

"They do."

"Greedy bastards." The lad smiles conspiratorially. His father calls him from a car, and he hurries off, tossing a wave before he opens the door and gets inside.

Mark takes a chocolate bar from his pocket and checks there are no more seagulls.

Why yew seeds, he thinks. It's an odd choice. He

remembered reading about a case in Dublin; the post-mortem showed no anatomical cause of death but analysis of the victim's blood and urine tested positive for taxine B. It's the most common alkaloid found in the yew tree, and its cardio-toxic. The coroner recorded an open verdict.

The vomit in the Pine Forest wasn't Jasmine Gardiner's; she'd been dead too long. Nor was it likely to have been caused by taxine poisoning. Cardio-respiratory failure happens quickly, and given the English yew is one of the most toxic (and toxicity increases during the winter months), no one can take it and survive, not if there is enough left over to be wiped away by a dishcloth. The murderer intended death. And whoever vomited under the tree, was in a pretty bad way.

From where he sits, the murder was planned. Everything required forethought, from the location to the mutilation to the mimicking of an unsolved homicide, and whoever wrapped her in sailcloth had connection to the sea – another problem for the case against Pierre. His family didn't own a boat. From what he read, his grandparents had been quarrymen.

And Jasmine Gardiner was not a sailor either.

Then there are the books, all over the floor, wiped off the shelves as if in a moment of pique. The study didn't adjoin the kitchen, so whoever went in there intended to do so, possibly in search of something. But what? There was no mention of a safe hidden behind the books, not in the newspaper reports anyway.

God, it's frustrating. He hates being Mark Roussel, Retired. Not having access to the files is like trying to walk without legs.

The only option is to see the house for himself.

Chapter Eleven

"You want to enquire about Pine Forest Lodge?"

"That's what I said."

The woman wheels her chair away from the desk and stands up. "Take a seat. I won't be a moment." A quick knock and she enters an office at the back, disappearing behind the door.

He bends to pick up a brochure from the coffee table and flicks through it. Glossy, designed for the Open Market. Basically, if you're rich enough to worry about taxes, then you're rich enough to pay seven figures for a house that would sell for a quarter of the price on the mainland.

"I hear you're interested in the Lodge?" A man stands before him, his hand outstretched. "Tim Mauger. Please, come to my office where we can chat."

He follows him into a room of black furniture and grey walls, and takes the chair as invited.

"It's not widely advertised," Tim says, his face to the computer screen. "For obvious reasons, of course. Can I ask after your interest in it? We've had a few unusual cases, you see, and with a local name like Roussel, I'm surprised you're looking at the Open Market?"

"The population laws, in a nutshell," he lies. "The Island's about money not heritage."

"Here we tend to talk about inclusivity…"

Cut the bullshit, his eyebrows say. "How much is the going price? I imagine it's dropped."

"It's certainly negotiable. But we're looking in the range of three million."

He guffaws. "Even with its history?"

"It's a selling point for some. One couple had plans to run a Ghostly Guest House or something like that."

"Except there's no ghost."

Tim smiles. "It's a substantial property. I'm happy to show you around. Bear in mind, it hasn't been lived in for two years. The owner used to let it but with the banks moving out, there isn't the same demand anymore."

Tim begins with the garage, a white space large enough to house two cars and a lot else besides, not least a body. The door at the back leads into the utility room.

"As you can see, the house was built in the 1980s. Strong construction and no damp to worry about. It could do with some modernisation, but the kitchen is open plan with a sizeable island, and the family room leads into the conservatory. Full of light. The last family had sofas and a television here, and kept the drawing room for formal occasions."

Mark nods. The body would have been on the floor, possibly where he is standing beside the island or over there in the family room with the step leading up into the conservatory. From there, it was probably dragged through the utility room into the garage and hidden. Alternatively, – he turns on his heels – it could have been hauled through the conservatory doors into the garden.

"I'm wondering about telephone sockets?"

Tim looks about. "Most people use their mobiles these days."

"I'm thinking routers."

In fact, he's wondering where the mainline phone would have been. She never called anyone, even as the taxine was attacking her heart, and that pointed to a rapid cardiac arrest. He goes to the window and looks out onto the garden. Where's the yew tree?

"Do you want to see the garden?" Tim asks, watching him.

"No, show me the rest. I'm looking for a large study."

"Got just the room, at the other end of the house. In the original brochure, we called it the library."

He can see why as he turns on his heels, surveying it. He had visualised a row of shelves beside a fireplace, not these wall-to-wall bookcases. Jasmine Gardiner was an avid reader, or a collector, or both of course.

He scans the walls for an inbuilt safe. It would explain why the books were thrown on the floor: the murderer was looking for money or something equally valuable. But there isn't one, so that's a motive scratched off his list.

"Upstairs we have five bedrooms and three bathrooms, and the attic, which could be turned into a large studio space."

A safe rule of thumb is 'quickest and easiest'. Pierre was seen fleeing the area about thirty minutes after death. Given nobody seeks the hardest option without good reason, it's highly unlikely he heaved her body up the stairs. Between a wardrobe and a garage, he'd choose the garage anytime. Especially if he was as weedy as Pierre Bourgaize.

Outside, he stands on the patio and scans the sweep of the garden, overgrown and chaotic with a few plants peeping up through the ivy and choking weeds. A gravel path runs around the side of the house and ends at the paved driveway, etched with dandelions. But there isn't a yew tree in sight. He crosses the lawn, clogged with daisies, and makes for the high wall that gives onto the Pine Forest. He paces its edge, past the cascading dog-roses and other bushes, and then stops. He pulls away the foliage to reveal a wooden door, rotten at the base with a rusted padlock. Over his shoulder, he glances towards the house and then back to the door. Here it is. The route down to the hanging tree.

"What is it?" Tim Mauger calls, walking towards him.

"A door."

"Oh that. You can't get through it. The brambles are too thick on the other side."

Brambles grow fast. In eleven years, they'd become a jungle. Before that? He needs the report, but if he were the murderer he'd drag the body through the house out of the conservatory doors, over the gravel and across the lawn to the door. The house isn't overlooked. No one would see.

Another thought comes to him.

He'd hide her body in the garage and escape through the door onto National Trust land, turning right to Jerbourg Point or left towards town. Leave it a few hours and then return the same way to get rid of it. He wouldn't take his bicycle out through the main gates and pedal up the lane onto the road for all to see.

Chapter Twelve

Who wants to be stuck on an island and not see the sea? That's what he hates about the mainland – no sea. Now he's back, and still no sea.

The best he can hope for is a sniff now and then, like a fucking greyhound with his nose in the air. The other day the winds were so high, they whisked up the waves and dumped their spittle all over the prison gardens. Sniff, sniff, he went about the place.

The only other things to smell are bleach and farts.

Gardens, please. They asked him where he wanted to work, and that was his reply. In the gardens. He wanted to catch the sea's breath.

And what the fuck – they've put him in the library.

Thanks for that.

"You like books," they said.

Yeah, right. He got an English degree in his last lock-up and now he's fucking Charles Dickens.

He's an islander, isn't he? And he wants to be by the sea, and if he can't be by it he wants to see it, and if he can't see it than he's bloody well going to smell it. So, fuck off.

The Accused

"You haven't been taking your medication, have you?"

Just piss yourself, won't you? Try taking mirtazapine yourself. Dry mouth, sick. How about the headaches? He wants to go back onto the old stuff.

Put a pill down his throat and chemicalise his brain – it's their answer to everything. Fetch his breakfast from the canteen, get the pills from the hatch and then back to his room to eat it all.

'I care for no man on earth, and no man on earth cares for me.' That was Dickens.

He likes his room. He'll admit that much. En-suite and all. Not the best hotel in the world, but not bad. He has a desk, TV, a safe and plastic crates to put his things in. And a board to pin up photos of his family. As if.

Mum and Dad at Christmas? Give me a break.

His sketch of Faustus is far more comforting. And it freaked out the chaplain.

Bloody funny that.

He copied it from a woodcut: Faustus in his circle of symbols, book in one hand and wand in the other, and a nasty-looking demon sitting on the floor.

It's the demon that makes him laugh, with its tail and barbed wings. It has a goatee too and horns.

Please, Mr. Chaplain. Give me some fucking credit, won't you? You think I believe in anything as ridiculous as that? *Solamen miseris socios habuisse doloris.* That's what Mephistopheles said, *It's comfort to the wretched to have companions in misery.*

The idiot can't see that it keeps him safe. In the other prison, they took one look at it and left him alone. The worse he ever got was a chin-check – then he muttered Marlowe and the idiot thought he'd put a spell on him.

Works like magic!

Except nonsense at the surface level is sense on a deeper one.

That's why it's called the occult, for fuck's sake: *celare, occulere...* it's covered-over.

Chapter Thirteen

He's lying on a towel with a phone at his ear.

"Is that the *Guernsey Press*? Can I speak with the advertising manager, please?" The rocks are warm and the sun is browning his legs. "Yes, I can hold."

High tide has always excited him. There's just something about it. The sea is so full, it's like being a toddler in an enormous bath. Ideas come best to him when he is floating in it, his eyes shut and his hands flicking now and then to keep himself afloat, which is why he has just scrambled out and is drying in the sun.

"Advertising Manager, can I help?"

"Hello, my name's Mark Roussel. I'd like to post an advert for three days starting from tomorrow. No, I don't have a picture, just the following: 'Information Wanted. Write to Mark with a contact number if you know anything about Jasmine Gardiner. PineForestMurder@gmail.com'."

The email address doesn't exist, but it will take moments to set up. Then all he needs to do is shift through the conspiracy theorists and nut-cases until he finds that titbit which promises a way forward.

The next person to call is the prison governor. He needs to speak to Pierre Bourgaize, but when he rings, he gets the secretary.

"The rules are no visitors."

"Not even family?"

"Family, of course. Are you family?"

"No."

"Then I'm sorry, you can't visit."

He calls another number. "Pete, it's me, Mark. I want to pick your brains. If you get this message, call me."

He lays back on his towel and looks up at the sky. It's so blue and boundless, and yet somewhere in all that colour are the stars shining brightly, hidden by the greater brilliance of the sun. The moon too. And he wonders what other things are concealed from him in broad daylight, not in the dark as everyone fears, but in the light. Because, right now, he can't ignore the tingling in his stomach and that quivering beneath the surface of his skin. He's back, and it feels good.

Lying sideward, he unlocks his phone and rifles through Google in search of Guernsey cleaning companies.

"Sorry, we don't employ a Mrs. Le Sauvage."

"No, our records don't go back that far."

"You've got the wrong number. This is a laundrette."

"Mrs. Le Sauvage, you say, her that lives at the Genats estate, eh? She doesn't work for us anymore – you want her number? I don't know if that's right, eh, giving it to a stranger – you say you're the police? Anyone can say that, eh, even the devil – Okay, I tell you what. You give me your number and she can call if she wants. What do you say to that? – Okay, I've got a pen and paper – 07781..."

Mark is stuffing his towel into a bag when his phone rings.

The Accused

"Is that Mark Roussel?"

"Yes."

"It's Tracy Le Sauvage, eh. 'Donkey Cleaners', they gave me this number, them." The accent is strong and he braces himself for the patois.

"Thank you for calling. I hope I'm not disturbing you. I'm looking into Jasmine Gardiner's death. I believe you used to work for her?"

"Cor chapin, and there I thought you were the lottery, eh!" Her laughter is thick and rasping.

"Sorry."

"Life, it's what it is, eh. You want to talk about Jasmine Gardiner, you?"

"Yes."

"A long time ago, eh. I scrubbed her floors for years, me. Why?"

"I'm doing some further investigations."

"You the *Press*?"

"No, nothing like that."

He hears her shuffle across a floor and puff as she sits down.

"She was a one, her, all that money and never happy, eh. Makes you wonder what they want from life. I used to say to her, I'd say, you know Mrs. Gardiner, you need to get a job, you do. And she'd say to me, she'd say: My bloody husband can keep me. Thing is, she was on the bottle, she was. I'd find all types in the bin, eh, wine, gin, whisky. It was sad, mind, what happened to her, eh? And her having married that man. Real bigwig, him, head of some bank, he was and running off with his secretary, eh. Local girl, her. That's what started it, is it. She hated all us locals. I used to tell her, I'd say, don't blame us coz of that trollop, but she couldn't see it, her. Said we were all witches, eh, which made me cross. I wanted to leave but I couldn't coz I needed the money, me. But I tell you what, Mr. Roussel, he used to hit her, he did. I know coz when he was still in the house, eh, I'd see her with the bruises. I told the police, I did, I said that man, he'd done it, him."

"I thought he had an alibi?"

"They said he was on the mainland with that trollop but I don't believe it, me. All I say is, thank the Lord those two boys were at boarding school, eh."

"I don't suppose you know if she had a safe in the house anywhere?"

"Cor damme là, how would I know that, eh? I wasn't her banker, me."

"Vère dja." A good point – eh.

He's struggling to hold onto his English. His grandmother spoke the patois and he remembered bits like *boudiax* and *I fait des sous coume d's écâles* which he tried to use once in English. "What kind of fuck-useless saying is that?" a mate asked, and he agreed – if he could make money like seashells, he'd be living on Herm and mining the beaches.

"I was wondering about the garage," he says. "What did she have in there?"

"Là là – it was a mess that place. I kept saying to her, I said, you need to send this stuff to the Bourg. They help people with cancer, them, but she didn't listen, her."

"Did she have a chest freezer?"

"On the left, as you went in."

"Was it full?"

"Cor heck, it was all frosted over, it was, I said, you need to thaw that, Mrs. Gardiner." She pauses. "You don't say – oh my giddy Aunt – you don't say he put her in there, eh?

As God is my witness, he'd have had to jump on top of it, him, to get her stuffed down. And that Pierre, I saw him once, I did, and he's a weedy little thing, is it."

"You saw him, at the house?"

"No, no. Only on the photos in the *Press*, eh. Mind, she did talk about a weird lad. Said she had met him, and he was into the witches and the black books, him, and it made her laugh. She said us locals were all weird, and I said to her, I said, look here, Mrs. Gardiner, we come from old stock, us, fairy stock. And that made her laugh even more."

"It is a silly legend," Mark admits.

"I said it on purpose, eh, just to make my point. I said to her, I said, that's why we're short and dark, and she said, that's why you're all funny in the head."

"Do you think she was talking about Pierre Bourgaize?"

"Faw saw. He was into the black books, eh. That's why the house was ransacked, is it."

"Not quite ransacked."

"Why would she do that, eh? She was house-proud, her. And she loved those books, even though they were full of dust and smelt bad. She showed me some of them, but I don't understand that sort of thing, me."

"Most of her books were old?"

"A mix, eh, but she had a lot, she did."

"And on the day of the murder, did you go to the house?"

"I told the police: it was me day off."

"One last question. Can you tell me what you know about Tom de Carteret? He was the one that saw Pierre Bourgaize on his bicycle around the time of the murder."

"Tom de Carteret." She laughs. "That one, eh? He was always round the house, him, chatting her up. He did work in the garden, all the time, he did, work that didn't need doing, eh. I'd love a coffee, Mrs. Gardiner, he'd say, him, and they'd talk, eh, all the time and he was charging by the hour, he was. Daylight robbery. He took the money right off her, eh, right in front of her eyes."

Chapter Fourteen

After lunch, he sits with his mother in the front garden, watching the sparrows peck at the seeds in the long grass. The lawn needs mowing but the Flymo is broken and he hasn't bought a new one. He enjoys watching the sparrows feed as nature intended, and he likes the dandelions and daisies. He likes the poppies by the gate too.

The clouds are high and thin, softening the sun's blaze and his mother dozes under a large hat, her chin on her chest. They sit there together, mother and son, each in their own thoughts.

"Good afternoon."

Jurat Martel is standing in the archway. "I like the meadow-look," he says casting his eyes over the garden. "You should get the *Press* to come and do an article on it."

Mark catches the sarcasm and stands up, holding out his hand. "Have you come to see Mum?"

Martel looks down at her. "Let her sleep."

"She'd be happy to see you."

"I'm not here for your mother."

That makes a change. In the old days, he came for nothing else. "How can I help you?"

"Let's take a stroll."

"Janice is inside doing the ironing, I can't leave Mum alone."

The furrow between Martel's eyes is deep. There is something of the patrician about him, there always has been, and he understands why his mother welcomed his visits in the old days, even if he resented them as a child. The brandy on the patio, the dinners at the White House. Martel used to pat him on the head, like a dog. Still, she never married him. The wolf is a handsome beast, she always said, but you never let him inside the house.

"I want to talk about your future, Mark. I have some ideas you might find interesting."

"The ones you mentioned the other day?"

"With elections in eighteen months, we need to increase your exposure."

"You're talking about me becoming a Deputy?"

"It's island-wide voting now. It should work for you."

"I've spent my career avoiding politics."

"You don't have a career."

Touché.

"But you could serve the island. With me as your seconder, it's in the bank."

Here it comes – Martel the Benevolent. Listen to me; do as I say. He became a teacher because of Martel, and then ran away to the other side of the world when he realised it was a mistake. The last thing he needs now is advice.

"I might not be staying. I'm here for the summer, to be with Mum."

"Your London flat isn't on the market?"

"I've left everything as it is."

The Accused

Which is true, even the car, the functional one, not the bubble-car he drove onto the ferry. The intention is to spend the summer with his mother and decide what to do next. The day the autumnal winds blow the sea onto the roads, he'll make his choice.

"I've been looking into Pierre Bourgaize's case," he says.

"I know. I heard you called the Greffe."

He's surprised. He thinks a moment. "Can you get me to see the transcripts of the trial? The forensic report would be helpful too."

"You're asking a favour?"

"I'm asking for your help."

"And the difference is?"

"I'm not exchanging anything."

Martel's smile is oily. "The Greffier will say no."

"Even to a man in your position?"

Martel raises an eyebrow.

"You sat on the trial," he continues, "you must be able to tell me something."

"Nothing you can't read in the *Press*."

Pull another.

"Look," Martel leans down towards him, "we understand you're finding your feet after London."

We – who is 'we'?

"I more than most. What happened was unfortunate, given your prospects. And I've told everyone who's asked that the rumours aren't true. But people gossip. And Guernsey's a small place."

What's he getting at? What rumours? From where?

"You don't want to go upsetting people."

"The only thing I'm upset about is my mother."

"Then find something else to get your teeth into."

"I am."

"Not Pierre Bourgaize. No one's interested in it anymore. He had his trial and now he's locked up. We've all moved on."

Evidently the man doesn't read the *Press* or listen to the radio.

"You should come and see Mum one of these days. I'm struggling to understand why her friends don't visit her anymore." If Martel feels the whip, he doesn't flinch. "Is a person less valuable because their mind's dying off? Or is everyone scared of it? I'm interested."

Martel glances over at her, still dozing in the sun. "She doesn't know who I am."

"She does."

"I don't know who she is." The statement is sharp and he's surprised by its anger.

"She's still Lilly, you know."

"I don't want to talk about it." Martel puts his hands in pockets. "Right now, I need you to listen, and if your mother could understand, she'd agree with me. Pierre's verdict was safe. I sat on the trial. Heaven knows what you're hoping to find."

"I'm making no judgement. I'm not asking to reopen the case. I haven't even asked Pierre to nominate me. I'm just doing some research. I can't see the problem with that."

"Isn't it obvious? You and I know the island has a dark side. It always has done."

"You sound like a Calvinist and that's a bit rich coming from your side of the family."

"Linda Martel wasn't a witch. She was a gifted child. A Christian. She gave a lot of people hope."

"I don't deny it."

"I was talking about the *grimoire*, a different kettle of fish."

The Accused

"The *grimoires* are a load of tosh. It's pseudo-science and fairy tales."

"Perhaps."

Martel's mother was one of them, with her séances and potions. He remembers her tales of ghosts and shape-shifters, of the little people sneaking out of a night and causing havoc.

"It's what they lead people to do that concerns me," Martel continues. "Pierre's a warning. Don't meddle, and you'll stay on the right side of the law."

Wait, now; this is interesting. "You're saying Pierre was locked up as a warning?"

"Of course not."

"What did you mean then?"

"I'm saying he must stay where he is for the good of everyone."

"I'm more concerned whether he's guilty or not."

"You're saying the verdict was unsafe? Good lord, man. I was chairman of the Jurats. I heard the evidence. Are you questioning my judgement? A man in my position..."

"Absolutely."

"Don't forget I was principal of Elizabeth College when he was there. I saw that man through his education."

"I know. So, here's a question for you: how did he get the body to the tree? He can't have done it on his own. He isn't strong enough. That's the first thing bothering me. There are more."

Martel stands still, his eyes fixed on his face. A few moments pass – a breath in, a breath out and a flicker of eyelids – then he cracks his knuckles and looks at his watch. "Send my regards to your mother."

"I'll wake her and you can say it yourself."

"I'm in a hurry."

"Off to play golf?"

"I don't play golf."

And that is the end of the conversation.

After Martel leaves, he takes out his phone and opens the PineForestMurder email account. The first person to contact him is a Ginny Bisson. If he wants to get the dirt on Jasmine Gardiner, she writes, they should meet at the White Rock Café at eleven. It's by the port, next to Channel Seaways; he can't miss it unless he's taking the boat to Herm, or blind.

Chapter Fifteen

He's no expert on island eateries, but the White Rock Café is as local as they come. It might aspire to grandeur with its ornate Victorian façade, but there's nothing fancy about the three old men sitting outside with their mugs of tea and cigarettes. It pleases him in an odd sort of way. No one is trying to ape London with glass-fronted buildings and warehouse chic. Take the black monolith that replaced the Royal Hotel, and Admiral Park's triangulated protrusions, for example: eyesores as far as he's concerned.

He nods at the men and pushes through the door into the café, hit first by the smell of chip-oil and then the size of the place; it's bigger than he realised. At the counter, he looks about for someone to serve him.

"*Warro!*" he says.

A fat woman pushes through the door from the kitchen. "What do you want?"

"Tea, please."

"Mug or cup?"

"Mug."

An old man sitting against the far wall raises his hand to him. "Strange weather, eh?" His beard is yellow about the mouth and salt crystals glisten in the cracks on his face.

"A nasty front last week," Mark agrees, and chooses a table by the window.

It has been wiped clean, as have the bottles of tomato ketchup and brown sauce. He glances at the floor. The café is spotless. The air might be thick with fat but the window has a grease-free sparkle to it.

He looks over at the specials board. It offers a Special Fry-up, Veggie Fry-up, Kid's Fry-up and the Jumbo Cod. There's fish and chips for £6 and scampi for £8.

"Any chance of a piece of toast?" he calls to the woman behind the counter.

"What?"

He gets to his feet. "A piece of toast, please."

"Egg on toast?"

"No, just toast."

She turns to the specials board. "You don't want chips?"

"No, just toast with butter and jam."

"Mr. Falla," she calls out to the kitchen. "Mr. Falla. We do toast, eh?"

When his tea arrives, it is the size of a workman's flask and just as strong; for that he's paid 40p extra. It's a bargain. Like the toast, which is three pieces high and dripping with butter the colour of marigolds. He bites into it and decides in favour of the White Rock Café.

"Didn't he jump out of your van window and run into the fields?" That is a young woman with pulled back hair and a tattoo on her neck. "He's always getting caught, eh."

"They turned up at the shed and said they wanted to speak to him. They said, where is he? and I said, cor heck, you aren't going to get him on one of my jobs, eh." That is the man eating his chips and eggs in the corner by the kitchen door. "I said, he's probably out at Jeff's and they said, if you don't tell us, we're going to arrest you and I said, I'm not being awkward, I'm just saying he isn't here, eh. They tried to put these handcuffs on me, but they were too small so they got all arsey and got on the radio, and I said to them, I said, it ain't my fault, eh?"

"They're bored, that's what's wrong with them. Got nothing to do, eh." That is the fat woman behind the counter.

He is nose-deep into his mug of tea when the door wings open and a woman appears. Dressed in tracksuit bottoms and a hoodie, she has the grey look of a drinker. She waves to the huddle by the corner and says '*warro*' to the old man with the yellowing beard, before walking over to his table and calling him, 'email-man'. Her accent is strong.

"Mark Roussel," he says, rising from his chair and holding out his hand. She ignores it and flops into the chair, choking him in spoors of ash and cheap perfume.

"Cup of instant," she calls out, then turns to him. "You don't come from these parts, eh?" Her eyes bob about the room.

"You mean town? I come from Câtel."

"Local, is it? Don't sound it." Sniffing and rubbing her sleeve across her nose, she settles on a point behind him and slumps her arms hard on the table. Stable, fixed to an unmoving point, she relaxes. "You want to know about the murder, is it?" Her knuckles are covered with tattoos: stars and asterisks and a line of uneven dots.

"That's what my email said."

Her coffee arrives, steaming hot with granules floating on the surface, and she slurps it, ripping open two sticks of sugar and tossing them in.

"What are you going to pay for it?"

"Pay?"

"What's it worth, eh?"

"That depends on what you're going to tell me."

"Yeah well, I don't do depends, do I."

Her tone is sparky but her eyes are tired and she needs more than caffeine to get her going. She takes a napkin from the metal container and blows her nose.

"How about a hundred for starters."

He bursts out laughing.

"Got a problem?" She stuffs the napkin in her pocket. "I sell, you buy. That's what me ol' man taught me, eh."

"Market economy?"

"Whatever."

There is something about Ginny Bisson he likes. Nothing so clichéd as a rough diamond (he doubts anyone could polish her up that well) but there's a sincerity of sorts.

Fiddling with the corner of the menu card, she runs her finger down the list.

"I'm having the Fry Up Special," she calls to the fat woman behind the counter.

"You're paying," she adds, grinning, a black hole where a tooth should be.

"What do I get for it?" he says.

"Bargaining, eh?"

"Capitalism," he smiles.

"Righty-ho." She scratches her armpit. "Jasmine Gardiner, she was no angel that one. That's my gem for the day."

"Priceless," he says. "And for ten times that amount, I'll get what? Something useful?"

"Hey mister!" the old man calls out. "You listen to our

Ginny. Bugger me, if that woman wasn't a right English bitch, her."

Ginny shifts her chair around to face him. "Spot on, Grandad."

"Why do you say that?" he asks.

"Her blog, eh. Never read it meself but they say it smelt like the *vraic* when it rots."

"It was wicked, that's what." The young woman with pulled-back hair and a tattoo on her neck speaks up from the other side of the room. "Me Mum read it. It did it for old Mr. Brehaut, didn't it?"

"Lost his job, is it." Ginny's eyes are sparkling and her hands are playing with the mug unaware – or unconcerned – that she's losing her monopoly on knowledge. "Nearly ended up in the Câtel with all the nutters, eh."

He looks from Ginny to the old man to the young woman. "What did she say?"

"That he was one of those paedos," the fat woman behind the counter explains. "She didn't give his name, mind, but you didn't have to be Miss Marple, eh, to work it out. He was at Amherst Primary School. Said they couldn't keep him on with all them rumours. He nearly topped himself."

"Crikey," Mark says, falling into the brogue. "Did he?"

"Caw heck, no," the old man laughs. "A bugger that one, but he's alright now. Like all them Brehauts."

"Which Brehaut is he then?"

"The one at Maurepas, eh. Just down from the infant school."

"So, was it true?"

No one answers.

The thin girl cleans a spot on the floor with the tip of

her shoe. "He'd have a few things to tell you about Jasmine Gardiner, I bet."

"Yeah," Ginny nods.

"I'm not saying she got what was coming, eh." The old man rubs his hand over his beard. "That Pierre Bourgaize, he's from bad stock, him."

"That ain't fair, Bill," the fat woman scolds. "It was his dad that handed him over. You know that."

"I wasn't talking about his dad, was I?" the old man mutters.

"Who then?" he asks, but no one answers and their silence is saved by a voice from the back of the café calling out: "Grub's up!"

The fat woman goes to the kitchen, switching on the radio as she passes by the counter. Island FM booms out with a phone-in complaint about a bus shelter that has been vandalised in Torteval. It's time to leave. At the counter, he waits to pay while the fat woman carries the largest fry-up he's ever seen to Ginny by the window. On returning, she takes his cash and when he asks if she knows anything more, she shakes her head. She wants nothing to do with it, not then, not now. You know how it is, there are some things better not to touch.

Outside, the old men are still smoking. The Liberation is in, and he waits for the disembarked lorries to drive past before crossing the road. He takes the steps up the wall and then down to the car-park. As he wanders about the rows looking for his car, he calls Viv.

"Any idea how I can get hold of Jasmine Gardiner's blog?"

"Hello, I'm fine," she says on the other end.

"What?"

"I just thought I'd tell you I'm fine."

The Accused

"Right." He has no idea what she's going on about. "The blog. Can you help me get hold of it?"

There's a moment's silence. "The domain name would have gone by now. You're not going to get much luck there."

He hasn't thought about that, although he should have.

"Anything else?" Viv asks.

"Nope, that's it."

"I can have my coffee now?"

"I'm in town," he points out.

"That's good to know."

"I can't stop you having a coffee if I'm in town."

"You're talking to me," she says.

She's confusing him. "There's one more thing you can do."

"Thought so."

"Have you got the *Yellow Pages* there? Can you look up Brehaut and find the one in Maurepas Road?"

Viv is silent.

"Viv?"

"Yes."

"Did you hear me?"

"Yes."

"Any chance of doing it?"

"You mean, any chance of me getting off my chair, leaving my desk, walking down the corridor to the hall and finding something you want?"

"Yes."

"The dog's in the way."

He didn't know she has a dog. "I'm sensing some resistance here."

"Well, blow me down. Mark Roussel, the detective. He's got there in the end. Try some charm and let's see how we go. You know, 'Hi Viv, my old friend, how're you doing?

Slept well last night? It was really muggy, wasn't it? You wouldn't do me a huge favour, would you?' That sort of thing."

For God's sake, people sometimes. "Hi Viv, my old friend, how're you doing? Slept well last night? It was really muggy, wasn't it? You wouldn't do me a huge favour, would you?"

"Enough. It doesn't suit you. I'll see what I can find." From the sound of her breathing, she's on her feet and walking down the corridor. She stops. "Right, give me a sec." She drops a book onto a surface. "Brehaut, you say?" She's flipping through the pages now. "Yup, got it. There's a hell of a lot of them. What's his first name?"

"No idea."

"That's helpful. Where did you say he lived? Maurepas Road, okay, I'm running my finger down the list. Here it is. Got it." She reads out the number.

"Thanks."

"You owe me one

"Noted."

Leaning against the side of his car, he dials the number and waits. The voice that answers is old and dry, and when he introduces himself, the line goes dead. Typical, and he lifts the canopy to get inside.

Chapter Sixteen

'Aumone' is a small terrace house set up above the level of the road, in walking distance of Amherst Primary School where Brehaut was caretaker. According to the *Press*, excrement was left on his doorstep and a dead bird posted through the letter box. No wonder he lives behind drawn curtains.

The doorbell doesn't work, so he knocks as loudly as he can. No one answers. He knocks harder. The door opens an inch and a flushed, puffy face peers around it.

"I'm Mark Roussel. We spoke on the phone."

"Go away."

"I just want to ask you a few questions."

"Leave me alone, eh. I didn't do anything."

"I know. That's why I'm here. Can I come in?"

"I'm innocent."

"Let me in and we can talk. I'm not with the police—"

"The *Press*?"

"God forbid me!"

He holds the man's gaze. It's a useful tactic. It speaks reliability and trust, as he expects, the door widens to let him in. He squeezes through the space and notices the piles of plastic bags filled to the handles with rubbish on the other side of the door.

The house smells of cigarette ash and something rotten, and he follows Brehaut into a small front room. It's dark and airless, and he widens the neck of his shirt. It's also a 1950's time-capsule. Stained antimacassars cover the backs of the armchairs and a mirror hangs on a chain over the fireplace. The television is thirty years out of date and the record player belongs in an antique shop. On the mantel is the black-and-white photograph of a young woman, framed in tarnished silver. Before it lays a bouquet of plastic flowers.

Brehaut isn't much better. His shirt sleeves are rolled up and held in place by garters.

He points at the photograph. "Is that your wife?"

"Died of cancer when she was thirty-three."

He nods out of respect.

The man has the swollen eyes of a drinker, and he looks about for the bottles. They're probably in the plastic bags in the hallway.

Outside, a moped roars down the road.

"Little shits," Brehaut spits. "They take the silencers off on purpose." He retrieves a handkerchief from his pocket, and wipes his mouth. "So, what do you want?"

"I'm looking into Jasmine Gardiner's murder. I suspect no one asked you at the time."

"Damn right they didn't." Brehaut blows his nose. "I'd have told them a thing or two."

"Would you tell me? I imagine you're bitter about what happened."

"She ruined my life, she did."

He looks over at the armchairs, either side of the electric fire. "Can I take a seat?"

The Accused

Brehaut holds out a hand to one of them and then takes the other, gripping the armrests as he lowers himself down.

Mark sits and crosses his legs. "Why do you think she picked on you? From what I understand, it was pretty vicious."

Brehaut rubs a hand over his grey hair. "I told her to move her car. One of those big Land Rovers, it was, and it was blocking the entrance, eh."

"The entrance to the school?"

Brehaut nods. "I told her, I did, I said, you move that car. She wouldn't, eh."

"What was she doing there? Her sons went to boarding school."

"I don't know, me. Picking up some brat for some friend of hers. Don't ask me."

"Then what happened?"

"Can't remember it all, eh. She called me a Guernsey donkey. I swore at her in patois. She said we were all witches and we had a row. I made her look a right fool, I did and after that she had it in for me."

"By spreading rumours? That's none too nice."

"A right bitch – excuse my French. I'll tell you something else too, she had a lover, eh. A young man, he was. I never saw him, but I could tell by his voice. Everyone went on about her husband running off with his secretary – poor Jasmine Gardiner and all that baloney – but she had a tallboy in her bed, eh. You know the secretary, she was local, that's why she started that blog, to get back at us all. Every one of us, is it. I was waiting for her to say something about the Bailiff, I was, but they killed her before anything came out."

He sucks his lips. "How do you know this?"

"The Masons, always the Masons, is it."

"Not about the Bailiff, I meant about the lover. How do you know?"

Brehaut shifts in his chair and runs his fingers down the sides of his mouth.

"It's important."

"Alright, keep your hair on. I went around to her house. Not on the day of the murder, mind. I went coz I was angry, eh. I'd lost my job and I blamed her. Right so too, the bitch – mind my French."

"I've seen the house. There's a high wall and gates."

"The gates were open. I stood there, eh, and I heard them talking."

"How do you know it was her lover?"

Brehaut's laugh is gravelly. "She called me a paedo, but I know love talk when I hear it."

Okay, he'll go along with that. "You don't know who he was?"

"Cor heck, Mr. Roussel, I'm no paedo – God bless my wife – and I'm no murderer neither. I'm related to Walter Brehaut, I am."

"Right."

"You don't know who I'm talking about, do you? He was that schoolmaster-turned-preacher down by Perelle. He converted all those fisherman in the 1920s, eh. There was so many of them, they had to build a hut for them all. He was my grandfather's cousin, he was."

"Right." It isn't the best character reference.

"I'm not sad she's dead," Brehaut continues. "She was a vicious woman. When she saw me by the gates, she shouted at me and she told me to get the hell out of there, eh. Those were her words. All dressed up in her fine clothes and jewellery, she was. She drove one of those big cars, Land Rovers, eh. I saw it in the drive. Like all those rich English women, bullying their way down the lanes, is it. I tell you, she was a right bitch – pardon my French. *La pute* eh?" His eyes twinkle. "If that makes me a bad man, so be it. I say it as it is."

He smiles. "*Coum aen l'âene Guernesiasie, eh.*"

"You speak the patois? I'm not ashamed of it. I'm a Guernsey donkey, me."

He sits in the car with the canopy open to cool it down. The sun is beating on his head and he stretches behind to get his cap from the back seat. Beside it is a notebook and pencil. He picks that up too and licking the pencil, he writes: *Brehaut heard her with a lover, young male. Avoided giving his name. Why?* Next, he calls Viv, tapping his foot on the pedals as he waits for her to answer. He looks up and sees Brehaut watching him from behind the net curtain. The old man points at the car and gives the thumbs up. Mark returns the gesture just as the phone clicks and he hears Viv's voice: "Sorry I can't come to the phone right now. Leave a message after the beep."

"Viv, it's Mark. Give me a call when you get this. Ta."

Chapter Seventeen

THE PATH TO THE GULLY IS WELL TRODDEN AND HE scrambles his way down it, worried that someone is already there with their towel spread out on the rock, reading a book. Ever since he was old enough to jump about in the sea, he's come here alone. Staked his territorial flag, so to speak.

To his relief, it's empty. The tide has come in and the rocks are warm. He takes off his shirt and shorts, and climbs down to feel the temperature of the sea, holding onto the side of the rock as he dips his foot into the water. Cold enough to energise; warm enough to be pleasant. He jumps in and swims to the end, where the gully meets the ocean. Then he lays on his back, loving the hugeness of it all, the sense of being suspended as if there's nothing holding him up. All praise to the sea, he smiles. Day in, day out, it always returns, the only sure thing in life, except for death (and taxes).

Without the sea, there's nothing. He missed it in London.

Afterwards, he lays on his towel, his arm over his eyes as

The Accused

he dries off in the sun. It's hot and he feels his skin burn. He turns over and checks his phone for messages. There's a voicemail from Viv.

"Hi, you. I had a client. Call me when you're free."

He does. After three rings, she picks it up. "Are you free to talk?" he asks.

"Totally. I'm sitting here, being Agony Aunt Viv. Right now, I'm advising a lad to tell his parents he's gay."

"Great."

"I hope so. They're Pentecostals. What about you?"

"I'm not gay."

"Good to know."

He hurries on. "Have you heard anything about Jasmine Gardiner's lover?"

"Wow!" She whistles. "Well done, Mr. Roussel."

"Are you taking the mickey?"

"No."

"Why the surprise then?"

"I had no idea."

"Even though most women are killed by a partner?"

"And men?"

"By a friend. It's like Poirot used to say…"

"Don't tell me you read Agatha Christie!" Her laugh comes from the belly.

"There are two aspects to every crime: the nature of the victim and the psychology of the killer."

"Did he really say that?"

"No idea. I remember it from a lecture. Right now, it's all I've got to go on, and I'd say a lover is high on the list."

"What about the Morse programmes?" She can't hide her amusement. "I bet you watch those of a night."

He does in fact (he's got the DVD set at home) but he isn't admitting it.

"About the lover..."

"I've absolutely no idea who it could be."

"Ask around, will you. See what you can dig up. You're mixing with these people, do a bit of research and let me know what you find out."

There is silence.

"How can I put this nicely..." Viv says. "I have a job. You don't."

He doesn't appreciate being reminded.

"Why don't *you* see what you can dig up? You're the detective. I get that in your old job you had lowly constables doing the boring stuff but..."

"Right." He's got the message. "I'll tell you what I find out." He hangs up.

That evening, he sits in the kitchen with his laptop and a glass of whisky. Janice is chopping vegetables and his mother is playing with a potato she has half-peeled and has no intention of peeling any further.

He opens the PineForestMurder email account and, as expected, the messages are lining up. Nineteen to be exact. He begins at the top and makes his way down. His strategy is simple: read the first few lines and ignore any that mention witchcraft.

If you want to know about what happened, read the Petit Albert. That says it all. DELETE.

Don't go talking to Pierre Bourgaize, he's the devil. DELETE

That Jasmine woman got what was coming to her. Not so nice. DELETE

There's a coven on this island that's set on cursing the

English. Mrs. Gardiner knew all about it. The big names killed her, not Pierre Bourgaize. DELETE

By the eighth, he's getting irritated, by the tenth he's bored. He introduces another strategy: trash any email that doesn't include a contact number (he specifically asked for one). That relieves him of six more. Three remain. He rings the first number and gets a lady from the Pentecostal Church near Delancey who wants to invite him for prayer on Sunday morning. He hangs up. The second is a man who was an avid reader of Jasmine Gardiner's blog, but on close questioning, offers nothing new. The third claims to have information that was never shared at the time of the investigation but when he calls the number, the answer machine clicks into action. He leaves a message and his phone number.

"I think we need some music," he says, knocking back the whisky and getting up from the chair. "You like music, don't you, Mum?"

She bites into the raw potato. He glances at Janice – *What's that?* he says with his eyes. *Don't worry*, she motions back and leans across the table to pull it out. Lilly won't let go.

"You're going to hurt your teeth, Lilly, let it go. Raw potatoes taste horrid. Drop it and we'll throw it away."

Saliva dribbles down Lilly's chin, but she clings on. A growl rumbles in the back of her throat.

"I've got an idea," he says and hurries out of the kitchen.

In the sitting room, he picks up an old record from the pile next to the gramophone and draws it out of its sleeve. Puffing away the dust, he lays it on the turntable and levers the needle down. First there is the crackle and then the sudden burst of guitars and trumpets. Increasing the volume, he jogs back into the kitchen and draws his mother off her chair, clasping her about the waist. The potato falls from her mouth and she lets out a screech of delight.

The rumba is fast and loud, beating a rhythm that moves her feet. Holding her close, feeling her smallness, he steps her forward and back and rocks her side to side. He has no idea what he is doing, but it she loves it.

"Olé!" she shouts, throwing an arm in the air.

Janice puts down her knife and claps.

"Cha-cha-cha," his mother calls out, and the next piece to play is just that.

Chapter Eighteen

Okay, so this is what he thinks – whoever's trying to get info on the Pine Forest murder needs their heads seen to. What are they after? Salacious gossip, gory details? He's thinking of sending an email: *'Dear idiot, go fuck yourself.'* Except he doesn't. For lots of reasons. He doesn't have an email address for one thing and he's practising his Ps and Qs. Not that it's easy. Swearing is *de facto* these days. He blames the Americans.

He blames most people for most things. Take his back ache: that's the mattress's fault; it's a piece of foam. And his gastritis? That's the shit coffee they serve.

'Wanker' is Mike's explanation, but he only knows three words and that's one of them – so not very informative. Still, he likes Mike. He just blames him for being a good guy; good guys are short on the neuron count.

Thing is, so is Tattoo-Trev. The bastard tripped him up in the corridor on the way to lunch. Retaliation was a piece of paper dropped on his food tray with a pentacle on it and some esoteric symbols. The man nearly pissed himself with fright.

Go fuck yourself, Tattoo-Trev.

Now, now, that isn't the way to talk, is it, *cherie?*

That's his gran. He wants to blame her for something, he just can't think what. For having a black cat and black books? She taught him everything he knows. Forget College and education. If you want people to fear you, get into the dark arts.

Not that his gran would approve. "I don't like your stepdad either," she said, "but I don't go putting worms in his lunch box, do I?"

He put a dead frog in his flask too, and got such a hiding, he couldn't go to school; his arse was black and blue and his face like a Picasso painting.

For his real dad – when he found out who he was – he served up a daily trot of spells cut out from the *Press* and stuck on A4 paper. Folded up in an envelope and stuffed under the door of Le Lievres before it opened. *For the Attention of Mr. Paul Ogier.* He got bored after a week, which was just as well coz an article appeared in the *Press* about it, saying the police were looking for witnesses. Temptation was to write in: *Dear Police, I've seen a short woman with curly dyed hair around there of a morning. She has a mole between her eyebrows and is quite pretty.* But he didn't. Despite everything, he loves his mum. She's an awful mum, but he loves her.

Not as much as his gran, though. It was his gran who went to see Mr. Martel, not his mum. She had the fright of her life when he got up from his chair and stretched out his hand – that stupid gown he flounced about in opened out like bat wings. *Cor damme là, I thought he was devil, him.* It didn't help that College's a fake castle, and his office a fake castle-room.

'Why, this is hell, nor am I out of it.'

The Accused

That's why he tried it, down in the dungeons where the Religious Studies department was. He hadn't put God down there, the school had.

I'm calling up the spirit of Wilson.

He set up his gran's Ouija board on a desk in the classroom. It was January so the place was dark after school had ended. Anyone brave enough came to watch, and Louis had agreed to sit with him, both their fingers on the *planchette*.

I'm calling up the spirit of Wilson. Are you with us, Wilson?

The *planchette* dragged their fingers to 'yes'.

Did you die in the cells in the attic?

The *planchette* circled the 'yes'.

Who locked you up there?

Their fingers moved to M and then A, then R, then T, then E and finally L.

"Your grandson violated the intellectual integrity of the college, Miss Queripel. I hope you appreciate how serious this is. This is his second term and already he is challenging God."

Pompous, Calvinist twat.

What he didn't like was his name being spelt out. Bat-wing Martel.

He had it in for him after that. Six fucking more years of it. And then the man became a Jurat.

Main de gloire, you little shit.

What does he care?

Chapter Nineteen

"You old rozzer, what are you doing back on the rock then? I'd heard you were over, and I thought: can't be. That run-away's never coming back here. Got too much London glitter in his hair. And then I see the advert in the *Press* and I think: that glitter's got into his brain, it has."

Robilliard flops down in the chair opposite and spills coffee over his hand. "Bugger," he says, licking it away. "They always fill them too much."

Café Victoria is a two-minute walk from the Priaulx library and set within an old Victorian bandstand. It gives onto the slopes of Candie Gardens and today it's empty. Mark has taken a seat by the window facing the statue of Victor Hugo. Herm and Sark sit on the horizon like a Greek archipelago, bright green and blue in the sunlight.

"So, what's this advert in the *Press* all about then," Pete says. "When you called, and asked for a chin-wag, I thought: yup, it's old Markers on the sniff again."

"I'm trying not to get bored."

"There are better ways to do that. Come out on the boat. There's lots of mackerel on the bank."

The Accused

"I hate fishing."

"And you call yourself a Guern?"

He shrugs his shoulders as if to say, 'Do I?'

"It's got tongues wagging, you know. Everyone thinks it's a nutcase. But hey, it's no skin off my back. You know me, never had much between the ears. Doing the same old. You remember when we were in College together, and you were set on going to Uni? Wanted to get into the Met and all that."

"Yup, and you said, to quote, "What do I want with the English, eh. They're as bad as those Jersey *crapauds*. I like my fishing, me.""

Pete laughs, slouching in the chair, heavy with uniform. He removes his hat and runs his fingers through his hair.

"Been on since seven. Got one drunk and a kid trying to sell pot at the back of the Jamaica. That's about it. Give me the Guernsey Police any day. So, what did you want to pick my brains about? Always welcome to the bits I've got." He stretches out his legs and slurps the coffee.

"Was anything stolen from the house, anything valuable?"

Pete puts the mug on the table. "Jasmine Gardiner's? You're really into this, aren't you? I can't make you give it up?"

"I've got doubts so nope, not for now."

"Okay then, nothing taken, just the books all over the floor."

"Any idea where she died?"

"You know the house?"

"Yup."

"Okay. They thought it was in the kitchen on the other side of the island-thing."

"On the day-room side?"

"Exactly. She'd dragged some stuff down with her. There was a plastic clock and the battery fell out. That's how they got the exact time of death."

"Eleven forty-three, wasn't it?"

"Something like that."

"Why didn't the murderer pick it up?"

"Probably didn't see it. Or didn't want to get his prints on it." Pete takes the flapjack from Mark's plate and eats it, saying with a full mouth, "everyone had an alibi except Bourgaize."

"What about Bob Brehaut?"

"Ah, him. Shifty character. He sent her these letters, you know, threatening her and everything, but they couldn't pin it on him. He was down at the Red Lion, as pissed as a newt."

"Anyone else?"

"The husband, but he was off-island with the lover..."

"The housekeeper?"

"Mrs. Le Sauvage? It was her day off."

"The gardener, Tom de Carteret."

"No way. He's a great guy."

"Did he have an alibi?"

"Yeah, he was working at Jurat Martel's. You can check, but I'm sure I'm right."

"They know each other?"

"It's Guernsey, eh?"

He nods. "That's true."

Pete looks at him. "You're not buying this, are you?"

"Something doesn't feel right."

"You've been in London too long. Over here two plus two equals four, it always does." Pete checks the clock hanging on the wall and gets to his feet. "Better be off before the Chief comes looking for me. A word mind, friend

The Accused

to friend – leave it alone, okay? The lad did it, and that's the end of it. No one wants to defend a witch."

"You don't believe that, that he's a witch?"

"It doesn't matter what I believe. That's why I'm still in uniform and I go fishing. Fish don't care about anything much. I like that about them."

He laughs and gets to his feet. "Good to catch up."

"Are you up for a barbie one of these nights?"

"Of course."

"I'll organise it. I know a rather... you know..."

He frowns.

"You know."

"What? A fish?"

"Cor heck," Pete says in despair. "You're pretty thick for a detective. I meant a woman. She's a friend of my wife's. Good body, nice smile..."

He holds up a finger. "Don't – don't even think about it."

Pete winks. "Leave it to me."

"I'm serious. Don't go there," but Pete is walking out of the café. He turns around and waves at him.

THE PRIAULX IS a two-minute walk up the hill from the café. He's so close, he might as well have a look at the black books, the *grimoire*. If he wants to understand Pierre, he needs to understand his hobby.

It also means he can stay away from the house.

His mother was in a noisy mood at breakfast, growling like a dog because she wanted to, sitting on the floor and refusing to move. Janice sat with her, watching over her.

"Off you go," she ordered. "I've got this." He mumbled

his apologies and hurried to the front door. Love might be love, but fear is hatred, and he hates seeing her like that.

Mrs. Boxall the librarian greets him with a paper-thin smile. Lovely weather, she says and he agrees, adding that – thank God – neither of them are walking down a London road breathing in the diesel. Her smile broadens. "Our emerald isle," she gushes.

"You can't beat the cliffs," he admits. "Even in the rain."

"That you can't."

"I was wondering if I could see the *Petit* and *Grand Albert*."

There's a moment's hush. The woman by the computer peers over the top of her glasses. The light from the window catches her profile and she is younger then he realised, early thirties perhaps.

"Pierre Bourgaize used to come in here all the time, asking to read them."

"We keep them locked in the safe," Mrs. Boxall says. "Better that way – being what they are."

"They're a hoot, if you want my opinion." The young woman says, pushing the glasses up her nose. "And they're titchy. That said, I kept a record of how often he asked for them. You know how it is. You begin to wonder after a while. I gave it to the police."

The third librarian – older and more serious, with short grey hair – pops her head up from behind a pile of books. "Odd boy. Looked a bit like Snape, you know, in the *Harry Potter* films."

He's been wracking his brain to place the likeness.

"Do you remember those rants he used to go into?" The young librarian is talking to Mrs. Boxall. "He'd got it into his head that his grandfather – or great-grandfather, I can't remember which – had the original copy. I told him it was nonsense; nearly every house on the island had one at some time or other. But he went on and on about it, saying they'd stolen it. Supposedly the Nazis were after it."

"You're right," the woman behind the books says. "It's quite a well-known story."

"I've never heard of it," he says.

"You have to be local."

"I am local."

"Anyway," the young librarian continues, moving her mouse and tapping a few keys. "Both the men and the Nazi died within days of each other, in odd circumstances, or so the story goes."

"No, no," Mrs. Boxall interrupts. "Nothing so mysterious. No one knows what happened."

"It got people talking though. And the book was never found. Which is odd if you go by the legend. They're meant to be indestructible and the only way to destroy them is to bury them or pour holy water over them."

"So, they buried it," Mrs. Boxall says with irritation. "It was the war. Everything went missing then. By the end of it, there wasn't a winkle left on the beaches." She leaves the congregation and walks towards the back door.

The young librarian raises her eyebrows and smiles. "She's got a thing about them. But don't forget, Hitler was into the occult. They must have been offering a lot of money for it."

"If it existed." That is the short haired woman at the back.

"Oh, I'm sure it did. No smoke without fire. You know how it is. Wait 'til you see them. They're titchy. It always surprises people. They expect some massive Bible-size tome." She laughs. "You can fit these in your pocket."

He laughs drily, having always imagined them to be enormous.

"You know Jurat Martel wrote a letter in the *Press* debunking the story?"

"Did he?"

"Oh yes." That's the short-haired lady again. "I keep it to remind people, in case they come asking. Here, have a read." She pulls open a desk drawer and takes out the cutting, leaning across the desk to hand it to him.

He takes it and reads it:

THE CONTINUED NONSENSE about a lost grimoire is polluting the island with superstition. Superstition is a pre-enlightened mentality that has no place in the 21st century and should be renegaded to the distant past when old ladies huddled about fireplaces and pretended to fly on broomsticks.

HE LOOKS UP. She is watching him. He continues.

FOR THOSE WHO have yet to progress in their thinking – who still believe in shadows in the dark and monsters under the bed – let me assure them that no such book ever existed. The rumours about the Nazis is only rumour, and the belief that Mrs. Gardiner was killed because she had found it, is also rumour. Let me repeat: there is no such book. I hope this will put the gossip to rest so we can get on with modernising the island for the good of future generations. Jurat Martel, address withheld.

. . .

The Accused

"You SEE. Trying to modernise the island," she says.

"I thought he was the bastion of good old fashioned values."

The young librarian laughs and swivels on her chair to face him. "He's trying to stop people looking for it. That's what my Pa says. He's probably got it, and wants to close the discussion down."

Mrs. Boxall snorts in disbelief. "He's Jurat, for goodness sake." She's just returned with two small books in her hands.

"That's never stopped anyone."

Mark's confused. "Does it or doesn't it exist?"

"Present tense, I've no idea," the young librarian says. "Past tense, yes."

"Nonsense," Mrs. Boxall snaps. "This island's full of rumours."

"But can you be sure?"

She looks at him. "You're the detective."

He leans back a little. "How do you know that?"

"Come on, Mr. Roussel, this is Guernsey." She enjoys his disquiet.

"There's sixty thousand people on the island."

"Very well. Pete Robilliard's my nephew. He's convinced you're Inspector Morse, 'brains the size of wine-vats'."

"I've only got one," he points out.

"Pete isn't good at detail." Mrs. Boxall hands him the two books. "Good luck."

The books are bound in cracked leather and sit in the palm of his hand, one thicker than the other. The paper is ragged, mass produced seventeenth-century style, and written in French. He takes them to a desk in one of the reading rooms and sits down.

Now that he has them, a childlike awe comes over him. There's something about them, a weight perhaps that isn't quite physical. The memories and hopes, of all the people that fingered them, huddled about the fire in their dark little cottages.

It doesn't help that the sun is lost behind a band of cloud and he's sitting in a gloomy room that smells of dying books.

Carefully, he turns back the cover.

His French is reasonable, and within minutes he is laughing out loud. Seriously? He glances over his shoulder. If you want to tell whether a girl is chaste or corrupted, you must fashion a crown (of what, he isn't sure) and force her to wear it. If she can't stop pissing, then she's corrupted, but if she can hold onto her urine, she's chaste.

He flips through the pages and stops at the section on how to win at cards. This is more like it, boiling up a wicked broth. All he has to do is take an eel that's died of thirst, add the gall of a bull that's been killed by dogs, throw in some vulture's blood and his own too, use hot manure to prepare an oven heated with fern gathered on the eve of St John and then cook it. Once he's inscribed the eel's skin with 'HVTY', he can wear it as a bracelet and win 'a fortune in all places'.

Simple really.

The section he's looking for is the 'Hand of Glory'. Pierre was accused of hacking off Jasmine Gardiner's hand to make it and when he finds it, he can't scoff any more.

TAKE the right or left hand of a felon who is hanging from a gibbet beside a highway; wrap it in part of a funeral pall and so wrapped, squeeze it well. Then put it into an earthenware vessel with zimat, nitre, salt and long peppers, the whole well powdered. Leave it in this vessel for a fortnight, then take it out and expose it to full sunlight during the dog-days until it becomes quite dry. If the sun is not strong enough put it in an oven with fern and vervain. Next make a kind of candle from the fat of a gibbeted felon, virgin wax, sesame, and ponie, and use the Hand of Glory as a candlestick to hold this candle when lighted, and then those in every place into which you go with this baneful instrument shall remain motionless.

HE'S MORE interested in how the Hand of Glory is made than what it does (which, in layman terms is 'scare the shit out of someone'). From what he's read, Jasmine Gardiner's hand was left in a terracotta flower pot, wrapped in a stained cloth. Perhaps the intention was to mix it with zimat and nitre and dry it in an oven. Or perhaps not. After all, what was the Hand of Glory without the candle? It is powerless, no worse than a mummy in the British Museum. Yet the body wasn't flayed; her fat wasn't removed. What was the point then? Felons don't swing in Guernsey's lanes; there's no chance of returning to it later to continue the gory task. Either Pierre had no idea what he was doing, or he had no intention of making it in the first place.

He looks out of the window. Witchcraft is about power, or the lack of it; it's about threatening people. Gangsters have guns; weirdos have spells. Guns are physical; spells are psychological, and Pierre's an insignificant lad. If he tried to make the Hand of Glory, he was posturing. It was unpleasant, grotesque, but bravado nonetheless – he is sure of it.

He takes the books back to the librarians, bids the ladies

farewell and walks out on to the front step. Standing away from the drizzle, he calls the prison.

"Can I speak to the chaplain, please."

Chapter Twenty

He parks in front of the main building and switches off the engine, leaning forward on the steering wheel to study it. The prison was built in 1989 to replace the old Georgian gaol in town. Twenty years later, they built St Sampson's High School next door. A clever bit of planning all things considered: a kid enters one institution at eleven, and five years later crosses the football pitch into the other. It is one of the State's better ideas.

The walls are white and the roof red, and only the bars over the windows distinguish it from a boarding school. At the Gate Lodge, he hands over his driving licence and phone, and is divested of everything else, even his sunglasses. He's given a lanyard to wear and from there taken to the administrative area where the chaplain is waiting, his hands behind his back and his dog-collar creased.

He removes a hand for Mark to shake. "Tony Le Cheminant. Prison Chaplain, for my sins."

The introduction is followed by an apology for not having an office and a general hand-wave at the starkness of the place. They pass through the security gates, along a white corridor into a room with a low coffee table, two upholstered chairs, an empty bookcase and a blind drawn against the sun.

"Coffee?" the Chaplain askes inviting him to sit.

He shakes his head.

"There are some bourbons somewhere, if you'd like."

"I don't want to take up your time."

The Chaplain laughs. "I'm the visible presence of the Church; time is what I have. All of time, supposedly. So, tell me, how can I help you?"

"I asked to meet with Pierre Bourgaize but my request's been refused."

"Policy at the moment, I'm afraid. We have the *Press* to contend with and the usual set of weirdos. Trophy hunters, the lot. Whatever you think of Pierre Bourgaize, he's got himself a following. I hear you're talking about reopening the case?"

"Not yet and possibly never. I have some questions first."

"I thought the case against him was strong."

"Strong-ish, but I have my concerns. Can you share what you know?"

The Chaplain rubs his thighs. "It might be easier if you started with those questions you have."

"Okay, here's an obvious one: Do you think he's guilty?"

"It's not for me to decide."

"From what you know of him, does he fit the profile?"

"He's got problems. He's probably capable of murder – most of us are – but, again, it's not for me to say. If you're interested in profiling, I'd describe him as introverted, very quiet, he doesn't relate to people. His parents haven't been to see him since he arrived back."

"How has he taken that?"

"Hard to say. He doesn't talk about his father but I'd say he's pretty upset with his mother. He's certainly more depressed than he was. He's written to her and tried to call her but she never answers."

"What about the attention he's getting in the *Press*? How's he coping with that?"

"I couldn't say. The inmates are scared of him. We had an incident the other day when he made one of the lads a cup of tea, and said it was a witch's brew. The guy tried to vomit it up in the toilets."

The Chaplain's eyes are soft but their edges are hard, and he likes the mix; it breeds confidence. "I need to talk to him," he says.

"I don't know. Unless you're serious about reopening the case, I'm not sure it's a good idea. We don't want to destabilise him or give him false hope. I'd have to talk to the governor."

He thinks a moment. "I don't buy all the witchery stuff. If Pierre's guilty, it's for some other reason."

"He peddles himself as a witch."

"We don't have to believe him. I'd say it was a useful tool if you want to be left alone."

"True."

"Does he talk to you about the black books?"

The Chaplain glances at the door. "Our conversations can be rather fractious. He doesn't like power, or other people having it. When I said the books were low-level alchemy, he got rather upset. Calling them 'trite' didn't much help either."

"You've read them?"

"Bits and pieces. It's not all potions and salamanders. There are recipes for making soap and keeping wine and useful things like that."

"That makes them okay?"

"Don't misunderstand me; they're a blight on the island, but alchemy began with the Christian Cabbalists. They thought you could prove Jesus was God by studying his name. Supposedly, if you take the Tetragrammaton – the name of God in Hebrew – and insert the Hebrew letter Shin in the middle of it, you get the name Jesus. Shin was likened to the breath of God. The Logos."

"Right."

He smiles. "I did my undergraduate thesis on alchemy, how it influenced Shakespeare and Marlowe. I studied English by the way, not theology."

"So, you've heard the rumours about an original copy?"

The Chaplain nods.

"What do you think?"

"There's mileage in it. Don't forget Isaac Newton was the last of the 'magicians'. It could be worth a small fortune if it's true he wrote in it."

"Isaac Newton?" He sits forward.

"Supposedly he scribbled in the margins. If that's true, the auction houses would scramble over each other to get hold of it. It would explain the Nazi connection."

"Hold on a moment." He takes out his notebook and bullet points the information. He stops and looks up. "You know Pierre claims his family had it and some people stole it off him?"

"That tale? Yes, I've heard it but I don't believe it. Life's hard, and for some people the occult offers a way out. Pierre's in the same tradition as the women they burnt at the stake."

"Possibly."

The Chaplain leans back in his chair. "I've often wondered what really went on, you know. It's the men, you

The Accused

see. If they were having wild orgies at the Catioroc, someone was playing the devil. It's always bothered me they were never caught. The women, yes, but seldom the men. Evil's forever disguising itself. It's never Satan that's gets lynched, only his minions." The Chaplain smiles. "Metaphorically speaking, of course."

He nods. "You agree with me then. Pierre's motive wasn't witchcraft."

"Ah, I didn't say that. I'm a priest, I believe in the supernatural."

"What are you saying then?"

"Not much, to be frank." The Chaplain chuckles and gets up. "I need to know that you genuinely want to help, otherwise I'd ask you to leave Pierre alone. He isn't a happy person."

"I don't guarantee I can do much, but if I take this further, I'm going to need his support."

"Very well," he holds out his hand, "let's stay in touch."

Chapter Twenty-One

"Good God. It looks like a snowstorm's passed through here."

He's standing in the kitchen door with a towel about his neck and his swimming trunks in his hand.

"We're making shortbread," Janice explains.

"There's flour everywhere."

"That's what happens when you get Lilly to mix the butter into it."

His mother's hands are in a pudding bowl, merrily working away, squeezing the yellow mix between her fingers. Lumps of dough are lined up on the table and Janice stands over them, rolling them out into sheets. The floor is a pebble-beach of crumbs.

"Want to join us? You can use the cutters to make the shapes. You better wash your hands first, though."

His mother is beaming up at him and showing her fingers, thick with dough. He thinks: *one day, I'll sell my soul to make biscuits with her again.* So, he dumps his towel on the floor by the back door and scrubs his hands under the tap.

The Accused

"Right, Mum, what do I do?" He draws up a chair and sits down beside her.

She pushes the bowl over to him and runs her fingers through her hair.

"Lilly!" Janice chides. "Don't do that. I washed it this morning. Give her back the bowl, Mark."

He obeys and adds his fingers to the mess inside it. "Come on, Mum, this is fun." It isn't but he's learnt to lie, and when she puts her fingers back in the bowl, he plays with them until she chuckles.

"Are you alright?" she says.

"I'm alright."

"Are you alright?"

"I'm alright, Mum. I love you."

"Silly boy." And then she says, "The bells."

His phone is ringing. He rescues his hands and wipes them on a cloth before taking it out of his pocket.

"Hello?"

"Am I talking to Mark? Mark of the PineForestMurder email?"

"You are."

"I sent you an email and you left me a message. We keep missing each other."

"You must be the lady with some 'surprising information'. Thank you for calling back." He gets up from his chair and walks out of the kitchen into the hall, down the corridor, through the dining room and into the vine-house. With his face to the glass, he looks out onto the garden. "How can you help?"

"My name's Cynthia Marshall. We bumped into each other at Port Soif the other day."

Oh dear. Those bleached teeth and jangly gold bracelet.

"The thing is, it's been rather difficult getting back to

you. I have the family over for the summer, you see. It's catching a free moment. I was hoping we could meet up but my husband's rather keen I forget about it all. You know how it is, too much gossip on the street. It's just there's something that never came up at the time and I thought you ought to know."

"Carry on."

"I knew Jasmine Gardiner, you see. We used to go to her house for dinner. Not often, but sometimes. It was all very tip-top, you know. Very kosher."

"She was Jewish?"

"No, no."

"I just thought – no worries. Carry on."

"We knew them before the divorce, and then afterwards, and – well – it was all rather difficult. We tried to sail a middle course, if you get what I mean. It's always a good idea with everyone swapping partners these days. It can get terribly confusing. Anyway, if you want my opinion, things didn't change much after he left, not with Jasmine anyway. She was never a happy bunny. All that drinking and laughing. So obvious. And she smoked like a chimney but she was discreet, I'll give her that. She stayed on the right side of the Rubicon, if you get what I mean. Never crossed it. Until she got into that blog of hers. Then – well – then everything changed. Heaven knows what happened to her. Some psychoanalyst probably told her to get things off her chest. That's the sort of thing they do, isn't it? Talk, talk. Except Jasmine wrote-wrote. By the end, no one wanted to have her around. We couldn't trust her with anything. 'Keep it within four walls' rather lost its meaning. We'd spy her coming and it was 'hush-hush'. Of course, she should have got a job. Not to earn money. She got a good settlement out of Barry. He wanted to get rid of her so she pushed a hard bargain. She wasn't short of a penny or two."

"Did you read her blog?"

"Oh absolutely. Everyone did. It was rather good, I must say. Very funny too. If you wanted the latest gossip, you just clicked 'The Viper's Nest' – that's what it was called. No disguising the fact – and there it all was."

"She must have got the information from somewhere."

"Totally, but heaven knows how. Some of it was probably made up. Other bits verged on the cruel. And then – well – then she got into the witches and after that it wasn't so much fun. It's dangerous to sow seeds like that over here, not because people believe it, of course, but everyone's interested in the dark side. You know she threatened to name all the witches on the island? Everyone was in a tizzy about it. You'd say, 'I don't believe in witches', and then you'd start wondering. You'd hear strange things like someone suddenly getting ill, or losing all their money just like that. And people are odd. You can't take them at face value. I knew this man once – friend of a friend, very charming, terribly good fun, he could do this clever trick with a wine cork – anyway, it turned out he was one of those, you know, one of *those*. Awfully embarrassing for his wife. Which just goes to show, you can never be sure. And Jasmine knew *exactly* what she was doing."

"Someone mentioned the Bailiff at the time."

"Now that was clever. She never *said* he was part of a coven, but she wrote in such a way that everyone *thought* she'd said that. But why the Bailiff? A lovely man. Did so much good for the island. I *absolutely* adored him. Quite the gentleman. I was so pleased when he was knighted. Anyway, why the Bailiff?"

"You have an answer?"

"Oh absolutely. He was a friend of Barry's. They were at Cambridge together. You see the pattern. Revenge."

"What about Pierre Bourgaize? You said you had some new information."

"I wouldn't say it's information…"

"What is it then?"

"More supposition. How can I put it? The evidence pointed to Pierre Bourgaize, absolutely. All that awful stuff about the hand and the pentacle. But, you see, if we ignore that for a moment…"

"Go on."

"…when I first heard she was dead, I thought she's committed suicide. Terribly sad and all that, but it didn't surprise me."

"She was suicidal?"

"Oh totally. I went to see her, you see. She knew a lot about old books because her father had been in the trade and she had some wonderful ones in her house. Worth a small fortune, I'd imagine. There was this first edition I had seen online and I wanted to get it for my husband."

"And?"

"She said they were asking too much."

"I meant about Jasmine."

"Of course, yes. Well, we had a coffee and she put brandy in hers and went on about the boys. She missed them terribly. Barry was fighting to have full custody and her drinking was working in his favour. She said Guernsey was the perfect place to drive a car off the cliffs."

"And you told the police?"

"Absolutely, but they weren't interested. It was the hand, you see. Everyone got so obsessed about it, they couldn't see past it."

He agrees.

The Accused

"Don't get me wrong, the Police couldn't *ignore* it. Terribly gruesome and all that. And poor Jasmine. No one wants to be dismembered. It's just it was all rather convenient, wasn't it? Jasmine threatens to tell everyone about the witches, and then – oh look, we've got a witch on the prowl. And..."

"If witches don't exist?"

"Precisely. If Barry hadn't been in London, I would have had him at the top of my list."

He is beginning to like Cynthia. "Talking about her husband – what do you know about her lover?"

"Gracious, no idea. We were never *tête-à-tête*, you see, but she was rather attractive. Quite the figure. Very Cindy Crawford. I'd be surprised if she didn't have someone knocking at the door. The fact I don't know means she was very discreet which, given how she was at the end, is rather intriguing, isn't it? I mean, you're filling up everyone's ears with gossip, and you've got your life under wraps. All very suspect. It had to have been off island, otherwise someone would have known. Nothing stays secret on Guernsey for long."

"That's true."

"Take Jurat Martel."

"What about him?"

"I know from good sources he pressurised the other Jurats to declare against Pierre Bourgaize."

That doesn't surprise him.

"A few were dithering, you see. Not everyone bought into the witchcraft thing. I'm not saying he was wrong. He was principal of Elizabeth College when that ghastly boy was there so he knew more than we did. Still, he pushed through the majority vote."

"You know this because?"

"The other Jurats. My husband thinks very highly of him. I'm not insinuating anything."

"Of course not."

"It's just worth noting. He knew the boy's character, you see – oh, am I disturbing anything?"

His mother is shrieking. He can hear her in the kitchen. Noise, pure noise. Anyone hearing it would think him in a madhouse.

"I'm going to have to cut you off, Cynthia. You've been most helpful. I've got your number if I need to call you again. Just one thing – do you have any photos of the time?"

"I don't take photos, I'm afraid."

"No worries. Thank you again. Goodbye."

"Mark," she says as he is about to hang up. "I don't want to pry..."

"What is it?"

"I'm so sorry about your mother. I remember some of the wonderful dinner parties at her house."

God, the conversation he was hoping to avoid.

"It's awfully tough – my darling Ma went quite nutty at the end – but you're doing the right thing keeping her at home. I just wanted to tell you that. She looked so well the other day."

"Thank you, Cynthia," and he taps off the conversation.

Photographs. He needs to get his hands on some. The obvious person to ask is the husband, but that means tracking him down. Easier to start with the *Guernsey Press*. They must have an archive. They're always printing photographs of social occasions and scenic views. Admittedly, they're usually of the coast, but it's worth a try.

"Mark!"

Janice is calling him.

"The door. Someone's at the door."

The Accused

He leaves the vine-house and walks along the corridor, into the hallway. There, standing in the porch, is Viv. She's dressed in stone-coloured chinos rolled up about her ankles and a light khaki shirt that sets off her tan. With sunglasses pinning back her hair, she looks ten years younger than her age, and for a moment he doesn't know what to say.

"How about getting a crab sandwich for lunch?" she says.

"Now?"

"Yoga's finished, the sun is out and I'm hungry."

He looks over his shoulder and back again. "I'm in the middle of something."

"How about Port Soif? You can bring your mum if you want."

"She's not too good in the mornings."

"Then come alone."

"I need a shower. I've just been for a swim."

"I can cope with you salty. Let's go before the crowds get there."

"It's ten thirty."

"God, you're a stickler. Lunchtime is hungry time, in my book anyway."

He hesitates. The photographs; they're his plan for the morning, searching online to see what he can discover. But Viv isn't moving.

"Coming?" she asks.

He taps his trouser pockets and then points inside. "I'll get my wallet and meet you by the car. It's parked round the back. Give me five minutes."

"I'm counting," she says, and disappears down the garden path.

"Why did you come back?"

Viv is leaning over his shoulder as he drives through the lanes. The engine is located behind her seat and she's shouting to be heard above its roar. The bubble car is little better than a moped with a roof over the top; it has two wheels at the front and one at the back. The aim is to enjoy the experience and avoid as many hills as possible.

"My mum was getting worse," he bellows.

"I heard you made some enemies in the Met."

He turns to look back at her. "Who told you that?"

"The grapevine," she shouts.

He doesn't answer. He knows about grapevines: they spread out from a trunk and grip onto anything that holds them up, knotting their way along walls and fences.

"Where are we going?" Viv interrupts his thoughts.

"Jerbourg," he says.

"What about Port Soif? I thought we were going to have a crab sandwich."

"I prefer Jerbourg."

"No one prefers Jerbourg." She sits back and crosses her arms.

They don't speak until the car stops in front of the kiosk and he lifts the canopy.

"Getting out?" he asks.

"Only if they have crab sandwiches."

They don't. He brings her a BLT and a cup of coffee.

"Keep it," she says as she climbs out of the car.

"I don't drink this type of coffee."

"I do."

A hand takes it away from him, and he turns on his heels to find Ginny Bisson standing on the tarmac, her lips about the black plastic lid.

"God, I needed that," she says after a noisy slurp. "Sure you don't want some, eh?"

Viv shakes her head.

"Suit yourself." She drinks again, her eyes on the sandwiches. "What about them?"

"All yours," Viv says.

He hands one over, keeping the other for himself. If Viv wants to starve, that's her problem.

"Cor, it's my lucky day, eh? I'm bloody famished."

Coincidence is a fact of life and he shouldn't be as surprised to find Ginny taking a cup of coffee out of his hand as if she's paid for it? Still, her presence is uncanny. More so given the general look of the woman: clean, neutral-smelling, in t-shirt and shorts, with a bulging plastic bag over her arm. The tattoos remain but her eyes are clear.

"Do you know Viv Le Prevost?" he asks.

"Blimey! You're the Agony Aunt?"

Viv admits that she is. She even smiles.

"I nearly wrote to you the other day, eh. My daughter, she thinks her dad's a dickhead and won't see him."

"Is he a dickhead?"

Ginny bites into the sandwich. "He's a fucking jerk," she admits, chewing as she speaks.

"Then good on your daughter."

"Yeah, good on her, eh."

Mark waits. He's never sure with women but it looks like the conversation has ended. Viv is watching a greyhound drag an old lady across the car-park and Ginny is scrunching the cup in her hand.

"What are you doing here?" he asks.

"Done a shift at the hotel, eh. Covering for a friend. What are you doing here?"

"Good point," Viv says.

Ginny opens her eyes wide at him – *upset your girlfriend, eh?*

Viv's made her point, he's got the message. Port Soif or nowhere. "We're heading to the benches over there," he points. "Great view and close to the Pine Forest."

"Still after info, is it?"

"Have you got any?"

She chews her lip. "Might do."

"Then join us."

They sit looking out to sea, Ginny in the middle, one leg bent up against her chest. A fan of sunlight pours through the clouds.

"What do you know about Pierre Bourgaize?" he asks.

"No one likes him, eh."

"No one liked the Birmingham Six," Viv points out, but the reference is lost on Ginny.

The sea is a flat expanse of blue, jagged here and there with white. A fishing boat comes into view, close enough inshore for Mark to see a man at the wheel and another in the back tidying the nets. Glints of sunlight skitter over its wake.

"So, what have you got for me."

"You're demanding, eh."

"Stubborn more like," Viv says.

"You did say you had something," he points out.

"I'm getting my life in order, see. I'm getting counselling from the States and I've got a job at the Co-op too. My counsellor, she said I had to change, eh. So, I'm changing. Giving you something for nothing."

"You just got a coffee and a sandwich out of me."

"Don't get in a tizz."

"Just clarifying things."

He leans back on the bench with his arms crossed,

The Accused

waiting as Ginny fumbles inside her shorts for a packet of Pall Malls.

"I didn't know Jasmine Gardiner, eh, not as a friend but I did go round to her house once."

"How did you know where she lived?"

"My sister."

"Who's your sister?"

"Blimey, and you're meant to be a detective. Tracy. Tracy Le Sauvage. You spoke to her, eh."

"The cleaner?" He whistles. "Right. I'm with you. Carry on."

"Well, see, I needed money and I'd heard stuff about a book, a real important book." She lights the cigarette and puffs smoke into the air. He wipes it away with his hand. "So, I told her, I said I could get it for her, eh, if she paid me."

"What's that got to do with Pierre Bourgaize?" Viv is kicking up dust with the tip of her sandal.

She glances at her. "You don't know? It's what got her killed, eh."

Mark looks at her. "I'll employ you if you're good at this."

"Don't listen to him," Viv says.

Ginny sucks on her cigarette. "My sister, Tracy, she lives at Les Genats estate, eh, but I want a place of my own. She's on the nice side, mind, if you're coming in from the Hougue de Pommier, is it."

"I know the place."

"She looks after my daughter when I'm up at the Co-op, but I need all the cash I can get, me, coz I've got to show the States I'm sensible if they're going to give me a place, is it. That's why I come here and help out when I can."

"Why don't you tell us about the book," Viv interrupts.

127

"Okay, okay. Keep your hair on. It's supposedly a really big thing, eh. My gran, she told me about it and then I read it in her blog." She turns to Viv. "You read it, eh?"

Viv shakes her head.

"Cor blimey, I thought everyone did."

"Why would it get Jasmine Gardiner killed?"

"Don't know, me, but I went and told her where it was buried, eh. She paid me a few quid and the next thing I know she's blogged about it. Anyway, a few days later she's dead and it's made to look like witches' work."

"None of this came up in the trial." Viv is interested now, sitting on one side and looking directly at Ginny.

"Did you tell the police?" He is looking at her too.

She laughs. "Cor heck! Who do you think I am, eh?"

"You're saying that whoever killed Jasmine Gardiner knew about the book?"

"I don't know, eh. I'm just guessing, me. Someone wanted the book and they thought she had it."

He shakes his head. "It's too conspiratorial."

"You're telling me. But – get this – my gran, she was a bit of a witch, her. She died last year. I told her what happened and she said the book was really powerful. That's why the Nazis wanted it, eh. She told me to leave it alone. It was bad stuff. But I told Jasmine Gardiner coz I needed money. I said it was buried under one of those stones at the fairy ring, you know, down at Pleinmont, is it."

"Le Table des Pions," Mark corrects her.

"Whatever."

"You're saying Jasmine Gardiner went and dug up the book?"

"Caw heck, no." Ginny puffs on her cigarette.

"Right, so it's still there?"

She shakes her head and blows smoke rings into the air.

"I'm confused. Who's got it?"

Ginny shrugs her shoulders. "You can't get rid of it that easily, eh. But they wanted it. That's what my gran said."

"So, where is it?" He's losing patience now.

"No idea." Ginny drops her cigarette on the ground. "I just made it up, eh. Thing is, she then went and blogged about it and all that, but that can't be right coz it wasn't where I said it was. But that's why she was killed."

Viv gets to her feet and walks to the cliff edge. She is excited, he can tell. "It makes sense."

"It doesn't help Pierre," he points out. "You're saying that none of this was in the trial?"

"Why would it be? No one told us." Viv glares at Ginny.

"Don't look at me like that." Ginny gets to her feet. "I don't talk to the police, do I."

He steeples his fingers and pulls on his bottom lip. It's a good story. It has tension, it has drama, but something doesn't add up.

"If she was killed because of this book," he says, "and you told Jasmine Gardiner you knew where it was, why didn't they kill you?"

Ginny opens her eyes so wide, they nearly shoot out across the car-park. "Cor heck." She stuffs her hand into her pocket and pulls out another cigarette. She puts it to her lips, and then takes it out again. "I just told a story. I needed the dosh. You keep me out of this, okay?" She puts the cigarette back in her mouth. "I don't want no one killing me." She hurries across the car-park at full speed towards the bus stop.

Mark blows a slow, flat whistle.

"What was that for?"

He gets to his feet. "More witches' nonsense. I don't

buy it." He walks around the bench and towards the car. Viv jogs up to join him. "The book's a distraction. Martel wrote a letter in the *Press* saying it was a myth, and I believe him. Murders are mundane. They're usually about money or love, things like that. They're not about Nazis and black books."

"You're saying what exactly?"

"Jasmine Gardiner had a lover. That's where we should be looking. He was a young man, he went to her house often enough and," he adds, "it wasn't Pierre Bourgaize."

Viv laughs. "Spare the thought."

"I need to find out who he was."

"I know someone who could help. Tom de Carteret. He was her gardener. He'll know who was coming and going. Meet me at the Cock and Bull at eight and I'll introduce you. It's band night. He plays the banjo."

Chapter Twenty-Two

NOT A 'WANKER' THEN.

"He thinks there are some irregularities." Those were the chaplain's words. Standing outside his cell while he was having lunch. "He wants to help."

What? With that fucking email address? He can go hang himself as far as he's concerned.

"He needs your permission to get access to the files."

Oh yeah? Does he know the etymology of permission? *Permissionen* – Latin for 'giving up'. He isn't giving up anything.

"Don't you want him to help you?"

Fuck you, Chaplain – except he didn't say that. His macaroni cheese was getting cold and he'd stuffed a forkful into his mouth.

Still, he had to say something otherwise the man was never going to leave.

Help, Mr. Le Cheminant, is when an advocate challenges the prosecution. Help is when a stepfather doesn't call the police. Help is when a mother believes her child.

Help is when the Jurats seek the truth. Help is when God doesn't execute his son for a bunch of losers.

Help, Mr. Priest, is a shit-useless word. Take away the P and you got Hel – Hel was the goddess of the underworld. Do you know about her? She ruled the World of Darkness where the shore was strewn with corpses and her castle filled with serpents. If you hadn't died in battle, there you went, and a dragon waited to suck your blood.

Go tell that to your Mr. Roussel.

Chapter Twenty-Three

THE COCK AND BULL IS NEAR THE STEPS WHERE THE women were burnt. Everyone knows the story, how a girl tied to the stake gave birth amongst the flames and the Bailiff ordered the baby to be thrown back into the fire. Just scratch the surface, and there it is, religious persecution and corruption; black dogs and potions. Even the family house has the obligatory witch's seat near the chimney piece where they can rest on their way to the Catioroc. The last thing you want is to be cursed, his gran used to say.

"You're early." Viv joins him in the porch.

He has his hand on the door, and opens it to let her through. The sounds of live Irish music pour out. He follows behind her into a beamed and pillared space, with orange walls and dim lights. The air is warm and smells of hops.

A crowd gathers about the bar listening to the quintet in the corner by the fireplace: three fiddlers, one guitarist and a banjo player. They sit in a circle, their music fast and jubilant, smiling as they edge each other on, playing louder and more exuberantly, their arms sawing and their fingers plucking. Within seconds, Mark is tapping his feet.

"That's Tom," Viv bellows in his ear.

"Where?"

"The one with the banjo. I'll get him to join us at half time."

"He looks young." And fit. His t-shirt is stretched over firm muscles.

"Not that young, thirty-two I think."

"That's young enough."

He needs a drink. It's those dark, narrow streets and their history. Proportionate to their population, Guernsey and Jersey hunted more witches than anyone else in Europe. He doesn't know the percentage that were killed, and perhaps it doesn't matter; he's on the side of anyone accused of witchcraft.

It's the 'because' word that bothers him, what it means to do something *because* of witchcraft. If the pentacle and severed hand were reasons for killing Jasmine Gardiner, then Pierre is probably guilty. He just can't tally how they are reasons. Does anyone really believe that a lad of nineteen said to himself one day: 'I'm going to kill a stranger; I'm going to string her up on a gibbet and then take her hand so I can terrorise the island'? Yet the Jurats did, and it points two opposite directions: either Guernsey's legal system is awash with superstition or Vernon's right: Pierre Bourgaize is a scapegoat.

"Get us a table upstairs." Viv is shouting above the music. "What do you want?"

"Pint of Guinness."

The gallery is empty, and he moves a table and two chairs to the front so he can peer over the balcony at the musicians below.

The Accused

"Front row seats," Viv says as she lays the pints on the table and passes him a packet of crisps. She sits down and leans her arms on the balustrade. "They're pretty good, aren't they?"

He admits they are.

"Lip," she points, and he wipes the spume away with the back of his hand.

He opens the crisps and offers it to her. She takes out a few, and together they munch and drink, listening to the music. In the quiet moment between one piece and another, he asks how she knows Tom de Carteret.

"Everyone does. He topped some trees for me, in the garden. He's the one who saw Pierre cycling away with the black bin bag."

The account he read in the *Press* struck him as odd. Supposedly Tom heard objects clanking in the bag as Pierre pedalled past, but how did a man hear much above the engine roar of an old van?

"He's promised to come up later."

"Right."

At the time, there was a lot speculation about what was in the bag. According to the police they were probably the paraphernalia of the murder which included wine glasses and/or mugs. Pierre must have disposed of them in the bushes along the way because they were never found at the Bourgaize bungalow, or anywhere else for that matter. Assuming the objects were in the bin bag, of course. Or there was a bin bag at all.

The prosecution assumed a lot.

The quintet plays two more tunes and then stops their strumming. He watches as they leave their instruments on the chairs, and make their way to the bar where the crowd is thick. Pats on the back, drinks passed over heads; soon he loses them to the muddle of their friends. The pub falls into the soft tones of mumbling voices.

"Ouch, that hurts!"

Tom de Carteret is behind Viv, his hands on her shoulders, massaging them. He is tall and dark, with impish eyes. And those muscles. It comes from living up a ladder, he supposes.

"You're full of knots," Tom says, removing his hands and taking the chair beside her. "You shouldn't be at your desk all the time."

"Tell me about it," she says, removing her cardigan.

Her top surprises Mark; it's electric blue and satin, buttoned at the base of her cleavage. He swings back on his chair's legs to check the rest of her attire. Capri pants and flat shoes. Stylish. Flirtatious too. He drops his chair forward and knocks back the last of the Guinness.

"Let me introduce you to a very old school friend of mine. Mark Roussel."

Tom holds out his hand. "The famous Mark. You're the one who put the advert in the *Press*. Everyone's talking about it."

He shakes his hand. "That wasn't the intention."

"Want another?" Tom points at his empty glass.

"No thanks."

"Viv will, won't you?"

"I'm on rations. I've got a heavy day tomorrow."

Tom laughs. "That's a cheap round then."

"You're not drinking?" Mark asks.

"Not on band night."

They fall into silence. It's more awkward than companionable, and he watches Tom's fingers tap the table top, as if he can't stop playing even when the banjo is leaning against the chair downstairs. They grow faster and firmer, and he realises that something is bothering the man.

"You know Pierre's guilty, don't you?" Tom says suddenly.

"So, I'm told."

"He's a nasty piece of shit."

"That's strong."

"Believe me, I know him. And don't let Viv feed your head with nonsense. I love her to bits, but she's way off on this one. Believe me. The guy did it."

"I'm just saying there were things the police didn't follow up on." Viv holds his hand still on the table. Motherly. Or maybe not. It's hard to decide. "People made a lot of assumptions about him."

"Come off it!" Tom pulls his hand away. "How many times have we been over this?" His exasperation is genuine. "I saw him."

"Sometimes we see what we want to see," Mark says.

"What does that mean?"

Tom's muscles are tense and his mouth tight, and he waits for the attack. Verbal, physical. It's bound to come. He's that type of man. Viv puts her arms around his shoulders and gives them a squeeze. He relaxes a little and leans his head on her shoulder and for a while he remains like that. There's a sexual force hidden in it somewhere – in the intimacy? In the tenderness? He isn't sure and before he decides, Tom sits upright and points at him.

"Haven't we met before?"

He raises an eyebrow. "I don't think so?"

"Elizabeth College reunion dinner?"

He shakes his head.

"West Show, perhaps?"

"Nope."

"What about carols in the town church? Schroeder's Bank usually does a sing-along."

His smile is lopsided.

Suddenly, Tom claps his hands. "I've got it! Liberation Day, about three summers ago. You won at the Crown and Anchor. I remember. You walked off with a hefty sum. Fifty quid or something."

"Fifty-five," he says.

His mother was with him at the time, on Jurat Martel's arm, and he asked her afterwards, 'What's it between you two?' and she said, 'A sad man's fantasy.' Except that the 'sad man' is nowhere to be seen any more now that his mother stands in dark corners and forgets his name.

Tom is talking to Viv. "See? I've got a memory like a microchip."

"And you're undercutting every gardener on the island," she adds.

"True enough. And yes, before you ask," he turns to Mark, "I worked for Jasmine. So, trust me on this when I say Bourgaize is a sick man. He was sick at College too. I saw him pedal away, hunched over the handles like a demented rabbit."

"He was a scholarship boy, wasn't he?" Mark adds. "Poor family, clever brain, a bit weedy, didn't fit in. Can't have been easy."

"You want me to feel sorry for him?"

"I'm trying to work out a motive."

"He wanted to do all his occult stuff. I don't know, read too much *Harry Potter* probably."

"Does that sound reasonable to you?"

"I have no idea. Life isn't reasonable."

The Accused

"There's always cause and effect. *Post hoc ergo propter hoc.*"

"By that logic, you'll have to tell me why you're digging this up again. He cut off her bloody hand, for God's sake!"

Tom's bark is sharp, angry, and the man turns away to rest his arms on the balustrade, his leg juddering up and down as he gazes at the people below.

"Let's forget about Pierre," Viv says.

Let's not, Mark thinks. This pressure-release of emotion comes from eleven years of something. Hatred, most likely, but why? He's interested; he wants to know. Viv promised him information.

"Tom's really good at card tricks," she says.

Oh God, not cards.

"He does them at the West Show every year. Raises money for Les Bourgs Hospice." She's trying to cajole Tom out of his mood. Like a mother – or a lover. "He catches me out every time. The Double Lift, that's what it's called, isn't it?"

Tom looks back at her, "spot on," and returns his attention to the floor below.

He's getting out before the cards appear. He pushes back his chair and stands up. "Can I ask you something, Tom? When you saw Pierre, he was on a bike, wasn't he?"

Tom lets out a long sigh. Hyperbolic, if he can say that of a sigh. "Yes. He was on his bike."

"Are you sure it was *his* bike?"

"Yes. I saw leaning it against the wall."

He clicks his tongue. "So, you and Pierre were at the house on the same day, around the same time?"

"I was her gardener. I had work to do. I can't remember. Dead-heading roses probably. I saw him peddle off when I was making my way home."

"Okay, so if you were both there around the same time, why weren't you implicated? You could have done the murder yourself, couldn't you? Or you could have done it together."

"Mark!" Viv turns on him. "That's outrageous. Take it back."

He has no intention of taking it back. The question's a valid one. Even she can see that, whether she fancies Tom or not. And she does fancy him, he's sure of it, from the top of his head all the way down to his toes. Tight t-shirt, tanned skin. She's old enough to be his mother.

THE RAIN HAS CEASED and the air smells clean and fresh. He crosses the cobbled lane and makes his way towards the steps that lead down to the lower part of town. At the top, by a lamp-post that doesn't shine, he stops. A realisation comes to him, one so glaringly obvious he can't believe he didn't think of it before. He punches the air. Of course! That's it!

He hurries back to the pub to tell Viv but when he reaches the blue door, he changes his mind. Voices spill out into the night and he hears the tuning of instruments. Tom de Carteret is inside, strumming his banjo. Everything about the man is sexualised, even the job he does, spreading compost, pruning branches. Down there with fornicating nature.

He gives his back to the Cock and Bull (Jesus, what a name!) and takes out his phone to make a call. It rings and rings. He taps his toes. Still it rings. Bloody hell, Viv. He switches it off and stuffs it into his pocket. Maybe it's better this way. He needs evidence. Insight is like spying the Pea

Stacks in the fog: suddenly seen but only in outline. He's going to need more to convince her.

The steps down to the Bordage are a tunnel of darkness with high granite walls either side. He slips on the wet stone and grabs the railing to catch himself, stopping a moment to let his heart settle.

Someone is following him. He looks up over his shoulder and sees a figure near the top. It has stopped too, a dark shadow in a dark place. He looks down to the Bordage. The street is tinged yellow by a light he can't see. Nothing to do but carry on. A shadow is only a shadow. Everything else is a trick of the mind.

With his hands in his pockets, he skips down the last few steps. The figure follows. He marches up the road and still it pursues him. Its footsteps are light but not too fast.

He reaches his car and turns around, leaning against the bodywork to wait for it to catch up. It's smaller than it appeared on the steps, and it's hurrying towards him.

"Mr. Roussel. Wait! I need to talk to you."

"Ginny?"

She staggers over to him and stops a few paces away, her hair hanging dank about her face.

"Are you following me?"

"I saw you go into the pub." She's stepping from foot to foot, her hands clasped in front of her.

"You've been outside all this time? Why didn't you come in?"

She looks up and down the road, chaotically, unfocused. "I didn't want to be seen, eh. People in there, they know me and not the good bit of me."

"You said you were clean. At Jerbourg, when we were talking, you said you'd turned a page."

"Yeah well, it flips back sometimes, don't it?"

"I can't help you with that."

"Yeah you can, you can keep quiet about it. Thing is, I've got to talk to you. Just not here, eh. It's important. It's about the thing. What you're looking into. You know." Her hands are going through her hair now, and she is biting her lip. "I haven't got time, eh. I'm meeting someone. I can't hang around."

"Why didn't you tell me when I saw you at Jerbourg?"

"I couldn't then. Not with that woman with you."

"She's a friend."

"Yeah, well I know a lot about friends."

"Okay. What's it about?"

She crunches forward and whispers. "The black bag."

"The one Pierre Bourgaize was meant to have ditched somewhere?"

Ginny nods. She glances over her shoulder.

"Tom de Carteret's the only one to attest to that," he says. "He's in the pub."

"I know. I couldn't go in, could I?"

"You're afraid of him."

"You're joking, aren't you?"

No, and neither is she. "What's wrong with the black bag?"

Ginny stamps her feet. "For f..." She bites her lip.

He holds up his hands. "Okay, okay. What about a lift? Where do you need to be?"

"You're thick or something?" She steps away, unsteadily. "You don't fucking get it, do you?"

"Why don't we meet up. Give me a time and place and I'll be there."

Her hand goes out to catch the lamp-post behind her.

"How about the White Rock, like last time? I'll buy you lunch."

The Accused

She nods.

"Tomorrow then? Say twelve midday?"

"Yeah, tomorrow," and she scurries off into the dark, half running, half falling down the hill towards The Front.

Chapter Twenty-Four

"What's this about you and Mark Roussel then?"

That was Tom's question in the pub after Mark left; the issue is how to answer it.

Mark's point was valid of course. Theoretically, he was as much a suspect as Pierre even if his presence on the Route de Jerbourg was innocent enough. He was driving towards the house not away from it; his claim to be going to trim her trees was confirmed by a note in Jasmine Gardiner's diary. Pierre, on the other hand, was pedalling in the wrong direction with no reason for being there in the first place. And that was the sticking point, the one that got Vaudin in the end (and the hand in the shed, of course). It was near impossible to offer an alternative explanation for his presence.

As for Tom, he's like a son to her, and she'll swear on the Bible he isn't a murderer. He's one of the most sensitive men she knows. Killers don't read Keats. Byron perhaps, but not Keats.

Sorry, Mark, you're wrong on this one.

And now, Tom's on her doorstep with a bag of croissants in his hand. It's quarter-to-eight in the morning.

"Breakfast?" he grins.

"I'm still in my dressing gown."

"Looking very sexy too. Make me a coffee and we'll have it on the patio."

"Are they warm?"

"Straight from Senner's."

Outside, the sun is peeking above the trees and the air is still.

"I don't know why he's got his teeth into it," Tom says, tearing his croissant apart and eating it. "It's not as if he knows the guy. And Jurat Martel's family, so I'm told."

She nods. "It's my fault. I told him the verdict wasn't safe."

"That's because you don't like Martel, and look, I get it. He's a bit pompous..."

"Conceited, more like it. Affected too. Do you want me to go on?"

Tom laughs. "I've heard the gossip."

"What gossip?"

"The dalliance at the White House. You missed the boat."

"Oh God, that!"

"Come on, what happened?"

"You want to know?"

"Absolutely!"

"He was tiddly-pink in his dinner jacket, and grabbed me by the pool."

"And?"

"We fell in, and my dress – it was strapless – slipped down to my waist as I tried to get out."

Tom claps his hands. "Wish I'd seen that!"

She blushes. "I was bit younger than. Anyway, he got the wrong end of the stick…"

"So to speak."

"So to speak, and held onto me. I thought he was trying to help me out. But forget gallantry. He got his hands on my tits and helped himself to a nice long fondle. That's when the Procureur and his wife stepped onto their balcony."

"They were in Room 7?"

"That's the one, and the little shit slid right under the water. I grabbed my tits with one hand and my sopping dress with the other, and scrambled out of the pool into the hotel."

"And you've never forgiven him?"

"He hasn't forgiven me, you mean. 'A man in my position' and all that."

It is why she's never been back to the White House either. Great chef, excellent food, can't beat the wine, Room 7 is a must-stay: forget it all! Martel's watery grope did it for her.

Tom leans forward to pick up the coffee pot. He pours the remains into her mug, and leans back in his chair.

"It doesn't make Pierre innocent though, does it? Martel might be a bit of a creep – I mean, I don't know, I'm not a woman – but the verdict was unanimous."

"I'm not saying Pierre is innocent *because* of Martel. I'm saying there were irregularities. The trial was over too quickly. That's my issue. That's what I told Mark."

"And Mark's gone off on some crusade."

"He's always been one for the underdog. And I think he's a bit bored. It isn't easy coming here with nothing to do."

"I weep for him."

She frowns. "That's not like you."

The Accused

Tom holds up his hands. "Amnesty?"

"Of course."

"Can I say just one more thing before we call it quits?"

"Okay."

"It's just, you're a bit of a tease, Viv. That's what I love about you. You dip your toe over the line and then hop back on it again. It makes great reading in the *Press*. You're really risqué with your advice and it's hilarious. But this time – I'm sorry, this time you've miscalculated. Mark Roussel's got the bit between his teeth, and he's going to make himself a lot of enemies, if he isn't careful. Take my advice, friend to friend. Stop him before he gets carried away. He'll take you down with him if you're not careful. Pierre's guilty. He really is."

She looks out across the garden towards the brick chimney at the far end of the field. It's all that remains of the old greenhouses.

Is Tom advising or warning? And if so, why? She glances at him. There's nothing threatening in his smile; nothing untoward. He's the same lad she drunkenly snogged one night at the West Show.

The problem is, she just can't take advice. Give it – yes. She'll tell an astronaut how to get to the moon if she could. Just don't think to counsel her. It's why her marriage ended. *'Tell that man to get his head seen to (not his dick). Better still, tell him to pack his bags and leave.'* It's why she makes a good Agony Aunt.

You don't fucking get *it, do you?*

Ginny's words keep spinning about in his head. Her

manner was paranoid. When he mentioned Tom de Carteret, she sounded anxious – *I couldn't go in, could I?*

He looks up at the Weighbridge clock. It reads twenty to eleven. Time enough to walk up the hill to Elizabeth College and down again for a haircut. He can even pop into Marks and Spencer's before the hour strikes twelve. The school is on holiday but the secretaries often work over the summer and, assuming they remember the days of Tom and Pierre, a quick chat should answer a few questions.

St Julian's Avenue cuts up through town, dividing Old Government House from the Canichers. It is the main road out of St Peter Port towards the West and a queue of cars wait on the gradient for the lights to turn green. Mark trudges past their exhausts towards St James' Church, keeping the Connaught Memorial to his left and the old Randall's Brewery to his right. Ahead, the remains of a granite arch mark the lower terraces of the hilltop site. Following the sweep of the road around, he tracks the black metal railings up and up until he meets the entrance gates to the school.

And there it is, a gothic citadel atop the town, seen by ships far out to sea. The turreted towers – one in each corner – have served as boarding rooms, stores rooms, punishment cells and now flats for teachers. The central tower rises high above the rest, each corner with its own decorated pinnacle. It was the library in his day, a sunlit version of the Priaulx with crumbling tomes and oak desks. Now it's obsolete.

Generations of his family were educated here, from its illustrious beginnings under Adrian Saravia in 1563, through the lean years of a pupil-less existence, to its resurrection in 1826 and later evacuation under German Occupation. He left in 1989 and hasn't walked its corridors since.

The Accused

But he remembers the layout: the central hall with its stained-glass windows and memorial boards, the high echoey rooms and the cells in the attic.

Today, the parade ground is empty of cars and the large doors into the hall are locked, so he walks up the side of the building and in through the staff entrance. Here he meets a small hallway with a white ascending staircase. Opposite are the blue doors he remembers from childhood, the ones he stood behind on the other side, waiting to be called into the Principal's office. It feels illicit, standing in the domain of powerful teachers, and he's surprised by the childlike awe that comes over him. He reads the notice board and peeps inside the staffroom where upholstered chairs line the walls. Behind the staircase is a corridor that leads to the pigeon-holes, a kitchen, a toilet and – down a step – three white-painted meeting rooms.

Back in the main lobby, he knocks on the secretaries' door.

"Come in."

The room is square and high, much like the classrooms with gothic windows and mullions. Two desks sit at right angles to each other and behind one is a round-faced woman with curly hair and ruddy cheeks. Behind the other a more severe version of the same. He chooses the former, and goes up to her desk.

"Mark Roussel," he says. "I'm here on the off-chance you might be able to put me in touch with someone who knew Tom de Carteret or Pierre Bourgaize."

"Heavens above," the woman says. "You're not the one that put the advert in the *Press*, are you?"

He admits he is.

"You'd do best to talk to Jurat Martel, he was Principal at the time. He'd have a tale or two to tell."

"He's not keen to share information."

The secretaries glance at each other, as if to say: well, that's a surprise.

"I wonder if James Mauger could help?" The chubby-faced secretary looks to her comrade. "He's chemistry. There's Andrew Springer too. English. Loves a gossip does our Mr. Springer. What do you think, Jane?"

"Not possible." Despite looking stern, Jane has a soft melodic voice. She is scanning her computer screen. "He's taken the CCF to Snowdon. There's Sally Birch. She's on island."

"History," the other one says. "She knows everything. I'm Babs by the way." She leans across the desk to hold out her hand.

He shakes it. "Nice to meet you."

"What is it you want exactly?" Jane looks away from her screen and rolls her chair along the desk so she can see him better.

"Can we start with their friendship?"

Both women guffaw. "Enemies more likely," Babs says.

"How do you mean?"

Jane thinks a moment. "I can't remember the details, but Pierre was sanctioned for threatening to put a spell on Tom. It was idiotic stuff but Martel took it seriously. As did the Dean. If I remember rightly, it was the Dean who pushed Martel to act. I've never understood why, if I'm honest. Teenagers will threaten the stupidest of things. That said, there had been a case earlier on, in an RE lesson, when Pierre had accused the teacher of 'persecuting his people'."

"Who did he mean?"

"Honestly, we weren't sure but the RE teacher – I can't remember her name, Foote, I think – believed he was talking about Satanists. He'd lifted his shirt to show her the bloodied face of some priest printed on a t-shirt. He'd boasted about digging up corpses in the Foulon Cemetery and things like that. He had a lot of issues."

Babs interjects. "He was on the register, you know. For vulnerable students. One of the PE teachers noticed bruises on his arms and legs. I remember him coming in here to talk about it."

It doesn't surprise him. He wondered about Pierre's home life.

"What about Tom de Carteret?"

"That one," Jane smiles. "He charmed everyone. Just couldn't help it. He'd charm a tree stump given half a chance."

His laugh is hollow. "Quite a favourite then."

Babs glances over at Jane. "He came in here once – about a year ago – offering to top the trees, didn't he? Oh, my goodness, I was quite lost for words. That smile. Well, you can imagine how difficult it was for the teachers, especially the women."

"He got away with blue murder," Jane admits. "Martel was far too lenient with him. He was no angel you know."

"I can imagine."

"There was the time he locked Pierre up in one of the cells in the attic. You know, the old Victorian ones. I think it was the one with all the carved names in the wood panelling. Quite scary for a young boy; he was only twelve. Martel should have gated him for it, but no, he just got a telling off."

He stops her there. "How long did he leave him there for?"

"I can't remember, a few hours. No one noticed he was missing. Personally, I think the teachers were relieved he wasn't in class. One of the cleaners found him. They heard him shouting. It must have been well after school had ended."

"And his father didn't do anything?"

Jane shakes her head. "I got the sense he didn't much like him. He came in with a black eye once. Walked into the door, the old story. I felt rather sorry for him—" She holds up her hand. The telephone is ringing. "Could you excuse me a moment." She picks up the receiver. "Elizabeth College, can I help you?"

Babs leans across her desk. "Jane's far too kind, you know. I'm not local, you've probably guessed. Personally, between you and me, I'd have left him up there. He and Wilson would have got on famously."

"Wilson?" He quizzes, and then remembers. "Wilson, of course. The boy that was locked in the cell and starved to death, supposedly anyway?"

"That's him."

Jane puts down the receiver and curls her hair behind her ears. "The truth is, Mr. Roussel, Pierre and Tom really hated each other. There were so many incidents: on the sports field, in the labs. If I'm honest – and I know I shouldn't say this, given what he did –, of the two, Tom was the real bully."

"Jane!"

"It's true, Babs. He was good at sports – and that goes a long way in this school. Cricket, football, tennis, swimming, you name it. The boys adored him, the teachers did as well. Pierre didn't have a chance. All that nonsense about Satanism and the Foulon cemetery, they were just ways to get his own back. That's my opinion, for what it's worth. As for what happened afterwards, I can't say. There's no excusing it, but no one's born bad, are they?"

"Psychopaths are," Babs interjects.

"I don't know. I'm talking from experience, that's all. Pierre went off the rails, but there're quite a few people who helped him along the way, that's for sure."

Babs shifts in her chair. "That's where we disagree," she says to Mark. "I don't think we can live our lives excusing people. A rotten heart's a rotten heart, and that's the end of it. You know they say one in ten people are psychopaths? Well, there you have it. Pierre Bourgaize was a psychopath from birth."

Jane raises her eyebrows, and straightens the diary on her desk. She glances up at Mark and asks, "Is there anything else we can help you with, Mr. Roussel?"

"I was wondering if I could see his school records?"

Jane pauses.

"I'll have to ask the principal," she says. "It's a matter of privacy, as I'm sure you understand."

"Of course." He didn't expect otherwise. "You don't have any school photos of Pierre, by any chance?"

Babs laughs. "You won't find one in the whole place. He refused to sit for the year photos and there wasn't a thing we could do about it, short of chaining him to a chair. He probably thought it'd catch his soul, you know, like they used to believe. I wouldn't put it past him anyway."

He nods. It is possible. "You've been very helpful. Both of you. Thank you. Don't mention any of this to Jurat Martel, will you, if he comes calling, or the Dean for that matter. Martel is family."

Outside, he stands on the steps and takes a deep breath. Tom and Pierre: it proves nothing, but underpins a lot. It gives explanatory force to the idea that Tom lied about seeing Pierre on the bicycle. Still, without evidence, it's just another schoolboy tale. Like Freddy tripping him up on Remembrance Day in front of the Lieutenant Governor.

Cars are roaring up the Grange, and he waits at the school gates until they have passed. Then he crosses over.

The haircut can wait. He's going to go to the *Guernsey Press* to look at their photograph archive. With his phone to his ear, he walks down the hill.

"Yes, hello. I was wondering if I could pop round and see your photo archive."

"It's online."

"All of it?"

"As I said, it's online."

He hears the receptionist tapping away at the keyboard. "I don't imagine they've all been digitalised yet."

"If you don't mind," she snaps. "I have a job to do."

The line goes dead. Very well, if that's her attitude. He glances at his watch. The Guilles-Àlles library in Market Square is worth a bet. They're bound to have computers.

The domed ceiling is two stories high, and the stained-glass windows at the far end lends it a sacred air. Amidst all the books, he finds a row of computers and sits down at one of them, clicking the mouse to enter.

Photos of Guernsey.

The first site he enters is GP-Digitel which is divided into the island's interests: Dance, Sports, Nativities, and the Best-Selling Picture of the last fourteen days. Not History or Ecology or anything that might inspire a wider audience. He clicks another: 'Guernsey Press pictures' and meets a page of thumbnails, beginning with Charlie Watts on the drums in 1964, performing at St Georges Hall. There's Bill Wyman with his bass guitar, then Mick Jagger; shots of the screaming audience, and then Keith Richards looking alarmingly young.

The Accused

He clicks the arrow at the bottom to see the next sixteen photos, only to be confronted with coloured snaps of people braving the Boxing Day Swim at Cobo the year before.

Odd archiving.

In the search box at the top of the page he types in 'Jerbourg'. Up come the generic pictures of the Doyle monument on a sunny day; a few photos are dedicated to a gorse fire on the headland, and then it's back to the usual athletic swims and runs along the cliff paths.

Nothing of interest. He types in 'social events' to no avail; he tries 'winter scenes' but nothing. 'Government House' is the next attempt and with it come pictures of the Lieutenant Governor and a 'Dementia Friendly' event on the Residence's lawn. All contemporary.

Irritated, he opens Google and types in 'Jerbourg, Winter Scenes, Guernsey'. Clicking through the pages, he comes upon a picture as rare as eagles – frozen trees and tyre marks down a snow-covered road. It's dated the year of Jasmine Gardener's death. He recognises the lane and the high entrance gates of Pine Forest Lodge. Parked against the wall is an E-type Jaguar and he's damned sure he's seen it before, in Martel's drive, a long time ago. He recognises the racing-green paint-work. He enlarges the picture to read the number plate: 6748. A high number and an unremarkable one to boot. On Guernsey, the larger the car, the smaller the number plate – both speak status.

He opens another tab and finds digits.gg, an online valuation service. 6748 cost £1,500 in 2016. To put it in context, 314 was valued at £14,000, and 007 cost some idiot more than £240,000. Martel's Mercedes carries the number for Pi as befits the man who taught mathematics for twenty years before becoming Principal of the College, and then a Jurat.

In other words, 6748 is far too plebeian for a man like Martel. But, frustratingly, Mark can't find out who does. It's a bloody nightmare trying to investigate a crime without the resources. He's beginning to respect those private detectives he used to mock.

Only answer is to change tack and search a meteorological site for historic snow falls in Guernsey. Worldweatheronline is the first he meets; it requires him to guess the day, month and year. That's easy enough. If Jasmine was killed on Tuesday March the 15th eleven years ago, he should start a week before and work backwards; there were no references to snow around the time of her death.

Within minutes he's made his discovery: on 6th March, there was a flurry which lasted for a day and a night before rain fell and washed it away. The conclusion? Someone rich enough to afford a vintage Jaguar parked outside her house ten days before she was murdered. He copied the link into an email and sent it to himself.

Outside, he walks down the steps to the Arcade and ambles through the shaded lanes of shops until he comes out onto the High Street. People are everywhere, in their flip-flops and shorts, sunglasses over their eyes, walking beneath the buntings hanging overhead. He steps down onto the cobbles, and is rammed by a pushchair.

"Watch it!"

"Keep your eyes in your head," snaps the woman.

"My shin," he says, but she's already on her way down the hill to Marks and Spencer's.

His phone chimes church bells and he pulls it out. "What?"

"Blimey, you woke up on the wrong side of the bed." It's Viv.

"I've just been butted by a pushchair."

"Metaphorically?"

"No. It's a woman – forget the woman, what do you want?

"Okay, let's try that again. Example: 'Hi Viv, how are you? Did you want to talk to me about something?'"

"You're being sensitive."

"I won't bother then."

"Bother about what?"

"You're as charming as a tinned anchovy. Look, I called..."

"Did you just call me a tinned anchovy?"

"Yup."

He pauses. "I like anchovies."

"That didn't work then, did it?" He hears the smile in her voice, and he remembers Tom. Is he a tinned anchovy? He doubts it. A bloody oyster, most likely.

"Anyway, listen, I've got some bad news. It's about Ginny Bisson. They've found her body at L'Ancresse... Mark? Are you there. Mark?"

He drops the phone.

Dead? She can't be. Last night...

He bends down to pick it up and puts it to his ear. "It's impossible. I'm meeting her for lunch."

Chapter Twenty-Five

THE POLICE HAVE CORDONED OFF THE CAR-PARK, SO HE leaves the car near the kiosk. Below is the German tank wall, and beyond, the sea. Brown-flecked seagulls are gathered at the edge of the incoming tide, pecking at the seaweed tossed about in the surf. On the sand, a father is playing cricket with his sons, and a couple are sunbathing on the rocks by the slipway.

He looks longingly at the water. Its edges are green, its depth a dark blue. Somewhere he read that we carried the sea in every cell of our body, an encapsulated drop of our original home. It's why he returned to the island. For better or for worse, he's come to be close to the many mothers that made him: mother-sea, mother-land, mother-mother. And though it feels right (noble, even), it's also frightening; the island is small, very small.

And Ginny is right – he doesn't 'fucking' get it.

A group of people are gathered at the top of the incline, standing in front of the cordons which stretch across the entrance to the car-park. One of them is Viv, with a dog by her feet, sitting on its haunches. She introduces it as Brandy.

"It's black-and-white," he points out.

"I know."

"Brandy is brown."

"Yes."

"Why did you call it Brandy then?"

"Because I wanted to. It doesn't have to be logical, you know."

The car-park is empty except for the police cars and an ambulance. He cranes his neck to see over them. The investigation is happening further along the path that curves away out of sight and he moves down the cordon to get a better view. Viv and Brandy follow him.

"It was busier earlier on," Viv says

Two policemen appear in uniform, talking to each other. Behind them comes another, on the radio. A while later, a plain-clothed official hurries into the car-park. He gets into his car and sits there, writing something. Amongst them, Mark catches sight of Pete Robilliard. He waves him over.

"What's going on?"

Pete's eyes are gleaming. "We have a woman, in her early thirties..."

"I know, Ginny Bisson. What can you tell me?"

"The body was found by a walker, Mrs. Davis, at 0715 hours. It's located 163 metres along the path, lying in a north-easterly direction, partially clothed..."

"Forget the report," he interrupts. "Give me the word on the ground. What are people saying?"

Pete beckons with his finger and takes them a few paces away from the others.

"To be honest, it's not clear. It doesn't look like murder.

There's no damage to the body so it doesn't look like she was attacked. She could have been suffocated but we won't know 'til forensics have finished and we've got the pathologist's report."

"You said she was partially clothed. Is it rape?"

"Not from initial findings, no. But her shirt was torn off and her shoes too, and it looks like she threw herself into the gorse bushes, the ones on the right of the path, you know, under the tower."

"They think she did it herself?"

Pete shrugs. "It's possible. There's this strange black paste all over her stomach. It smells pretty odd. It's on her clothes and her hands as well, so she either put it on or she tried to take it off. The juries out."

"Any idea what it is?"

"Not without testing it, no."

"What's the chatter?"

"Honestly?"

"Yup."

"'What the fuck is that?'"

"And the cause of death?"

"Heart attack's the going theory at the mo."

"Not the black paste?"

"It looks like mushed up olives if you want my opinion."

"Tapenade? You've got to be joking," Viv says.

"Who knows. It doesn't look lethal, if that's what you mean." He motions his head towards the scene. "Look, I better get back."

Viv touches his arm to stop him. "Is she facing up or down?"

"Up. Why?"

"If she's head down, I'd say someone pushed her. Head up, she's looking at the sky."

"Good point," Mark says.

"Excuse me."

A plain clothes policeman is walking towards them. He stops at the cordon, and gestures for Pete to get back to work. "I know who you are," he says to Mark.

"I can't repay the compliment." Mark offers his hand.

The man looks over his shoulder, and back again. "Meddlers aren't welcome. I'll ask you to leave now."

"Meddler? I happened to be on a walk with a friend and stopped to observe."

"As I said, leave now please."

"I'm a citizen expressing his interest."

"Leave, Mr. Roussel. We don't need you."

"What's the problem? Because I'm Met or because I'm asking about Jasmine Gardiner?"

"Sergeant!" the man calls to Pete. "Make this man leave, will you."

Viv takes Mark's arm. "Come on," she says.

He pulls against her like a dog on a lead. "I have every right to be here."

Pete is before him. "Come on, mate, go home."

He points after the disappearing man. "What's his problem?"

"I told you. They don't like you looking into Jasmine Gardiner. And they don't like what they've got here either."

"And that's my fault? If they'd done their job better..."

Viv tugs at him. "Leave it, Mark. Let's go."

ON THE BEACH, Mark takes off his shoes and rolls up his trousers. He's angry. Fuming, in fact. He wades into the surf to cool down. Pig-headed bastards exist everywhere – he's met enough in his time – but he's never been called a meddler before, like some fussy old dot poking her nose into things. Accuse him again, and his not only going to sniff out Pierre's innocence but every bloody case the police have investigated since.

And he's never broken a promise to himself, ever.

Viv joins him on the sand, throwing Brandy a ball. They walk in silence, listening to the waves. L'Ancresse is his favourite beach with its wide spread of sand and curving edges, piniomed by eighteenth century fortresses either side.

"Penny for your thoughts."

He looks at her.

"Let me guess. 'Bloody Guernsey police'? Or 'What the hell happened to Ginny Bisson?'"

He smiles and carries on walking. "She wanted to tell me something about the black bag, the one Pierre was seen with. We were meant to meet for lunch at the White Rock."

Viv throws Brandy the ball, and he watches the dog dash after it, tossing seagulls into the air as it goes.

"She had to meet up with someone, that's why she couldn't talk. She was nervous. Something was bothering her."

"You think they're linked?"

"It feels like it."

"It could be coincidence." Viv takes the ball from Brandy's mouth and throws it again. "She was a drug addict. Maybe she needed to get a fix."

"I don't think so."

They walk on. A wave crashes over his legs and soaks his trousers. He jumps over the one that follows.

"I tried to call you last night," he says.

"When I was in the pub? You disappeared off pretty quick."

"Something came to me. It was what you said about Tom and card tricks."

"Ah Tom. We need to talk about Tom."

"Why?"

"What you insinuated, that he was involved in the murder."

He stops and faces her. "I didn't insinuate it. If he was there at the same time..."

"Look, it's obvious you don't like him."

"That's not the point."

She strides on, calling Brandy to follow her. The dog is more interested in sniffing the bottom of a Shih Tzu. "Brandy!" she snaps, and the dog pads after her.

"Imagine I'm doing that card trick, the Double Lift," he says catching her stride. "It's about a sleight of hand. What I want you to believe is that I've lifted one card from the top of the deck when in fact I've lifted two. To you, it looks like I'm showing you the top card, when in fact it's the second."

"And?" She isn't looking at him.

"It's the same with Jasmine Gardiner. It's made to look like a single event when it's actually two unrelated ones."

"Sorry, I'm not following."

"Cause and effect. You think something happens because of something else, when in fact they're not related at all. Correlation not causation. We have a murder and we have a severed hand, okay? The fallacy's in assuming the murder happened *because* of the hand. Or, to be more specific, the murder happened because of the witchcraft."

"Someone did the murder and someone else did the mutilation?"

"Exactly."

Viv takes the ball out of Brandy's mouth. "You're saying, someone found her hanging in the Pine Forest and thought: Oh look, I can cut off her hand." She throws the ball and Brandy runs. "That's got more holes in it than a crumpet."

She has a point.

"I'm not saying the mutilation was accidental. There was a reason for it, but the reason had nothing to do with the murder. If we work from that hypothesis, we might get somewhere."

"How?"

"Let's work on the possibility that Pierre did the mutilation."

"Because of his interest in the black books?"

He nods. "That means he didn't do the murder, so if we can find who had it in for Pierre, then we might find who killed Jasmine Gardiner."

"You're saying the murderer wanted to frame Pierre?"

"He's a self-proclaimed witch. He's an easy target. Let him take the blame for both acts. Someone wanted us to believe it was all about witchcraft."

"When it wasn't."

"Exactly."

Brandy is bored of trying to catch Viv's attention. She drops the ball and sits down in the sun to watch the seagulls. Her tail is making rainbows in the sand.

"I've been doing some thinking of my own," Viv says. "About the book, the one Jasmine Gardiner was interested in. I was talking to my gran and she said it belonged to Victor Hugo. Supposedly – so the rumours go – he brought it with him when he came over from France, and used it in his séances. You know he held them in the house, don't you?"

"The reason I won't read his books."

She smiles. "Whatever. His mistress – what was her

name? He put her up in the house down the road, in Hauteville."

"Juliette Drouet."

"That's her. She stole it and gave it to a Mrs. Queripel as payment for some witchery she did. According to my gran, Mrs. Queripel was meant to have cursed Victor Hugo, just before they returned to France."

"So that's how they got hold of it."

"Who?"

"Pierre's family. His mother was a Queripel."

Viv is surprised. "How do you know that?"

"They told me at the Priaulx. It would have been his great-grandfather who tried to sell it to the Nazis."

Brandy has given up on the seagulls. She is snapping at Viv's heel. Viv tells her to be quiet but Brandy is having none of it and continues to yelp in her high-pitched way until Viv bends down and picks her up.

"You know the last woman convicted of witchcraft in Guernsey was a Queripel," Viv says. "I mean, her maiden name was Queripel. It was in 1914."

"Family business, evidently."

"She was had for selling powders. It's a fact."

"The powders or the witchcraft? You know it's nonsense, don't you?"

"'There are more things under heaven and earth than are dreamt of in your philosophy,' Mr. Roussel."

"I hate it when people quote Shakespeare," he says, not too gallantly.

Viv bursts out laughing. He looks at her. He really does hate it. Worse, it is one of the most overused quotations in literature.

"Witches aside," she says, "perhaps Jasmine Gardiner was onto something. If the book was as valuable as people say, then maybe she got hold of it and that's what the murderer was looking for. It would explain the books being thrown off the shelves. And," she adds, "as reluctant as I am to say this, Pierre had a reason to want to get hold of it. He could have killed her *and* done the mutilation."

"Why kill someone when you want something from them?"

"Maybe he got angry? I don't know. It's just conjecture."

"I thought you championed his innocence?"

Viv doesn't answer.

He raises an eyebrow. "An evening spent with Tom de Carteret and you've changed your mind?"

"I'm trying to be the devil's advocate."

"You know he's young enough to be your son?"

"Pierre?"

"No – yes, probably. I meant Tom."

She stares at him. "Seriously? That's what's bothering you?"

He doesn't answer. 'Bothering' is the wrong word; it's something else and he doesn't care to name it. Name it and you pin it down; you make it concrete. Concrete cracks.

"Most murders are domestic," he says, changing the subject. "I'm putting my money on the lover, and the lover stitched up Pierre."

They reach the rocks that separate L'Ancresse from Pembroke. He turns around to head back the way they came.

"If we follow your hypothesis," Viv says, following him, Brandy still in her arms, "and Pierre did the mutilation, how did he know where the body was?"

"Someone told him."

"Who?"

"The person trying to frame him."

The Accused

"What was his motive?"

"I've told you. Not to get caught."

"I meant the mutilation. Why did Pierre do it?"

"I don't know. A sick interest in the occult? A desire to try it out – 'Oh look, at last a corpse I can hack away at.' I don't know. That's why it's a hypothesis."

They carry on, past the girls hopping about in the shallows and the woman striding down in her cap and goggles; there is a Labrador paddling and a little boy howling at the water's edge. Finally, they reach the rocks beneath the cliff path. Above, he sees the police working in the shadow of the round tower, its loopholes like square perforations.

"What if we start with the book," Viv says. "Someone wanted it, they thought she had it, and they killed her for it. The book's about black magic, the body had the pentacle on it and a severed hand. It's obvious they go together."

"If we keep looking at the same evidence with the same set of glasses, we're going to see the same thing. The point is to change the spectacles. Let's separate the murder from the mutilation and see what comes up."

"You've forgotten what the island's like."

"That's a *non sequitur*."

"No. The place might look anglicised, but the old beliefs haven't gone away."

"Meaning?"

"My glasses are seeing things very clearly. You can't ignore the superstition."

He shakes his head.

"You can't and you know that."

"Tell me about it!" he vents. "I'm related to Linda Martel, for God's sake. The child-mystic, who cured people. You remember her? I can't tell you how many times I was taken to her grave to pray for my eczema."

"Did it work?"

He glares at her.

"Only teasing."

Just then, his mobile rings. He taps the screen to answer and puts it to his ear. It's the Chaplain. If Mark is free, he's managed to arrange a visit with Pierre for eleven thirty, in half an hour. It's short notice, he admits, but he's taking a risk. Can he come?

Most definitely, and he hangs up.

Chapter Twenty-Six

"We'll go to the visiting room."

Mark follows the Chaplain down the corridor. He hears the clanking of a door and a voice yelling at someone to 'piss off'. Of the eighty-two prisoners, thirty-six are locked up for drugs, sixteen for sexual assault, fourteen for violence and nine for public disorder and property fraud. Only one is for murder. He's done his research.

"It's not bad," he admits, looking at the newly painted walls.

"We're rather proud of the place. It's based on the hotel-corridor layout."

"Do the prisoners know that?"

"No," the Chaplain admits.

"They're not complaining about the minibar then?"

The Chaplain laughs. "Room service isn't quite to their liking. But here we are." He stops outside the door to the visitors' room. "Shall I sit in with you?"

"I don't imagine he's very fond of chaplains." The Chaplain opens his mouth to reply but Mark interrupts, "I'm used to it, don't worry."

"I should warn you, he's got access to the internet. He's checked you out."

"I assumed as much."

"He wasn't too keen on the meeting. Heaven knows why, but I've convinced him to give you a chance."

"Thanks."

"He's still very much into his beliefs too. It's what we talked about the other day."

"The need to straighten out his synapses a bit?" Mark says.

"That's one way of putting it."

The room is empty except for tables and chairs laid out in rows. It's stark with its spread of white paint and pipes running along the tops of the walls. Vertical blinds bar the windows and filter the light, and the smell of disinfectant is strong. He sits at a table and waits for Pierre. The guard by the door has a bird-splat of a birthmark on his face. It's bright red and he keeps looking at it.

A few minutes later, Pierre shuffles in and Mark gets to his feet and holds out his hand. Pierre refuses it and flops down in the chair. His hair falls over his face like a mask.

"Thanks for seeing me," Mark says.

Pierre grunts.

"The Chaplain might have told you why I'm here."

Silence.

Mark sits back and crosses his arms. He studies Pierre: the small build, the thin body; the shoulders curled forward and the neck sunk down between them. His arms are long, his fingers delicate. There isn't a tattoo in sight. When he flicks back his hair to reveal his eyes, they are green and set deep in his face; they have a serpentine look to them but he never relies on the face to reveal a character. True, the years can set the sinews of a body and the eyes flicker with the mind, but though the mind has its habits, it isn't set in stone and what he sees today, he might not see tomorrow.

"I've read up about you."

Mark cocks his head.

"You were in the Met. You were earmarked for the top, and then you left. Just like that. You came back to this crappy island to look after your mum. I don't buy it."

He doesn't answer.

"I bet you upset someone, or did something illegal. Are you one of those cops that bend the rules? You see them on TV. You're not married either. Are you gay? Trans?"

The skill is to listen but not to feel. If he feels, he reacts.

"I'm trying to make conversation, you know." Pierre drops his eyes and looks sideward to the floor.

"I don't want a conversation."

"What am I doing here then?"

"Look at me," he orders. He puts his elbows on the table and links his fingers. Pierre flips his hair away and glances up. "I want information."

"What about?"

"Why you're here."

"The Chaplain threatened me."

He raises an eyebrow. "I want to know about Jasmine Gardiner."

"Oh that." His smile is fake.

The clock on the wall needs a new battery; the minute hand is trembling at five past the hour. Mark catches the guard's eye and motions to it with his chin. Pierre notices and turns around in his chair.

"Tell me about her death."

Pierre turns back. "I don't know anything about it."

"Why?"

"Coz whoever did it had Gyges' ring. It made him invisible. He used it to kill the king. It's in *The Republic*."

"I know."

"Plato."

"I know that too."

"JG's killer has the ring."

"You say that in the present tense."

"You don't believe me?"

"Should I?"

Pierre's eyes are as green as the seaweed washed up on the rocks, but there is something brittle about them.

"You don't believe in much, do you?"

"I'm a detective, I look at the facts."

"Ah, facts. Weird things, aren't they? You know the word comes from the Latin *factum*? It means an event, something that's happened. It assumes truth, but I don't think it guarantees it."

Pierre is digressing, trying to control the conversation. "What happened?" Mark says with authority.

His smile is dry. "*Nihil, niente, nada.*"

"Stop being clever."

"I am clever."

"Then tell me what happened."

"Nothing happened. I didn't kill Jasmine Gardiner. They say I did, but I didn't."

At last, he's got him there. "Tell me more."

"Crime: murder. Motive: black magic. Verdict: guilty. In a nutshell."

"And?"

"Wrong, all of it. I didn't do it." There's a scratch on the table and Pierre runs his finger along it.

"Tell me about the pentacle carved into Jasmine Gardiner's chest."

The Accused

Pierre frowns. "You think I did that?"

"Well, didn't you?"

"Are you serious? It's straight out of *The Da Vinci Code*. Give me some credit."

"Why?"

"It was badly done, for one thing."

"How do you know?"

"I saw the photos. They showed them to me. 'You did this, you son of a bitch,' that sort of thing. Look, give me a pen and paper."

He leans to his right and takes out his notebook with the small pencil attached to it. He flips it open to a clean page and pushes it across the table. "Show me."

Pierre draws a line down the middle of the paper. In one he does a pentacle, basic in shape and uneven; in the other he draws something far more complex. Mark recognises it from the *Petit Albert*.

"If I'd carved it, I would have done it like this." Pierre points to the double-circled star with its strange letters. "You don't just cut a body for the fun of it. There's always a purpose. I'd have done a decent job and I'd have had a reason for doing it too."

"So, who did it?"

"I don't know. Someone who didn't know what they were doing, for starters."

"Was this mentioned at the time?"

"What do you think? They'd found their witch, that was good enough for them. A real coup for those Masons, eh. They've been persecuting us for centuries. You think it's going to stop because we're in the scientific age? Don't make me laugh."

Mark doesn't laugh. "What about *la main de gloire*. Can you explain that to me?"

Pierre chews his bottom lip. "You know what it is?"

"Yes, I've read the *Petit Albert*."

"Wow." He pins his hair away from his face and Mark sees its contours for the first time, the hollowed cheeks dotted with pock marks and the chafing from a blunt razor.

"Your dad found it, didn't he?" Mark says. "He handed you over to the police before you could finish the job."

"I couldn't finish the job because I didn't start it."

Mark takes back the notebook and leans sideward to slip it into his back pocket. He needs a coffee. His mind wanders to his beans, roasted to perfection...

"I was framed."

The word brings him back. "Who wanted to frame you?"

"I've got my ideas."

"And?"

"You won't believe me."

Mark senses a closing off, a folding inward. Self-pity, even narcissism perhaps, but given the lad's eleven years of incarceration he's willing to be generous. He changes tack.

"There was vomit found by the body, in the Pine Forest."

Pierre shrugs his shoulders.

"You didn't know about that?"

"No."

Little point pushing it then. "Okay. Tell me about the yew seeds. Why use them?"

"I didn't use them."

"Okay, why do you think someone would use them?"

"How should I know?"

"What significance do they have, apart from being deadly?"

"How do you mean?"

The Accused

"Are they used in magical rites or something?"

Pierre massages his temples. "The tree is associated with immortality – renewal, regeneration, that sort of thing. It's sacred to Hecate. I don't know much about the seeds. Some people claim you'll get a vision of the afterlife if you take them at the alignment of Jupiter and Venus, but I've never tried so I don't know."

Mark blows out his cheeks. The nonsense of it all. "And you believe that?"

"What does it matter what I believe? I didn't give them to her."

"But it's the sort of thing you would do?"

"What's that supposed to mean? I'm not an idiot."

"The thing is, Pierre, you were seen pedalling away from the scene of the murder and given your" – he tries to find the word – "interests, it's not surprising people put two and two together and got four. I'd have done the same."

"I didn't have my bike. Someone stole it."

"You could have borrowed one."

"Who was going to lend me a bike? I'm a weirdo, remember."

"Did you report the bike as stolen?"

Pierre shakes his head.

"So, I only have your word for it?"

"Is that a problem for you?"

He smiles. "It is for you. Tom de Carteret's a reliable witness. I'm inclined to take his word for it."

"Like everyone else," Pierre grumbles.

"Exactly," or not as things stand, but Mark knows his prejudices. "What I don't get is this: if you're innocent, why didn't you appeal the verdict?"

"Are you stupid or something?"

He opens out his hands as if to say, come on.

"No one's going to help me, are they? My ma, my pa? They can't stand the sight of me. And I don't have the money, and what advocate's going to stand up for a convicted witch?"

"You weren't convicted of witchcraft."

Pierre laughs. "Not on paper I wasn't, but a piece of paper doesn't mean anything, does it?"

"If you're innocent, you could go free. Don't you want that?"

Pierre picks at his shirt. "I don't have friends. You've probably gathered that. I don't have any money, either. Where would I go?"

"I don't know. Go somewhere. Anywhere. Timbuktu."

Pierre glances up at him.

"It does exist, you know. It has an amazing library. The point is, you could start again. Try a new life."

Pierre closes his eyes and takes hold of his neck, rolling his head from side to side. Mark feels his weariness.

"One last question. Tell me about the book. Why was it special? It's not as if the *Petit Albert* is particularly rare..."

"Our one was." Pierre's hands fall from his neck. "My gran saw it once, when she was little. The family kept it hidden up the chimney piece. She sneaked up and got it and said there were notes written in the margins which she couldn't read. I've always assumed they were in Latin. There were rare talismans as well... Then they stole it."

"To stop it being sold to the Nazis."

"That's a frigging lie."

"Okay, I don't really care. Jasmine Gardiner lied in her blog, that's all that matters. She didn't know where it was and she hadn't found it."

Pierre falters a moment. "You mean it wasn't in the house?"

The Accused

He bangs his hands on the table. Mark flinches. "Ginny Bisson. That druggie good-for-nothing bitch!" He raises his hands and clenches them over his head in a strange prayer-like gesture.

"You know Ginny?"

He glares at Mark. "Of course, I know her. I used to meet her at the top of Pedvin Street. That's when I was experimenting with drugs. Her boyfriend supplied half the island. I couldn't afford them and he's not someone you mess about with. I tried some spells on them both but they didn't work. And don't scoff at me. I couldn't get all the ingredients." He lowers his arms and clenches his fists before his chest. Suddenly, he leans across the table and grabs Mark's arm. "You've got to find it. The book." His grip is strong. "Get hold of Ginny Bisson, make her tell you what she knows."

"I can't, she's dead."

Pierre slumps back and drops his head. "Jesus!"

OUTSIDE, he finds the Chaplain waiting in the corridor. His face is cherub-wide and shiny. "How did it go?"

Mark doesn't answer.

"That bad?"

"He contradicts everyone. It could be a game, it could be fantasy. I'd keep an eye on him though. I think he's got a death-wish of a sort, and that doesn't help matters."

"It hasn't been easy for him. Everyone was up in arms when they brought him back, as you well know. Petitions and the like. He's a dark presence around here, I don't deny it. The lads play tough, but they're convinced he's conjuring things up in his room. It doesn't help his parents haven't been to see him. They see it as confirmation. He's so evil, even his mother keeps away."

"And you?"

He presses his thumb into the small of his chin. "I keep an open mind."

"About his guilt or his witchcraft?"

"Both. Judgement isn't my job, thank God."

Chapter Twenty-Seven

Okay, so the Chaplain didn't threaten him. He just said he had. The man looks like a cross between a Teletubby and Barney the Dinosaur. Menace a bee and you get stung.

He agreed to meet the Roussel-man coz it got him out of the library. Stopped him bumping into Fat Bill. Get a baked potato and scale it up to human size, and that's Fat Bill. Cut open his head and it's all starch inside. Plato? He thought it was Italian for 'plate'.

Roussel isn't stupid, and he doesn't look like a cartoon figure either. He didn't peddle some moral claptrap and he didn't make any promises. He hasn't even offered to help him.

He'd have got up and walked out if he had.

Thing is, he doesn't know what the man is offering – except Timbuktu and another bloody library.

But he told him the truth. And he hasn't done that in years. Truth hasn't much worked in his favour. Always tell the truth. That was his mother's mantra.

Oh yeah? Well maybe she shouldn't have given him

salt-water to drink when he did, and that monster of a husband shouldn't have fisted him one either.

Think about that, Mum?

College was the same. Everyone knew Tom de Carteret locked him up in the cell in the attic. But guess what? Tom got a merit and he got a detention. Then Tom said he tried to do a spell on him, and he got a week at home 'to think about it'. Thanks, Mr. Martel. A week at home meant a week in his room with rations and a morning thwack to make sure he got out of bed.

Sorry, world, if he doesn't much like truth.

Spells and black magic are far more useful. They scatter people like sheep. And it isn't a question of 'working'; it's all about the 'doing'. He couldn't stop laughing when he shouted, 'main de gloire' in the court. Fucking hell! They looked like they'd seen the devil. There to you, Mr. Bailiff, and to you Jurat Martel and to you too, my useless, smarmy advocate.

That said, he begged his mum to believe him when the hand was found in the shed. He'd been scared then. Oh yeah. The only dead body he had ever seen was his gran, lying on the bed in the funeral parlour, congealed like wax and most definitely inert. She'd gone off – flown away – and he hadn't forgiven her. All the séances in the world couldn't get her back down to earth. Magic circles, incantations – he did them all at low tide, at night, down at L'Ancresee. Nothing. He was furious. No one wanted to be left behind. He thought about it then – jumping off the cliff – but he didn't.

That was before they found the hand. It still had its ring, and the nails were painted red.

"You fucking little creep. The devil's own son you are, eh? What the hell is this?"

That was his dad.

The Accused

"I didn't do it." That's what he'd said. "I didn't do it."

His mum started to cry. Not because he was black and blue from being 'taught a lesson', mind. Shame. That was the word she kept using. Shame. As if this shame thing was all his fault.

Yeah, well, tell another. He hadn't got anyone when they were stacking shelves at Le Lievres, had he? He didn't care that his gran smoked cigars and got pissed down at the Albion; he didn't even care when he turned up at her place on Cambridge Steps and found some old man doing up his flies in the kitchen.

What got him was his mum's bloody crying. "Get a grip, Mum." His eye was swelling up like a football and all she could do was sniffle.

"And here we have exhibit number eight. A drawing found in the accused's bedroom, copied from the *Petit Albert*. It was recovered during the police search. As you can see, we have a severed hand in the palm of which is a lit candle."

Okay, so he drew it. And what? Louis Duquemin drew Catherine the Great having sex with a horse. That didn't make him a pervert; it made him a really bad artist. And what about Seb Langlois? He drew a penis in ethanol and set light to it in chemistry. It didn't mean he was gay.

Vaudin told the Jurats it was 'well executed' – which wasn't the best term given the hand had been cut off, but anyway he said it showed what a talented artist he was. He showed them some of his other drawings. His best one was from Albrecht Dürer. It was a naked old woman riding a goat. She had long wavy hair and droopy breasts, like his gran. They were dark, full of distorted images and hidden symbols. That's why he drew them. That's why he liked them.

Celare – occulere – incantare.

The Jurats didn't get it. Martel whispered something to the guy on his left, and the guy nodded.

Fuck you for manners; whispering was rude, so he shouted at them: "*Sit crudeliter scelerate hac poena mali omnibus diebus.*" May you be cruelly and wickedly punished by evil all your days!

The guy spoke Latin, which did it for him.

And his mum – she did it for him too. They made her take the stand.

"Now Mrs. Bourgaize, did Pierre get a phone call the day Jasmine Gardiner was killed?"

"Yes, in the evening, on the mainline. I know coz I answered it. Pierre was upstairs and Dad – Mr. Bourgaize – was watching TV."

"Who called him?"

"I don't know. Some man."

"Can you tell us anything about him?"

"He was young. He didn't have a local accent. He told me to tell Pierre to go to the Pine Forest because there was something waiting for him."

"What time was this?"

"I can't remember but it was after ten because we had just finished watching the news. I went to Pierre's room to tell him. He was in bed with a migraine and didn't want to know. He didn't have the light on and he was under his duvet. He can't take any light or sound when he gets one of those."

"Can you be sure Pierre didn't leave the house?"

"We went to bed about ten thirty."

"Could he have slipped out afterwards?"

She dropped her head. "He thought someone was playing a prank. He told me to go away."

The Accused

"And you went to bed?"

"Yes."

"Thank you, Mrs. Bourgaize."

Yeah, thanks, Mum. You missed out the key point: 'I never told him it was the Pine Forest. Even if he'd gone out afterwards, he wouldn't have known where to go.' That was all she had to say. That was the truth. Not her little speech.

Fuck you, Mum!

Chapter Twenty-Eight

THE PHONE'S RINGING. SHE BENDS DOWN TO PICK IT UP off the floor where it's charging.

"Hello?"

"Hi Viv, it's Mark. I thought I'd update you."

"Okay." It's nine forty-five in the morning and she's tetchy.

"Are you okay?"

"Too much work. I've got a client turning up any moment now. What do you want?"

There's a pause. "Can't you call them something else?"

What's he going on about?

"Client – it makes you sound like a prostitute."

She's stumped. "What would you advise?"

"I don't know. Flipped-in-the-head? You're counselling them, aren't you?"

"That's objectionable."

He doesn't answer.

"People normally apologise when I say that."

"I suppose they do. I'll call you later," and the line goes dead.

The Accused

She drops the phone on the table top, and gets up, stretching her arms over head and arching her back. It's a squabble over nothing. There's no client turning up. No 'flipped-in-the-head' pursuer of her rather expensive advice. It's her ex-husband. The man with the wayward dick who is now living down the road in an old house with greenhouses collapsing in on themselves. He doesn't own it, his partner does – a nice arrangement, all things considered. There isn't much there which he can bankrupt; the woman was wise enough to put everything in her name. Josie, that is, her once-friend, who knew everything and still thought him worth screwing behind her back.

The question is 'What does her ex want?'

Last time, it was about a life insurance; the time before that to claim a painting by Sir Alfred East, a small oil sketch of spring in Japan. Supposedly, her father had given it to him as a present, which is bollocks of course; it belonged to her great-grandfather, and is a family heirloom. "I'll take you to court," she threatened, at which he capitulated. As he always does. He's like a feral dog that scarpers at the first shout, then crawls back for another try.

Except he isn't quite as pathetic as he seems. It's an act. He's hidden a shed-load of money in the Caymans, or so she suspects, which is about the same thing as truth when it came to James de Moulpied.

Frankly, she isn't averse to a little 'witchcraft' to get him off her back. A few frights might do him good. Nails down the windowpane at night; straw dolls in the fridge. She can try the Queripel-trick and send him packets of brown powder. Or better still, letters through the post with pentacles drawn all over them.

The doorbell rings and there he is, as expected, in a panama hat and chinos.

"Yes?" she asks, standing on the doorstep.

"You're looking tanned."

She ignores the comment. "What do you want?"

"To come in."

"Sorry, the place is a tip and all the paintings are in the attic. You're going to have to tell me what you want here, in the sunshine."

"It's a bit awkward."

"Go ahead, I'm all ears. It must be important to have booked an appointment."

"You're not helping."

"Well what a surprise. You're pretty good at helping yourself, from what I remember."

James rolls on his heels. He isn't heading off and that's a bugger.

"Look, it's about the chap you're seeing."

She widens her eyes.

"He isn't good for you."

"Who?"

"The man."

"I'm not 'seeing' a man." Her fingers etch inverted commas in the air.

"The ex-policeman."

"You mean Mark Roussel. Detective. Met. A bit more than a policeman."

"Whatever. You need to be careful."

"You're worried for me? That's novel."

"Don't be unfair. I'm here as a friend."

"I don't screw my friends."

He blows out his cheeks. "I can't talk to you."

She smiles. "Are you worried he'll start looking into your business deals?"

"I came with the best intentions."

"No, you didn't."

"You're wrong. Josie sent me."

"Ah, so Josie has the good intentions. Didn't think it was like you. What's her problem? Still doesn't have the guts to come and see me."

"If you're going to be like that, I'm off."

"Cheerie, then."

He moves from foot to foot. "Josie was only thinking of you."

Just piss off. Her smile is caustic. "How kind of her." And she shuts the door on him. She takes a few deep yoga breaths and then goes into the kitchen to get a glass of water.

Bloody James. Bloody Josie – J-squared, the two of them. The woman has acrylic nails, for God's sake, and injects her lips with fillers.

It sets her thinking. Josie used to volunteer at the Société Guernsesais. If anyone knows anything about island witchcraft, it's the Société. A quick check online, and she taps in the number.

"Société Guernsesais, can I help you?"

"Hi, yes, good morning. I've got a question. Is there anyone doing research on witchcraft at the moment?"

"Are you a member?" the man asks at the other end of the line.

"I'm not, I'm afraid."

"Could I encourage you to join? We have some fascinating talks."

"Absolutely. Of course. I'm just in a bit of a hurry right now. And the question is rather important, the one about witchcraft."

"A lot of interest in that again, isn't there?"

"Unfortunately, yes, but I'm not into anything weird."

"That wasn't what I meant."

"No, no of course not." She tries again. "Is anyone doing historical or sociological research into it? I'd be interested in talking to them."

"Let me have a look." She hears computer keys tapping. "I'm just checking on our database." More tapping. "Nothing, I'm afraid. Except – I've got an idea. Hold the line. Yes, here we are. I don't know if this would be of interest, but Mr. Torode has been researching the herbs the witches used to use. He lives at Le Catioroc House, the one Barry Jones the actor owned. He might be able to help."

"That's great. Thank you. Do you have his number?"

"I'm sure he won't mind me sharing it. Bear in mind, he's rather old."

"I'm sure we'll get on famously." She jots the number down. "Thank you," she says again.

Chapter Twenty-Nine

Washed and dressed after his swim, he combs his hair flat and dabs shaving lotion on his cheeks. Downstairs, he goes into the garden and kisses his mother good morning.

"Old Spice," she declares, sniffing his neck.

It isn't, but he doesn't mind. Old Spice was his father's cologne.

She's sitting upright on a lounger with a floppy hat over her head and her face has that sunken look, as if all the air has been sucked out of it. Like a cadaver, he thinks, and he plays a game with himself, a version of Hide-and-Seek, searching her features for the ones of old, the green fleck in the iris and the slight bend of the nose, and the smile that bursts into laughter.

"How is she?" he asks.

"Being naughty," Janice says. "Now Lilly, what did I say? Leave it alone."

She is lifting her skirt up her legs until it she is close to exposing her nappy. Janice leans over to rearrange it, giving it a strong tug to straighten it out. Lilly slaps her wrist.

"Mother!" Mark says.

She turns and smiles at him.

"You mustn't treat Janice like that."

He perches on the edge of the lounger and takes her hands. They're fragile and bony and he lifts them to his lips, gesturing to Janice to pull the dress down.

"You're alright?" she asks.

"I'm alright."

But she's already looking away into the garden. She's forgotten about the skirt. And him.

He gets up and goes to the telephone to call the advocate, Vaudin, on the mainline.

"He's away," the secretary says, "but I'll leave your contact details on his desk."

Next, he calls Viv and leaves a message: "Got things to tell you about Pierre and Tom. Call me when you're free."

He doesn't like Pierre – that's a fact – but he doesn't much like baked beans either or cheap coffee. What bothers him is a system that pretends at justice and lets the criminals go free.

True, the lad's pretty fucked-up. He seeks power through make-believe and fear but what he needs is a shrink, not a gaoler. If the mutilation was part of the murder – and the murder was motivated by anger – then it's odd that only the hand was cut off. He would have expected more of the body to be mutilated, the face slashed perhaps and possibly the breasts too. So, yes, the hand speaks of witchcraft. That leaves two options: witchcraft or innocence. And since he doesn't believe in witchcraft, innocence is the likely answer. He's willing to bet his car and hoard of Ethiopian coffee on it.

Coffee. He looks at his watch. Any hour is coffee hour, and eleven twenty-three is selling its heart to be one. He

The Accused

makes his way to the kitchen, and is stalled by the telephone ringing.

"Hello."

"Mr. Roussel? It's Tracy Le Sauvage, eh, Ginny Bisson's sister."

"Mrs. Le Sauvage, I'm so sorry to hear the news. Please accept my sincere condolences."

"Thank you, thank you." A child is shouting in the background.

"How can I help?"

"I want to talk to you, eh. It's about Ginny. Can you come to my house? I've got my hands full, me, and I can't get out. I'm at the Genats estate eh, down by the Hougue du Pommier. You know it, eh? It's the second house on the right."

He says he knows where it is.

"Can you come this afternoon, eh, before teatime?"

Teatime – does she mean three-ish?

"No, no, *tea*time. Before seven, is it."

"Okay, I'll be there."

He really does need a coffee. Filtered water, freshly ground; the preparation is part of the experience. He goes into the kitchen and sets himself to the task. Later, he enjoys it in the vine-house looking out over the back garden.

There's a man on his list he needs to visit.

"Got drowned, eh?"

Old Dorey is standing behind the counter, filleting a fish. His apron is splattered with blood and his shirtsleeves are rolled up. Before him lay a selection of brill, bass, turbot, pollock, with the snout of a pink John Dory poking up through the ice. There are scallops and mussels and crabs too.

"Chancres look good," Mark says. "How many?"

"What you see is what I've got."

A storm has come in from the south-west with fifty knot winds. Waves as high as houses are flying over the seawall, and they drenched his car as he drove into the Castle Pier. They also drenched him as he parked next to an untidy huddle of pitching dinghies and clanging masts. Head down against the wind, his face whipped by the rain, he scurried across the road towards Old Dorey's shop, pushing against the metal door and hurling himself inside.

Now he waits as Dorey drops the fillet onto a piece of paper and folds it, handing it across the counter to a tiny old lady who is peering over the top. Wiping his hands on his apron, he takes her money and pings open the till. "*A la perchoine,*" he says.

"*A la perchoine,*" she squeaks, letting go of the counter and tottering towards the door, her basket over her arm. When she opens the door and a gust rushes in, she declares, "*Cor chapin. I plleut ogniet,* eh?"

"I'd wait if I were you," Mark advises.

"I'll be okay, cherie," she says. "*J'té verrai dmoïn,*" she peeps to Ol' Dorey before disappearing into the storm.

"Last of her kind, eh. Won't hear much of that once she's pushing up daisies. So, what can I do for you?"

He points to the crabs stacked in the corner. "Four of those wouldn't go amiss. And some of the brill too."

Dorey lifts the brill and lays it on a piece of waxed paper. He weighs it on the scales and then wraps it up, stuffing the package into a plastic bag and tying it closed with a knot.

"I hear you're the one that's into the Pierre Bourgaize

stuff, eh? Don't know what a man like you's doing wasting your time on that *caongre*."

"Trying to keep out of trouble."

"Cor damme là. That's the opposite of what's happening, is it.

"Actually," Mark says, "I thought I'd pick your brains."

"I'm not a chancre for picking, me."

He laughs. "You're about as wily as one though. Look, I just need to know what you think."

"He's a *sorcière*, him, and that's about it."

"Witches went out with the electric light. And don't raise your eyebrows. You know I'm right. Tell me something interesting."

He's known Old Dorey since childhood, holding his father's hand when they came to inspect the fish. He always teased him and pinched his nose, giving him a handful of mussels to take away.

"How about this then: keep out of his way. He's a *caongre*, eh, and I'll tell you why. The conger, he hides in the dark him, waiting to ambush. Then suddenly – snap! – it's taken your finger off."

"Maybe. He's passionate about some book the Nazis were after though."

Dorey cleans the counter with a bloodied rag. "You keep away from that too, eh. It brings bad luck, it does."

"How do you know?"

Dorey throws the bloodied rag into the sink and looks at him. His white eyebrows are as thick as bushes and the seams of his face are red. "My grandfather, he was one of the ones that tried to hide it from the Nazis."

He leans forward a little. "So, it did exist?"

"Cor heck, yeah. That's why you listen to me on this one."

He is listening. Eagerly in fact. "I've been told it was given to the Queripels by Victor Hugo's mistress when they left. Is that true?"

"You know what they said about her, eh?" Dorey puts the packet of fish on the counter top. "She was hot blooded and beautiful that one, and jealous too, eh. She got that Queripel woman to put a spell on him. Then she gave her the book, to get back at him. That's what they say, anyway."

"It couldn't have been much of a spell. He didn't die for fifteen years."

"Don't forget his daughter, eh. She ended up in a mad house, her."

"She'd been ill for years. Whatever, I want to know what happened to the book afterwards."

"Who knows, eh? The rumours started during the Occupation. They said old Queripel was trying to make money selling it. He was a nasty piece of work, him. Always snitching on his neighbours. When my grandfather heard about it, he told Stan De Carteret and they hatched this plan with an Englishman."

"That must have been quite early in the Occupation."

"That's the problem, eh. My grandfather, he was the brains behind it, but come the night he couldn't go, coz the Nazis were doing a raid in the house next door. It was Stan de Carteret, he was the one that stole it, and the Englishman, he said he'd hide it. Best that way, eh, in case anyone got caught. Problem is, the Germans sent the Englishman to Biberach, to the camp eh, when they deported all the English in 1942, and that was the end of him."

"He never told anyone where it was?"

"Nope. Not my grandfather and not Stan de Carteret either. It's lost for good."

Mark takes the packet of brill and holds it a moment.

The Accused

Then he puts it back down on of the counter. "Stan de Carteret. Which family did he come from?"

"The ones in the Forest, eh. The young one's a gardener. Tom de Carteret."

"Never!" Mark punches one hand into the other. "I knew it. God, I'm good." His smile cuts from ear to ear. "Tom and Pierre had history. Not just at College, but this as well. I smelt a rat from the start."

Dorey points an arthritic finger at him. "You don't call Tom de Carteret a rat, not in this place, eh. I've known you since a boy, Mark Roussel and I know that look of yours. Cock-sure, is it."

"Okay, okay." He holds up his arms in apology. "It's just there's a lot of windy lanes going through all of this." He stops a moment. "What else do you know?"

"Pierre was off his rocker, eh. Jurat Martel, he always said so. He knows a lot more about Pierre than I do. And about the book, eh."

"The book? Are you sure?"

"I'm sure."

"He's done a good job of pretending otherwise. He wrote a piece in the *Press* saying it was a legend."

Dorey gives a deep smoker's laugh. "I bet he did."

Mark decides to lie. "There're rumours he's got it, you know."

"Na. That can't be true." Dorey picks up a crab and puts it in a bag. "How many again, eh? Four, is it?"

He nods. "Why can't it be true?"

"Coz he doesn't know where it is. He asked me to help him find it, eh. He wants to give it to the museum, as a national treasure or something like that. I don't know, me." Dorey picks up three more crabs. "Thinks it will make him famous. He's a bit of one, he is."

Mark has a few choice words to add to the description. "Have you helped him?"

"Cor heck, no. Not wasting my time with all that. You'd have to dig up the whole island to find it, eh, and I've got better things to do." He hands Mark the bag. "Sixty-eight in total."

"Cor damme là," Mark jokes, mocking the accent. "The prices, they've gone up, them, eh."

Dorey waves his hand at him. "Be off with you, *pieuvre*." The smile is genuine.

He takes his card from his wallet and taps it on the machine. He doesn't tell Dorey that *pieuvre* – the Guernsey word for squid – has entered the French language thanks to Victor Hugo; it might go to his head. Dorey is as close to an island-nationalist as you can get. With a cheerful *a la perchoine,* he leaves the shop.

He knows where he's off to next.

Chapter Thirty

THE WALL IS LOW-LYING BUT THE RAILINGS GIVE IT THE height of a prison yard. On the other side is a lawn cut in half by a path leading to the house. It's fifteenth century, possibly earlier, and the entrance is arched like a Norman church. It's famed for its carved fireplace the size of a baronial hearth, but with walls two feet thick and windows like peep-holes, he's never much liked the place. It's Norman, yes, and steeped in history, but it has a heavy, unhappy feel to it.

He waits in the car, watching for the door to open and Martel to walk out. Instead, Tom de Carteret appears pushing a wheelbarrow, dutifully shirtless and looking rugged in khaki shorts. When he notices the bubble car, he lowers the wheelbarrow and walks over to investigate. Mark turns the ignition.

"Neat," he says, bending down to talk through the window. The man oozes a grassy, manly scent. "I wouldn't have put you down as quirky-car type of guy."

Mark forces a smile. "Have you heard from Viv by the way?"

"No, should I have?"

"Just wondering."

Tom points at the house. "Martel's out if that's who you're wanting."

"I'll leave him a note."

He switches off the engine and lifts the bonnet to step out onto the road. Giving Tom his back, he walks off in his bobby-stride, through the gate and around the side to the back of the house.

It's the book. It's been bothering him ever since he spoke to Dorey. If the rumours are correct and Isaac Newton wrote in the margins, then it's a treasure. Priceless in fact. Martel 's letter to the *Press* was a deflection. But why? Why would he risk his reputation? More importantly, did the book have anything to do with Jasmine Gardiner's death? He doubts it, of course. Life isn't a Dan Brown novel and murder is nearly always domestic. Still, it's a question worth asking, and here he is, free to wander through the house alone. If it's open, of course. In the old days, no one locked their doors, but that was then and this is now, and Martel isn't a man to trust his fellows.

The place is tastefully renovated with a glass corridor linking the house to the barn. He tries the stable door, and it opens into a flagstone corridor. At the end is a room that looks suspiciously like an office. He strides in and pulls the door closed behind him. The heavy Victorian furniture and the thick beams darken the place to the point of obscurity. He switches on the light and meets rows of leather books lining the panelled walls. The flagstones are covered in Persian rugs and the monstrous partner's desk is like something out of Dickens. The old granite fireplace sits to one side, and carved into one corbel is a smiling face and into the other, a sad one; hanging over it is an oil painting of a stormy sea.

Unsure where to begin, he tries the books to the right of the fireplace, flanked by the smiling corbel, and reads their spines, his head on one side. Nothing interesting along the middle shelves. He bends his knees to read the ones beneath: leather-bound copies of Pope and Coleridge, and Métivier's *Rimes Guernesiaises*; there are also essays by Montaigne and Francis Bacon. Again, nothing to excite his interest. Looking up, he lets his eyes stray along the upper shelves. Here the books are older, their spines badly cracked; many are French and range from sermons to the history of the Roman empire. He walks to the other side of the fireplace, to the left of a frowning granite face, and meets what he never thought he'd meet: *Le Petit* and *Le Grand Albert*, larger in size and seemingly older than those at the Priaulx. There are books on legends and myths, and a heavy tome of Guernsey history. He pulls it out and opens it at the page marked with a slip of paper; it's the account of Fanny Le Page's murder in the Pine Forest. Evidently, Martel did his homework.

He looks about the room. By the door is a bookcase of box files. He strides over to it and runs his finger along the printed labels. Dates, inventory letters; he pulls one out and opens it, but it is full of bank statements. He carries on. Names of investments, names of properties. He pulls out another, labelled 'SDL', and meets a collection of sepia-stained sheets. Closer inspection shows them to be facsimiles. He flips through them and then carries the box to the desk, taking the first few out and laying them on top to read better. They're in French (late nineteenth century from the typescript) and seemingly unrelated to each other. There is one sheet titled *Les secrets mystiques de la magic naturelle du Petit Albert*. Nothing unusual about that given Martel has a copy of the book. It has a diagram of something that looks like a woman's cap but which was called *Hipomane* (he recognizes it from the original he saw in the Priaulx), and in the bottom left-hand corner are two tiny initials with a flourish of circles about them. He takes his phone from his pocket and clicks a photograph, and then looks closely at it, enlarging it on the screen. Is that a 'VH' or an 'IN'? VH would indicate Victor Hugo; IN Isaac Newton.

He's getting fanciful. They could just as easily be Vincent Heaume and Ian Naftel, or Vincent Hamon and Irvin Nicolle. They have calligraphic aspirations, that's all, and rather ornamental ones at that.

Still, it points to Martel's interest in the black books, and either this is because he researched everything he could about Pierre Bourgaize before the trial, or – as Dorey said – he knows of the book and is looking for it.

There's one other sheet that catches his attention. It's poking out from beneath the others at the bottom of the box file. It's a list of initials and at the bottom is written *Le Société du Livre,* with a thick line scratching it out. He takes a photograph, and then slips it back underneath the others.

That's enough for one day. He shuts the door behind him and walks down the stone corridor, through the glass passageway and into the kitchen of the ancient house.

And stops.

Martel is leaning against the Aga. He's dressed in jeans and a linen shirt, opened at the neck to display a forest of grey hairs.

"Tom said I had a visitor."

"I popped round. I thought I'd wait in here."

"Except you weren't in here, were you?"

Mark flips his phone in his hand, thinking fast. "I came

The Accused

through the barn door and was admiring the Brenda Munson on the wall. I didn't know she'd painted the house."

Martel sniffs. "It's an early piece."

"A nice one. I took a shot. I hope you don't mind. By the way," he adds, holding his phone against his chin. "I didn't know you knew Jasmine Gardiner."

"I didn't."

"I've seen a photo of your car outside her house."

Martel's surprise is candid.

It's a tactic he's used often enough: shift attention and catch them unawares. It also keeps the conversation away from what he was doing in the house. "I'm wondering why you never mentioned it."

"I didn't know I was under investigation."

"You were the chief Jurat."

"And I take my integrity seriously." There's a moment's pause. "Are you accusing me of something?"

"I'm just trying to get a picture of things."

"Such as?"

"Who was in contact with Jasmine Gardiner before she died."

"A lot of people, I imagine."

"Someone in a vintage Jag?"

"Possibly. There are a lot of rich people over here."

"But not you?"

"Not me."

"It's just I'm damn sure you had one like it. Who did you sell it to?"

"Mark," Martel begins, and then stops. He puts his hands in his pockets and walks to the door that gives onto a yard. He opens it and invites Mark to leave. "Let's have this conversation another day."

Mark joins him on the threshold. "Thing is, some new facts have come up. And now we have Ginny Bisson dead."

"Ginny Bisson?"

"The girl found at L'Ancresse."

"Oh yes, the drug addict."

"She told Jasmine Gardiner about the book, the one that was stolen from the Queripel house. She lied about knowing where it was, but that's beside the point. She was the one who got Jasmine Gardiner interested. The question is whether the book was involved in the murder. Some people think there's a link."

"What people? That airhead Viv Le Prevost. She'd say the Queen was an alien if it got her enough readers."

Mark scrubs a piece of moss away with the tip of his shoe. "Why did you write that letter in the *Press* telling everyone the book was another Occupation rumour? A man in your position, and all that."

Martel fixes his eyes on Mark's face. A few moments pass – and then he cracks his knuckles and looks at his watch. "I have an important phone call in five minutes. You know your way out."

Chapter Thirty-One

Dear Ma,

PLEASE READ THIS LETTER.

It's important you hear me out. I don't expect anything else from you, only a listening ear. That's probably asking a lot given your silence over the last eleven years. If I didn't know better, I'd assume you were deaf. Perhaps you are deaf, or maybe you prefer to tear my letters up and throw them away.

DON'T TEAR THIS UP.

I've met a man called Mark Roussel. He used to work at the Met. He came to the prison to ask me questions about the case, and he's got me thinking.

God damn her!

He says it as loud as he can, just in case the Chaplain is creeping about the corridor.

GOD DAMN HER!

He's thrown away three sheets of paper trying to get the tone right. Not too angry, not too sweet; little boy's grown up but he still remembers darling Ma and her rice pudding. Yum, yum.

Now read my fucking letters, and fucking well answer them too, you bitch.

He's got an idea. A chance for her to make amends for the shitty little life she lived: yes husband, no husband, let me rub your feet husband so you can kick my creepy son up the arse.

Yes, creepy. She's called him that to his face.

And he had got kicked up the arse too, outside by the shed. It sent him flying onto the gravel, literally. He ended up with bits of flint stuck in his forehead. He used his compass to dig them out.

"Caught the pox?"

That was Tom de Carteret. He grabbed him by the collar and pushed him into a locker down in the basement and shut the door. Fucking downsizing, it was – the last time was an attic room, now it was a metal box for school bags and books. Literally stuffed him into it and left him there 'til break, his knees under his chin and his arms squashed into his ribs. His nose was up against the air vent. He tried to think he was a moth in a chrysalis, tightly wrapped up, waiting to get out.

It didn't work.

He screamed. Really screamed, and the Latin teacher forced the door open to get him out.

And what did Tom bloody De Carteret get for forced imprisonment? A rap on his knuckles. Some kind of justice that, Jurat Martel.

He deserved the spell he got. It just didn't work, but who cares – Tom and his mates were freaked out. Their fault for following him into the science lab after school. He

The Accused

was going to make the magic candle, the one that made whoever lit it appear headless.

God, that would have been hilarious if it had worked: Tom frozen with terror.

He took the snake skin from the bottle on the top shelf of the lab, and he found some wax at home. He improvised with chicken rather than donkey blood and though he had no idea what 'Greek pitch' was, he tried some tar. He put it all in a tube and boiled it over a Bunsen burner, filled with mucky water he got from the garden. Then he separated the mass from the liquid, and knowing Tom was watching him, said out loud "shroud from the Foulon cemetery, let me dip you into this mix." Which he did – and that's when Tom and his mates got him, arms pinned behind his back, and dragged him down the corridor.

If that's Tom de-effing-Carteret's take on magic, someone tell him why he made Jasmine Gardiner get in touch with him all those years later?

She called his home. "Hi Pierre, Tom's told me all about you" – the fuck he has – "he thinks we should meet up for a chat. I understand you know a lot about the black books. Why don't you come to my house?"

And he did.

Chapter Thirty-Two

The carpet is cold, and when he lifts his foot, he notices it's wet. The storm woke him in the early hours, throwing rain in through the open window. That was after his mother wandered in and dropped herself onto his bed. Deep in sleep, he leapt out and grabbed the first object he could find, which happened to be the sidelight, ripping it from the socket and thwacking the plug against his shin.

"Fuck!" he roared, dropping the lamp and grabbing his leg.

Then he realised who she was.

"For God's sake, Mum."

"You alright?" she said.

"I thought you were – heaven knows what I thought."

"You alright?"

"Mum!"

"You alright?"

"No – yes – it doesn't matter."

He limped round to where she was slumped on the duvet and put his arms about her, feeling her bones and thinking of a charnel house. That was when he smelt the urine. He leant over to switch on the wall light.

"Janice! Janice!" he called

"What is it?" Janice came running into the room, dressed in oversized pyjamas.

He held his mother out to her. She was wet through and the stench was in the back of his throat.

"I can't ... this isn't my thing."

Janice took her by the shoulders and led her out of the room. "It's okay, Lilly. Everything's alright, eh. We just need to get you to the bathroom. That's it, keep walking and mind the furniture."

Now it's morning. The clouds are breaking apart and letting through the sun. The birdbath is full and a thrush is splashing about in it, head down and wings out, tossing water everywhere.

Downstairs, the washing machine is tumbling sheets and his mother is sitting in the vine-house, *The Week* on her lap and her eyes shut in sleep. Janice is flipping through an old copy of *Country Life*.

"Coffee?" Mark asks.

"Love one," Janice replies.

"Did she get back to sleep in the end?"

"Almost immediately."

He wants to thank her for being a barrel-sized angel. Without her, he's like a boy scout in shorts, no more able to wash his mother as gut a fish. The wetness, the intimacy – worse, the smell; it repulses him. The very thought of it...he can't even go there.

"I'm really grateful..." he begins.

She waves him away. "You should read the letter in the *Press*. I've left it on the table. It's all about the black paste on that girl's body."

The letter is printed in the centre of the editor's page. He draws the newspaper close and leans over the table to read it, his hands either side. The writer is Anonymous with 'address withheld':

THERE ARE people on the island who know what the paste means. They're silent but they know. The police would do better to read the old witches' books than rely on toxicology reports.

THERE IT IS in black and white – the old superstition bubbling up again. He can't get away from it. He needs a toxicology report, not a witch's book. Except he doesn't know anyone in pathology and it's possible the paste is linked to something esoteric: Ginny was crazy enough to try it out. The only other option is to go online.

After making coffee, he joins his mother and Janice and opens his laptop to Google 'witches, black paste'. The search leads him to Halloween emojis, pumpkins, and some pagan site about moon-worship. He adds the word 'sabbath' and meets images of black pointed hats. Ridiculous, he thinks and scrolls down to the bottom, where he finds the Wikipedia site for 'flying ointment'. He clicks on the link and scans the article. Point seven reads 'possible opiate component'. Now he's interested. He follows the search-leads in the references, and clicks his way through the web, learning about the *solanaceae* family which include datura, nightshade, belladonna, henbane, wolfsbane and mandrake. Supposedly the witches mixed them with animal fat and blood to create a hallucinogenic drug.

He carries on and discovers an article from *The Spec-*

tator which references Frances Bacon. He knew all about the flying ointment: *'Witches believe they transform themselves into other bodies, not by incantations or ceremonies, but by ointments and anointing themselves'*. On Encyclopedia.com, Bacon is further quoted as writing, 'The *ointment, that witches use, is reported to be made of the fat of children, digged out of their graves; of the juices of smallage, wolfebane, and cinque foil, mingled with the meal of fine wheat: but I suppose that the soporiferous medicines are likest to do it, which are hen-bane, hemlock, mandrake, moonshade, tobacco, opium, saffron, poplar leaves, etc.'*

So, so, so... there he has it: deluded women tripping on drugs. Admittedly, none of the sites mention black paste rubbed onto the abdomen. The colour is never discussed (but given the binder was fat and blood, it's possible). As for application, it seems a broomstick was used to rub it between the thighs. Absorption was quicker on the genitals and more erotic too; it sent them soaring into the heavens.

Everything depends on the toxicology report.

The question is why anyone would bother to resurrect an ancient recipe when they're cooking meths in their baths and hauling cocaine up from crab pots.

He steps out of the vine-house and into the garden to call Viv. He wants to tell her about the black paste but ends up talking about Tom.

"You've got it in for him, haven't you?" she says.

"I think he knows more than he's saying."

"Don't go down that road. Jasmine Gardiner helped him set up his business."

"More reason for him being around there a lot."

"He owed her everything. She gave him his clients. He was hardly going to kill her, was he?"

"Lovers kill each other all the time."

"For goodness' sake, Mark."

"What? He likes older women. It was pretty evident the other night. He was all over you."

"I've known Tom for years!"

"That's not the point. He's good-looking and he's probably..."

"What? A good lay?"

"I didn't say that."

"You meant it."

"I was just saying he's fit and young, and guys like that often go for older women because they're..."

"Okay. Stop there. Just stop."

"I was trying to say..."

"Don't."

"If you'd just listen to me."

"Drop it, Mark. Okay? Enough. Don't try to explain. Don't try to say anything. Tom's off limits."

Not as far as he's concerned, he isn't. First, there's an alliance between Tom and Martel; then the feud with Pierre, and now an unhappy connection with Ginny Bisson too. Ginny didn't go into the Cock and Bull because of Tom de Carteret.

"To change the subject," Viv is saying, "I'm off to see the old man who lives at the Catioroc House."

"Say that again?"

"The Société put me in contact with a man that lives at the Catioroc. He's researching the plants the witches used to use in their brews."

"What made you do that?"

"It was an idea I had."

"A bloody brilliant one. I was just on Google reading up

about flying ointment. That's why I called you, to tell you. When are you off?"

"Shortly. Do you want to come?"

"I can't. I've got a date with Mrs. Le Sauvage. Can you delay him?"

"Doubt it. Can you delay Mrs. Le Sauvage?"

"Probably not."

"He's quite old by the way. You know, just in case you're worried."

"About what?"

"Okay, forget it."

He's confused. "Call me after you're done with him."

She guffaws. "You've got a really bad turn of phrase."

He doesn't know what he's said. "Stay in touch." He hangs up before he makes another blunder.

Chapter Thirty-Three

He steps over a decapitated doll and kicks a pink walkie-talkie across the floor. When he stoops to pick it up, he stands on a soft toy with a loud burp.

"A bit tight in here, eh?"

Mrs. Le Sauvage squeezes past him, and with her Marigolds still on her hands, throws the toys out of his way. She is nearing twelve stone and the space is tight. He steps sideward to get out of her way.

"It's a miracle I don't have the kitchen sink and all the pans out here too, eh, with the way that Pebble's been behaving, her."

"Pebbles?" He isn't sure he's heard correctly.

"Like the ones near Fort Doyle, eh. Fontenelle Bay, it's full of them, is it."

"Right." He's none the wiser. "Is she upstairs?"

"No, she's round at a friend's, eh."

She rips the gloves off her hands and apologises again before throwing them onto the pile of toys.

"Please." She stands aside to let him through into the sitting room.

The Accused

The place smells of cigarettes and boiled milk. It reminds him of his grandmother's house in the old days before she died. It's comforting, like buttered gâche and hot chocolate.

He sits down on the settee. "Lord!" He springs up. A toy phone pokes out from under the cushion. He pulls it out and lays it on the floor.

"Sorry. Pebbles, she's in for a walloping, her."

Cautiously, he sits down again.

"Do you want coffee?"

"No, thank you."

"Cream crackers?"

"I'm fine."

Mrs. Le Sauvage takes the chair opposite and he waits for her to speak, but her hands are doing all the communicating, clenching and unclenching themselves. So, he looks about the room, at the over-sized television and the shelf of DVDs. On the mantelpiece is a porcelain shepherdess with a broken staff and above it a faded print of a country scene; on the hearth is a toy cannon with black wheels.

"I wanted to talk to you, I did." Mrs. Le Sauvage is speaking to her lap. "I want you to get the man who killed my Ginny. I don't trust the police, them. Ginny wasn't the type the police care about." She takes a tissue from her sleeve and pats her nose.

"The police don't have favourites, Mrs. Le Sauvage."

Her snort is part snigger, part sob. "Look at that big house down by Cobo, eh? If you've got money, you can do anything on this island. The rich, they get special treatment, them. I know all about it. The English, they come here and get away with blue murder, them."

That's the States not the police, he's about to say and

then stops. There's no point in arguing. "Why are you sure Ginny was murdered? There was no sign of a struggle."

"You're joking, eh?"

"The body wasn't damaged."

"He hurt her all the time, him, Pebble's dad."

"Pebbles is Ginny's daughter?"

"Cor heck, didn't you get that?"

He tries to smile. "Just getting things straight in my mind."

"You see him in town, eh, with that bad leg of his always getting into trouble. That's where I'd put my money, me, but the police, they don't listen, them."

Mrs. Le Sauvage blows her nose and stuffs the wet tissue up her sleeve.

"When I last spoke to Ginny, she said she had something to tell me. Something about a black bag. It seemed important. You wouldn't know what that was about, would you?"

"A black bag, eh? What black bag?"

"I was hoping you could tell me."

The fat around her neck wobbles as she shakes her head. "What about that black stuff found on her, eh? What was that? On her stomach, they said. A *bouzat*, is it?"

"Not a cowpat. Some sort of paste. They're sending it for testing. It could be a drug."

"Caw heck," she says.

"We won't know for a while."

"She was trying hard, you know. She told that boyfriend, that waster, that she was going clean, her."

"I know."

"There're some bad words I could use about him. In and out of prison, is it. And there's the Chief Minister, him, he takes my taxes to pay for those wasters so they can have fun,

The Accused

eh. Well I tell you what, Mr. Roussel, I'd go to prison, me, if it meant I got free food and TV all day long."

"It isn't all beer and skittles."

The 'huh' he gets in response settles the issue. He returns to the drugs.

"What can you tell me about her boyfriend? He's Pebble's dad, I'm assuming."

"Là, là, he is alright. He got that leg from making meths, he did. With a friend, is it. They blew the windows out of the house, them. The house, eh, just on the other side of the estate. You'll see it when you drive out. Set the house alight, eh. Didn't use the fire extinguishers, that's what Ginny said. Ended up in prison, him, but it made no difference. He said he'd changed, eh, but he hadn't. He's just as bad as before."

"Was she seeing him recently?"

"He kept coming round, him, telling her he loved her, is it. I told her, I said, you don't listen to him, eh. He just wants your body. And she said, he wants to see his daughter and I can't stop him doing that, can I?"

"Do you think he was into the occult?"

"What's that, eh?"

"Witchcraft."

"Cor damme là, one of those, eh? I don't know. He's into everything, him."

"And Ginny?"

"Now you don't go dirtying her name, Mr. Roussel. She had her problems, her, but she was no witch. She was interested, eh, like lots of us locals, but she told me, she said, I know Gran was a witch but she wasn't happy, her, and I want to be happy, me."

"Did she tell Jasmine Gardiner about a special book?"

"Look, I told her, I said, you don't go bothering Mrs. Gardiner, but she wasn't listening to me then and she told her all that silly nonsense about the fairy ring, eh, which isn't even a fairy ring coz the fairies, they came out of L'Eree not Pleinmont, them."

"Do you think she knew something about the murder? Maybe something important she hadn't told the police? She wanted to talk to me, you see. I bumped into her the night before she died, and I know she had information."

"You tell me what, eh. She didn't know Mrs. Gardiner, and she didn't know that Pierre Bourgaize either, him."

"I was wondering about the black bin bag, the one that Pierre was seen carrying."

"I don't know nothing, me. Those bin bags, they're everywhere. The Co-op sells them in packs."

The roar of a motorcycle tears into the conversation. Mark looks over his shoulder and sees a man sitting on a bike, revving the engine, waiting – he assumes – for someone to come out of the house opposite.

Mrs. Le Sauvage motions at the window with her head. "He's not a bad lad, him. I know this estate has a bad reputation, eh, but there're some good people here too. He just likes that bike, him. Drives me potty, mind. Like my Ginny."

A smile lifts her face, and then it falls, and a wretched sob accompanies it. He waits, expecting her to cry, but she clenches her hands to her chest and shuts her eyes. When she opens them again, she looks directly at him.

"The woman next door, Mrs. Falla, she wants me to go to church, her, but I won't go coz I don't like feeling bad, me, and that's what they do in church, eh, always telling you what you do wrong. I like my brandy and my ciggies, and I get a bit tipsy of a night, eh, but life, it's difficult and I don't need a vicar telling me off."

The Accused

He doesn't have much to say about vicars, and he knows from experience to leave someone alone with their grief.

"Thank you, Mrs. Le Sauvage. You've been a great help."

"Voul-ous enne coupaïe d'coffee?"

"Nen-nin merci," he says. He draws the line at instant Nescafé. "Thank you again."

She heaves herself up from the chair. "You find who killed my Ginny, won't you, Mr. Roussel."

"I'll do my best."

Outside, he pushes through a crowd to get to his car. A kid yelps with excitement when he lifts the canopy.

"Caw heck, Mum. Did you see that? It's a kiddy's car, is it."

He drives off as fast as he can, weaving his way along the roads that turn and twist through the estate until he reaches the Route de Carteret. Turning right, he heads down towards the coast. There the orange-pink rocks glow in the afternoon sun, like embers in the sea. Turquoise water washes over white sand, and he parks by the German bunker to go for a swim.

Chapter Thirty-Four

SHE'S FAST COMING TO THE CONCLUSION THAT MARK needs a therapist. Not that he'd agree, of course. Men like Mark have a Perspex wall around their hearts. Tell them they're troubled, and they say they have a good view of their inner states, thank you very much - which they probably do. What they don't have is access to them.

His dislike of Tom is almost Freudian. Transference and reversal – she's trying to remember her study of the Wolf Man. He wants to be Tom (virulent and popular), but isn't, and feels he is more like Pierre (outside and rejected), so the hatred he has for himself, he directs onto Tom to avoid being the failure he fears himself to be.

Or not.

She isn't a Freudian. To be a Freudian she'd have to bring in his parents and the Oedipus complex and, to be honest, she's no interest whatsoever in going there. Sex and Mark – she's parking her thoughts.

What she does suspect, however, is Mark's jealousy. It just depends what he's jealous of – her affection for Tom or Tom's affection for her? The latter is problematic; the former rather charming. She hopes it's the former. It always helps to have her fancies echoed back at her; it avoids a solipsistic sad-show.

Like this chat with herself.

She's driving down L'Eree and has just met Rue des Bordes. The road is narrow, and the lane on the right is narrower yet. She parks the car tight into the hedge, and gets out. From here, the walk up to the old man's house is short.

Mr. Torode meets her in the doorway, his hair like gossamer combed over a speckled head.

"Miss. Le Prevost," he says. She takes his outstretched hand and the bones seem to crumble in her grip. "I see you carry the name well."

"Thank you, but you're going to have to explain that to me." She follows him into the narrow passageway of the house.

"Prevost is like provost. Dean and chancellors – your ancestors were officials in Old France. And you, I understand, are taking charge of us all with your column."

"Oh that!" She laughs. "It's just a way to keep me busy."

He laughs too, in a dry, crackly way, and shuffles into a room with a large bay window. From there, she views the flat marshland where the geese feed and beyond it, Fort Saumarez and Lihou Island. Streams of sunlight break through the clouds and shine on the sea, and she wishes she were a painter to capture the beauty of it all.

Instead she says, "Great view".

"Your father loved it," he is standing beside her. "He tried to buy the house off me many a time."

"You knew him?"

"Le Prevost Flowers were quite famous in their day."

She nods. "He never accepted the end of the growing

industry. When it was all over, he still had freesias in the back garden."

"And the Guernsey Lilly too. He wrote a paper for the Société on it. That's how we met."

"I've never read it – to my shame. I don't really share his in interest in flowers."

"But people, yes?"

"Absolutely. A flower is a flower but people are harder to classify. You find a trend, and then someone comes along and breaks it."

"Please." Mr. Torode invites her to take an armchair. "We can look out and talk in greater comfort." He's getting old, he confesses; having turned ninety the month before last.

"You'll have to share the secret," she says.

"If I knew the answer, I could make a fortune. Truth is, I think I'm just lucky. So, tell me Miss. Le Prevost..." he cracks his knuckles.

"Viv, please."

"Very well, tell me, Viv, what I can do for you?"

"I understand you've been looking into the plants the witches used to boil their brews."

"Ah, you have come about the paste found on that young woman's body."

She hadn't. "There's a connection?"

"A writer in the *Press* believes that there is."

"And you agree?"

"It's possible."

"So? What do you think?"

"Without analysis, I can't say with any confidence but you have to ask yourself, why would a former drug addict smear something rather disgusting over herself? Now, I am fully aware that there are neater and cleaner ways to take drugs, but I'm also aware that if you want to make drugs and not get caught by the police, you are going to have to be inventive. Boiling up meths in the bathtub is rather passé, wouldn't you say?"

"Honestly? I have no idea."

"Of course, it could just be a harmless poultice to cure colic."

"The witches made those too?"

"Most certainly. Most of them were women who knew their plants – a bit like your father. And the monks too. Think of *Romeo and Juliet*. The problem is, patriarchy has always feared women..."

"Tell me about it."

"There was this man on the island called Martin Tulouff. He told the authorities he saw his mother straddle a broomstick and disappear up the chimney. He must have hated her very much to say that."

"They killed her?"

"Absolutely. It was 1563.'"

"Bad times."

"They were, which is why, my dear, this paste everyone is talking about might just be a mix of things like turmeric, ginger, eucalyptus, garlic, onion – charcoal would give it its black colour. And an oil as a binder. It doesn't have to be an opioid or hallucinogenic. Without a toxicology report, I'm only presuming. But you see where I am going with this?"

She does. When it comes to old ladies with warts and hooked noses, she draws the line. It lights the feminist in her. That said, she's willing to keep an open mind about most things, and she's sure many a woman fought her suppression by threatening potions; she'd probably do the same.

The doorbell rings and footsteps are heard in the hall.

"Torode?"

A young man limps into the room and within moments Mr. Torode is on his feet, grasping the back of the armchair, his liver-spotted skin flushed red with anger. Embarrassment too, Viv thinks. Pure anger would say, 'Get out of my house!' Embarrassment says, 'What are you doing here?'

"What are you doing here? I told you not to come back."

She struggles to get a sense of the man. There are so many tattoos on his arms, neck and face, it's impossible to see him. When he speaks, it's like hearing a ghost.

"Yeah well that's it, isn't it, old man. You told me and I didn't listen, right. So, look, I've got this stuff and I want you to look at it." He holds up a jam jar filled with a pesto-like concoction.

"I have no intention of doing anything of the sort." Torode is standing as tall as he can, but he's bird-like and withered. He tries to shoo the man away but the man just stands there, enormous, like a hillock, shaking the jar in front of him.

"Go! Go!" Torode orders.

The man says nothing. His gaze falls on Viv, and then on Torode. A smile creases his face. "I get it." He winks. "You want me to go. Alright, I'll go, but I'm coming back, old man, so get that lab of yours ready, eh, coz we've got work to do."

Lab? Viv frowns a silent question. Torode ignores it. After the man has left, he sits down, his hands trembling on his lap.

"I would be grateful if you could go now, Miss. Le Prevost. I think our conversation has ended."

Outside, she walks down the shaded path towards her car. Just as she nears it, clicking the key to unlock the doors, the tattooed man steps out from amongst the trees.

"Hey."

She stops.

"D'ya want to try it?" He has the jar in his outstretched hand. "Give it to you for twenty."

"Don't you want Mr. Torode to have it?"

"I got more at home. It's good stuff. Try a bit, on your wrist. Here, I'll show you."

"What's it for?"

"Everything."

"Snake oil?"

"What's that?"

"Just a term. What's it meant to cure?"

"You don't half ask questions, do you? Come on, try it. You look like you could do with a bit of livening up? Can't be much fun with old Torode."

"Thanks for that."

Viv takes the jar and opens it. The stuff smells earthy, with a hint of warm hay. "Not bad." She sticks her finger into it. The consistency is like pesto but thicker, fattier. "This isn't the stuff they found on Ginny Bisson's body, is it?"

"Don't know what you're going on about." His response is too quick, too forceful.

"I bet," she says. She screws the lid back on. "I'll give you a fiver for it. That's all I've got. Take it or leave it."

The man hesitates.

"I could just drive off with it," she points out.

"Okay, fuck it. Give me a fiver."

As she reves off in the car, she feels as thrilled as a little girl with a new toy. Wait 'til Mark finds out what she's done. She's damn sure it's the same stuff that was on Ginny Bisson.

On reaching the coast road, she turns left rather than

right, and drives into the small car-park on the corner opposite Le Trépied Dolmen. The best place to try out the stuff, all things considered. Not that the headland is particularly mystical in the summer. Still, it's the place of the witches, and whatever the stuff in the jar is used for – be it an aphrodisiac (much in need) or some harmless concoction for curing piles – she's going to give it a go.

First on her wrists. A thin greasy smear. She waits. Nothing. She focuses her eyes on the horizon. It's still; the clouds are clearing. Turning her head to the right, she looks out across Perelle Bay with its black rocks towards Fort Richmond. Nothing at all.

Feeling warm in the car, she opens the door and gets out for a walk.

Chapter Thirty-Five

"Mark, this is Tony Le Cheminant, the chaplain at the prison. Call me if you can. I have news on Pierre."

He's standing outside the Cobo Village Centre with the phone in one hand and a box of tea in the other – Yorkshire tea, as it happens, being the only type they sell apart from PG Tips. A cyclist pedals past him, and then a van, which stops at the filter. He crosses over the road and walks through the lay-by to the sand-splattered path beyond where his car is parked in front of an upturned boat.

"Tony," he says. "I've just heard your message. How can I help."

"It's not good news, I'm afraid. He's in hospital. He tried to hang himself. It happened after breakfast this morning."

His first thought is 'No surprise there'; his second is 'That's the end of it then'.

"He'd tried it once on the mainland – a knife from the canteen – so they had him on suicide watch but we didn't think it was an issue over here."

"I warned you the other day. I said I thought he had a death wish."

"A death wish isn't the same as being suicidal."

"You've got me there."

"He didn't show any signs of self-harm. It was totally unexpected. He finished breakfast, got his sheet and tied it to the railings outside his cell, the ones that surround the floor; then he jumped. A chap called Le Cras saw him and rushed to lift him up. Another pressed the panic button. The guard got there as fast as he could and cut him down, just in time."

"And the parents – how have they taken it?"

"I've only spoken to the father. He just said 'okay' and hung up.

"And the mother?"

"I can never get hold of her."

"That means they haven't visited him yet?"

"Exactly."

"Do you know why he did it?"

"On that particular day? At that precise moment? No. He didn't leave a note, and they usually do. But there's nothing usual about Pierre."

"You really should have had him on suicide watch. His mother hadn't been to see him. That could be excused when he was in the UK, but how do you square it when she lives down the road?"

"Literally, too. They have a bungalow on the Route Militaire."

"There then. Everyone hated him."

"Not quite. He had a listener, Mick Tostevin. After he got beaten up on the way to lunch, Mick stepped in – that was about a week ago. We moved him to the VP wing, for vulnerable people. Le Cras was okay with him too."

The Accused

How convenient, he thinks, to have Pierre Bourgaize dead. It draws a line under things, stops the rumours. They call it justice, but it smacks of retaliation, an eye for an eye and all that.

"Do you know if he was interested in appealing the case?"

"He never mentioned it, and considering what he's just done, I'd say 'No'. You don't try to kill yourself if you hope to be released."

"True."

"Some people feel safe in prison. They know the rules."

How safe is killing yourself? he thinks. "Is he in a coma?"

"An Alpha coma, so they say. There's a high chance he won't recover though sometimes they do."

A group of youngsters sit on the seawall, their legs dangling over the side. They pick at chips in paper bags and laugh.

"Thanks for letting me know," he says.

"I thought you should hear it from me."

"Yes. Thanks. I need to go." He hangs up.

Coma or not, he's going to see him. He gets into the car and drives to the Vauxbelets, the box of tea on the seat behind him. At the Bailiff's Cross, he catches the red light and taps his hands on the steering wheel. A car crosses in front of him and then another until suddenly a stream shunts by, bumper to bumper.

The lights turn green. He screeches the gears into third and speeds downhill, turning right and driving up the road to the hospital. At the main entrance, he walks through the glass doors and straight into a restored clinker that sits keeled to one side. A large display lauds the prisoners who worked on it. After reading it, he spends a moment inspecting its painted planks and the rivets that hold them together. An idea comes to him: he could donate his skiff to the DT department at Elizabeth College. A generous gift from a grateful pupil. Shut Martel up and relieve him of being technologically incompetent. Once completed, the Combined Cadet Force can teach the lads how to sail in it because – from memory – the CCF does a lot of marching up and down outside College's steps and nothing much else. Except paper aeroplanes. He remembers making them in the gym after school. 'It's all about aerodynamics, boys!'

Filing the idea away, he walks through the foyer and takes the lift to the second floor where the ICU ward is located.

There he finds Pete Robilliard and a constable in conversation. On seeing Mark approach, Pete walks over and steers him towards the wall.

"You can't go in," he says.

"I didn't expect to. He's in a coma, isn't he?"

"Yes."

"I'm not going to get much out of him then. On the other hand, you just happen to be here and we just happen to be chatting."

Pete looks over at the constable and leads Mark further away to a large window that gives onto the car-park. Mark rests his arms on the metal railing that separates them from the glass.

"Will Pierre come around?"

Pete shrugs. "The guard's only for a few days, so that says everything, doesn't it? If he comes out of here, it won't be in his right mind. But..." he taps his nose, "I've been talking to some of the lads, just asking out of interest, what they remembered, that sort of thing."

"About the attempted suicide?"

The Accused

"No, the murder, back then. You know, the one they got him for."

"And?"

"Looks like Pierre might of had an alibi coz there was a sighting of him. Problem is, the witness wasn't reliable and no one took any notice of it."

"What was the alibi?"

"Old Falla saw him cycling down by Bordeaux around half twelve."

"You can't kill up at Jerbourg and get down to Bordeaux for twelve thirty."

"I guess you could if you pedal fast and there isn't much traffic."

"No way. She died at eleven forty-three. It's impossible."

"Yeah, but that's the thing, Old Falla was a drunk. Supposedly Pierre knocked him over. He said he went to the chemist coz he had bashed his elbow and he had cuts on his face."

"Which was substantiated by the pharmacist?"

"No, that's the other problem. No one remembered him going in and Pierre couldn't produce the bicycle. And Old Falla was his great uncle, so he could of been trying to cover up for him."

"You believe that?"

"That's what they were saying."

He pinches his bottom lip. "I don't know. Pierre said his bike had been stolen, so he shouldn't have been on one."

"Exactly, but don't forget, he never reported the theft, so he could have lied about that too. Or he could have used someone else's."

"Except he denied being on the bike, and he doesn't hit me as fit enough to do the murder, hide the body and get to

Bordeaux in time to knock over his great uncle. So, one of those scenarios is wrong. Can I talk to Old Falla?"

"He died last year. Liver cancer."

"We're back to square one."

"Looks like it."

He turns around and rests his back against the railing. Opposite is a photograph the size of the wall, depicting Fort Grey at dusk with the last streak of sunset on the horizon. It's a dramatic mix of colours.

"If we can put someone else in the Jerbourg area at the time Pierre was knocking over old men," he says slowly, "we might have a new lead."

"You can do that?"

"Tom de Carteret. He was the main witness against Pierre."

Pete snorts disbelief. "He's a decent guy. He had an alibi. I don't buy it. He was with Jurat Martel, working his garden."

"I know. It's convenient though, isn't it?"

"He hadn't left Jurat Martel's place when she was killed. I know coz I was there when they interviewed the DHL guy who delivered a parcel to the house. Tom signed for it."

Chapter Thirty-Six

"You have one new message. Press 1 to listen to your new message."

He presses 1.

"*Warro*, Mark, it's me, Viv. Viv-viv-vimmm. I'm having a walk or I think I am. Anyway, I'll call you later when I get home. I've got so much to tell you, about absolutely everything. You're going to go bonkers. Really bang-wang nuts. You just ain't gonna believe it. Sorry, can't do American accents. Oh, can't forget this: I met a guy who's seriously off the wall. Intrigued? Ha! See? I know how to catch a detective. Cheerie-o. It's Viv by the way, just in case. Viv here, signing off. *A la perchoine*. It's Viv by the way. Cheerie."

That's some chat with an old man. Quite the cocktail maker by the sounds of it. Bang-wang nuts (who in their right mind says something like that?). Viv-viv-vimmm is pretty embarrassing too.

He's sorry he missed the party. Sorry too that he wasn't there to take her home. Pissed and going for a walk? That isn't much of a problem on the West Coast where the land is flat. Pissed and going for a swim? That's dangerous. As for pissed and driving? He remembers the young couple who drove their car off the Catioroc headland, possibly worse for wear, certainly driving at eighty miles per hour; they miscalculated the corner and ended up on the rocks. Their death horrified the island.

And Viv sounds like someone about to fly off.

He wanders into the kitchen and picks up the post Janice has left in a pile. Two bills forwarded from his flat in London, and a request from *The Week* to renew his subscription. There is also a letter from the States of Guernsey. He tears it open and draws out the headed paper from the Population Management Office at Frossard House. Odd. Concerning too. He reads on. A question has been raised about his right of residency. Having spent three years off island, from the age of ten to thirteen, he hasn't completed the required period to qualify as local. He is to present himself as soon as possible to discuss the situation.

What situation? He's a Roussel, for God's sake. The name goes back to the Norman Conquest, to the family who were lords of Rosel, near Cherbourg. If they aren't happy with that, what about his other connections? Geffroi Martel was a knight with William the Conqueror, and to push the point further, Charles Martel was grandfather to Charlemagne. Okay, so he isn't saying he is descended from royalty, but he has a bloody right to live on the island, and a lot more than most of the people they let on with their gold coffers.

But then everyone knows Guernsey doesn't 'do' heritage. It does money. It also does cars and buildings. And now they're after him. A few phone calls might resolve matters. Martel perhaps, then the Procureur, maybe even the Bailiff. Or not. He doesn't know either, and he's damned if he is going to go cap in hand to Martel. He'll finish getting

The Accused

to the bottom of the Pine Forest murder, and then he'll leave. Has to anyway, by the sounds of it. Perhaps that's what they want – to get rid of him.

With his phone to his ear, he calls Vaudin the advocate, Viv's old boss. The man should be back from his holidays by now.

"Mr. Vaudin, I've caught you at last. This is Mark Roussel. I've been leaving you messages."

The voice at the other end is smiling, he can tell in the tone. "Mr. Roussel – Mark, if I may – I've been rather flattered by your insistence. What can I do for you?"

"Two things as it now stands. First, I would value a chat about residency rights. Second, I'm looking into Pierre Bourgaize's conviction."

"I've had a message from Viv about that. She's always had a bit of a saviour complex. I'm free in two days' time, if that's any good? For coffee? How about ten forty-five at Le Petit Café in the Pollet? Does that work for you?"

"I'll be there."

"As for residency, I'm sure it's a misunderstanding, unless," and here he laughs again, "you've been upsetting people. *À la perchoine.*"

SHE RUBS the paste further into her wrists, but still it looks like she's fallen in a cowpat. The answer's to get to the water and wash it off – except the scramble from the Catioroc Point down onto the rock doesn't appeal, so she walks over the grassy verge and onto the road down to Fort Saumarez. There she turns onto the lower stretches, and sees the tide falling fast. Lihou sits in the sea, less sunken then before, and she decides to clamber over the rocks and around the corner towards it, to see if the causeway is open.

She isn't a water-girl. The sea's dangerous, fickle. Yet strangely, for the first time ever, it seems to beckon her. Come, come. It's still – magnificently still – save for the tip of the retreating tide fizzing about the rocks. She can take a dip, wipe the stuff off her wrists, and go for a float. The weather's warm enough.

And there's Venus' pool on the other side of Lihou. An amble along the causeway, up on the grassy verges, past the monastery's ruins, over the top and then down the rock face. All very adventurous. And exciting too. Venus seems apt for how she's feeling now – light, remarkably light, an emptying out as if she's got air in her veins, not blood. A lifting up, a floating away...

She ought to call Mark.

Chapter Thirty-Seven

"What's happened to life?"

He takes his mother's hands and leans forward to kiss her on the forehead. It is the most lucid thing she has said since he arrived back, and he doesn't know how to answer it. Her eyes are looking, yet not looking, at him. He's noticed this: how he struggles to find the point of her focus. The hallucinations have begun too; the children in the corner of the room or outside in the garden, and her agitations because he isn't caring for them. "Nasty, nasty," she yelled at him yesterday; supposedly a boy was crying by the door and he had pushed past him.

He opens out her hands and strokes them. They're the only part of her that hasn't changed. When she talks, they move in the same way as they did when he was a boy. The same long fingers, the same painted nails (courtesy of Janice); liver spots and raised veins too, and he loves them for it.

His laptop is by his feet and he bends down to pick it up. His mother's chin is on her chest and she's drifting. Laying her hands on her lap, he puts the computer on his own, and opens it, drawing up the photographs he took of the pages in Martel's office. The one he's interested in has the list of initials and the words *Le Société du Livre* scratched out which could either mean The Book Society or The Society of the Book, and they aren't the same thing. There are Bank Societies and Food Societies; Wine Societies and Fine Art Societies, but there's no Society of the Bank, as far as he's aware. He doesn't need a grammatician to tell him there's a difference between a collective noun and a proper noun.

As for the list of initial, who do they stand for?

F could be Falla, Fallaize, Ferbrache or Foote. C could be Carey, Carre, Collas, Cohu, Collings. He followed his eyes down: D for De la Rue, Dobrée, Duquemin, Dorey.

Go on like this, and he may as well name the whole island. If the piece of paper didn't look so distinctly Victorian, he'd say SDS means Safety Data Sheet and FLF, Front-line Force.

He's barking up the wrong tree. Everyone's getting to him with their lost books and Double Lifts, their bin bags and yew seeds. He closes the laptop and gets up.

What he needs are links. How each piece of information relates to the other. Then he needs to see where they lead.

In the kitchen, he takes a box of greaseproof paper from the drawer and draws it out until it covers half of the table. He tears it free and pins it down with a mug in each corner. A pencil doesn't work, nor a biro, but he finds a permanent marker in a drawer and writes JG in the centre and frames it in a bubble. Around the bubble, he writes a list of adjectives: mother, attractive, wealthy, not working, blog, revengeful, unhappy, drinking, possibly suicidal. Completed, he draws a cloud about each one and off these

The Accused

he draws the arrows, leading to the names of people associated with her, each with their own set of adjectives, each in their own clouds. Then he stands back and looks – and looks. He draws a line here, a line there, connecting people to each other. Nothing. He keeps looking. Motives are cancelled by alibis. He adds 'Venus and Jupiter' to the yew seeds – and keeps looking. Still nothing. He includes the book – the one Pierre is obsessed about – as a character and looks again. More links, more associations, but the web of connectivity goes around and around and nowhere in particular.

What he seeks is that line which breaks free and announces itself: follow me and I'll show you where the murderer hides. But the line doesn't materialise. It exists – it has to – but he can't see it.

In the right-hand corner he writes 'vomit' and looks to see who may have been drunk enough, high enough or sick enough to puke on the ground under her body – and he realises it's just about everyone. In the left-hand corner, he writes 'drugs' and looks again. In the bottom, right he scribbles 'witchcraft' and looks again. In the bottom middle, bin bag. Nothing comes to him.

Wherever he looks, Pierre's shadow lurks, straining to be the answer: it's him, it's him! Yet Pierre's a waif – he's sure of it – but there's no way he can prove it.

There's one person he hasn't talked to and that is Mrs. Bourgaize herself. According to the Chaplain, she lives along the Route Militaire. Finding her in the *Yellow Pages* will be easy.

"Janice!" he calls as he takes the car keys from the dish in the hall. "I'm off. Mum's in the vine-house asleep."

"Cheerie," she calls back from somewhere deep in the utility room.

"Do you want anything? I'm going via the Bridge."

"Pint of milk, if you're passing. Blue, not red. You got red last time."

"Okey doke."

The Bourgaizes live in a pebble-dashed bungalow along the Route Militaire. It's post-war in design with the four sides of its roof meeting atop its four-square walls. It's unremarkable in every regard, including its name, *Belle Fleur*. Bright red begonias border the tarmacked drive, and set between these and the boundary fence is a silver Ford Fiesta with a dent over the back wheel. Beyond that is a garden wall, a gate and a shed of over-lapping slats. Squeezing between the car and the fence, he walks to the wall and peers over it, at the shed. Its door is shut but there's no padlock to secure it. Easy to access, he thinks; easy to break into. The only window that gives onto the shed has frosted glass, and the neighbour's bungalow is hidden behind an overgrown leylandii tree.

Here is one theory supported by evidence: So-and-So crept up the drive in the early hours of the morning, went through the gate and opened the shed, planting Jasmine Gardiner's severed hand in a flowerpot. It was a decoy: look here so you don't look there.

Bingo.

Now to talk to the parents.

The front door is plastic-framed and set back inside an arched porch. He rings the bell and hears it peal on the other side of the wall. He waits. He steps back out of the porch and looks left and right at the windows either side. Patterned net curtains shield the rooms from prying eyes. Back into the porch, he rings the bell again. More waiting. Another step out, and then the sudden flick of a net curtain. One more ring, and at last there is the jangling of chains and locks. The door opens a crack and a face appears around the side of it.

"Mrs. Bourgaize?"

All he sees is a flop of greying hair and an eye.

"Mrs. Bourgaize, I'm Mark Roussel. I know Pierre. I was wondering if I could come in for a chat?"

The eye flickers.

"I won't take long."

"Go away." It's a rasp.

"A quick chat, that's all. I might be able to help Pierre. But we need to talk."

"Go away."

She keeps the door ajar, her eye watching him. The hesitation gives him hope. He fumbles for his wallet, telling her to wait a moment as he opens it and draws out a calling card. He hands it to her.

"If you change your mind or need to talk, give me a call. Any time."

She snatches it out of his hand and slams the door shut. From deep within, he hears a voice growl, "Who was that?"

"Postman."

Back in the car, with the windows open, he checks the PineForestMurder account. The emails are few, and all are offensive; one is threatening. Time to close it, he thinks. Time also to check on Viv. He calls her number, and it rings and rings. He calls her mainline, but again no answer. She's either sleeping off a hangover or still angry with him about Tom. If her message is anything to go by, her head will be a train wreck.

Chapter Thirty-Eight

THE ATLANTIC HIGH CONTINUES OVER THE ISLANDS. The pressure reads 1032 millibars, and the blue sky goes high into the heavens. He overtakes a few cyclists and a stationary horsebox but otherwise he has the West Coast to himself.

The morning swim cleared his mind. He feels energised and ready to take on the world. Pushing the speedometer to thirty, he passes Perelle's butchers and forces the car up the hill towards the Catioroc headland, famished for breakfast at the Imperial. Eggs and bacon, and some Guernsey tomatoes on the side; a hash brown too, if they make them. The car begins to judder and slow, and when it reaches the top, it's all but gasping. Luckily, as it transpires, because it gives him time to spy Viv's car in the lay-by on the corner. He swings into the parking lot and switches off the engine.

The Volvo is oversized and in need of a wash. A glaze of salt covers the windscreen. He peers inside but she isn't there. A dog's lead and a water bowl, empty Waitrose bags and a summer jacket, but no Viv. It should be a relief – she was sensible enough to take a taxi home – but he's been in the police long enough to suspect an empty vehicle. He rings her mobile. She doesn't answer. He leaves a message: "The car's still here. The sea hasn't washed it away. If you get this, call me back."

A thought comes to him. Perhaps she's slept it off in the old man's house, in a spare room, overlooking the sea. Or she's having breakfast with him now, sunglasses over bloodshot eyes as she stares at a plate of toast.

The corner is blind and he dashes across the road and up the steps to the worn path. On one side is Mont Chinchon battery, built against the French in the last years of the eighteenth century. The two twenty-pound cannons command a stretch of sea littered with rocks. On the other side is the Trépied with its views of the marshes and the German defences at Fort Saumarez. In the old days, when the fishermen at L'Eree ventured out to sea but never to town, it was the wildest part of the island. There was no coast road then, and the witches of legend met here on Friday nights to cavort with the devil, Baal-Bérith, dressed as a goat. They danced naked and shouted obscenities to the hermit reciting his prayers on an outcrop nearby. *Tcheit, d'la haout, Marie d'Lihaou.*

Yet read the historical accounts and another story emerges. Take Collet Du Mont (who was burnt because she ate Satan's food) - she complained about the rough bread and low-quality wine the Devil gave her which shows the guy – whoever he was – to be a miser as well as a megalomaniac. And let's be honest, the dolmen is pretty small; it doesn't really fit its reputation. At best, it accommodates two crouching figures – a cadaver with more ease – and of the three capstones, only one is flat enough for a man to stand on it and pretend to be Lucifer.

He passes it now and walks along the escarpment,

between high hawthorn hedges and windswept trees. The sun is brilliant and the shadows sharp. The air has its morning thinness still and he hears the birds chattering in the hedgerows. It's a beautiful day. Stepping over granite slabs buried underfoot, he passes beneath old pine trees with their gnarled trunks and witchery branches, into their cool speckled shadows. Further along he meets the boulders of long lost dolmens that form the start of a garden wall. A few yards ahead, Le Catioroc comes into view. He has always liked that place with its higgledy-piggledy shape and small white window frames, but it stands on prehistoric tombs and an ancient fort, and its round squat tower was built by the Germans during the war.

When he rings the bell, no one answers. He rings it again and steps back to look left and right. Still no answer. He walks around the house, calling out 'hello'. The stillness is eerie. There's no one about.

"Hello!" he calls out louder.

A pigeon coos. A crow caws.

He peers through a window, hands about his face so he can see better. The room is small, with two armchairs and a side-table, nothing unusual, nothing interesting. The next window gives onto a kitchen. He moves on and notices a small window close to the ground and, getting onto his hands and knees, he looks through the dusty pane of glass at a stone floor and brick walls and a table laden with all the paraphernalia of a laboratory; he identifies a pestle and mortar, a Bunsen burner, test tubes and their rack, evaporating dishes, a weighing machine and a thermometer. There is also a microscope.

No wonder the man has something to say about the witches' potions.

"Excuse me?"

Mark scrambles to his feet and stands upright. Before him is an elderly man, with a straw hat and a pair of secateurs in his hand. There are grass stains about the knees of his trousers.

"Can I help you?"

Mark hides his hands in his pockets. "I'm Mark Roussel."

"Can I help you, Mark Roussel?"

"I was looking for you."

"Congratulations, you've found me."

"A friend came to see you yesterday, Viv Le Prevost."

"Ah, yes. We had a chat. She left. You seem surprised."

"Yes."

The garden slopes down away from the patio, with a rockery to the right and a hedged-off area to the left.

"Frank Torode, by the way." The man takes off a glove and extends his hand. Mark takes it, feeling the bones scrunch under his grip.

"I came up because I noticed her car is still in the lay-by."

"She must have gone for a walk, or met a friend for dinner. The Indian down at L'Eree is rather good you know. Perhaps she got a lift home."

Perhaps. Possibly. His smile is lame. Frank Torode is studying him, his brown irises fading blue about the edges. The man must be ninety at least.

"I know she came to talk to you about the plants the witches used to use. You had something to share with her, I understand."

"Ah yes." Frank Torode puts the secateurs in his pocket and removes his other glove, pulling at each finger until it's free. "I can tell you what I said."

Mark scratches his chin. He didn't shave and it's itching. "I looked up something similar on the internet."

"The internet! I imagine you're an expert now."

Mark catches the derision. "No, but I have an idea what the black paste in the news might be."

"Really? How clever of you."

Now the scorn.

"The witches used to make a hallucinogenic mix from plants like hemlock and wolfs bane. Taking a lead from the letter in the *Press*, I surmise it is something similar."

"It could be. Without a toxicology report, we can't know for certain."

"True."

"The Solanaceae family are very common. They are the nightshades, you see, but a diverse genus of plants. They have a range of alkaloids, but the tropanes are the most well-known. They are poisons. You would have read about them on the internet. Scopolamine and hyoscyamine. Nicotine too. The name tropane comes from Atropos, the Greek Fate whose job it was to cut the thread of life. Interesting, no? More interesting of course is that they are powerful anticholinergics."

"I'm sorry, you're going to have to translate."

"They block one of the neurotransmitters in the central and peripheral nervous system."

"Killers, then."

"In large doses the person taking them will get dilated pupils, ataxia – that means losing control of their movements – then hallucinations, convulsions and finally death. In very small doses, we use them medicinally all the time."

"So, it's possible Ginny Bisson – the girl at L'Ancresse – could have died from an overdose?"

"It's possible. But you usually have to take them orally

The Accused

to die from them. The witches learnt to mix them with oils and fat and put them on the skin. That lessened the effect. And from what we read, the balm was green in colour. We have a reference from Andreas de Laguna who was physician to Pope Julius III. We should also remember that the witches did not always use an ointment. They often burnt henbane and inhaled the smoke."

"So, the paste might have nothing to do with her death?"

Torode opens his hands as if inviting an answer. "A poultice, most likely. The last woman tried for witchcraft was in January 1914 and that was Mrs. Lake, nee Queripel."

"I've heard."

"The worst she did was read teacups and sell a powder to ward off demons. It was made of cornflour, paisley, flour, brown starch and baking powder. For that she spent eight days in prison. Of course, the powder used in the sixteenth century was most likely made of fern seeds. Fern seeds were said to have the power of invisibility."

The old man is interesting – he has a scientific approach to the subject – but there's something unsettling about him; he is dry and crackly like an old leaf.

"The problem we have, Mr. Roussel, is simple causation. People really do not like it. It is far too boring for them. But look!" He points towards the marshes. "Can you see it? The osprey, over there, hovering. What a magnificent sight."

They stand in the garden watching. Lihou sits high in the water now, the white of the waves breaking against the rocks surrounding it. The sea sparkles all the way to the hard line of the horizon and Mark is silent. He wants to enquire after the basement but chooses to gaze instead.

"I am blessed to live here," Torode says.

"Yes. Viv told me about your herb garden in the lower terraces." It is a shot in the dark, but not without aim. The man has a laboratory and he knows about hallucinogenic plants.

"Most certainly I do. On your next visit, you are welcome to see it but I am surprised the information came from Ms. Le Prevost. She never saw it and I never mentioned it to her, but I understand that detectives have wily means to extract information. Now – if you don't mind – I have things to do. I have been invited to lunch and it takes an old man time to prepare himself. Please," he holds out his hand in the direction of the house, "since you found your way in, I am sure you can find your way out."

Viv's car is still in the lay-by. He walks around it one way, and then around it the other, peering through the windows and trying to the open the boot. He bends down to look underneath. It makes no sense. He checks his phone but there are no missed calls. His voicemail tells him he has no new messages either.

He needs to think through the options, consider the possibilities. There is a logical explanation, he just has to find it. A taxi home or a walk home, a lift from a friend, a flat battery, a broken mobile, a really bad hangover, a foul mood.

It doesn't mean she'll wash up at Rocquaine.

Most probably, she's in bed with a packet of Panadol and a jug of black coffee. If she has any sense, she'll have switched off her phone as well. Cheap wine and a bad curry can put anyone's head in the toilet.

He ought to drive past her cottage and check if she

needs anything, and if she is well enough – or happy enough – to talk, he wants answers to her cryptic message and the name of Mr. 'You'd never guess who'.

The Vazon stretch of road is empty and he's pushing the car to its speeding limit when his phone ding-dongs on his lap. He indicates and swerves the car into a parking spot along the seawall and grabs his phone.

"Viv?"

"No, it's Pete."

"Oh." He tries to sound upbeat. "How are things?"

"I thought I'd keep you updated."

"Excellent."

"It's about Ginny Bisson's death. It's heart failure. She had a congenital problem that no one knew about. Nothing suspicious. I thought you'd like to know."

"What about the black paste? Any news from toxicology?"

"They take ages but I asked this guy. He's a friend of Jen, he works up at the hospital. They're talking about some sort of plant compound. It's still hush hush so keep that to yourself."

"Do you know what's in it? What type of alkaloid?"

"Foreign language to me. It's strong enough to knock a horse out, mind."

"What if I say to you someone's trying to make drugs the old-fashioned way."

"Nah, I don't buy it."

"Why not?"

"The big gangs have their guys over here already. They drop it from planes. They stuff it into torpedoes and stick it to the bottom of boats; fishermen pick it up in their crab pots. You get my drift."

He does but there's mileage in his theory. Ginny's heart

didn't stop without a reason, and she didn't just happen upon a new herbal cream. She had information to share and her dud boyfriend has already blown himself up once before in the bath.

"Okay hear me out a moment. Imagine you're some low-life dealer who's not in with the big guys, you get your hands on an old recipe using plants that you can grow yourself and no one suspects because they're found everywhere – you're with me? Okay. So, you start selling it as a paste. Problem is, you don't know the dose and you've ended killing someone by mistake. I'd say something like that is going on."

Chapter Thirty-Nine

THE SUN IS GETTING HOTTER AND THE AIR HAS LOST ITS fresh morning scent. He calls Viv from the lay-by at Vazon. Still no answer. He begins a message – "For God's sake, Viv, answer my bloody messages" – then he stops, tapping his phone on his chin. Instinct tells him something is wrong. He turns the car around and heads back to L'Eree.

Parking below Fort Saumarez, he walks down the path to the beach and looks out towards Lihou island. The causeway is disappearing under the rolling waves and there is no getting over for another six hours. If he'd come earlier, driven straight here in search of her, he could have made it over because it's obvious to him now that Viv is lost. The options have changed – swept out to sea, picked up by some weirdo, lying in a ditch, stuck on Lihou.

He walks back up the path onto the grassy embankment and looks about. The best place to start is Rocquaine and then Pleinmont, first the slower stretches and then the cliffs. Except now he's looking at the German Observational Tower and a thought comes to him. Beneath its concrete brutalism and slit windows (which remind him of the helmet worn by the knight in the Monty Python film), is a trench system that zig-zags down to a tank turret and a bunker.

Perhaps... he hurries up the path and through a field, up again into the tower's shadow where the trench begins. Granite walls covered with grass and ivy pen him in. The space is one-man wide and reaches to head height with enough room to stand akimbo. The ground is still damp from the rain. He follows it right and then left, then right again. "Viv? Viv?" he calls. Another left until he meets a T-junction. For a moment, he hesitates before carrying on into a deeper, darker trench which ends in a steep incline cutting underground. At the bottom is an iron gate and dripping water. Perhaps he's wrong. Wasting time again. Back he treads, and takes the other trench. A few paces more and he trips over a log.

"Fuck!"

He hits his forehead on the ground. He wipes it with his hand and sees blood on his fingers.

"Fuck!"

That's when he feels the log beneath him and realises it's something else. Scrabbling to his feet, he looks down at Viv collapsed on her side, her legs crooked and her torso half hidden inside an old ammunition store. She's as sodden as a fish and shoeless. For a moment, he's lost for thoughts – then he's on his knees inside the bunker, checking for signs of life, feeling her jugular vein and holding a hand over her nose to feel her breath.

She's alive.

Her legs are covered with cuts and scrapes, her toes are bruised. The arms are no less battered, and the nails on her fingers are torn.

He sits back against the wall of the trench, his knees

crunched against his chest, and shuts his eyes. A moment of silent gratitude – then he's back checking her. She doesn't respond. He raises her arms and notices more cuts and bruises. He smells urine and rolls her over. Her clothes are inside out, and something sticky is on his fingers. He takes away his hand and sees that it's covered in a black mud. He puts it to his nose. Mown grass and bacon.

It's on her t-shirt, it's on her shorts. He lifts her top and sees it smeared across her stomach like war-paint. It sticks to everything.

He gets to his feet and leans over the trench, wiping his hands in the grass, trying to clean the stuff off. He finds a stone and scrapes at his skin, spitting on it and rubbing it until it's clean.

Bloody hell, Viv!

Memories topple out of his brain. The Catioroc, Frank Torode, the weird message on his phone.

Bastard! He'll get him with his lab and congenial smile, his twisted rationality. He nearly killed her.

First, he has to call the hospital.

"Emergency. I need an ambulance. There's a woman in the trenches below Fort Saumarez. Suffering exposure and an overdose of some sort – yes, there are signs of life – no, she isn't conscious – she's about forty-eight. Yes, I know her – yes, I'll stay with her."

There's nothing more to do but wait. He crouches down and thinks to tidy her up, but the black paste is everywhere – in her hair, on her cheek, over her hands – and he doesn't know what to do.

The sun is still brilliant, still burning, but the trench is in the shade and it is dank. He crawls under the concrete ceiling of the bunker and lays down beside her, taking her hand in his.

He thinks of the monks who lived on Lihou once, not in poverty but in medieval splendour with painted glass windows and carved walls, coins and pottery and gold. They murdered one of their own in the dark of night. They ran him through with a sword, and fled.

He thinks of his mother alone in the farmhouse. She refused to leave the island to live with him in London. "I'll miss the sea," she said, "and I'm not leaving your dad alone in the graveyard."

He thinks too of Jasmine Gardiner's death. Why is it proving so difficult to solve a crime on an island of twenty-five square miles with more lanes running through it than the capillaries in his arm?

He thinks of many things until, in the distance, he hears the ambulance's siren.

Chapter Forty

A STAR GLITTERS HERE AND THERE, BUT THE MOON IS slow to come out. He sits in the car and waits, unsure what to do next. Rectangles of light make up the hospital frontage, and he watches a nurse appear in a window and flick the curtains shut; in another he spies a man in a chair reading a book. To his right, a couple wander out of the large glass doors, arm in arm, talking – a burst of laughter – and then the talking again. There's nothing for him to do, he ought to go home, yet he remains where he is, watching a world settling down for the night.

He tried to keep up with the ambulance as it sirened its way through the centre of the island, losing it somewhere around King's Mills and arriving at the hospital half an hour late. Hanging about the receptionist's desk, he waited for news, but none came. He asked where Viv was and received the curt answer that visiting hours had ended and he should leave, if he didn't mind. He did mind, and he swapped the reception for his car, where he sat doing the puzzles in the *Press* until he finished them. Then he listened to the news on his phone. It's ridiculous of course, hanging around, waiting for something. He went home for a while, and then returned, but if anyone asks him to explain his behaviour, he's stuck for an answer.

The police could turn up?

That's possible but unlikely given the hour.

They might need to talk to a family member or a close friend?

True, but he's neither.

He wants information and isn't going to rest until he's got it?

That's it in a nutshell. He's an intolerable son-of-a-bitch when a case is serious. Except Viv isn't a 'case', and there's nothing he can do. Either she will make it through the night or she won't, and it isn't up to him.

He really should get home. Dinner will be waiting in the bottom shelf of the Aga and his mother will be in bed, asleep. There's always Netflix to watch if he can't nod off.

He turns the ignition key and drives away.

Chapter Forty-One

THE SKY IS A BRILLIANT BLUE, AND THE AIR SMELLS fresh. With his mother on his arm, he walks out of the old gate and onto the lane. She's been up since three in the morning, and neither he nor Janice have slept much. First, she was restless and then she was angry. Now she's happy to shuffle beside him, looking down at her feet despite the beauty of the day. From time to time she lurches forward, taking him with her. She's forgotten how to lift her feet and no amount of reminding helps her. That part of her brain has died.

He hums 'Morning has Broken' to distract her. He can't stand the hymn and he hasn't been to church for years – he isn't one for spirits and gods – but he knows his mother loves it and it's the least he can do.

"Come on, Mum," he says, squeezing her arm. "Sing along with me. *Morning has broken, like the first morning…*"

She joins in, a bright smile on her face. Her warble on 'morning,' with its four descending notes, is hoarse but anyone can hear the joy in her voice. They carry on.

"*Blackbird has spoken like the first bird. Praise for the*

singing, praise for the morning. Praise for them springing fresh from the world."

By the time they reach the lynch gate, they've sung the first verse multiple times and la-la-ed their way through the other two, throwing in the odd word here and there.

"Look, Mum, can you see Vazon Bay?"

Together they stop, and he looks out across the field towards the island's fringe but Lilly is studying the ground. He lifts her head so she can see the yellow stretch of sand, but she drops it the moment he lets go.

Bells toll in his pocket and he takes out his phone. It's Advocate Vaudin, asking to bring the meeting forward half an hour. "Right," he says, none too pleased, and stows it away.

"Righty-ho, Mum. Time's running away with us."

They have come to dribble whisky over his father's grave, to wish him well. It's a ritual they've devised over the years. Sometimes they bring a blend, other times a malt – it all depends on what's in the cupboard at the time – but only Scottish, never Irish, and certainly not American.

He tries to hurry her along the path, toward its end where the grass begins. The lawn has been cut and with it the daisies and dandelions.

"Come on, Mum. Dad's getting bored down there."

Her legs stumble over the uneven ground. She's breathing heavily. They pass Mr. Le Cocq under his cross, and Mrs. Ozanne beneath her headstone.

"Hello, Mrs. Aubert," he says, patting a slab of granite. "A few more rows, Mum, and we're there."

That's when his mother screams.

He stops. "What is it?"

She screams again.

He looks around, seeking the cause. "What's the matter?"

"Home, home. I want to go home."

"Dad," he says, pointing towards the row of graves near the hedgerow.

"I want to go home."

Mucus dribbles out of her nose and her hand is gripping his arm so tightly he feels a bruise form. Something has spooked her – a rustle in the trees, a moving shadow. He takes her in his arms and holds her close, leaning his chin on the top of her head. Snot wet his shirt.

"Okay, okay," he says, kissing her hair. "We'll go home."

Le Petit Café is at the end of the Lower Pollet, in a round-fronted building with Parisian doors and Belle Époque calligraphy. It keeps faith with history, eschewing the Londonisation of newer developments. He likes it, always has done, but he prefers it in winter when the wind blows the waves over the seafront. In summer, he wants to sit by the water and watch the boats.

Inside, Édith Piaf is singing away. The only customer is a man with greying hair who sits at a table near the bar. Expensive suit, silk tie, exactly what he expected. He crosses the floor and flicks the chandelier of hanging spoons. There is the old grandfather clock and the bicycle hitched onto the ceiling. The décor has a quirky charm to it: the velvet curtains and the old cabinet of wine bottles; croissants piled high on the counter and the bottle of champagne cooling in its bucket.

"Peter Vaudin?" he says, holding out his hand. "Thank you for meeting me."

Vaudin half rises from his chair to shake his hand, and then invites Mark to take a seat.

"Coffee?" he asks.

He holds up his hand. "No, I'll just have a croissant."

Vaudin turns to a waiter in braces and a peaked cap, polishing glasses behind the bar. "Croissant," he orders.

Mark notes the tone and the gesture. He notices the man's hands too, manicured with a pale band of skin around the wedding finger.

"How can I help you?"

"I'm reviewing Pierre Bourgaize's case. He's keen for me to help him."

"I imagine it's rather moot now that he's in a coma."

Mark takes the plate from the waiter and makes a point of thanking him. He tears apart the croissant and eats. Using the black napkin, he cleans his fingers and flicks the crumbs off his shirt.

"Possibly. Unless, he recovers of course."

"The truth is, Mr. Roussel…"

"Mark, please."

"The case against Pierre wasn't strong but – and this is the point – the outcome was inevitable. The main witness, Tom De Carteret, was credible whereas Mr. Falla – you know about Falla, yes?"

"Yes."

"Then you'll understand what I'm trying to say. The alibi was weak and his character condemned him."

"And Jurat Martel?"

"If we accept the rumours, yes. But I wouldn't waste too much time looking into that."

"Some say you were sat on."

"They can say what they like. The Jurats were never

going to give the benefit of the doubt to a dangerous misfit who cuts off people's hands and tries to do sorcery."

"*If* he did cut off the hand."

A young couple push open the door and stand a moment, deciding where to sit. They choose the high chairs under the spoon-chandelier and heave themselves up, holding hands across the table. The waiter hurries over to greet them.

"Tom spoke of seeing Pierre cycle away with a black bag full of stuff," Mark says. "I find that curious."

"Why?"

He moves his plate away and wipes the crumbs off the table. "It isn't easy to hear items clunking about in a bag if you're driving at the same time. And no one seems to have found the bag."

"We tried pushing that. Pierre denied ever having it. Just as he denied the bike. But Tom said he had slowed down to overtake a parked car and that was when Pierre cycled by, so it was possible. He had his window open." Vaudin orders another coffee. "Are you sure you don't want anything? I drink far too much of the stuff."

"I'm fussy about my coffee, I'm afraid." He waits for Vaudin to place his order and then continues. "I'm keen to rethink a key assumption. That's why I wanted to talk to you. What happens if we say the murder and the amputation are two separate crimes. They aren't linked but are made to look as if they are."

"Interesting."

"Someone had the motive to kill her, that's obvious. But why hang her in the Pine Forest? Say the murder was for love or revenge – the usual things – and the hanging was to frame Pierre, then we are looking for someone with two motives."

"Who's going to frame Pierre? You usually frame people for money or revenge. Pierre didn't have the former and as for the latter, he was all bark and no bite. He didn't have a police record, remember."

"True."

"So, let me remind you of their case: it's rather unfortunate, isn't it, that Pierre just happened to do the same mutilations to the body as the ones in 1908? And it's unfortunate, isn't it, that he just happened to be a self-professed reader of black books?"

"Unless he didn't do the mutilations either."

Vaudin chuckles. "You can't get him off both crimes. And I'm not sure why you'd want to. He's a total misfit." He takes the second cup of coffee from the waiter without acknowledgement, and carries on. "Unless you can find new evidence, everything points to Pierre." He stirs it, and drinks. "And don't forget, people achieve remarkable feats when they have to. They can lift cars. He could have strung her up."

"That's pushing it bit! Let's talk about hiding the body then. Whoever killed Jasmine Gardiner put her somewhere. There wasn't any forensic evidence in the garage, was there?"

"No."

"So, the next best bet is a van of some sort. The one person who was always at the house and who had a van was Tom de Carteret."

Vaudin shakes his head. "I know Tom. It doesn't fit."

"He has the physique to carry her to the tree and string her up."

"Yes, it's possible. It's equally possible Pierre left her in a sail bag in the garden, near the back gate, and dragged her down at night as the prosecution claimed."

"The grass would have been flattened. Or the gravel would have had drag marks. None of that was noted as evidence."

"True. The garden was clear."

"And it's a long way down to the tree," he adds.

"He had the whole night to do it."

"You can see where I'm going with this though? There's no evidence and there's no motive."

"I wouldn't say 'no motive', I'd say 'weak'. Which is why I decided to defend him. But the Jurats decided against him, and I'd have done the same in their position."

Mark runs his finger over the table top. "Indulge me a moment. Tom de Carteret and Pierre have history. Tom's always hated him – he thinks he's a freak. He's the perfect person to frame. He tells Pierre where the body is hanging with the expectation that he's sick enough to go and do something to it."

"Let's say I accept Tom had reasons to dislike Pierre, that doesn't amount to – or even point to – his guilt, which you're insinuating."

"I'm posing it as a possibility."

"I can pose the end of the world tomorrow as a possibility."

"You're missing the point."

"Am I? Give me one good reason why Tom would have killed Jasmine Gardiner?"

"I don't know."

"There, then."

"No, wait. Most people murder because of love, money and revenge. My instinct tells me money is irrelevant."

"You can't present a case on instinct."

"I'm not. I've learnt to trust it, that's all. Like a compass:

head north, not south. So, putting money to one side, that leaves us with love or revenge."

They sit looking at each other. Vaudin drops his gaze and shakes his head. "You're way off mark."

"I disagree."

"That's your prerogative. Just take my advice: the island's small. It's not worth making enemies." He pauses. "How are your taxes by the way? Actually, wait a minute, didn't you mention something about residency issues when we spoke on the phone?"

Mark takes a breath. "I did."

"What's the problem?"

"I've been called to Frossard House. Someone's found out I went to the mainland after my father's death and spent two years at a prep school in Surrey."

"They're saying you didn't do enough of your education to qualify for local status?"

"In a nutshell."

"You were born here and one of your parents was local?"

"My father."

"If you did ten years in twenty, then you're fine. What's the issue?"

Mark thinks a moment. "Evidently, I've upset someone."

"I'd says it's a warning. Toe the line; keep your nose clean – that sort of thing."

"Head below the parapet, in other words."

"If you want a military metaphor, yes."

Vaudin drains his coffee and puts his cup down on the table top. Standing up, he holds out his hand.

"It's been a pleasure talking to you, Mark. Take my

advice. Forget about Pierre and chat up the powers that be. If you want to stay on island, of course."

Chapter Forty-Two

THE WALK FROM LE PETIT CAFÉ TO THE CAR-PARK takes him past the roundabout and across the road to the Weighbridge. Tables are laid outside and people sit under its clock tower eating waffles. Further on is the Liberation Monument, its obelisk casting a shadow on the stone seating behind. There he spies Mr. Brehaut, beer can in hand, slumped against the carved words of Winston Churchill: '*Our dear Channel Islands...*' Brehaut is covering the word 'dear'. Mark sits down beside him and quickly shuffles away: the man reeks.

People are queuing to take the Herm boat. The sun is bright, and everyone is dressed in t-shirts with beach bags over their arms; there are sunglasses and hats, flip-flops and phones. Children poke each other with plastic spades and dogs pull on their leads. The predominant colours are red, white and blue (with the odd green towel thrown in) and he thinks it all very patriotic until he remembers that Guernsey's flag is red, white and yellow.

"How are you doing?" he asks Brehaut.

The man grunts.

The Accused

"Do you remember me? I popped round a while ago. Hot, isn't it?"

"Piss off." Brehaut's gaze is fixed on the ground.

He stays where he is because he's just noticed Mrs. Le Sauvage in the queue for the Herm boat, dragging a little girl towards the steps that lead down it. Pebbles by all accounts who happens at that moment to be throwing her bucket and spade on the ground and stamping her foot. Mrs. Le Sauvage stops to pick them up, causing the queue to stall and then shuttle around her. She drags Pebbles a few paces more, but now the girl tears off her sunhat. Down it goes. Again Mrs. Le Sauvage picks it up. Next comes the heart-shaped sunglasses.

"That's it!" Mrs. Le Sauvage shouts. "The Herm boat, we're not going, okay?" And she storms off, leaving the little girl alone. The crowd moves down the steps onto the boat, but Pebbles stands where she is, her arms crossed and her mouth puckered.

"Jasmine Gardiner must have been a pretty awful person to do what she did to you," he says to Brehaut, "about as spoilt as that little girl over there."

Brehaut sucks on his beer can. "You don't know the half of it." He knocks it back and crunches it flat. At his feet is a Co-op bag and he opens it to take out another can. He pulls back the tag and lets the fizz bubble over his hand. Then he slurps.

"The last time we spoke you said she had a lover."

"Don't remember."

"I was wondering who it was?"

"Cor heck, you don't half like your questions, do you? My memory, eh, it's got to warm up, it does." He lets rip a deep stomach burp, waits a moment and then says, "nope, nothing's coming. Piss off and leave a man to his drink, eh."

Mark leans back on the stone seat and shuts his eyes to the sun. The lover is still his preferred thesis even if the murder was too calculated for enraged passion and there were no signs of resistance on her body. It has to point to trust. She knew the person who gave her the yew seeds. She took them *because* he gave them to her. The only person who came and went from the house without suspicion was Tom de Carteret.

"Was it the gardener?"

"Fuck off."

Tom would know better than anyone that yew seeds kill. Not the fruit, just the seed. And Tom likes older women. The problem is motive. A lover killing without passion requires a wider context, a need that overpowers the love and justifies the violence. Hatred of Pierre would explain the mutilation: he framed him. But it can't explain the murder.

"If you remember anything," he says to Brehaut as he gets to his feet, "give me a call. You've got my card."

He goes over and picks up the heart-shaped glasses that are still on the ground. Mrs. Le Sauvage has long since disappeared with Pebbles in tow, and the Herm boat is sailing out of the harbour; he puts them in his back pocket for safekeeping. She's Ginny's daughter after all.

With a new item on his tick-list – call Tom – he takes out his phone and waits for Martel to pick up. When Martel answers, his tone is incredulous.

"You want to invite him for dinner at the Copenhagen? Whatever for? The two of you have nothing in common."

"I just need his number for now."

"I've been thinking about the elections..."

"I'll only stand on a promise to tax oversized cars."

The Accused

"The last person who tried to do that had to leave the island. You can't take a Guernsey man's car from him."

"Precisely. So, can I have Tom's number please?"

With an 07781 still in his head, Mark calls Tom and is put straight onto his voicemail.

"Tom," he says, sounding as affable as he can. "This is Mark Roussel, Viv's friend. I was wondering, are you free for dinner at the Copenhagen? I was thinking tonight or tomorrow night? Give me a call when you can."

He's walking towards his car, parked at the far end of the jetty, when his phone rings. It's Tom.

"Just got your message. Jolly nice of you. Totally unexpected."

The joviality smacks of guile and it irritates him. Tom de Carteret the incontrovertible charmer. Does he know Viv was missing and is now lying in a hospital ward?

"I can't do tonight, but I'm free tomorrow," he continues. "What time were you thinking?"

Mark is about to say seven-thirty when "bloody hell" escapes his lips. A piece of paper is pinned under his car's windscreen-wiper. He pulls it away and reads it.

"The bloody warden's given me a ticket." He looks at his watch. "I'm ten minutes late, for God's sake."

"Take my advice, pay it immediately, otherwise they'll add on the pounds. Happened to me and I ended up with a sixty quid fine."

"Thanks, I'll do that." He stuffs the ticket into his pocket.

"About dinner," Tom continues. "You said eight, didn't you?"

That was slick.

"Eight's perfect for me. I've got a job to finish in St Peter's and when the weather's good I tend to work late.

And why not the Rockmount? Make the most of the sunset."

This is irritating. "I haven't booked it."

"Don't worry. I know the guys. They'll get us a table. Eight at the Rockmount then."

There's no point arguing. Let the man believe he has the upper hand. Tomorrow will be another matter.

Right now, he needs a swim.

Having a hot shower after a dip is as good as whisky on a winter's night. He scrubs his hair and watches the flecks of seaweed wash out from between his toes. Free of salt and thoroughly rinsed, he steps out onto the bathmat and - Lord! There's an intruder!

Or not.

The mirror is wall height and covered in steam. Vanity is lost the instant he recognises himself. There's no hiding the bulge. He pulls in his stomach, then lets it out; pulls it in again and stands to one side to see how far he can flatten himself. Not far enough. Time to redesign the bathroom. Tiles on every wall and a mirror the size of a pudding bowl. He turns his back on himself and grabs the towel. Back-and-forth and back-and-forth until he's dry.

It comes from not having a job. Like his morning rises that are getting later each day; the lazy amble down for breakfast, the indecision over muesli, granola, porridge or toast: hmm, maybe toast with marmalade today – but then, no, wait, there is the new pot of honey he bought from the hedge-veg down at Perelle. He can dribble it over his porridge, which is healthier than sugar and a lot less calorific than buttered toast except – well – buttered toast

The Accused

goes better with coffee and he doesn't like porridge, and life is short, and... no wonder he is getting fat.

He chatted with Viv after his swim at L'Ancresse, the phone to his ear as he dried in the sun and watched two toddlers chase each other down the sweep of sand towards the sea. She thanked him for having found her. If it hadn't been for him, she might not have made it. Her voice broke. The good news, she said a few breaths later, was her 'clean bill of health'; no renal failure, no liver malfunction. She was free to go home. Would he pop round to the cottage for a natter? Work was on hold, and she had no intention of reading the Agony Aunt letters clogging up her mailbox – unless, of course, he wanted to help? It was free titillation, and she'd let him choose the juiciest.

Oh wow, he said, he couldn't wait. Then he changed the subject.

Chapter Forty-Three

There isn't room on the dashboard for his phone, and given the windscreen sits at a 40-degree angle, there's little point attaching it there either – he'll have to hunker down and angle his head upwards to read it, and the cockpit is enough of a squeeze already – so, he sits with it on his lap (Google Maps working), and tries to navigate his way through the lanes to Viv's cottage.

It's a case of interpretation. The *ruettes tranquilles* are as narrow as alleyways. They twist this way and that, until he has no idea whether the sea is to his left or his right. He passes cows and sheep. Tarmac gives way to water lanes and ditches to hawthorn trees, and after reversing up a lane to let through a hedge-hugging 4x4, he performs an eight-point turn because the satnav has led him onto a cliff path and nearly sent him over the edge. Granite boulders guard entrances to fields and disguise themselves under lumps of vegetation, and by the time he finds Furzedown – bumping and crashing over the drive that is hidden between gorse bushes and blackthorn – he's ready for a drink. A strong one.

The Accused

"I can get you a Wheadon's," Viv asks.

They're sitting in the lean-to conservatory at the back of the cottage, facing a long garden that's actually a field and in need of sheep to keep the grass under control.

"What's a Wheadon's?"

"Gin. It's local. You can have the rock-samphire and grapefruit, or the lime and something else."

God, all those botanicals.

"Or a brandy smash?" she adds.

"You don't have a whisky?"

She shakes her head. "Brandy smash then?"

"Go for it."

It turns out to be brandy and soda with mint and sugar, and after the first sip (which is a touch too sweet), it slips down fast. Very fast. Brandy has never been his tipple and he doesn't think much of it as a dog's name either, but he's willing to change his mind.

"It was shock to find you in the trenches," he says. "What happened?"

Viv stretches out her legs. "It's all a jumble. Like a pile of dirty laundry. I'm still trying to work out what bit goes in what pile."

He must look bemused because she explains, "you know, colours and whites, that sort of thing."

The analogy is losing him. "How did you end up in the trench?"

"No idea."

"Chat me through it."

"I don't know where to start. Ask me something specific. You know, a question."

She sits forward in the chair and takes a deep breath, squeezing and opening her eyes until she falls back with a puff.

"What's wrong with your eyes?" he asks.

"They've been fucked since I took the stuff."

Took?

He lets the word pass. A rabbit is munching dandelions outside and Brandy, that little barrel of black and white fur is jumping up with her paws on the window and barking, her snub-tail going back and forth like a joy-stick.

She opens her eyes. "Brandy! Come here."

The dog looks back at her, and then returns its focus to the garden. The rabbit has hopped away, but Brandy keeps her nose to the glass.

"When you went to the Catioroc, do you remember seeing a lab in Frank Torode's house?"

"No. I never went further than the sitting room, the one with the bay window. We talked about my father."

"How did you get hold of the black paste?"

"Not from him." She unwraps the band that's holding back her hair and scratches her nails deep into her scalp. It's like she has ants eating away at her. When she stops, she wipes her hands over her head and reties the band. "I got it from a guy covered in tattoos. He came to the house."

Getting up from her chair, she walks to the conservatory door, tickling Brandy behind the ears as she goes to open it. The dog pushes past her and dashes like a greyhound over the lawn.

"Why did he give it to you?" He wants to ask, *Why were you stupid enough to take it?*

She squeezes her eyes. "He caught me by my car."

"You didn't drive home?"

"No."

"Why not?"

"Heaven knows."

"What did you do instead?"

"I ended up on Lihou."

"Jesus."

She smiles. "That's when I called you. I know that because a black-back watched me from the rocks and it reminded me of you."

Thanks. "They eat the ducklings."

She laughs. "I was thinking more of their sharp eyes and stocky build."

"Right. Thin legs, fat stomach ... I don't see it personally." He sniffs and carries on. "When you left me the message, you sounded as high as a kite."

"Did I? I must have called you after I put it on. That would have been by the ruins."

"No one else was around?"

"Nope. Not that I remember."

"After you put it on, what happened?"

"It was like some badly made pesto."

"You didn't think, this is the stuff that killed Ginny?"

"I did, but I don't have a bad heart. It could have been a poultice, that's what Torode said, and anyway, it didn't work immediately. I mean, I waited quite a while before I tasted a tiny bit of it."

"Tasted?"

She ignores him. "Nothing much happened, so I dug out the whole lot and smeared it on my stomach."

"Like Ginny."

"Like Ginny."

"Then what? When I found you, you looked like you'd been attacked."

She presses her hands against her face and rubs her eyes. She waits and then drops them on her lap, her eyes still closed.

"It's like a horror film live-streamed in my mind. There's no logic to it."

"You were hallucinating."

"Yes, but I've still got this sense – it's quite overwhelming – that it was all real. Not a hallucination but like it really did happen."

The drug had taken a while to get going, and then suddenly she was whirling, in her head, like a spinning-top. She was trying to stand upright and walk, but she kept falling over. Things were in her way, big things, small things; rocks perhaps. Her vision was distorted. She kept thinking 'I can see, but I can't see'; it was like wearing the wrong prescription glasses, everything was out of focus. One minute as light as a feather, really, really light – whoosh! She was up and off. Amazing. Exhilarating. She was flying, truly flying, like a bird, going wherever she wanted, here and there. Then – she had no idea what had happened – she was on the ground again. Up she got. Walked – fell over – crawled – and then got up again. Dizzy, so dizzy, not really seeing anything at all and then – whoosh, up she went, soaring towards the clouds. Astonishing. Incredible. There was a bit of vertigo now, and she was thinking: I've got to tell the scientists. I've got to tell them we can fly. Great for the environment. No more planes.

All of this was going through her head when suddenly a woman leant out of the clouds with an enormous white face and a telephone to her ear. Viv called out to her: This is great, isn't it? The woman put her finger to her lips because she was talking, and her voice was so loud that Viv could hear everything she said. And it was important. Viv told herself: Remember this, this is going to change the world. The woman was like a goddess, and she wanted to catch her attention. Find out who she was talking to. Here, over here!

The Accused

The woman ignored her and carried on talking when suddenly, Viv was on the ground again, on her back, listening to music. Orchestral. Violins, horns. Beautiful! Until it screeched into static, getting louder and louder, becoming a storm of white noise. She rolled onto her stomach and put her hands over her ears.

Night. The stars were out. She was on her back again, looking up at a spread of blurry lights. So close, so beautiful. She raised a hand to touch them, but they shrunk away so she got to her feet to try again – and, whoosh, she was off. Flying. Or not, because she was on her feet, trying to walk. Over she fell and smashed her knee on something hard. The pain!

There was a lamp in the distance. Bright, like a street light. She made her way towards it. It illuminated the whole area and she thought: At last, it's day, I better switch it off... Except – suddenly – it exploded, like a bulb that had been shot. Blue electrical sparks everywhere, spraying out and falling to the ground. And it was dark again, but not pitch black. She could see the ruins of the priory. A strange, anxious feeling came over her, like a blanket over her head, that sudden, that engulfing. There were creatures moving about the ruins. Get away from them! Hide! She stumbled and fell. She crawled away, her nails breaking on the rock, trying to escape. Now the grass. It was rough and thorny. Gorse bushes under her hands and knees. Over there, not far away, was a row of glasses. Where had they come from? Her mouth was dry, really dry, and she wanted a drink. They were full of something white, ice-snow white, and she was so desperate, she kept trying to get to them.

Someone was there.

She didn't like them. Yet she was talking to them. Asking them: Can I have a drink? It was dark, sliding type of a person. A shadow-person. It wouldn't keep still. Others appeared, and she followed them to the beach – yet she didn't follow them – she just suddenly found herself there, on the pebbles. And they were there too and she talked to them.

Dark. So, so dark. And cold. Wet, too. She was in the sea, right up to her knees and beneath her the water pulled at her, tightening itself about her legs. She thought: I'm swimming or I'm drowning.

No, she was flying.

But she had to be swimming, surely?

Yet she wasn't doing that either.

Darkness came thicker, like coal dust pouring over her. Sneezed. Coughed. She couldn't breathe. It wouldn't stop falling.

Suddenly it was light, and she was on the beach and there was something crawling over her. She tried to bat it away, but it kept appearing – and then disappearing – and then appearing again. Bat-bat, here there – where was it? WHERE WAS IT?

"Viv?"

She turns to Mark.

"Where was what?" he says.

"I'm not making sense, am I?"

"Not really," he admits.

"It wasn't a good trip."

"Evidently."

"I did quite a lot of drugs at Uni, but never like this. It's not nice stuff, believe me. There's something about the hallucinations. It's not like LSD or ketamine, you know, when you get these lucid but sort of dissociative experiences. This is something else. More like delirium. I can't explain it."

It went on and on. She was in some world – a real world – just not this one. There was no way to describe it. Ineffable, but not in a religious sense. Where she had gone was dark, almost satanic, and she came around, face down in the grass. Her mouth was like paper and her eyes stung. She was freezing cold, naked, down to her pants and bra. It had to stop, truly stop, halt – kaput! She'd had enough.

But it didn't. Things came to her, monks and goats the size of houses. Weird ghost-like creatures and insects decked as armies. She was getting desperate.

The next time she came to, she was dressed again and she remembered thinking: I must get home, I'm feeling sick, I've got to get a drink. Her eyes were sore, as if something had tried to tear them and squeezed them tight.

Scrambling to her feet, she started to walk and the joy of feeling the ground stay firm underneath her was rapturous. Thank God! Terrestrial Viv, forever heavy-boned and rooted. She was putting one foot in front of the other, delighting at the feel of the grass.

And that's when she saw him. Right in front of her. A tall, tall man with a strange thing atop his head. Small eyes and a crooked mouth. Her neck hurt from looking up at him. She knew who he was. No one had to tell her, she just knew. He smiled at her, and bent his finger to beckon her.

"No!" she shouted.

He undid his trousers and drew it out. Enormous. Swollen.

His finger beckoned her again.

"NO!"

She cups her hands over her face and scrunches her shoulders. Her breathing is fast. Mark leans across and takes hold of her arm.

"I'm here," he says. "It's okay. I'm here."

They sit like that, together, waiting for her breath to

ease and her hands to fall onto her lap. He watches the dog sniff about the field.

"Are you alright?" He eases her hands away from her face. She is sucking her lips and her eyes are red-rimmed but dry. "Can I get you something?"

She shakes her head.

"Do you feel better?"

She nods.

"Quite an experience, eh?"

Her smile is shy.

"Do you think it was the stuff they found on Ginny?"

"It's likely, isn't it?" She looks at him. "The doctor was sure it was belladonna mixed with other nasties. It wouldn't have been so bad if I hadn't eaten it."

"You could have called me *before* you took it, you know."

"I know." She pauses. "Those women, the witches. It was real for them, Mark. It really was. They flew, they saw the devil. It wasn't like 'this is happening to me but it isn't true'. They cavorted with Satan. They had sex with him. It happened to them."

"That's just what the delirium told them."

"Yes, but it *feels* real. Satan wasn't a myth to them. It's hard to explain – those things happened to them. They happened to me."

"They happened in your head."

"Everything happens in the head!" Viv snaps.

He takes a breath. "I suspect it was more insidious." His voice is quiet. "I'd put my money on a gang of men getting them as high as kites and using them for orgies."

She relaxes into her chair. "It's possible. They wouldn't have known the difference."

"It would have been easy enough. All they had to was

get the women hooked on the stuff. If they tried to stop, they'd have threatened them."

"The poor things."

"The men had to be powerful enough not to get caught, of course."

"Nothing new about that," Viv says.

Neither speaks. He's thinking about the court papers from the time; whether he can read them and test his theory. Most confessions were gained under torture, but a parallel investigation into the douzeniers and constables of each parish might reveal how endemic corruption was at the time. Hadn't Adrian Saravia written to William Cecil, Secretary of State, complaining about the godless nature of the Jurats and how they treated the people with contempt, rather seeing a man hang then tell on a friend? He knows this because he wrote about it for the College's history competition as a boy, and the Principle disqualified him for bringing the island into disrepute.

Viv interrupts his thoughts. "This stuff is seriously bad. We really need to get the police onto it. People like Ginny could end up hurting themselves. They aren't going to be calling St John's, you can be sure of that. Do you know how much an ambulance costs if you don't have a subscription? I bet that's what happened to her. She didn't call because she didn't have the money. We're talking hundreds."

"Why didn't you call the ambulance?"

"I'd lost my phone. I wouldn't have been able to see it to use it anyway."

"The same with Ginny, I suspect." He sucks his lip and thinks a moment. "Frank Torode and the tattooed man are in it together. That's my thesis. Torode makes the stuff, and the tattooed man sells it."

Viv shakes her head. "When Torode saw him, he was furious."

"I bet he was. You were there; you made the connection."

"No. He was *really* angry, not just caught out. I thought he was embarrassed at first, but then I changed my mind. If he'd been younger, he'd have given him one."

"Either way, the police need to check his lab."

"They need to find the tattooed man, that's for sure."

Chapter Forty-Four

The evening sky is clear all the way to heaven, and he smells the scent of gorse flowers in the air. Climbing down Burton Battery, he meets the coast road and crosses over to the other side.

There he stops a moment to stare at the orange rocks of Albecq, glimmering like amber in the sea. Turquoise green, blue, navy – the colours are washed in lines to the horizon, and he rests a moment in the gorgeousness of it all.

Then he turns away and ambles down the hill towards Cobo, past the parking spaces filled with vehicles. The place is abuzz with people, some on the beach, some in the sea, others sitting on the seawall gossiping. He approaches the Rockmount and sees the crowds at their tables watching the sun go down. They're young and beautiful, chatting in a lazy animated way. It suits Tom de Carteret with his suntanned fitness and charm. And there he is, standing up, his hand raised to catch Mark's attention. He should have guessed he'd booked a table on the veranda; he's a friend to everyone, with a smile to open doors.

They shake hands. Mark settles himself down in his seat.

"Good spot," he says.

"The manager's a mate from College."

Tom pours him a glass of wine. "Viognier quite young but pleasant. It's one of my favourites. I was surprised when you called, you know. I'm guessing it's about Pierre."

It is, but now that Tom has said it, he decides to the contrary. "Actually," he says, taking the menu from the waitress and thanking her, "I wanted to talk to you about something else."

"Tell me." Tom casts his eyes over the options. "I'll go for the moules," he smiles at the waitress, and then adds to Mark, "You should try them."

"I'd rather the scallops." He isn't sure about the pea purée but if there's samphire on a menu, he is eating it. "So, tell me about the book, the one the Queripels lost."

Tom snorts. "It's nonsense."

"Tell me what you know."

"Honestly? Nothing more than anyone else."

"That's not what Martel said."

Tom stiffens. Good. He wants him less sure-footed. "Don't worry, Martel filled me in, so let's say I'm in on the secret."

Tom tops up their wine glasses. "What did he say?"

"Bits and pieces. I know he's been looking for it."

Tom is cautious. "He told you that?"

"He said it's unique."

Tom nods. "I'm not an expert, but there isn't another one like it. It's not the same as the *Petit* and the *Grand Albert*, that's where people go wrong. The *Alberts* are this sort of an amalgamation of Albertus Magnus' work. They have some of Paracelsus' ideas in them as well, though heaven knows who thought to put them together. They're perversions really. Albertus Magnus never said the four elements had four elemental beings, for example."

"Right." Mark has no idea who Albertus Magnus is but he's heard of Paracelsus. "Who told you this?"

"My grandfather. Albertus Magnus wasn't an alchemist, he was a philosopher and a theologian."

"So, we're agreed, this stuff is nonsense. Salamanders with fire, and dwarves with earth – I've read them. They're full of it. So why would anyone take it seriously?"

"Albertus Magnus might not have been an alchemist but he thought stones had occult properties. And we all know Isaac Newton was one of sorts."

"And?"

Tom looks at the other tables and then leans forward. "The book's an original copy of an earlier collection of manuscripts that had put all of Albertus Magnus' ideas together. We don't know who did it, but it was written in Latin, not French, and somehow Newton got hold of it. That's why the Nazis wanted it. Newton had written in the margins, supposedly amending his prediction for the end of the world."

"Newton predicted the end of the world?"

"Yes. There's a letter he wrote – I think it's in Jerusalem's university – where he says the world is going to end in 2060, or sometime after."

"God, how disappointing. I thought he was a genius."

"The point is, he supposedly gives an earlier date in this book, and a different rationale for calculating it. That's why it's so important. That's why the Nazis wanted it."

"Hitler was a crackpot, I'll give you that."

"It's more than that. Newton didn't note this down

anywhere else. It's a one-off. Priceless. It's also everything Albertus Magnus ever wrote, in one volume."

The waitress weaves her way through the tables to reach them, a plate in each hand raised above the heads of the other diners. When she finds them, she lays them down and hurries off.

"It's busy here," Mark says, pointlessly, and then adds, "So the book's important because it's of academic interest, esoteric interest, or because it's worth a lot of money?"

Tom flicks his napkin onto his lap and moves the finger-bowl over to his right.

"It depends on who you are. For the Nazis, probably all three. For Victor Hugo, it has to be the esoteric. Have you been to his house in Hauteville? It's amazing, but I'd rather shoot myself than spend a night in that place."

"Agreed."

"The Garibaldi room is famous but I swear to you the time I went in..."

Mark interrupts. He knows what he is going to say: he felt the cold air. Everyone does. They'd say it even if they haven't. "What about you? Why are you so interested in the book?"

Tom doesn't answer. His mouth is full and he's busy pulling apart the shells. For his part, Mark is grateful the pea purée is smeared across the plate and not left in a dollop to be eaten. The samphire, however, is salty enough to prick the tongue and the scallops are cooked to perfection.

"I wouldn't say the book's important to *me* as such," Tom says, twiddling his fingers in the bowl of lemon water. "It's connected to my family, that's why I'm interested in it."

Mark eats a scallop. Tom digs out another mussel.

"Your great-grandfather stole it, didn't he? From the Queripels."

The Accused

"He didn't steal it. He saved it from the Nazis. There's a difference. Queripel didn't care a toss about its historical value or what Newton had written, he just wanted the money. And barrel loads of it too. He had a reputation." He breaks open another shell. "He was always snitching on his neighbours. He's connected to the rounding up of the three Jewish girls, you know."

"Connected or guilty?" Mark asks.

"Can't say, but he was a nasty piece of work. It runs in the family."

"As you would know, of course."

Tom flashes him a look. "I'm repeating what my family told me."

"Right. So, how do you think Jasmine Gardiner got to hear about it?"

"I've no idea."

"I'll fill you in. You were having an affair with her."

Tom holds his gaze. A little too long. People always make that mistake. A fraction of a second and he doubts everything they say.

"I also know about Ginny Bisson," he continues. "She wanted money for her drug habit. Her grandmother told her about the book and her sister worked for Jasmine Gardiner. Mrs. Le Sauvage. You must know her."

Tom nods.

"Ginny got this idea to make up a story about the book. She'd read the blog and knew bits and pieces. That's why she went to see her, ringing on the doorbell. Were you there at the time?"

"No."

"A shame. The story continues with Ginny telling Jasmine Gardiner that the book was buried under the fairy ring – the Table de Pions – at Pleinmont. For that she asked for a wad of cash."

"I didn't know."

"Well, here's the odd thing – before Jasmine Gardiner had a chance to blog about the book, someone went along to Pleinmont to dig it up." He's lying now. "Apart from vandalising a historical monument, it means someone must have heard the conversation and decided to get there before she did. I assumed it was you."

"Why?"

"Because you're the only person who could have overheard it."

"Why would I do that? I'd heard about the fairy ring theory, and I didn't believe it."

Mark raises an eyebrow. "Are you sure?"

"Yes."

"You don't want to rethink what you've just said?"

Again, that stare. Just a few seconds too long. "No."

"That's a shame, because Ginny made it up."

Tom drops his gaze. He twiddles his fingers in the water bowl and then dries them on a napkin. He extends a hand to take the wine glass, holds the stem a moment, lifts it – and then puts it down again. Sitting back and crossing his arms, he meets Mark's eye.

"I knew about the fairy ring because Jasmine told me. She also told me it had come from a druggie wanting money."

"You did a lot of chatting for a gardener."

"She was a chatty person. Look, I told her not to blog about it."

"Come on! You were worried it might be true and someone might get hold of it."

"We didn't want it to get into the wrong hands."

The Accused

"We? You mean, you and Jurat Martel?"

Tom doesn't answer. He unfolds his arms and dips a piece of bread into the moules marinière sauce, leaning over the bowl and tossing it into his mouth. There is more to consume, and once he has finished the bread, he takes a spoon and slurps the last of it. Mark waits. He is enjoying the spectacle of Tom de Carteret hiding in his dinner.

"The thing is," Tom says, putting down the spoon, "she had a genuine interest in antiquarian books. She got that from her father. Her collection was amazing. I just wanted her to look the other way, if that makes sense. That's how I got her to meet Pierre."

Mark didn't expect that. He puts his elbows on the table and points at him. "You introduced Jasmine Gardiner to Pierre?"

"Don't look at me like that. She was always going on about the Guerns being witches, I thought she'd get excited about it. 'I've met a real *sorcière*', that sort of thing. She could blog about it."

"Playing with fire, wasn't it?"

"I hadn't gambled on Pierre knowing anything about the book let alone being obsessed by it."

"Come on. Your family stole it from his family."

"We didn't steal it!"

"Whatever. You led Pierre right into Jasmine Gardiner's home."

"You don't have to rub it in. It's haunted me every day of my life since. How do you think that makes me feel?"

"A shit?" Mark says.

"Thanks."

The sun is slipping out of view, leaving a fan of orange and pink across a mackerel sky. The sea is turning purple.

"Of course, Pierre might not have killed her."

Tom's arms go into the air. "What's this Pierre thing you've got? He asked her about the book and she refused to tell him. That's why he killed her."

Mark clicks his tongue. "He put her in a sail bag and hid her in the garage."

"Something like that."

"Then he sneaked back at night and carried her all the way down to the tree, where he hung her up, carved her chest and cut off her hand."

"Yes."

"Then he took it home and planted it in a flowerpot."

"Yes."

"Come on, you expect me to believe that?"

"Why not? No one else is that sick. The man's a creep. And he's obsessed by the book."

"So are you and Jurat Martel; that doesn't make you murderers."

"I don't get your point."

"There's no way he carried her down to that tree, let alone strung her up. He's hardly got a muscle on him. If he killed her, then given what I've just said, someone must have covered it up but I can't see who and why. Ergo, he didn't kill her."

"That's your case?"

A shadow flashes behind Tom's eye and it's enough to tell him he's right, that Tom is hiding something. His next comment confirms it.

"It's not up to you to decide anyway. The law did that. End of story."

The Accused

It's ten at night and the air is filled with evening sounds: the call of the gulls flying down to rest on the water's edge, and the chatter of youngsters sitting on the beach wall. Cars are backing out of the car-park, and he makes his way over the German bunker and past the kiosk, onto the path that leads uphill. The band of fire encircling the horizon is fading fast. The air is growing damp.

That's when the idea to call Mrs. Le Sauvage comes to him. He stops on the path and taps the number into his phone. He holds it to his ear.

"Gorgeous, eh?" An old man potters past, pointing his stick at the rocks shimmering in the sunset.

"Gorgeous," Mark agrees.

"Doesn't matter what's happening in the world, the sun she always does her bit, eh?"

"She does indeed." He hears the click of a receiver being lifted at the other end of the line. "Mrs. Le Sauvage?" He smiles at the man and turns away from him. "It's Mark Roussel. I'm sorry it's a bit late, I just wondered if you could spare me a few minutes."

"Faw saw. The TV, I've just switched her off, eh. I was going to the kitchen, me, to make a cup of Ovaltine."

"I won't keep you then. It's just a question. Did Jasmine Gardiner have a lover?"

"Cor heck, I bet she had more than one, eh. Not that I'd know, is it."

"I was wondering if Tom de Carteret, the gardener, could have been one of them."

"Blow me down, Mr. Roussel, he was always round there, eh, with his smile and big muscles. I heard them having bargy, I did, and that was before she died, eh, a few days, is it. And you don't have an argument like that with any old gardener, eh. They were shouting, them. You this, you that. On and on. Cor damme là, I thought."

"It was that bad?"

"She was a right nutty Norah, her. I thought, the neighbours, what are they going to say, them, with all the racket, eh? Bloody English, is it. Bet he went to College, eh, coz he didn't sound like us locals."

"Why didn't you say anything at the time?"

"I didn't put two and two together, me."

Mark snorts. "Come on, Mrs. Le Sauvage. An argument like that? You know the police would have been interested."

There's a moment's silence. "Hang it, Mr. Roussel. I was worried, me. I heard Ginny's name, and I thought to meself, I thought 'What has she been up to?', eh. I didn't know what to do, is it. Ginny'd been to see her, you see, and I thought, cor heck, Ginny's been selling drugs, coz Ginny was doing drugs then, eh and I thought, if I say anything, me, she's going to get caught."

"The argument was about Ginny?"

"Blimey, Mr. Roussel, I don't know do I? I just heard her name, me, and more than once, and I went into a tizzy fit coz Ginny was such a one, is it, just like Pebbles."

"Why didn't you tell me this the other day?"

"You didn't ask, eh."

"You could have said. Anyway, look, do you have any idea what the argument was about?"

"If I knew I'd tell you, eh, coz it's strange she died a few days later, is it."

"Do you think I could pop round tomorrow, for a quick chat?"

"You come when you want, eh. I like a nice natter, me. Want some cake and a cuppa?"

"No thanks. I'm trying to keep trim."

The Accused

"Tell me about it, those pounds, them; they never stop piling on, eh? Chips and beer, that's what killed my old man. I like the Mr. Kipling cakes, me. And them pizzas you get at Iceland, eh. Four cheeses, it's called, and only costs a quid or two. A bargain, eh?"

"A bargain," he agrees.

"Well, cheerie then."

"Cheerie."

Night is switching on the stars and the moon is a thin smile in the sky.

Chapter Forty-Five

His immediate concern is a house full of pink telephones and plastic saucepans, so when he walks into a vacuumed hall with only flip-flops in the way, his relief is genuine, even more so when he sits down on a sofa and finds it free of hidden objects.

"The weather, it can't make up its mind, eh? Driving me nuts."

Mrs. Le Sauvage is dressed in t-shirt and slacks. The short-sleeves pinch her fat arms and sweat glistens on her upper lip.

He smiles. "It's certainly an unsettled summer so far. I hear May was good."

"Faw saw. The sun, he came out to say hello, eh, got the flowers all excited and then went back to bed. Just like them men, eh – except you, Mr. Roussel," she adds quickly. "I don't mean you."

He laughs. "Tell me about the gardener and I'll forgive."

She snorts. "What about my Ginny, eh? I thought you'd come to talk about her."

The Accused

"Ginny. Yes. I want to talk about Ginny. But first, tell me about the gardener."

"You promise?"

"I promise."

She hesitates, deciding whether to believe him or not, and then drops into a chair. "Blow me down, if I know. He's good looking, him, and he has a big van, eh."

"You're sure they were having an affair?"

"Not my job to look, eh, but I tell you, he was there a lot, him, and they were always giggling and kissing."

"Except when they had the argument."

"Cor heck, she was furious, her."

"And what about the day of the murder?"

"It was my day off."

"Right."

"About my Ginny then, eh." She has her hands on her stomach. "What do you know?"

"Not much more. She had a poor heart, and the black paste was most probably a drug."

"That's it then, eh? All her fault, is it? The police, they've given up, them. They don't care about the likes of Ginny. And with that dicky heart of hers too, they've stopped trying, them. You said she had something to tell you, eh. What was it? You tell me that."

"I don't know. I've got nothing to go on. It looks like it was a dreadful mistake."

She heaves herself out of the chair and waddles to the corner of the room. Bending over so she is more balloon than woman, she drags a large plastic box across the floor. He gets up to help her – "Let me," he says – and he takes it to the sofa where he sits down.

"That's all of it," she puffs. "Ginny's stuff. Go on, have a look."

Mark leans over and removes the lid.

"She was a hoarder, her. Kept everything, even milk bottle tops. There's lots of photos in there. She never kept them on her phone, her, coz she was worried about losing them, eh. Used to go the Guilles-Àlles library to print them off."

He thanks her and takes out the first object, a knitting book with a cracked spine and torn pages. He lays it on the floor and takes out a shoe box. Inside are hair bands, costume jewellery, batteries and perfume samples. There is also a pocket book on positive thinking.

"Sure you don't want a coffee, eh?"

"Sure."

"I'll be in the kitchen, me. Give a shout if you want anything, eh."

"Will do."

He picks out a large envelope and pulls from it a folded bundle of A4 paper. He opens it and checks the sheets. The images printed on them are too blurred to decipher. He tries another envelope and meets the blue and yellow lines of an ink cartridge about to run out. More books, more odds and ends, and then a diary held by an elastic band.

"Any luck, is it?" Mrs. Le Sauvage is back in the room, a mug of coffee in her hands.

"Not yet. It's going to take a while."

She points at the book. "Don't waste time with that, eh. She never wrote a thing, her."

"Right."

The band snaps in his hand as he removes it. He flicks through the blank pages, and then stops. He draws out five folded sheets of paper and opens them. Each is printed with a sharp-edged colour photograph.

"That's Mummy's stuff."

The Accused

A girl stands in the doorway, her hands on her waist and her chin tilted upwards. Her knees are covered in dirt and the t-shirt she wears has 'top girl' written across it. He recognises her.

"Pebbles, this is Mr. Roussel. He's Mum's friend, eh."

"Hello Mr. Friend." She walks over and sits down on the sofa beside him, a fearless twig of a girl. "That's my dad." She points at the photograph in his hand.

He glances up at Mrs. Le Sauvage. The man is tattooed, with long hair.

Pebbles pulls the sheet of paper out of his hands so he can see the one beneath. "That's Mum. I wasn't born then, that's why you can't see me."

He looks closely. It's Ginny, younger, prettier, less haggard too. She's sitting on a red-painted bicycle, grinning at the camera. At the front of the bicycle is a basket and inside it an empty bin bag. Printed at the bottom in neon yellow is the digital date. The photograph was taken a few days after Jasmine Gardiner's death.

Pebbles puts her hand about his ear. "Do you want to hear something?" she whispers. "Don't tell anyone coz it's a secret, eh."

"I won't." He has his eyes on Mrs. Le Sauvage.

"Dad gave it to Mum, the bike, is it."

In the next photograph, Ginny is holding up two finely decorated mugs.

Pebbles leans forward and puts her hand about his ear again. "Mum's pissed off in that, isn't she? Fucking useless, they were, eh?"

"Should you be using language like that?" he says, and Pebbles throws herself back on the sofa, laughing. He turns his head to look at her. "Where did your dad find these things?"

"Don't know. She said Dad's presents were always crappy, eh. She said she wanted a proper present, like from a shop, is it. She said he got all his presents out of dustbins, coz he was a stinking bastard. Like that black bag in the photo." And she laughs again.

"And you know this because?"

"She told me, eh." Pebbles folds herself into a ball and scowls, her feet on the cushions.

So, so, so... this was what she wanted to talk to him about. The black bag and what was in it.

Mark holds up the photograph for Mrs. Le Sauvage to see. "They're odd presents to give someone, don't you think?"

Mrs. Le Sauvage leans forward a little to see it better, screwing up her eyes. Quickly, she straightens herself.

He turns to Pebbles. "What else do know you about this?"

Pebbles shrugs her shoulders.

"This is important. I want you to tell me everything."

"Don't want to." Pebble sticks out her tongue and slumps further down the sofa.

"Don't you speak to Mr. Roussel like that," Mrs. Le Sauvage barks, wagging a finger at the child. "Coz if you do, I'm going to give you a hiding, eh, and when I give a hiding, it hurts."

Mark interrupts. He suspects Pebbles will take a 'hiding' out of bloody-mindedness. "Thing is, they look very much like something a rich woman would have," he says to Mrs. Le Sauvage. "Have you seen them before? The mug is quite distinctive. Wedgwood, I'd say."

She doesn't move.

"Be honest with me, Mrs. Le Sauvage. None of this can hurt Ginny. Just tell me, do you recognise them?"

She nods.

"Pebbles," Mark says, "would you do me a favour and get me a biscuit, please?"

"Nope."

He raises an eyebrow. "I'm asking politely, Pebbles."

"You do what Mr. Roussel says, or else."

"Or else, what?" Pebbles grumbles.

Mrs. Le Sauvage's arm rises above her shoulder and her hand opens out like a fan. Pebbles wriggles off the sofa and runs from the room.

"I don't hit her, eh, but that girl, she'll be the death of me, she will. She breaks things and shouts, and she won't sleep in her bed. She used to sleep with her mum, eh, and I said to Ginny, I said, that's not right. And now look. I've got a monster in my house, me."

"It must be hard for you, but we do need to talk about this."

He invites her to take the armchair opposite, and she squeezes herself down between the arm rests.

"Let's think this through," he says. "I don't want you to worry. I'm not going to ask why you didn't show these objects to the police..."

"I didn't know," she interjects. "I never saw them. Cor heck, Mr. Roussel, I couldn't have handed her over to the police, me, but I'm no thief, eh."

"I know. But they came from Jasmine Gardiner's house, didn't they? The date on the photo more or less confirms it."

"I don't know, Mr. Roussel. I say they look like they belonged to her, eh, but that's all. There are a lot of rich people on this island, and he's a thief, he is, and he could have got them from anywhere."

"Okay. Let's assume for a moment they are what I think

they are. Do you think Ginny's boyfriend – Pebble's dad – could have murdered Jasmine Gardiner?"

"What d'you mean?"

"It looks like this: he killed her and then he smuggled out the incriminating evidence – that's the mugs – and was going to get rid of them but changed his mind and gave them to Ginny instead, as a present."

Mrs. Le Sauvage fiddles with the edge of her shirt. "He didn't know her, eh."

"He dealt in drugs. Perhaps he was her supplier and she wouldn't pay up."

Mrs. Le Sauvage shakes her head. "She liked the bottle, her, but she was no druggy."

"How did he get hold of the stuff then?"

"I don't know. He's a loser, him, and a druggy. He gave Ginny a black eye too, he did, so he's no friend of mine, but – cor heck – you say he's a murderer, eh? I don't think so. He's too much of a coward, him."

"If you give me his name, I can find out."

Mrs. Le Sauvage shakes her head. "I don't give names, me."

"Let me have the photos then, and I'll find out. But you could save me a lot of time."

She glances towards the kitchen where Pebbles is splashing about, and leans forward. "Luke Guille," she whispers. "But you don't go telling anyone I told you, eh."

"It's HIM? You're sure of it?"

They're sitting in the middle of the garden with Brandy curled up at Viv's feet. The grass is long and there are dandelions everywhere, bright yellow heads of sunshine.

The Accused

Viv hands back the photograph. "He has more tattoos now, but it's the same guy."

Mark's stomach tingles with excitement. The hunt is closing in. This is it. He can't take his eyes from the man's face.

"Unless it was Pierre who dumped the bike and the stuff, and he just happened to find them," Viv says.

"What was Pierre doing on a woman's bike?" He looks over at her.

"He'd lost his bike, and he borrowed Jasmine Gardiner's."

"If she had a bike," Mark points out.

"You seem doubtful."

"I just think Tom's involved somehow."

"That again. You don't like him, that's why."

"Give me a break. I'm been doing this for years. I know a feeling when I have one. They're like these knots on a piece of string. The more you have, the more you've got."

"That doesn't make him a murderer."

It makes him a knot, and knots needs to be untied. "You remember the card game, the Double Lift? I think I might have got it back to front." He pauses. "Where can I find Tom on a Sunday? Just to talk to him."

She shrugs her shoulders. "Rousse maybe. He's helping Bob Perchard with his boat."

Chapter Forty-Six

THE ACCESS ROAD VEERS LEFT ON A TIGHT CORNER AND he drives past before he realises it's there. A stream of cars follow him in his rear mirror and he carries on to L'Islet, cuts into the local supermarket, turns the car around and heads back the way he came, turning off and bumping down the incline to the small lay-by.

He parks the car facing the sea, and looks out at the turquoise bay. The tide is falling, and the water is white with children jumping off the end of the pier. Fishing boats loaded with orange buoys bob in the surf and on the other side of the water, the spire of the Vale Church breaks free of the treeline.

Stepping out, he crunches over shingles and dries seaweed. To his right is an upturned rowing boat tied to the ground with thick rope. A few paces further on is the boatyard with all kinds of vessels perched on their stilts. It's small, chaotic and has a quaint, discarded feel about it.

To his left is the kiosk which sits in the shadow of the pre-Martello tower. It's a squat granite building with a hatch window and a blackboard of specials. Bright blue picnic-tables and a Walls ice cream sign lend it a holiday feel, but there's nothing touristy about the place. It's down-to-earth and hearty, like everything in the North. The menu says it all: beanjar for lunch and *gâche melée* for afters.

He orders a cup of tea and walks with it towards the yard, where a man is scrubbing the underside of a fishing boat. He has grey hair and saggy skin, with a torso as tough as a thirty-year-old's. The last time Mark noticed any definition in his six-pack was after a bout of dysentery in Laos.

The old man is not alone. Tom de Carteret appears from behind the other side of the boat with a sanding machine in his hand. They are both shirtless and tanned, looking like an advert for 'Keep Fit, Guernsey'.

He balances his mug on the top of his car, and waits for Tom to see him. When he does, he puts down the sanding machine and walks across the yard and up the path towards the car. He even waves.

The man is irritatingly virile.

When he reaches the car, he leans over it and crosses his arms on the canopy-hood. Mark grabs his mug before it falls.

"I love this thing," Tom says. "I didn't get it at first, you know, why you'd have such a quirky car, but it's growing on me. I told Martel there was a rebel in you somewhere. If you want status on the island, you go big, really big. But not Mark Roussel, he goes Noddy-size."

He fakes a smile.

"It's quixotic, you know." He taps the roof. "There you are, always running after the runt. First a kiddy-car and then a murderer."

That's below the belt. "I don't think so."

"You wouldn't."

They stand facing each other, the sun glinting off the car's paintwork.

"Okay, look," Mark says. "I've got a question for you. Did Jasmine Gardiner have a bike? I'm not thinking of one of her sons', but a women's one. Red, with a basket at the front."

"Why should I know?"

"You were sleeping with her."

Tom lays his chin on his arms and holds it there. Mark waits. A flock of sparrows are squabbling in the bushes, and somewhere music is playing.

Tom is looking at him. "You've really got it in for me, haven't you?"

He doesn't answer.

"You want me to admit it, don't you? Fine, I'll say it: I was seeing her. Okay? Does that make you feel better? You sussed it out. Well done, Mr. Detective. Got where the local bobbies never did." The chirpy chap has gone. There's a weight about his eyes and his voice is heavy.

"This isn't about me."

"Yeah, well, it's probably because she was older than me, isn't it? That's what gets you. Fourteen years, to be precise, but it was love whatever you want to think, and it wasn't my decision to keep it secret. I'd have shouted it from the clifftops, but she was worried about her husband. He's a piece of shit. Vindictive as hell. He'd managed to get custody of the boys and was threatening to cut off support. If he'd found out about us, that would have been it." He pushes himself away from the car and looks out across the water. "She was a lovely, lovely person. She didn't deserve what happened to her."

The Accused

Mark waits. "What drugs was she taking? I know you had an argument before she died."

He turns to him. "Who told you that?"

"You were overheard."

"Jesus." His arms go back down on the car's roof. "Okay it's true. I worried she was getting them from Ginny Bisson. Her sister cleaned for Jasmine. But I was wrong." He thinks a moment. "Don't tell me it was her? She told you, didn't she? God, that woman! She had her nose in everything. That's how Ginny came around in the first place. She turned up looking like a bag-lady and as high as a kite. She said she wanted to see her sister. What she actually wanted was money."

"What about the argument?"

"With Jasmine?"

"Yup."

He rubs his neck. "I don't know why I'm telling you this."

"Because you need to?"

Tom shakes his head, but the gesture isn't negation; it's comfort. "Look, I accused her of taking drugs. She denied it. We had a row. I was furious and I left. I didn't go round for days. She kept leaving messages on my phone. I gave in and drove round to see how she was. That's when I saw Pierre on the bike with the black bag."

"Clunking away," Mark adds.

"Yes, clunking away. I had to stop to overtake a car and he pedalled past, head down like some manic weirdo. It was odd though, I mean he was on a woman's bike…"

"You said it was his own bike, the one he had at school."

"Did I? Whatever, it wasn't. It had this basket in the front and the bag was inside it. I laughed it off. Fruitcake, that's what I thought. Wacko. And then I got to the house.

That's when I found the room in a mess, and Jasmine nowhere to be seen. I put two and two together."

"You assumed she was dead?"

"Yes."

"Straight away? You didn't think she'd popped out to see someone or gone for a walk?"

"She wasn't the walking type."

"Your first thought was: Jasmine's not in; she must be dead. Sorry if I find that odd. Did you call the police?"

"No. I thought she'd gone off somewhere in a hurry. So, I left."

"You just said you thought she was dead."

Tom is getting angry. "No, I didn't think she was dead straight away. I thought something was wrong. Then I thought she was dead."

"This isn't very clear."

"I can't remember everything perfectly. It was years ago."

"I'm trying to work out why you didn't tell anyone. The house is in a mess, she's disappeared, you think something is wrong, you've seen Pierre pedalling away with a clunking black bag, and then you just – how did you put it? – you just left." Mark takes the car keys out of his pocket and dangles them from his finger. "The man you saw on the bike wasn't Pierre, was it?"

"No. It was Pierre. I'd swear on the Bible."

"Really?"

"Yes."

"Are you sure, given what you've just said about remembering things? It was Ginny's boyfriend, wasn't it? He was supplying her with drugs, she wouldn't pay, and he killed her."

"That's ridiculous!"

The Accused

"The man's been supplying drugs for years. He ended up in prison for making meths and now he's brewing up the flying ointment, the one the witches used to use. He gave it to Ginny and it killed her; it nearly killed Viv too."

"Viv?" Tom looks genuinely shocked. "What was she doing with the stuff?"

"Trying it out."

"Jesus! I love her to bits, and I know she's got this crazy side to her, but to do something as stupid as that? I can't believe it." He thinks a moment. "Are you telling me that this guy was making the stuff when Jasmine was alive?"

"I can't say."

"It doesn't calibrate. I saw Pierre. I swear to God I did. He knows about yew seeds – that's his sort of thing – and he knows about pentacles and the like. This guy and his ointment – what's his name?"

"I can't tell you."

"You're saying he killed Jasmine and then mutilated the body? Is he a witch or something?"

"He decided to frame Pierre for it. He cut her up and put her hand in his shed. A perfect set up, and it worked."

"Why would he do that? Did he even know about Pierre? It doesn't make sense. Don't forget about the books all over the floor. What would this guy want with some antiquarian books? Pierre was looking for it. He killed her and cut her up because he's a sick bastard."

"I admit the books are a problem. But there's nothing to say they were involved in the murder."

"Come on!"

"Jasmine could have done it herself, in a fit of pique. When the man turned up, the books were already on the floor. He killed her, hid the body and then went back later hoping to frame Pierre."

Tom shakes his head. "Sorry, I don't buy it. How did he know Pierre? And how did he know Pierre was caught up in all this occult nonsense? How did he know where he lived?"

Exactly, Mark thinks. Tom de Carteret has just said it. There are too many unknowns. And it breaks his theory of 'two events–two perpetrators'. But it fixes another idea brewing in his head.

Chapter Forty-Seven

"Hi Pete, it's Mark. Just wondering if you had any news for me."

"It's not a good time, Mark."

He hears voices in the background, and a telephone ringing. "Why are you whispering? Are you in the station?"

"I'm not meant to be talking to you." The ambient sounds lessen as Pete walks to another place.

"What? A memo's gone out?"

"Tongues are wagging and I don't need problems."

"Neither does Mark.

"Okay, I've got a quick question and then I leave you alone. What do you know about Luke Guille?"

"That shit? Look..." He hears Pete move his head away from the mouthpiece, as if checking for listeners. "I'm out on patrol in half an hour. Bring a bottle of something and meet me at the Dehus."

"The Dehus?"

"I'll be down round the Vale, it's pretty private."

"You know this is ridiculous, don't you?"

"I don't care."

"Why a bottle?"

"I can pretend I'm arresting you for drunk driving. Dehus in forty minutes. See you there."

MARK SHARES his theory about Ginny's boyfriend.

"We've just arrested him for drugs. You know that black paste they found on her? Well, a Mr. Torode came to the station to testify against him."

"Torode, the ninety-year-old?" That's a clever way to avoid suspicion.

"He explained everything. Seems Luke was helping him with his research and then raided his garden for plants and started using them to make this brew. We found pots in his back garden."

"That's a neat explanation."

"It fits and the man's ancient."

"That doesn't mean anything. He's got a lab in his home. I'd check out his bank account, if I were you."

They are at the entrance of the passage grave, pretending to read the information board, three paces away from the lane where they've parked their cars. He presses the black switch by the door and bends his back to step inside. The burial chamber is filled with an eerie yellow light. Enormous granite slabs line the space and in the centre, is a pillar that stands alone and disconnected from the ceiling. On one of the capstones is the *Gardien de Tombeau*. His father showed it to him when he was little. "He's got a beard. And can you see his hand and the strung bow as well?" he said, making him lie on the ground and look up. "He's guarding the tomb and you must always show him respect."

Pete is holding his phone out before him, pretending to take a photograph. "We've got Guille for illegal supply and if we can show he knew it was possibly lethal, we've got him for manslaughter too."

"You can probably get him for Jasmine Gardiner's murder as well."

"Pull another!"

"I'm serious. Yew seeds are easy to use if you can get the person to take them. Clean, no strangling, no blood. Like giving a drug: 'Here, try this, it's something new. It'll knock you off your feet.'"

"He's a nasty bit of work but – I don't know – why would he do that? He's a bully and a crook, not a cold-blooded murderer."

"She owed him money."

"Did she?"

"She was buying drugs off him, and stopped paying. It happens."

"Do you know this for sure? He did a piss poor job of getting it back then, didn't he? There was a wad of cash in her desk, and all her jewellery was in its box. And what about the computers? He could have made a fortune if he'd looted the place. We're talking fifty grand just in the bedroom."

That's the problem. As it stands, his theory is conjecture. The photograph in Ginny's box points to a random discovery, nothing more. That it happens to be a bike and a mug puts him by a dustbin, not the scene of the crime. He walks out of the tomb and onto the road turning around to face Pete who remains at the entrance, ready to nip inside if anyone comes along.

"Put Luke Guille to one side for now and hear me out on the mutilation," he says. "If someone wanted to frame Pierre, what was the best way to do it? Cut a pentacle in the body's chest and hack off its hand."

"Who'd want to frame him?"

"Tom de Carteret."

Pete's eyes bulge. "You're way off."

"It's not so crazy. I know everyone likes him but it works. The two guys hated each other at College. They'd also inherited this issue with the book, the one the Nazis were after. Their great-grandfathers fought over it. Add to the pot Tom's affair with Jasmine Gardiner and things begin to take a different hue."

"Stop there. Affair? What affair?"

"She helped him set up the business. I think he was pretty smitten."

"He's never said a word."

"A bit suspicious, don't you think?"

It takes Pete a while to answer. "If he'd loved her, he'd never have killed her, let alone cut her up like that. And don't forget, he wouldn't have known how to do it either."

"Why not? I know what a pentacle is, and if you've read *Harry Potter*, you'd know about the Hand of Glory."

"You've read *Harry Potter*?"

"That's beside the point. The thing is, he could have easily known about the Fanny le Page murder too."

"How? He's a gardener, not a historian."

"You can't rule him out on occupation."

"You can rule him out on motive. Why kill her?"

"I'm not saying he killed her."

"Mutilated her then. That's even more sick."

"He did it to get back at Pierre."

The Accused

"Why?"

"Because he hated him and thought he'd done it. No surer way of getting him caught. Tom went round to the house shortly after the murder."

"He never said that at the time."

"Of course he didn't, but he's just told me. They'd had an argument, he was worried about her and went to see her."

He's has been thinking about Tom's confession. There's something that doesn't add up. If Pierre killed her and fled on the bicycle, he had to hide the body somewhere – that would explain its absence. But where? There were no drag marks across the lawn or the gravel, so it must have been in the house. Given Pierre's build, it wasn't going to be in the attic, and surely Tom would have searched upstairs and down anyway; he would have gone into the garage too. The fact that he can't corroborate whether he assumed her dead or out on an errand, furthers his doubts.

"It goes like this: Tom went round and found Jasmine's body on the kitchen floor. He was sure Pierre had done it – he'd just seen him cycle past with the black bag and he wanted to get him any way he could. Remember their hatred. He put her body in the back of his van and kept it there until night. Then he drove back to the house when everyone was asleep and took her down into the Pine Forest and cut her up. Forensics said she'd been wrapped in a sail-bag. He could easily have had one in his van. It adds up."

Pete's arms are over his head, as if to hold his thoughts in place. "You're saying he found Jasmine and he was the one who hid her body? And then cut her up…"

"And planted the hand."

"He isn't that kind of guy."

"I agree. It would explain the vomit found at the scene, wouldn't it? It's been bothering me all along. Why vomit? He probably knocked back a bottle of scotch to do what he did."

Pete shakes his head. "No, no. He'd never do that."

"But if he did...?"

"Who killed her?"

"Exactly. Enter Luke Guille, Ginny's boyfriend. He gave Ginny the bike and two mugs used in the crime. I've seen the photos."

"I bet she was pleased.

"Thrilled, from what I gather."

"But Tom said he saw Pierre cycle away with the black bag, not Luke Guille."

"True, but if he wanted to frame Pierre, it's the easiest story to make up."

"Except you can't tell me why Guille wanted to kill her and I can tell you why Pierre did."

"Can you?"

"'Course I can."

"What? A weird kid playing at witchcraft?"

Pete shuts his eyes a moment. When he opens them, he points at Mark. "He wanted the book you were going on about. She wouldn't give it to him, he got cross, gave her the yew seeds and then destroyed the bookshelves looking for it. He also mutilated the body."

"And you think she'd have taken the seeds from Pierre Bourgaize?"

"If he put them in a cup of coffee she would, yes."

"She didn't know, you mean?"

"Spot on."

"That would hold for any number of people, including Luke Guille."

The Accused

They cross the road to their cars, and as Pete backs to drive away, he winds down his window. "You know they've removed the guard, at the hospital."

"Pierre won't make it?"

"Not according to one of the nurses, he won't."

Pete waves as he drives off.

Chapter Forty-Eight

It isn't a question of losing interest. Pierre's attempted suicide is heart-breaking; it speaks of despair, and in the face of injustice, despair is the last step before ruin. She knows that. She learnt it from her husband. That's why she cares.

It's just she's had enough. Weary is the word, the sense that nothing matters anymore. She doesn't see things as well as she used to; she doesn't understand them so clearly either. Her life isn't ordered; it isn't happy. She's knitted herself a nice story of success, and now it's disintegrating.

Blame the paste. Blame Ginny Bisson. Blame Mark and his investigations. Blame herself for telling him to research it.

She hates blame.

What she wants is to stop. Stop trying, stop striving. Just stop. Like a trek up the mountain: no more. Here is far enough. Let her sit down and roll over.

The Agony Aunt letters are piling up; her clients are leaving messages.

Back to work, old girl.

Just, no, not yet. Please.

Her life is haunted. Images, sensations – they come back. At night, when going upstairs to bed. In the evening, when walking down an unlit corridor. It isn't fear as such, but it is anxiety.

Which is why she wanted Mark to stay. After sharing her experiences, she hoped he would kick off his shoes and lay out on her bed. Hold her close. Make love perhaps, but that wasn't necessary, it was just being with her.

Instead his kiss lingered on the corner of her mouth. He hovered in the doorway, and for a moment she thought he would push past her, into the cottage.

Except – no. He got into that stupid car of his and drove off, back to his mother. Fucking Oedipus complex.

Perhaps he's gay.

No, it's Oedipal. Has to be. Ticks all the boxes. Infantile libido directed to the wrong object. Mark screeching with delight as his mother tosses him into the waves down at Vazon. She remembers those summers. Burying each other in the sand, up to their necks. Mark's father was never around, and Lilly was everywhere, with flasks of milky tea and cheese sandwiches. And those huge towels she brought to the beach – she used to rub them dry like dogs.

Freud and Little Hans, perhaps?

No, that's unfair. It's cruel to accuse him like that when Lilly is lost in her dementia and more a cadaver then a living human being. A man can love his mother without Freud's finger pointing down at him. She's jealous, that's all.

The bell rings. And then rings again.

Go away!

It rings again.

Persisting bastard. It's probably Mark. She heaves herself up from the sofa and goes to see who's bothering her front doorstep.

"Peter Vaudin, well I never."

"Can I come in?"

Yes, no – she wants to be alone.

"I've been dreaming of your homemade lemonade all day."

Like hell he has.

"And you never answer your phone."

"I lost it – in the sea, at Lihou."

He's looking dapper in his chinos and open necked shirt. Straight from work with the faint smell of sweat that comes after a day in the office. Handsome isn't the adjective to describe the man, but he compensates with the clean lines of wealth. So much so, he's almost attractive.

Offering him a chair on the lawn, in the warmth of the afternoon sun, she brings two glasses and a jug of lemonade filled to the top with ice.

"So, what do I owe the pleasure to?" she says, passing him a drink.

"A visit from a friend of yours."

She clinks his glass. "Never one to charm the ladies, are you Peter."

The laugh is genuine. "You don't need charming, Viv, and you know it."

She isn't so sure. "I guess you're talking about Mark Roussel."

"The one."

"And there I was hoping you had come with flowers and chocolates. And don't look so surprised. I've been off sick."

"I'm sorry to hear it."

"In hospital, actually."

"I didn't know. Your friends aren't going to phone me up to tell me, are they?"

"True." They're loyal in that regard; have heard her side of the story and don't need to hear his. Not least because she lost her job and he stayed on to make a nice fortune. But that's what comes from sleeping with the boss.

"Why do you want to talk about Mark?"

"He's making enemies."

"That doesn't surprise me."

"I've been sniffing around. He needs to leave the Pierre case alone."

She looks at him. "What do you know?"

"Less then I'd like, but enough. I know you disagreed with the choices I made at the time."

"That's one way to put it."

"I did what I believed was right. Pierre didn't have a chance. This isn't a fair world, but it balances out in the end. This little residency threat is only that, a threat. But it means the weather cock is pointing in one direction, and he better heed it."

"What residency threat?"

"He hasn't told you? I assumed you were an item."

"What, a bit of cutlery?"

"Never a bit, Viv. Never that."

"It doesn't matter. I've been ill." She's thinking. "Why do you care anyway? I mean, you don't know the man for Adam and suddenly here you are."

Perhaps he's jealous. Vaudin married a pretty little intern at Credit Suisse but rumour has it he is bored. She looks for the wedding ring and spies a pale band of untanned skin, which says it all really.

He finishes his glass and lays it down on the ground. "I like him. He has honest eyes."

"I don't believe you."

The corner of his lips twitch. "It's true. I know an honest man when I meet him. And I know there's a cloud over him. The Met and all that?"

"And Indonesia."

"Indonesia?"

"He taught there for a bit. Something happened when he went into the jungle but who knows what. He's a closed book."

"Well, he's opening up a pretty big one over here."

"I know. And if you mean the lost black book, the one Martel wrote a letter about in the *Press*, it never came up in the trial and it should have. It featured in one of her blogs."

"Lots of things did."

"You should have looked deeper into it."

"What do you want me to say? Sorry? You can carry on accusing me – that's nothing new – or you can listen to me."

She clasps her hands in mock obedience. "I'm all ears."

"Good. Tell Mark – I know it will come better from you – tell him that there's one big name blocking him. Jurat Martel. He's telling everyone he's having a nervous breakdown. That's the gossip on the street. My take on it is this: anything Mark tries to produce now, anything new on Pierre's case, is going to fall dead. No one's going to listen to him."

"You mean, he's silencing him."

"Basically, yes."

"Before he can get anything together?"

"In a nutshell."

"Meaning, he might as well give it up."

"Exactly. This investigation into his local status, it's

useful if it unsettles him. If it doesn't, it can be swept away as some administrative error. Either way..."

"It's got Martel's fingerprints all over it?"

"Precisely. So, again, my advice is this: let Pierre die in hospital, and move on. This Island's got more problems than Pierre Bourgaize, believe me."

Chapter Forty-Nine

HE WALKS ALONG THE CHARROTERIE TO SIR CHARLES Frossard House, through the glass doors and into the foyer. It's cramped and functional and he waits in line to talk to the receptionist. Viv has relayed her conversation with Vaudin over the phone, and he's spoiling for a fight.

"I'm here to speak to Mrs. Stone. We have an appointment."

"Take the chair and she'll be with you in a moment. Can I ask what it's about?"

"My residency."

"With a name like Roussel?" She smiles. "Very well, I'll let her know you're here."

Mrs. Stone is thin with short cropped hair. 'Functionary' is written in her blue suit and white shirt and the large circular table she's sitting behind. The room is pleasant enough: white walls with posters about immigration, pensions, taxes, even a government charity event. What is concerning is the file Mrs. Stone has on the table.

He relates the details to Janice over lunch later that day.

"I asked, why am I here? And she said it's because you

don't qualify as local. And I said, how come you're suddenly so interested in my residency? For that I got a smirk but not an answer. She opened the file and began to ask me about my education. It was okay, I said. Nothing spectacular. Elizabeth College isn't Eton or Winchester, is it? I'm not talking about the quality of your education, she snapped, but where you had it. Very well, I said, Castel Primary School, prep years in Surrey and then College. Precisely, was her answer. You didn't complete your education in Guernsey. No, I said, but I bloody well did more than ten years of it here, so what's the problem? We need to be sure of the dates, she said not too kindly. Phone Castel Primary School and phone the College, I said; they've got the information. We've done that, she said. So? I asked. We've further enquiries to make. What enquiries? You've got all the dates entering and leaving the island, you've got my school records. What is this? Someone's got it in for me, have they? Mr. Roussel, I advise you to change your tone; it isn't helpful. Damn right it isn't, I said, and stormed out."

"Cor heck." Janice gets up from the table and clears the plates. "She isn't going to like you for that, eh. You've got to be nice to them otherwise they can get nasty. I know. My son, he's married to a Madeiran and they ended up leaving coz they said she wasn't legal. They swapped one island for another, and he's as happy as Larry. Says it's hot over there."

"Good for him."

"'Course you've got friends in high places, eh. Always useful that."

"Right now, I'd say it's the problem."

He looks over at his mother. She sunk into her chair and her back is so bent, she is more roulade than human being. Her eyes are staring at the table top.

"Mum!" he says loudly.

There's no response.

"Mum!"

She lifts her chin, then flops her head down again.

"It's the food. Makes her sleepy. I'll put her under the tree for a siesta."

He nods. "By the way, have you seen a sheet of greaseproof paper? I left it on the sideboard a while ago."

"The one with all the writing on it? And those bubbles?"

"That one."

"Ah," Janice begins. She's wiping the table now, and lifts Lilly's arms to clean under them. "It ended up in the bin."

"What?"

"Lilly tore it up."

"You didn't stop her?"

"She was in one of those moods. And it would have torn anyway if I'd tried to get it off her."

"You didn't think to keep the pieces?"

Janice stands up and looks at him. "You'd have needed a whole roll of Sellotape to get it back together again." She walks to the sink and rinses the cloth under a running tap.

Bloody hell! It was his thinking-sheet. To have his mother destroy it hurts. More than hurts, it feels like betrayal, as if she's saying along with the rest of the island, give it up, forget about it: you're not up to this.

But he is 'up to it' – and that isn't a mantra put on his reminder list, timed to pop up on his phone every morning at 7 am (and yes, he does have one of those, it just isn't *that* one). It is a fact. Now he's got to start all over again. Bring those sheets before his mind's eye and look, and look again. Enter that state of seeing without thinking... wait for a line to emerge from one of the bubbles, growing brighter and brighter until it's neon-coloured and heading in one direction.

The doorbell rings.

He goes to the front door to open it. Tom de Carteret stands in the porch. What the hell does he want?

"Have I come at a bad time?"

"We've just finished lunch."

"I'm meant to be in Torteval. I just wanted to say something. After our talk the other day, you know."

Mark steps out onto the threshold, and draws the door behind him. "Okay."

"It's about Jasmine. I need to be honest with you."

"Right."

"I haven't told anyone this." There is a pause. He takes his hands and presses them prayer-like in front of his mouth. Except he isn't praying. "It goes like this. I really did see Pierre on that bike, and it was Jasmine's. I recognised it. It was red. And he did have a bag in the basket."

"But you didn't hear anything clanking inside it?"

"No."

"Why did you say you did?"

"It didn't make any difference."

"That's debatable."

"It's just – look, I'm not what you think I am. I really thought Pierre had killed her – and I still do. But she was going through a bad patch. She was struggling with things, with life in general. She was in a bad way. That's why I went round to see her, after the row." He pauses. "I really loved her, Mark. I know you won't understand. She was old enough to be my mother. But – she was just this wonderfully sad, lovely person. And I – I'd walked out on her."

"You found her body, didn't you?"

He doesn't answer, blinking away the tears in the corner

of his eyes. "I'd never have hurt her. Not ever, not when she was alive." He looks at him. "I really believed it was Pierre. I still do."

"But you can't be a hundred percent sure?"

He drops his head. "Ninety-nine point nine is as good as proof, isn't it?"

"I don't know. Sometimes yes, sometimes no. Your testimony did it for him, you know that, don't you? He didn't have a chance, did he?"

"No." The voice is a whisper.

Chapter Fifty

The room is built to keep out the cold with its low ceilings and thick walls. The fireplace takes up most of the wall and is large enough to sit in, which was the intention once upon a time. If you want the light you have to huddle about the stone windows, your head inches below a beam. Which is where he finds him, in the front room facing the garden, a cafetière on the table with two china mugs, a jug of milk and a plate of buttered gâche. When Mark greets him – "Great summer we're having" – Martel peers over the top of the newspaper and gestures at him to take the chair.

He sits down and taps his fingers on his thighs. The rain has stopped, but the sky is still grey and wet. There's no view here, only high granite walls and the mulberry tree in the middle of the lawn. A few crusts of bread have been left out for the birds to eat.

"You can pour the coffee." Martel folds the newspaper and lays it on the floor by his feet.

He performs as bidden. "Here you are."

Martel takes the cup in one hand and a piece of gâche in the other. "Won't you have one yourself?"

"You know a proper cup of coffee is my one indulgence…"

"One!" comes the guffaw. "You can add that ridiculous car as another."

It's like being back at school, in the Principal's office. He crosses his arms, and then decides against being defiant and uncrosses them.

"Why did you want to see me? You were only here the other day."

A seagull dives down to gobble up the crusts on the lawn. Three others swarm overhead and then land, huge in size and voracious.

"Before I forget," Mark says, clearing his throat, "I've got a brill and some chancres in the deepfreeze. I got them from Old Dorey."

"I don't eat crab."

"Very well, you can have the brill."

"Thank you. Now, your reason for coming?"

There are a number. His anger wants to know about the residency; his grief about his mother. To both, Martel will retort 'assumption' and remind him with highhanded condescension that detectives investigate facts, not emotions.

"When I got the brill from Dorey he told me about the book, the one you said was a myth. It looks like you've been economical with the truth. I want to know why."

Martel wipes the corners of his mouth with his fingers. "Island living requires – how shall I put it? – a certain attitude. There are opportunities here, but you must show respect if you wish doors to open and stay open. You understand what I'm saying?"

The Accused

"Are you alluding to the letter from Frossard House?"

"I don't know what you're talking about."

"Then we've got something in common. I don't know what you were talking about either, when you wrote that letter to the *Press*."

Martel places his hands on the armrests and draws himself to his feet. "Witchcraft has always been a curse on this island. Pierre brought it into our living rooms. The process of normalisation is ongoing and dangerous – even the museum has a display about it now. He must stay in prison where his nasty little habits can be kept out of view and silenced."

"He's very silenced; he's in a coma."

Martel shakes the crumbs from his jacket. He walks across the room towards the door and the inner darkness of the house.

He follows him. "There's a Frank Torode who lives at the Catioroc. He's a member of the Société. He's writing a paper about witchcraft. No one is silencing him." He bends his head to pass through the doorway.

"Frank Torode is a chemist. He is trying to break the island's superstition, not encourage it."

"Was that Jasmine Gardiner's mistake? She started sticking her nose into things?"

"I have no idea."

"You wrote that letter."

"Yes, but since it wasn't a crime, I don't believe I have to explain myself and certainly not to you."

Okay. He raises a hand in acceptance, as if to say, 'you've won that round.' He can swallow his pride to move the conversation on. He takes out his phone and flips through the photos until he finds the one he wants.

"I found this the other day and I thought you'd be able to help me with it."

The phone shines brightly in the dark corridor. Martel takes it from his hand and squeezes his eyes to read.

"Where did you get this?" He looks up at him, frowning.

He lies. "Dorey showed me."

"What was he doing with it? I didn't know he had a copy."

He shrugs his shoulders as if to say, 'he's a wily one is Ol' Dorey', and hopes to God Martel doesn't phone the old fisherman after he's left and demand an explanation. "I know it's related to the book, but I've no idea the list of letters. I'm assuming they're initials."

Martel hands the phone back. "Victor Hugo created a society around the book. It was the sort of esoteric thing he would do. These were the names of its protectors."

"It's the original list?"

"I have no idea. The monogram in the corner is VH so I'm assuming it is."

"Do you know who they were? D could be for Dorey and M could be Martel. It would explain your fascination."

Martel says nothing. He clasps his hands behind his back.

"It's got me thinking. If I were you, I'd be trying to work this list out because – let's be honest – I'd be hoping the Englishman who died in Biberach had left it with one of their descendants."

"How do you know about that?" His voice is a growl.

He smiles. "I've spent my career getting information from people. Look, there's a DC on the list as well. Reasonable conjecture tells me it stands for de Carteret. Tom's great-grandfather helped steal it off the Queripels, which

The Accused

explains the connection. The question is, who did the Englishman leave it with?"

"That's for you to work out. I've no idea. Goodbye. You can leave by the back door."

Outside, the wind has blown the front through to England but the ground is still wet. He walks over the grass and into the yard where the old barn stands in its original state a few feet from the garage. The wooden doors are rotting at their base, and the single window above it is shuttered. It sets him thinking. Many a thing can get lost in a barn, large as well as small, buried under forgotten objects. An E-type Jaguar for example.

A pinprick of red, like a ruby caught in a tree, flashes in the corner of his eye and he turns his head. A cluster of berries still wet from the rain glisten between the thorn-shaped leaves of a yew. The tree is old, with a gnarled trunk and a canopy of spindly branches. Most of it is lost behind the back of the barn. Perhaps that's why he never noticed it before.

Chapter Fifty-One

"Excuse me." A woman is loitering at the gothic entrance to the cemetery. "Are you going to the cremation?"

"No."

"You know Pierre Bourgaize died the other night in hospital, don't you?"

"Everyone does."

"Can you share your thoughts? I'm from the *Guernsey Press*."

"Sorry, no."

"Not even a comment?"

He shakes his head and hurries past into the quiet garden of the dead. The cedars spread their branches overhead, motionless in the summer air. Beneath them, the silver birches grow amongst the graves. Paths split off from each other, edged with granite, leading here and there through the fields of tombstones. Everything is green: the leaves, the grass, the ivy clad tree-trunks, even the moss that grows on the old stone crosses. Up the hill he walks, past them all, towards the chapel that stands waiting for him with its two spires, one shaped like a chimney.

The Accused

Inside, light pours through the double-arched windows and fills the open space. The walls are cream and the ceiling is wooden-pitched like the hull of a boat. He walks through the vestibule and down the short aisle to join the other person sitting there, Mrs. Bourgaize. She nods at him as he takes a chair and the first thing he notices is the mole between her eyebrows. The second is the set of her face, strong-boned and attractive. With her hair pinned back and rouge on her cheeks, he struggles to recognise the woman who peeped at him from behind the front door. He considered her brow-beaten and terrorised, but evidently, she is neither.

They wait in silence, facing the coffin that rests on its rollers. There's no hiding the purpose of the place, with the double doors that led to the furnace. The chapel is airy and light, but it isn't a church. There's little hope in the presence of an all-consuming fire.

His father was cremated so he knows what he is talking about. And he wishes to God he'd asked Viv to join him; he glances over his shoulder in the vain hope that she may appear.

"Mr. Roussel."

He turns in his chair. "Mrs. Bourgaize."

"I want to give you something." She retrieves an envelope from her handbag and hands it across to him.

He takes it and looks down at the spidery writing. "Pierre's?" he asks and she nods.

"Don't judge me harshly. Everyone is let down by someone."

He says nothing, and slips the letter inside his jacket pocket. Not a tear in her eye, not a flush of sadness. Her son committed suicide, and she can only think of herself.

Footsteps.

The Chaplain is walking towards the lectern in his black and white gowns. He stops, crosses himself, and then raises his head. Mark catches the sadness in his face.

"We are here to bid farewell to Pierre and to remember his life, not as we would wish it to have been but as it was in all its complexity." He turns to the coffin. "Pierre, I never expected to officiate at your funeral. We didn't know each other long and I'd hoped for more time together. You spent your short life searching for the truth. It took you to dark places and for that you were judged and reviled. But you tried, and that merits our respect. If we believe the journey is important because it teaches us the roads to take and the roads to leave behind, then only the brave choose to go it alone. I'm sad you chose to give up when you did. As I told you once, so I say again: 'The Lord upholds all who are falling, and raises up all who are bowed down.'" He turns to face Mrs. Bourgaize. "Pierre has gone to stand before God. God is merciful. God is just. There was goodness in his heart, he was not without hope. You spoke of his love of animals. You said that he refused to kill the ants in the garden. Any soul that can love an ant, that is here today and gone tomorrow, is a soul that can stand before God. I'm sure that Pierre is looking into the eyes of Jesus right now, and is learning – perhaps for the first time – what love truly means." He pauses. He raises his hand and gives the sign of the cross. "In the name of the Father, of the Son, and the Holy Spirit, Amen."

After the coffin disappears behind the doors and the curtains are drawn in front of them, Mark shakes the hands of both Mrs. Bourgaize and the Chaplain, and leaves. Pierre is being consumed by flames and he doesn't need religion to tell him the fires of hell are earthly.

A few steps along the cemetery path, he stops to take

the envelope from his jacket pocket. He pulls out the letter and reads it.

Dear Ma,

PLEASE READ THIS LETTER.

It's important you hear me out. I don't expect anything else from you, only a listening ear. That's probably asking a lot given your silence over the last eleven years. If I didn't know better, I'd assume you were deaf. Perhaps you are deaf, or maybe you prefer to tear my letters up and throw them away.

DON'T TEAR THIS UP.

I've met a man called Mark Roussel. He used to work at the Met. He came to the prison to ask me questions about the case, and he's got me thinking.

Mark looks up and over his shoulder. A thin wisp of smoke is escaping through the top of the chimney, and he thinks of the witches hoping to fly high and of Pierre trying to be free. What a shit-awful world we live in, everyone trying to escape.

He turns back to the letter and reads it to the end. It's very much as he thought, except for two important differences.

"Do you judge me, Mr. Roussel?" Mrs. Bourgaize joins him on the path. "I saw you reading the letter."

The question irritates him. "He was your son."

"He was difficult to like. It wasn't easy, you know."

"You're not the one who's dead, are you?"

Her eyes are dark bullets, and she fires them at him. "Do I have to explain myself?"

"I think so. I came to your house because I wanted to help him. You shut the door in my face. I gave you my calling card. You could have got in touch."

"They found the hand in our shed, Mr. Roussel. The hand!"

"But why assume he put it there?"

"I couldn't swear a hundred per cent he hadn't gone out, could I? And Dad – Dad was furious. He told me to keep quiet about him having a migraine."

"I'm guessing they didn't get on?"

She lifts her chin defiantly. "He wasn't Pierre's father, but that's got nothing to do with anything. He's a hard-working man. Everyone respects him."

No remorse, not even a flicker of it. He takes a breath. "You're a Queripel, aren't you?"

"What's that got to do with it?"

"I was thinking about the book the family had."

She sniffs. "My mother filled his head with all that nonsense. He used to go round after school every day. She spoilt him rotten and turned him against me. Said I was a stuck-up mutt with my net curtains and dishwasher."

"That must have hurt."

"She didn't live to see what Pierre did." She pulls the handbag towards her chest and holds it there. "He was very upset when she went, you know. That's when it started. Obsessed, he was. He wanted to change his name. He told

The Accused

Dad he wasn't a Bourgaize, and there was a huge row, I can tell you. Dad said he didn't care who he thought he was, but he wasn't changing his name coz that would get tongues wagging and he hadn't worked as hard as he had to have a weirdo like Pierre make him look a fool."

"And you agreed with him?"

"My mother was an ignorant woman. She lived in a mess. Never washed her clothes. Pierre was an ungrateful..." She hesitates to find the word.

"Bastard?"

"I don't use bad language, Mr. Roussel."

"I was meaning it literally. Tell me, what do you know about Jasmine Gardiner?"

"That woman? Nothing. Except she wrote all those things about us locals. Dad was furious when he found out Pierre had been to her place. Everyone knew about the blog down at the garage and he was embarrassed, you see. He banned Pierre from seeing her. Pierre told him to mind his own business and when she called the house, he spoke to her. She told him to come to the house."

"She called on the mainline? He knew her well enough to give her your phone number?"

"Not so confident about him now, are you?" There's a nasty sneer on her face. "She said she had some proposition to make."

"How do you know?"

"I listened in."

"There are two phones in your house?"

"Yes." She's sounding like the Stasi.

"Okay, so when was this?"

"The day of the murder."

The plot is shifting fast. "What time was this?"

"After breakfast."

"Did he go?"

"I think so."

"How did he get there?"

"Bus, I suppose. His bike was stolen. I don't think he'd have walked. It's too far."

The bike story holds firm then, but the fact he intended to go to her house turned everything on its head. Think fast. Intending and achieving aren't the same thing, and it's always possible he never made it.

"Do you think Pierre killed Jasmine Gardiner?"

Mrs. Bourgaize sucks in her lips. She frees them, chews on them and then sucks them in again.

"The Chaplain said he wouldn't kill the ants in the yards. Is that true?"

"Pierre was a weakling. That's what Dad hated about him. A wimp, he used to call him."

Nice family. "Did you ever talk to social services about your husband?"

Her eyes flash and she clutches the bag so tight to her chest, he thinks it might come out the other side. "My husband, he's been very good to me."

"You had a duty to your son."

"I have a duty to my husband. He put food on Pierre's plate and clothes on his back. What did Pierre do for him, eh? Shamed him. That's what he did. He shamed all of us."

She turns away and hurries down the hill.

Chapter Fifty-Two

HE HAS A QUICK SHOWER AND DRESSES, THEN HURRIES downstairs. "I'm off to the Gouffre," he tells Janice and no, he won't be back for lunch, not even for salmon parcels. Yes, they're his favourites and yes, he's very sorry to be missing out but no, he won't be joining them. He's donating his to their party à deux. If they can't eat all three, he'll have it tomorrow. With salad? Yes. And avocado? Of course. He looks at his watch. Running late, he says, and kisses his mother before leaving.

The road to the Gouffre is steep. Cars are squeezed into the hedgerows, bumper against bumper with no space to add another. The car-park is no better and he watches a BMW do a five-point turn and drive away. Big car, big problem. His Messerschmitt, on the contrary, slips in between a Range Rover and a bush at the far end, by the cottage where the cliff path begins. Nifty. The issue is getting up the hill afterwards.

Walkers and couples are seated at the tables, sunglasses on their heads and dogs at their feet. Arrayed in front of them are baskets of fried fish and burgers; chips, BBQ ribs, ice cream and Coca Cola. It's a colourful, noisy sight, and Viv is nowhere to be seen. He crosses the patio and walks to the side of the restaurant, where he finds her at a wooden table overlooking the cliffs.

"You're looking better," he says, kissing her cheek. It's an understatement given she has styled her hair and is wearing lipstick.

"Nothing like a near-death experience to justify a spa day. St Pierre Park is pure magic. I was looking like a pumpkin and now I'm tip-top amazing!"

He isn't sure how to answer. A poorly placed word and he can say bye-bye to lunch. He smiles and askes for the menu.

"What does a Mark Roussel smile mean?" Her eyebrow is raised.

There, he was right. The only hope is to speak so fast he can get to the end of the sentence before she's heard the beginning.

"It means you look lovely – always tip-top - and I'm starving, and I don't know anything about pumpkins. What are you having?"

Viv rocks her head, deciding how to respond. A pause, a decision and then she says, "I'm having the seafood linguini. It's really good."

He's made it through, thank God. "The same then, and a bottle of Chablis."

Pasta is designed to be eaten without conversation. It takes focus to twist the linguini onto the fork and get it to the mouth without sauce splashing down his front. It isn't until he has consumed all £22-worth of crab, mussels, prawn and calamari that he's able to drink the wine and think again.

The Accused

"You eat far too fast." Viv is dipping bread into the sauce. "It's like running a marathon keeping up with you."

"I hate tepid pasta."

They're silent, sipping wine and watching the sun play far out to sea. He finishes first and Viv holds up the bottle to see if there's any left.

The day is hot. Very hot.

"They've arrested Luke Guille," he says.

"Who's he?"

"The one who gave you the paste."

"The guy with the tattoos? Thank God for that. The stuff was evil." She holds the bottle upside down to let the last drips pour into her glass. "I hope he gets years."

"I thought he might have killed Jasmine Gardiner, but now I'm thinking it was suicide."

"Are you serious?"

"It's the only scenario that makes sense."

"You've moved on from Tom-the-evil-gardener, then?"

"Not exactly."

"So?"

"My theory goes like this. We start with Ginny Bisson. Her half-sister worked at Jasmine Gardiner's house, so when Ginny read the blogs and realised Jasmine was into witches, she went around pretending to know about the location of the book, the one the Nazis were after. She wanted money for drugs. But it was a lie; she had no idea where it was. She only knew it existed because of her grandmother. Jasmine didn't know this, of course, and when Tom got to hear about it, he panicked. He was connected to the book through his great-grandfather – he'd helped steal it from the Queripels during the Occupation – and he didn't want Jasmine getting her hands on it. At the same time, he was, having an affair with her."

"Tom and Jasmine? Are you sure?"

"Very sure. He told me. Tom decides to get Jasmine to meet Pierre, thinking he'll distract her with his occult nonsense. She can get to meet a real live witch. Pierre goes to the house and they get talking. What Tom didn't bank on was Pierre's obsession with the book."

"Okay."

"Things get complicated because Tom and Jurat Martel know each other. Tom works on his trees and Martel is also interested in the book."

"You're thinking your Frossard House letter is linked to Martel?"

"Yes. You know Pete, the sergeant at L'Ancresse? He's got the wind up him. I had to meet him at the Dehus. The idea was to dive inside if anyone came past."

"You're joking?"

"No. Thing is, the knot's around Tom, Martel and Pierre. Look, a few days before Jasmine's killed, she and Tom have a massive row and Tom leaves. He won't answer her calls and to all intents and purposes the relationship has ended. Jasmine is already depressed, drinking heavily and missing her sons. My conjecture then is as follows: feeling suicidal, Jasmine invites Pierre to her house – I know this happened because his mother confirmed she'd called him on the mainline phone. Pierre sets off on the bus because his bike's been stolen. He assumes Jasmine wants to talk about the book, but in fact, Jasmine has other plans. She's read that if you take yew seeds when Venus and Jupiter align, you get a vision of life after death. Before she kills herself, she wants to know what's going to happen to her."

"Wait, stop there a moment. Where did you get that from?"

"Pierre told me."

"Which bit, that she wanted to die or that stuff about Venus and Jupiter?"

"Venus and Jupiter. I've checked it online, on those esoteric websites."

"And were Venus and Jupiter aligned on the day of her death?"

"Yes, and it isn't such a rare event. Supposedly it happens about once every 13 months."

"That's helpful to know."

He frowns at her.

"I'm being sarcastic. What about her being suicidal?"

"That was from a friend of hers. I told you this."

"I know, it's just a jump from feeling down to wanting a trip into the next life."

"Let me finish.

"Okay, okay."

"Pierre brings the seeds with him, already ground up, and puts them in the mug of coffee. She takes it and has a cardiac arrest. In a panic, Pierre throws away the mugs – he must have wrapped them in a cloth because they didn't break. He finds Jasmine's bike in the garage and pedals away as fast as he can. He dumps the stuff – including the bike – somewhere near the Bouet where Luke Guille finds it. Luke takes it to Ginny as a present. At the same time, Tom – worried about Jasmine – goes to see her. On the way, he passes Pierre. When he gets to the house and finds Jasmine dead, he assumes Pierre has killed her. He guesses that Pierre has come about the book, and learning nothing, has killed Jasmine in fury. He messes up the books to make it look like there's been a fight or disagreement, and wraps Jasmine in a sail bag and hides her in his van. He's heartbroken and consumed by guilt, so he devises a plan to get Pierre. That night, he carries the body down to the tree in the Pine Forest and cuts the pentacle – he does a bad job of it – and also hacks off her hand, then he hangs her up. He's as drunk as a lord, and vomits."

"Woah! Stop there." Viv hold up her hand. "You're saying that Tom cut her up? I don't believe it."

"He all but admitted it to me."

"He wouldn't do that."

"He said, to quote: 'I'd never harm her, not alive.'"

"That's not a confession."

"It's a slip of the tongue."

Viv clenches her hands in front of her. She knocks them rhythmically against the table top as she thinks. She stops. "Why didn't someone report seeing his van? If he'd come back, the neighbours would have heard the van, especially if it was late at night."

"One of those things. No one was looking out of the window at the time. He drove into the drive and took her out through the small gate in the wall. It's overgrown now, but it's still there."

"I need a coffee. I can't get my head around this." She looks over her shoulder and through the glass windows into the restaurant.

"It fits the evidence."

"What evidence?" She swings back to face him. "You don't know if or why Pierre gave her the yew seeds. It's all conjecture, and there's a difference between doing it to help her have some weird mystical experience and doing it to kill her."

"Suddenly you're happy to think Pierre's guilty? Is that because I've implicated your friend?"

"No."

But he knows she means yes. Her voice has a defensive ring to it. And it riles him.

The Accused

"You can't let him go, can you?"

"Oh, for goodness' sake, Mark. What is this? Jealousy?"

"No!" A man strolls along the path that passes before their table and climbs the steep steps to the cliffs above. "I've racked my brain over this," he says as calmly as he can, "and I can't find a single motive for Pierre killing her. Not one."

"The book."

"Why kill her for the book? If he wanted the book, he wouldn't have killed her, would he?"

"She refused to give it to him and he got angry."

"But the body wasn't damaged. An angry killer hurts the body. This was neat, ordered, planned. Nothing about it points to an act of fury. The mutilation happened hours later."

Viv is shaking her head. "I can't believe it. Tom wouldn't do that to the body."

"Put belief to one side and look at the pieces. Line them up. You'll see it's the only order that makes sense."

"You say he was in love with her?"

"Hence the vomit."

"And he hated Pierre that much?"

"If he thought he'd killed her, then yes."

"So, it was an act of passion."

"The mutilation was, yes. Not the murder."

"Pierre did murder her then? You've just said it."

"No, he didn't murder her. There was no intention to kill. Whether she asked him to do it for a weird esoteric experience or because she wanted him to assist her in suicide, I don't know. But from what Mrs. Bourgaize said about him, I don't think Pierre would have agreed to it. He believed he was helping her get a vision of the afterlife, it's a simple as that."

Viv throws her arms in the air and then drops them down onto her head. "God, I wish I'd never got you to into this." She looks at him. "What are you going to do about it?"

"I don't know."

"Want some advice? Leave it alone. It's over. Pierre's dead and nothing can come from it except problems. Your friend, Pete, would agree with me. We're telling you – leave it."

Chapter Fifty-Three

LEAVING IT IS AN OPTION. THE WISE ONE. NO ONE WILL thank him for exposing Tom de Carteret as a mutilator, given the man will probably never do it again. But that isn't the point of justice – keeping the world happy. Justice is about absolutes. It isn't an ideal or a vague concept. It has an ontology of sorts; it is or it isn't, there's no fiddling around with it.

Since he parted ways with Viv, the clouds have stormed across the sky and covered the sun. A south-westerly wind has whipped itself into a fury and he's sheltering from it behind a rock, watching the ocean. It's warmer than the air but the swell is voluminous and he knows better than to swim in an angry sea.

Even the gulls have hunkered down.

Still, there's nothing like a wind to shake up his thoughts. It tosses them about, and then dumps them on the ground. Rearranged. So, he sits in his rocky alcove, sea-spray in his face, and lets the wind do its magic. And what he realises shocks him. He jumps to his feet and nearly flies off in the gale. He sits down again.

His theory doesn't work. It's fiction. And bad fiction at that. He's forced the story.

Suicide? It's possible but the rest of it's nonsense: wanting a vision of life after death before she killed herself? Come on! There's simpler explanation; there must be. Love, revenge, greed... he's missed something. It's a maze. Somewhere along the way, he's taken a wrong turning and found himself at a dead end. He's going to have to retrace his steps, all the way back to the starting point.

But which starting point? There are multiple.

The only option is to flip the coin. Instead of beginning with Pierre he should begin with Jasmine, with the break-up of her marriage and her revenge on the islanders. Or – no - not her marriage, the book. What was her interest in it? Rethink who she was too. Discard the narrative of some rich, stay-at-home mother with too much time on her hands who was jealous and sought revenge by writing a blog.

That diminished her.

He remembers something Pete said: the books on the shelves were old. And he recalls Cynthia Marshall's comment about the father being an antiquarian bookseller.

God, it's been staring at him all along! She not only valued the books, she dealt in them too.

He takes out his phone and does a Google search using her maiden name. Pete gave it to him, but he hasn't considered it important until now. And there it is, on the screen: *David Fletcher, 1935–2001, dealer in rare books and manuscripts. Areas of interest: early scientific manuscripts and medieval esoterica.*

This is it. This is the starting point. Jasmine Gardiner was her father's daughter, continuing his legacy.

He taps in the number. "Mrs. Le Sauvage, sorry to call you but I've got a question."

The Accused

"That's okay. I'm just cleaning the house, me."

"Do you recall anything about the books Mrs. Gardiner had? I was told the ones in her study were old."

"Cor heck, Mr. Roussel, they were old alright, eh. I wasn't allowed to dust them, me. Only her. When they said they were all over the floor, I nearly wept me coz she adored those books."

"Do you recall her saying anything about them or anyone coming to buy or sell the books?"

There's silence. He hears breathing. "I don't know, eh. She'd got her hands on a horrible old thing. It was really dirty and the leather, it kept flaking off it. She showed it to me, she was so excited, her. Said it was so special she wasn't going to put it on the shelves with the others."

"What was it, do you know?"

"I don't know me, but she had this glint in her eye, that I know. Said it would really upset that Martel man, the Jurat, eh. She didn't like him. He'd come to the house..."

"Wait a moment. Rewind, Mrs. Le Sauvage. You said Jurat Martel would be upset that she had it?"

"Yes."

"And you said Jurat Martel had been to the house?"

"La la! I can't remember when, me. There was lots of snow, eh, coz I slipped on the way from the bus. They were arguing in the kitchen, them. Cor damme là, they were really going for it. Martel stormed out, him. Nearly knocked me over. Mrs. Gardiner was all in a fluster."

He thinks. "Do you think it was the book, the one Ginny was going on about?"

"I don't know, is it. I just heard him tell her it belonged to the island, it did. She said she didn't care about the island."

"What else did she say?"

"Bugger me if I know."

"Did she show Jurat Martel the book you'd seen?"

"I wasn't peeping, me. He offered her a lot of money, he did. Made my eyes water, it did, the amount he said. I thought, I did, I thought – cor heck, I'd live like a queen, I would, with all that money."

So, so, so.

Jasmine Gardiner found the book. Martel was trying to get it. She refused.

What he needs now is evidence. He begins with that photo of a Jaguar parked outside in the snow. The number plate, what was it? 6748. A high number, not one Martel would be happy to don. Unless it has significance. Day, month, year: 6th July 1948. Date of birth, perhaps?

Chapter Fifty-Four

THE HOUSE IS LOCKED. NO ONE IS ABOUT. HE WALKS around into the yard and then through the gate that leads to the garden. Empty. With hands either side of his face, he goes from window to window, peering inside. Martel is out.

Looking about the garden, he returns to the yard where the old barn sits with its ivy-covered walls and lichen on the roof. The doors are held together by a loose iron chain. Pulled apart, there's enough of a gap to squeeze between them, wriggling sideward to enter the darkened space.

Earth, damp – he tries to identify the smells. Age, if it has a scent. And rats. Perhaps a hint of hessian too. Using the torch on his phone, he spins the beam about the place, down onto the earthen floor and up at the wooden struts overhead. Old furniture edges the granite walls, grey with dust; there are tomato crates and machinery left over from the days of farming. He walks towards a shape covered with a tarpaulin, on top of which are cardboard boxes and two tennis racquets. Lifting the cover and sneezing from the dust that comes off it, he crouches on his knees and shines his light underneath.

There it is. 6748. And the racing green paint of an E-type Jaguar.

He drops the tarpaulin and gets up - and then bends down again to take a photo, a few in fact, enough to serve as evidence. Quickly, he squeezes between the doors into the yard and dashes across the cobbles to his car. On goes the ignition and off he drives, down the *ruettes tranquilles* and onto the road towards Icart. An awful truth is dawning on him. He could be wrong – he has been several times already – and there's no saying Martel has done anything worse than cover for Tom de Carteret.

Yet it isn't looking good.

And there's the yew tree in the yard to consider as well.

He needs to speak to someone. Someone he trusts.

THE SHOP IS empty when he arrives. Old Dorey is on the telephone and he raises a hand to say, 'be with you in a moment' as he carries on taking an order, writing it down on a piece of paper. Mark casts his eyes over the fish, a veritable harvest of bream, red mullet, mackerel, whiting and pollock. There are also some chancres, scallops and lobsters on display.

"So, what do you want?" Dorey says, putting down the phone. "There's some brill coming in later, if you want to wait."

He shakes his head. "Not shopping today."

"Come for a chat, eh?"

"Sort of. It's to pick your brains."

"Still into the Pierre stuff? He's dead. No point sorting out the dead, eh."

The Accused

"Maybe not, but then when it concerns a Jurat, it's more about getting to grips with the living, isn't it?"

Dorey raises an eyebrow. "What're you thinking?"

"Martel."

"Oh eh, and what've you got on him then?"

"It's delicate. I need to know I can trust you."

"Your father did."

"I know. But this is about Martel."

Dorey crosses his arms. "He's your family, eh, not mine. What have you got on the old bastard, then?"

"The book. Jasmine had it, Martel knew that and he tried to get it off her. My concern – and yes, it is a concern – is he might have killed her for it. I don't say he mutilated her – I know who did that – but killed her, yes. Be it by accident or design, he's guilty."

Dorey stands motionless, his arms still crossed. He casts his eyes towards the door, and then walks around the counter to flip the 'open' sign to 'closed.'

"No point having eavesdroppers, eh."

He nods.

"How many people have you told about this, then?"

"No one."

"Right, good. You say Martel killed Jasmine Gardiner. That's your theory, is it? Let me tell you this, and I tell you coz it needs to be said, but you don't go doing anything clever with it, alright. You just listen, eh. Martel came to see me the day before they found her body, and he said, 'Don't go talking about the book, Dorey. I've found it but it must be kept a secret.'"

"Why did he say that?"

Dorey shrugs. "Maybe he'd got it from her house."

"Killed her."

"I didn't say that, eh. I said he might have got it from there."

"You know there's a yew tree in his yard, don't you?"

"He might have poisoned her. He might not have. Who can say, eh? I keep my promises, and so do others. If someone knows the truth, they're not going to go talking, are they? Martel, he's a fox. He has information on everyone. People, they're going to be careful, eh, and they're going to be taking what they know to the grave with them."

"I know he's the one that got Population onto me, saying I didn't do all my education on-island."

"There then. Martel – he knows about your little goings-on, so you don't go talking. You keep quiet. Same for everyone."

"You're saying people knew or at the very least they guessed? They convicted Pierre because they were worried Martel might spill the beans on them?"

"I don't say anything, eh. Note that. I'm just warning you, là. Jasmine, she's dead and Pierre too. All very sad, eh, but nothing you can do about it now. So, you turn around and walk in the other direction. You forget all about this. You smile at Martel and you pretend you don't know. Justice, she doesn't exist, her. She's just a nice word people like to use to feel good about things. You remember that."

THE WALK from Dorey's place takes him past the old slaughterhouse and along the edge of the Albert Marina towards the town church. The sun sparkles on the sea. Cars drive past and people amble along. Gulls laugh from their perches.

The Accused

He has no idea where he's going – he just needs to walk, to think. Crime exists in duality: there's a victim and there's a perpetrator, and the former requires the latter to be convicted. Now, though, everything's shifted – not away from justice but away from his comfort with it. Justice is objective, detached; it's easy to wield it when its sharp edge falls on the other side of the divide. But when it falls close to family?

Perhaps he's like all the others and afraid of Martel's power. Or maybe he fears the smallness of a community he doesn't understand but which he's shackled to.

A cruise ship is anchored out in the Little Russel, between Guernsey and Herm. He leans against the railings to watch the small boats bring the tourists ashore. He takes out his phone and calls Viv.

"You want my honest advice?" she says after listening to his amended theory. "Don't do anything. You've got no proof."

"It works, the scenario works. Think about it this way: if Tom hadn't been driving past and seen Pierre on the bicycle; if he hadn't been so enraged, decided to hang her up and do what he did, Jasmine's death would have passed as a cardiac arrest. Unexpected but not suspicious. Martel would have got away with it."

"Okay, so how did he do it and get the book?"

"She could have been showing it to him. That would explain why he never picked up the clock as it fell, he was too focused on stealing the book and leaving."

"The place was cleaned."

"Right, so he got the book, quickly wiped down the surfaces and left. I bet the coffee machine was still on. He poured her a coffee as she got the book. Easiest way to get the seeds into it. He'd have brought them already ground from his garden. It's simpler than all the nonsense about Jupiter and Venus."

"I don't know anything about a coffee machine. I can't remember anyone remarking on it."

"It's what happened, Viv, I'm sure of it."

She's quiet a moment. "If you're right – and I can see you might be – no one wants the case reopened, not now that he's dead. And without concrete evidence, you haven't got a chance."

"It's a point of principle."

"What principle?"

"I want to clear Pierre's name."

"Why? You didn't even like the man. You told me yourself. And it won't make any difference to him, will it? You're not God."

He purses his lips. "Martel needs to be exposed."

"Who for?"

"For everyone. Who's to say he won't do it again?"

Viv laughs, not unkindly but with dismay. "You're saying he's a serial killer now? Come on, Mark. Keep your head in gear."

"He can bloody well lose his seat as a Jurat, then, and Tom de Carteret can be pushed off his pedestal."

"That sounds like revenge."

It is, and he wants a bucket load of it. He wants Pierre's name cleared, his parents consumed with guilt, Tom de Carteret arrested and Martel humiliated. He wants the whole bloody lot tarred-and-feathered through the High Street.

Especially Martel – get the man once and for all. His sense of entitlement is boundless, but everything in the universe has limits and he's going to show him where his lay – right at the end of his nasty little nose.

The Accused

Maybe vengeance isn't justice. But it bloody well is the desire for it, and he doesn't need anyone unravelling the strands and laying them out on a table for him to see. He knows his own self-righteousness is there, in amongst the mess of it all.

The question comes down to this: What is he willing to sacrifice? His hatred of Martel? Justice for Pierre? His mother? If he stands up to Martel, he's going to be waving goodbye to her from the boat.

Perhaps everyone is right – if he's going to stay, he needs to learn to live on a small island.

Chapter Fifty-Five

"Have you got an appointment?"

"No."

"You need an appointment."

"I just wondered if he was free, so I don't have to make one."

"Sorry. By appointment only."

He takes his wallet out of his pocket and draws from it his calling card. At the bottom is his former warrant number. He hands it to the sergeant.

"Ex-Met," he says.

The sergeant takes it and reads it. "You still need an appointment," he says, handing it back.

He strides to the glass doors and walks outside, stepping down into the quad. Opposite is a granite wall with two entrances, one an arched gateway and the other wide enough for vehicles to drive through. It's an austere place with a single, charmless tree. It was the poorhouse once, with 'solitary cells' on the ground floor to punish the runaways. Later it became the hospital. Now it's the police station. An interesting evolution, all things considered.

The Accused

He walks back in.

"I would like to make an appointment with the Chief Officer. Can you tell him that Mark Roussel, former Detective Chief Inspector of the Met, needs to talk to him about something important?"

"Of course, Sir," the sergeant smiles as he telephones through Mark's request. A moment later, he puts the receiver back in its cradle. "You're in luck. He'll see you in ten minutes."

The Chief Officer is not much older than Mark but a good foot taller. He steps around his desk to shake his hand and cordially invites him to take a seat opposite the desk. The windows are opened but it is still hot inside.

"Your investigations have come to my attention," he says, leaning back in his chair and steepling his fingers. "I can't say it has pleased people around here. I took over three years ago so I don't consider my reputation dependent on the investigation, but my men do, especially those who were involved."

"Yes, one of your sergeants would prefer not to be seen with me in public. We went to College together."

"I'm sorry to hear that but you can understand the situation. Esprit de corps is important in the force. Still, if you have new evidence I'm interested to hear it."

"I've enough to warrant a reopening of the case, that's all. I can't give you any hard evidence, not without the means or resources to delve further. But my conclusions are justified and I'm confident they merit further investigation."

"Very well, tell me what they are."

The Chief Officer sits forward to listen as Mark presents his thesis. His elbows rest on the desk and his fingers are clasped. Now and then, he nods.

"Impressive, Mr. Roussel. You've managed to turn the

case on its head and incriminate one of our Jurats. There's a logic to what you say and I respect a man of your experience. The problem is evidence. Given the serious nature of the allegation, we need more than a theory to reopen the case. Bear in mind, Pierre Bourgaize is now dead and Jurat Martel has done a lot for the island."

"There's the letter Pierre wrote to his mother."

The man smiles. "Would you put valuable police time into a letter?"

"No," he admits, looking down. "Probably not."

"You see my predicament?"

He does.

MARTEL IS SITTING behind his desk, stabbing at a notepad with a pen. The wooden beams of the office are low over his head but the sun is shining in through the window, framing him in a bright halo. It is misplaced as a metaphor but as a tactic, it is effective. It speaks of power and authority.

"You're willing to believe a letter he wrote to his mother? A Senior Investigating Officer from the Met. I thought better of you."

He says nothing. He can play at authority too, play all day long if necessary; he's nothing else to do. Few men can bear silence. It smacks of disapproval, and as he expects, Martel begins to fidget.

"What do you want?"

He uncrosses his legs. "I'm interested to know why you went to Jasmine Gardiner's house a few weeks before she died."

"I didn't."

"You were seen."

"That's only possible if I was there. I wasn't so I can't have been seen."

"There's a photograph of your car in the lane outside the house. It was snowing."

"Show it to me."

"Later. What I want to know is why you went. Was it to get the book?"

"Why would I do that?"

"Because you wanted it, and you thought she was trying to get her hands on it. That's why you wrote the letter in the *Press*, to stop the gossip."

"Hypotheticals," Martel snaps.

"They're usually a good way to test a theory."

Martel glances at the door. "Very well, let's play this game of yours. Let's say, hypothetically, I went to her house. And let's say, hypothetically, I was worried she was after the book. That doesn't implicate me in murder, does it? Let's continue with this theoretical scenario of yours. Say I made her an offer. I write a letter to the *Press* to silence everyone, and then I give her the information I know. She uses her contacts and if she finds it, we share the ownership."

"You were assuming – hypothetically, of course – that the book had left the island."

"Putatively, yes. It was an avenue to investigate."

He flicks his nose with his finger. It expresses perfectly how he feels about the story.

"Tom de Carteret mutilated the body. He all but confessed it. He was in love with the woman and thought Pierre had killed her. He did it for vengeance. It's a crime under statute law to interfere with a body's right of burial."

"What are you saying?"

"You misused your position as a Jurat to protect him. You did that because of his connection to the book. Keep it all in-house, so to speak. By doing so, you implicated an innocent man and convinced the other Jurats to follow your lead."

"Innocent? Don't make me laugh! All I did was encourage the other Jurats to see what I saw. Pierre was as guilty as sin. He prepared the concoction and he gave it to Jasmine Gardiner. He left her to die while he searched the house for the book. That is murder."

"If Pierre was the one who gave it to her."

"He prepared it!"

"Are you sure?"

"Of course, I am!"

"What if someone else had got to the house before he did?"

"We'll never know, will we? He's burnt to ashes."

That's kindly put. "But we do know. It's in the letter. Read it. I've made a copy."

Martel leans over to take it from Mark's hand. He scans it, expressionless.

DEAR MA,

PLEASE READ THIS LETTER.

IT'S important you hear me out. I don't expect anything else from you, only a listening ear. That's probably asking a lot given your silence over the last eleven years. If I didn't know better, I'd assume you were deaf. Perhaps you are deaf, or maybe you prefer to tear my letters up and throw them away.

. . .

The Accused

DON'T TEAR THIS UP.

I'VE MET a man called Mark Roussel. He used to work at the Met. He came to the prison to ask me questions about the case, and he's got me thinking.

I'M GOING to ask him to open the case again but I won't do it unless you support me. It's the last thing I'm asking of you, as my mother, that you support me in this. I'm going to wait for your answer. I'm going to wait and wait, but if you don't, then there's no point, is there? Everyone needs someone; everyone has someone. If I don't hear from you, then I'll say cheerio because that's what you've always wanted, for me to say cheerio and get out of your life.

I DON'T KNOW why you didn't tell the police the truth, that I had a migraine that night. You could have told them I didn't cut her up. I had no idea where to go. Have you forgotten that? You came into my room and said someone had left me a message. I didn't care. I didn't want to know, I felt so ill. I told you to go away. You never gave me the message, Ma.

I NEVER KILLED HER. I went to her house but when I got off the bus and walked there, this car was in the drive, an old green Jaguar. I didn't want to talk to her with someone else there, so I walked into the Pine Forest and down to Divette Bay. When I came back up, the gates were still open but the car had left. I rang the doorbell but no one answered.

. . .

I WENT OUT onto the road to get down into the Pine Forest, but I heard voices down in the valley and I thought they were coming up. So, I went back to the garage where I'd seen a bicycle up against the wall. I jumped on it and got away as fast as I could.

THAT'S the truth of it.

NOW WRITE TO ME, and I'll get this ex-detective to help.

WRITE TO ME.

WHEN MARTEL HANDS IT BACK, he says, "What convinces you this is the truth?"

"Instinct," he says

"I've never found that very reliable."

"Not when it conflicts with self-interest, no. The problem is this: there's a green E-type Jag in your barn. The same car that was photographed in the February snowstorm. Here." Mark held up his phone to show a copy of the photograph he'd found online.

"I'm willing to bet it's the same car that Pierre saw in the drive."

Martel clasps his hands and rests them on the desk. "Are you now?"

"There's one thing that's been bothering me though. The clock. It fell with Jasmine and broke, giving the police the time of death. Why didn't you pick it up or hide it? I'm wondering if you were surprised by how fast she died. Or perhaps you knew you'd never be caught so it didn't matter."

"Is that a trick question?"

"No."

"Are you hoping you'll trip me up?"

He shrugs his shoulders. "Perhaps. The same goes for the black bag, of course. Dumping in the Bouet wasn't that clever, given it was found." Then he adds, "You know Tom vomited all over the crime scene, don't you?"

"Which crime scene are you talking about?" Martel is irritated.

"The Pine Forest. That confirmed it for me. A psychopath doesn't vomit nor does some lunatic witch high on drugs. It had to be a normal person."

Martel is staring at him.

He waits.

"What do you intend to do now?"

He smiles. "That's the question. Family is family, after all. Isn't that what you used to tell me as a child, when I came back from school and found you in the bathroom?"

Martel gets up from his chair and steps away from the window. He extends his hand to touch the glass. "Life isn't about right or wrong, black or white. That's what we teach children. It's about negotiation, moving objects. Cost-benefit analysis. There are no absolutes.

"Is that your defence?"

Martel's eyes flash as he turns to look at him. "I'm not under caution. I don't have to answer to your fantasies. When your father died, I made him a promise: I'd look after you. I've tried to keep it.

"I remember. You sent me away to England. Just when I needed my mother the most, you separated us. You convinced Mum it was for the best and she listened to you. You sent me off to some prep school in the home counties."

"It was for the best. Your mother was a wreck.

"I was a wreck. I saw him cremated and the next day I was on the boat to Poole. You say that was helping me?"

"Children adapt."

"Sure, they do."

"Your mother needed time."

"Yes, time with her son."

"Time to recover. She couldn't look after you and herself. She needed help."

"Which you gave her, of course. You made yourself indispensable – until she lost her mind, of course. So, just in case you're wondering, I went to the police."

Martel stands very still.

"They don't consider the letter sufficient evidence."

Martel's eyes are motionless. "And?"

"They won't reopen the case. For now."

Is that a smirk? He can't be sure. Perhaps it's a nervous twitch, or just relief.

"But given what I know, I think it's prudent you negotiate with me."

"You're cocksure for a man without a mandate."

"My report is with the police. Money is the issue, not interest. Not everything depends on the letter – which is why I've got a proposal to make."

Martel raises an eyebrow.

"You get the Population department off my back, and you retire as Jurat. Your tenure is coming to its end anyway. You can dress it up however you like – 'Let another person have a chance'; 'I believe in the young'. I'm sure you can think of something."

"And why would I do that?"

The Accused

"Things could slip out. I'm not the only person who knows. Imagine if the *Press* got wind of it?"

Martel turns his back on him, and stands looking through the window. "Get out," he says.

Viv is sitting by the glass wall in the Octopus overlooking Havelet Bay and the castle beyond. It is high tide and the sun is lost behind a band of cloud. Children are jumping off the pier into the sea.

"What can I do for Mr. Roussel on my sunny day off?" she says with a lazy smile.

"Share a glass of champagne with me." He pulls back a chair and sits down.

"What are we celebrating?"

"I've got Martel by the short and curlies. You won't be hearing much from him anymore."

"I'm intrigued."

He tells her about his visit to the police and the advice he gave Martel in his study.

"Does Tom know?" she says.

"No."

"Are you going to tell him?"

"Not unless it's necessary."

She smiles. "You're learning to live on a small island."

"Looks like I am." He calls to the waiter. "A bottle of Veuve Cliquot and a dozen oysters, please."

"Am I reading something into this?" Viv teases.

"Maybe." He takes hold of her hand across the table.

Pronunciation Guide

Most Guernsey names are Norman. Here, I give a sense of how they are pronounced locally:

Bourgaize (Borgaze)
    Brehaut (Bre'ho)
    De Carteret (de Cártret)
    Dorey (Dórey – with stress on the 'o')
    Duquemin (Dukman)
    Falla (Falar)
    Guille (Gueel)
    Le Cheminant (Le Chéminon)
    Le Prevost (Le Prévo – with stress on the 'e')
    Le Sauvage (Le So'varj)
    Mahy (May'ee)
    Martel (Martél – with stress on the 'e')
    Mauger (Major)
    Moupied (Moo'piay)
    Priaulx (Pri'yo)
    Queripel (Kériple – with stress on the 'e')

Pronunciation Guide

Roussel (Roosél – with stress on the 'e')
Torode (To'roa[d])
Vaudin (Voedan)